T0113847

TAVIN
Shire

Discovering courage, love, and God's
goodness on the embattled frontier.

JENNIFER BROOKS

WESTBOW
PRESS®
A DIVISION OF THOMAS NELSON
& ZONDERVAN

WestBow Press books may be ordered through booksellers or by contacting:

WestBow Press
A Division of Thomas Nelson & Zondervan
1663 Liberty Drive
Bloomington, IN 47403
www.westbowpress.com
844-714-3454

Scripture quotations are taken from the Holy Bible, King James Version (Authorized Version). First published in 1611. Quoted from the KJV Classic Reference Bible, Copyright © 1983 by The Zondervan Corporation.

ISBN: 978-1-6642-8465-4 (sc)
ISBN: 978-1-6642-8464-7 (e)

Print information available on the last page.

WestBow Press rev. date: 01/10/2023

CONTENTS

PROLOGUE

I write this today as an ancestor of German Palatines who experienced the miseries of fleeing from their own country due to the devastations of war, exhaustive taxation, religious persecution, and famine.

Centering on the tragic circumstances of families of both Native American and white settlers in the Pennsylvania wilderness of the mid-1700's, a quick overview highlighting the historical background and surrounding events of the day is warranted.

Palatine German immigrants arrived in America in the 18th century ready to begin a new life. Native peoples felt the encroachment of white settlers pushing them further and further west. The French feared losing control of the Ohio Valley and with it, the flourishing fur trade, while the British sought more and more of it all.

Soon Britain declared war with the French, and the gates of fire encircled settlers living on the fringes of civilization. Of course, the full expanse of these historical facts cannot be summarized in such a brief synopsis yet covering a bit of the specifics describing the behind-the-scenes of the account offered here will help in understanding how the story itself is well within the context of feasibility, even probability.

POOR PROTESTANT PALATINES

The German Palatinate, located between the border of France and the left bank of the Rhine, was known for its rich farmlands and vineyards. This coveted land saw thirty years of misery and devastation. Between 1684 and 1713, the people of the Palatinate lived with constant political/religious chaos and physical suffering.

War and Taxation:

Virtually the entire 17th century was one of continuous turmoil as King Louis XIV of France sought to expand his empire. During the War of the Grand Alliance (1689-1697), the French sent soldiers time and time again to ravage the Palatinate. This war ended in 1697, with the Treaty of Ryswick, leaving a badly battered Palatinate.

Unfortunately, peace was not to last. In 1707, the War of the Spanish Succession began. Once again, towns, villages and farms were burned and plundered. Money was demanded from poor peasant farmers, taxed so heavily that many resorted to beggary or thievery.

Religious Persecution:

The reformation in Europe had encouraged the growth of Protestantism. By 1648 three churches were officially recognized: Lutheran, Catholic and Calvinist. Yet at the same time, the populace was expected to follow the religion of the reigning king. As a result, the Palatinate became a rollercoaster of religious requirements, based on whomever came to power at any given time, bringing great persecution to those whose faith was contrary.

Queen Anne came to the British throne in 1702. She was ambitious to secure religious and civil rights for all Protestants in England and the continent.

Longing for Land:

A royal charter had been granted to William Penn in 1681 for Pennsylvania. The people of Amsterdam and the Rhine Valley were very familiar with "Penn's Province", and with the Palatinate all but stripped by war, the enticement to emigrate to the New World was powerful.

The Deep Freeze:

A final and devastating blow came in 1708-09 with one of the most severe and deadly winters ever recorded. The diary of twelve-year-old Conrad Weiser noted that the sea was frozen to the shore, animals froze in the forest and birds dropped dead from the sky.

The Migration:

Queen Elizabeth recognized the dire suffering of the Palatinate and authorized refuge. Traveling down the Rhine took four to six weeks to reach Rotterdam, where ships would be used as transport to England. Once in London, they became charges of the government. Most of the refugees were in rags, with no money. Public sympathy rose, with Londoners providing food and shelter for those in need, yet the burden soon became overwhelming. By early June 1709, one thousand people were arriving each week. The sheer numbers made it an unmanageable situation, and England closed its border to German immigrants.

The Board of Trade met during that summer to consider proposals for resettling refugees. Most wanted to be sent to North America, but with England's ships engaged in warfare, and with many other considerations, there was some hesitation.

In July 1709, the Council of Ireland proposed that the refugees be brought to Ireland. There was a desire by the English for a stronger presence of Protestant settlers in Catholic southern Ireland. In August of that year, approximately 790 families were relocated.

Thousands still remained in England. Making an economic decision, the Lords of Trade proposed that a group be sent to the Hudson Valley in New York state to train in the production of naval stores (turpentine, pitch, tar and ship masts) for the British fleet. Of more than 2,800 who made the trip, nearly 500 died on the way or shortly after.

A number became indentured apprentices, while many made their way further north and settled land along the Mohawk River, invited by five Mohawk chiefs who had witnessed their plight in London. Others recalled the luring descriptions of Pennsylvania from William Penn and settled there.

FRENCH and BRITISH CONFLICT

The Seven Years War (1756-1763), or French and Indian War as it became known in America, proved once again that the long imperial struggle between France and Britain was far from over. Although it was a complicated global war, the unfriendly embers that smoldered for control over the Great Lakes region and the Ohio Valley finally ignited into a raging fire of brutal conflict across the entire territory.

Shortly after the French built Fort Niagara in 1726, the English began construction of Fort Oswego, establishing a British presence and threatening the French stronghold.

The remote forests of the western wilderness beckoned to British citizenry and government ambition. The French rightly feared the Great Lakes trade system would fall into English control, blocking their fur trade supply routes. Determined to defend their territory, in 1754 the government of New France took steps to prevent British intrusion and constructed Fort Duquesne where the Ohio, Monongahela and Allegheny rivers converge (modern day Pittsburgh), making it a strategically important fortress.

A series of battles erupted (or continued as the case may be), including the defeat of General Edward Braddock, with over two thousand soldiers, which contributed to the official British declaration of war on May 20, 1756.

Amid these cold hard facts lies the unfelt truth. Real people, real families, and real tragedies were caught up in the turmoil. Whole communities were ravaged by brutal, deadly attacks. Whole counties were all but abandoned, leaving their possessions and property in exchange for their very lives. If captives were not tortured, put to death, or adopted into the life of an Indian village, they were exchanged for either money or some valuable commodity, to fill a labor void as slaves and to increase population in Canada. Once native tribes discovered that selling captives was a lucrative business, a steady stream of captives became the norm. Hundreds were taken.

Raids were relentless and well planned, designed to inflict the most pain and suffering possible. Prowling war parties successfully caught settlers who were unprepared to defend themselves. British and Provincial Militia proved ineffective against guerilla warfare techniques used by French and Indians. During times of crisis colonists gathered in defensive buildings that had been fortified, referred to as blockhouses or guardhouses.

There was little early success against the French. Superior in military leadership and numbers, and with the strong support from their Indian allies, they made it difficult for the British. Eventually the tides of war began to shift in Britain's favor, bringing a swing of allegiance from many Native Americans who had once allied themselves with the French.

In 1758, Fort Duquesne was captured by the British and renamed Fort Pitt. Now able to focus on French forts in Canada, the British took Fort Niagara, then going on to capture Quebec. Once the British took Montreal in 1760, the fighting in North America ended.

NATIVE AMERICANS (INDIANS)

The use of the term "Indian" became universal originating from Christopher Columbus who, once encountering the inhabitants of the new world, believed he had arrived in "the Indies." I use it in this writing intermittently, as the reference is generally considered acceptable and was used throughout the time frame of the 18th century and thereafter.

Native support for either side did not erupt in an isolated bubble. Years of tribal conflict as well as developing relationships with the French and the English helped to lay the foundation of native assistance. Indian tribes fought alongside both the British and the French and shifting loyalties occurred with the winds of war.

Many tribes, such as Lenape, Algonquin, Ojibwa, Ottawa, Shawnee, and Huron allied with the French to keep British expansion at bay. For the French, enlisting Native backing was relatively easy. Issuing presents and convincing them that the English cheated, lied, stole their land and should be forced out was an effective influence.

The English attempted the same thing, but with lesser success, as their attitude toward Native Americans was, in general, much less respectful and, in many cases, utterly contemptuous. Yet the Six Nations of the Iroquois (Seneca, Oneida, Tuscarora, Mohawk, Onondaga, Cayuga) sided with the British. The reasons were many, but primarily they had become dependent on the British for European goods, and the French had allied themselves with the Algonquins and Hurons, traditional enemies.

Brutalities were not only sanctioned but encouraged on both sides in this bitter struggle to gain control of the North American continent. To oversimplify the lasting effects would be a mistake. After the peace negotiations of 1763, the French gave up all of their lands west of the Appalachian Mountains to the Mississippi River. With the British victory, settlers began moving west taking more and more land. Indian peoples rebelled, and once again the wilderness burned with raids and attacks.

Human nature does not change throughout the centuries. It wrestles with the ever-present issues of good and evil, fairness and injustice, truth and deceit, God's love and human suffering, always walking a tightrope of seeking to live well in the midst of life's uncertainties and the inevitability of death. As our tale of Tavin (TAY-VIN) Shire demonstrates, there is only one who makes sense of this confusing, violent world and offers a hope that goes beyond justice to grace - Jesus.

Jennifer Brooks

CHAPTER

1

Early-November 1755

The Pennsylvania Frontier

Tavin stood motionless. Slowly lifting the rusty barrel of his grandfather's old musket, he waited. A fleeting movement came from behind a gnarled, ancient oak. A branch snapped. Listening, his eyes darted in quick nervous twitches. He licked his lips and held his stance. Nothing. Crisp, amber-colored leaves whipped up in a gust of wind, swirling around his legs. Noisy rustling chaos broke the silence. A grey squirrel scurried around a nearby sapling, circling in frantic, chattering annoyance, breaking Tavin's uneasy posture.

Dropping the long gun to his side, he breathed deeply, *"Doltish squirrel!"* Disgusted, Tavin took one more nervous look around. Maple trees appeared to scrape the sky, their barren branches spitting the last remnants of dead foliage. The warm sun had begun inching across the morning sky and an earthy smell permeated the air. Tavin had only a scrawny hare to show for his patience. Thunder rumbled over the mountain to the south. *"Looks like rain. That would be a relief after this summer's drought,"* remembering the hardships of the arid hot summer that had baked the crops useless. Wiping his brow with his sleeve, he stood for a while soaking in the coolness of the autumn breeze, before carrying home the disappointing prize for his morning's effort.

"Mother will be disappointed," he casually commented to the floppy, mottled carcass slung over his shoulder. *"But you will have to do."* Thick underbrush intertwined with grasping vines, and dark pines cast silent shadows across the leaf covered, crunching forest floor. Tavin became aware of how much noise his steps were making as he worked his way back to his family's cabin. Slowing his pace, he began to pay more attention to his surroundings, hesitantly mumbling reassurance to himself, *"There is no reason for the willies. The defeat of General Braddock will not affect us this far east. Colonel Washington and the provincial army will see to it. The problem with the French will be settled once and for all and the Indians will be pacified."* His buoyant self-talk did nothing to appease his jittery nerves.

He could not shake the nagging blanket of dread that wrapped itself tightly around him. That very morning, before dawn, an ominous dream had stripped calm resolve bare, leaving in tatters any small amounts of optimism he clung to. It was vivid with color, swift flowing flashes, and gaping horror. He awoke, sweat dripping from his body, motionless on his cot in the darkness, listening. Waiting. Turning his head toward the bolted door on the other side of the room, he half expected garishly painted warriors to break it down. Bloodthirsty raiders with devilish purpose. Tavin's imagination plunged into the dark waters of a shoreless ocean. Ghostly images drenched his mind. A sea of terror.

Arriving back home by mid-morning, his nerves remained unsettled. Feeling hungry and disappointed with the hunt, he complained to his mother, *"Just a sorry hare. I'd hoped to bring something with more meat on the bones."* His mother smiled, as she handed her anxious son a steaming bowl of porridge, *"Meat is meat, and we are thankful to God for His provision. I will skin it, drop it in the pot with a few carrots, turnips and potatoes and it'll make for a fine evening meal."*

Tavin sat absentmindedly pushing the oat mush around his bowl with a piece of dark rye bread, waiting for it to cool. *"Your thoughts seem far away"*, his mother noted, giving him a quizzical look, the light from the fire dancing across her tired face. *"I just wish father were home. I had a most terrifying dream this morning. Indians attacked. It felt so real and with the French on the move and the Lenape already incensed, it could truly happen! Everyone says so. Attacks could be launched on the frontier at any moment."*

She stood stirring the large, blackened cauldron that hung over hot flames, looking haggard for her thirty-eight years. Streaks of grey tinted her auburn hair, loosely braided, and piled on top of her head. She calmly remarked, *"The nightmare that you had this morning was naught more than that…a nightmare. You cannot allow your imagination to run away with your peace. Fear is like wings, delivering you to the dark side of hades or soaring to the highest points of God's comfort. Allow those wings to carry you in strength and courage."*

Tavin smiled and wondered at his mother's ever enduring faith. *"Mother, the Lenape and the Shawnee are decidedly with the French. The Huron are filled with vengeance. No one can say if we are in harm's way. Nerves have been on edge up and down the frontier for months. Since General Braddock's defeat, the Indians with the French have free reign with no one to stop them. It is just a matter of time. And we have had no word from father."*

"Gustav Shire," she firmly stated, using Tavin's full and proper name, *"rumors of possible attacks spread like wildfire and have no merit."* He quickly realized that he was in for serious correction, as his mother continued, *"Your father would not remain away from us if he believed us to be in any real danger. We are safe. Fincher's Mill is but a few miles off, and should there be cause for serious alarm, the watch house, over the mountain, will be our refuge."* She smiled, her sorrowful, hazel eyes shimmering in the firelight, and added in her German tongue, *"Alles ist gut."*

"I hope you are correct, but I am not so sure that all is well," he huffed.

In his heart Tavin wanted to believe that his mother was correct. Yet, he could not ignore his apprehensions. Stepping out onto the front stoop he yawned, and stretched his long arms over his head, *"Georg!"* expecting to see his scruffy yellow dog bounding toward him. *"Georg!"* he called more emphatically. A loose chicken came running around the corner of the barn. *"You're not Georg!"* Tavin gave a short, irritated laugh.

Scratching his head, he stopped his twelve-year-old brother, *"Henryk, have you seen Georg?"* *"Nope."* Henryk replied, not looking up, as he continued sauntering toward the nearby stream. Tavin noted the slumped shoulders and the sullen expression on his little brother's face, as the empty bucket swung absentmindedly back and forth. With his shirt hanging to his knobby knees and his yellow hair sticking up as if he had just stepped out from a violent windstorm, Tavin shook his head in amusement. Henryk was never one for words. Tavin appreciated his solemn brother's no-nonsense ways.

Finding sixteen-year-old Jakob in the barn, Tavin asked the same question, *"Have you seen Georg?"*

Jakob raised his head from milking the cow and with a blank, unconcerned look on his round, freckled face, flatly commented, *"That mangy old mutt is always skulking around out here somewhere, especially when he thinks there might be a few scraps of food. He is about as useless as any dog I have ever seen. I don't know why you like him so much. He is not even good for hunting. And who names a dog Georg? Ridiculous."*

"Jakob, I don't need your opinion, as ready as you always are to give it. I only need a 'Ja" or 'Nein'." Tavin rarely used his parent's German.

"Nein", replied Jakob with a pretentious smile.

Tavin walked away, frustrated at the disagreeable attitude that Jakob invariably offered. After having also questioned his two younger sisters, Katherine and Berta, who were busy with a game of tag, their matching blond curls bouncing in the cool breeze, he finally decided that Georg had simply run off after some female in heat. *"Dimwitted dog,"* he mumbled to himself, unsure if he was truly referring to Georg or reminding himself of his own lovesick behavior over Agnes Rose Bowen. *"Chasing after a fickle female is a useless waste of time."* He frowned, his foul mood only increasing.

Grabbing the axe, he headed for the woodpile and angrily began chopping. After a few minutes, a heartfelt voice came from behind him, *"Tavin, it appears as if you are as stirred up as a hornet's nest."* His mother had followed him outside, the limp hare dangling from her calloused, red hands.

Tavin's pent-up emotions spilled out, *"I don't understand why we ever left Germantown to live in this isolated, primitive wilderness with nothing to show for our efforts. And now we are potentially in danger from Indian attack. I know that we are 'poor German Palatines', as grandfather always reminded me, yet would not the city have offered us more? There was work to be found there and community, as well as women to potentially court and...*" his voice trailed off. He quietly added, "*I just wish we'd never left. I think that the Palatinate would have been better than this.*"

His mother frowned. "*Tavin, you know nothing of the sufferings your grandfather endured in the Palatinate.*" She paused and continued, "*I know that you are unhappy. It will take time for your wounded heart to heal. God will reveal your future in His good and perfect time. Leave it in His sovereign hands. Be patient,*" Shifting the lifeless hare to lay across her arm, she took his rough hand in hers; "*Trust Him to direct your path.*" She had a pointed intuition that predictably led back to God.

Tavin hesitated to say more, but something in him required that he continue. "*Why was I rejected? If we had remained in Germantown, I would never have known who she was, and my life would be filled with joyful social junctures. Now, I courted the most stunning girl, and she will marry Reinhard "Renz" Millar,*" pronouncing the name with disgust in his voice.

Wincing, his mother responded firmly, "*Tavin, Agnes is spoken for. Jealousy is an ugly and dangerous companion. I have no doubt that she holds fond feelings toward you, but you must resolve yourself to the fact that she is betrothed to another.*"

"*It was her father who guided her inclinations toward Renz, considering nothing but wealth and status,*" Tavin spewed.

"*It is true that Mathias Bowen is a formidable man, but to judge him unfairly regarding his intentions over his daughter's future is wrong. He wants the best for her. You are young, Tavin. Trust in God. Remember, Der Herr ist mein Hirte.*" At that, she turned and walked away.

He cringed, feeling like a wolf caught in a trap, angry and helpless. "*If 'The Lord is my Shepherd', why do I feel so lost?*" he muttered under his breath.

Images of Agnes assumed their usual, precarious place across his mind as he chopped wood. Her smooth honey-brown hair, always parted perfectly in the middle, with a thick braid falling loosely across her back, was rarely covered with an appropriate mop-cap. She held an air of sophistication, even as she milked a cow or worked the garden. Her countenance was one that could easily be mistook for arrogance. But Tavin understood her. It was not sinful pride, but rather, simple pleasure. She would happily hum as she worked and found delight in small things. Her mind was quick and genuine, although he wondered at her lack of personal judgment in accepting Renz. While Tavin understood that he had no right to pursue her, he thought of little else.

His last conversation with Agnes refused to loosen its grip on his wounded heart. It clung to him like pitch sealing the seams of a ship, adrift across an obscure ocean with no end in sight. Her words seemed to both save him from sinking to the depths, while sticking painfully to his sides. He'd rehearsed them so often they'd seared word for word into his memory, *"I am fond of you Tavin. However, my father's decision is mine as well. I will marry Renz. I have entertained no other."*

Pausing for a moment, vibrant images of Agnes resounded and encircled his troubled thoughts. Her piercing eyes, black as night, held an instinctive softness, stabbing at Tavin's very soul. Her strong chin and straight nose. Her broad smile revealing pearl white teeth. Smooth skin lightly tanned in summer, accentuated a childhood scar just above her eyebrow. Her hands were most often red and chapped from gardening and housework. She was slender, but not fragile, with a tendency to run rather than walk wherever she went. Not as ladylike as most would find acceptable, yet there was something magical about Agnes.

A stiff gust of wind suddenly blew across his face, breaking off his daydreaming and catching his attention. Decisively, he shook her from his mind, and returned his energies to the wood pile throughout the afternoon. Iron grey clouds grew heavier to the south, gradually blotting out the warmth of the sun. Thunder echoed like cannon in the distance. A chilling breeze drove dust and dirt reeling into the air and the nearby trees seemed to mournfully sigh, swaying in sad rhythm. Tavin failed to notice the shadowy figure move like a cat stalking a mouse from the side of the barn.

The ringing of Tavin's axe filled the blustery air when down the narrow lane came Johann Schaffer, racing on his spirited black gelding. It was unusual to see him. He lived with his wife several miles to the west and rarely socialized. He was hollering as he pulled back hard on the reins, bringing his horse to a skidding stop. The wind carried his imperceptible words away with the whirling dry leaves and Tavin strained to hear what he was shouting. Johann's face was as wrinkled and red as a crab apple, his heavy overhanging eyebrows veiled his dim eyes. He gracefully leaped off and planted both feet on the ground. It was hard not to wonder how a man of his age remained so agile.

Magdalena stood from the old tree stump she sat on and wiped her bloody hands on her apron, laying the half-skinned hare on the ground. "*Mr. Schaffer...*" but before she could finish, he blurted, "*Mrs. Shire, I bring frightful news. Lenape warriors massacred a settlement, near Penn's Creek, some days passed. I am riding to warn families settled along the Swatara to be on the watch. I know your husband, Josef, to be with the colonial militia, so you best take extra care to be on the alert. The Terrence post is serving as a refuge house along the Blue Mountain ridge, ten miles or so above Bethel. I know it is a trek, but it might be best for you to pack up and head that way. If you choose to remain, your boy here will be your best defense,*" nodding toward Tavin, who now stood next to his mother, towering over her small frame.

Tavin quickly responded, "*Yes sir! I turned eighteen last month and know how to use a musket and shoot straight as an arrow.*" A bit of pride swelled up in his spirit to think that a capable and respected man such as Johann Schaffer, viewed him in such regard. Magdalena frowned and added, as she scanned the darkening sky, "*We shall wait until there are indications that we are in imminent danger. Penn's Creek is a good distance from here. It may be but an isolated attack. We cannot afford to leave our livestock and our crops to suffer without sufficient cause. Lord knows we have lost enough through this drought. I thank you for your warning and we will be vigilant.*"

Johann, breathing heavy, mounted and pulled the reins taut, spinning the big black horse tightly around. "*God be with you,*" he said and kicked his heels hard into the muscular flanks. The horse reared up and he was gone. Sneezing, Tavin turned to his mother, who already had her skinning knife posed to continue meal preparations. Squinting his icy-blue eyes, he gloated, "*See mother, I told you that things could get bad! We should not stay here.*" Magdalena smiled at her son. "*Yes, indeed, you told me, but may I remind you that we are in God's hands and in Him we hold our confidence. An isolated attack is not reason enough to pull out and lose everything we have.*" The admonition hit its mark and Tavin said no more.

Magdalena watched Tavin sourly march back toward the woodpile, his sandy-blond hair tied in a messy queue at the base of his neck, his shoulders broad and square. Just under six feet tall, his gait was long and sure, like his fathers. Thunderclouds resounded again in the distance and Magdalena shuttered. She believed the warning to be valid enough. Deep seeded anger had been building among the Indian peoples for many years, but she could not allow fear to have a foot hold. She had to remain strong and pray that Josef would soon return to them. She closed her eyes and recited, *"The Lord is my light and my salvation; whom shall I fear? The Lord is the strength of my life; of whom shall I be afraid?"*

With her eyes toward heaven, she silently prayed, *"He's been gone too long Lord. Hold my dear husband in your protection and bring him home. Your will be done. Amen."*

CHAPTER

2

Agnes sat down heavily on the teak-wood chest and sighed loudly. Leaning over she picked up an ivory-colored, delicately embroidered shawl from the floor and slid it through her rough hands. It had belonged to her Grandmother Switzer, making its way across the Atlantic from Germany, by way of London. A prize possession, a rare luxury for a German-Palatine widow traveling to a new and better life, only to die five years later. Folding the fabric carefully, Agnes stood and re-opened the chest, laying it neatly on top of the carefully placed clothing already packed inside. A whiff of musty, stale air filled her nostrils as she snapped the seasoned lid back down.

Stretching, she yawned. After a restless night's sleep, the thought crossed her mind to curl up on her bed and go back to sleep. Although only a fleeting contemplation. There remained too much to do. The news that Johann Shaffer had delivered early that morning had prompted a flurry of activity and Agnes would not neglect her duties to simply indulge herself. She promptly focused her attention on the tasks ahead.

Her mother was busy packing the few cooking supplies that they would take with them. *"Agnes, could you please sand the table?"*

Agnes chuckled and teased, *"So you are afraid that wild Indians might be offended by a table that is not properly sanded?"*

"Agnes Rose Bowen…" her mother laughed, *"…I am not afraid of Indians or their opinions on my housekeeping. We will return in a few weeks, after the threat is vanished and I want the house clean."*

"I am not certain that we will return so quickly. The French have thrown wood on the embers of discontent. Trouble is certainly coming."

"You forget that God is sovereign, Agnes. His will be done," her mother flatly stated, her native German brogue seemingly accentuated, ended the discussion.

Agnes believed that her mother's words were aimed at bringing comfort, but underneath, there was the familiar twinge of worry. Their lives had been uprooted when her German-Palatine family moved from New York to settled along the upper Tulpehocken Creek, northwest of Reading. Plans had not gone as expected. Agnes's father and his business partner in the construction of a refinery forge had had a falling out after several years of hard work and significant investment. The circumstances of the feud Agnes was never privy to. However, for whatever reason, the result was the Bowen family reestablishing themselves north of the Blue Mountain just a year earlier to begin in a fresh, new way.

Thomas, Agnes's older brother, joined them as well. Thomas was a rover with an adventurous spirit which all too often landed him in trouble. By nineteen he had amassed a gambling debt that he could not pay. Agnes's father settled the debt, rescuing his only son from the unsavory element seeking recompense. The move over the mountain seemed a smart and healthy option for Thomas's future. Agnes was happy to have her brother living back at home during this past year. It seemed that at twenty-one years of age, he had finally sown his wild oats and was ready to make an honest future for himself.

Stepping outside, Agnes yelled across the yard, *"Mother and I are packed! We are ready to load supplies into the wagon!"*

Thomas came around the corner of the house. *"You don't have to shout, I'm right here. You might hurt that dainty little voice of yours."* he laughed.

"Oh stop. You flatter me so," she mocked, fanning herself dramatically with her hand. Spinning around, she stepped back inside the house, to sand the table.

CHAPTER

3

As Jakob finished the afternoon milking, the old cow stretched her head around to nip his leg. *"So that's how you're going to be today?"* Jakob scolded, giving her a solid slap on her beefy hip, and shoving her hard. Picking up the milk pail, full and heavy, he turned to head back to the house coming face to face with a bold, stocky Indian in the doorway of the log barn. Naked to the waste, black zigzag tattoos covered his arms and chest, with the image of a turtle design etched along his neck. A perfect line of red paint ran from ear to ear across his hawk-like nose and his left eye circled in black. Jakob dropped the pail and milk puddled around his boots.

Hearing his sisters scream, Tavin dropped down behind the chopping block. Cautiously he lifted his head to peer over the top. Two warriors danced merrily about the girls in mocking imitation, their medicine bags flopping around their necks. Tattered strips of colorful trade cloth fluttered gaily as they yapped like dogs, muskets in one hand and scalping knifes in the other. Each of their heads were shaved at the sides with a scalp lock of black hair running over the top. Red and yellow porcupine roaches shook in sinister rhythm. Their faces, ornately painted in black, white, red, and yellow designs, appeared eager and wild, like ravenous birds of prey circling their victim. Inside the house Tavin heard pottery smashing and his mother screaming in German.

Glancing toward the barn, Tavin's heart sank when a sinister looking Indian emerged wiping his scalping knife on his buckskin leggings. The Indian calmly turned and locked eyes with Tavin. Running was instinctive. With his axe still in his hand, Tavin instantly jumped up and over the woodpile, taking flight. Without looking back, like a deer darting about in fear, he ran across the parched field toward a steep ravine. Jumping hard through the air, his arms and legs flailing for balance and control. Rolling head over heels, he plunged down the rocky embankment. Losing his axe, he slammed into the trunk of a large tree, abruptly stopping his fall, his head bleeding and his body bruised.

The forest spun in nauseating gyration as he quickly came to his senses. His eyes flashed back up the hill. He saw nothing but the clawing forest. Scrambling behind a large boulder, he waited. A loud guttural whoop echoed from the ridge above, *"Peureux!"* sending chills down his spine. Frantically feeling around in the soggy leaves for his axe to no avail, he quickly gave up and worked his way further down the hill, uncertain whether he was still hunted. Rain sputtered. Tavin's heart pulsed like the constant rhythm of ominous drums. Splashing across a shallow stream, he came to a fallen hollowed-out tree, its roots a mangled chaos of mud and moss. Grabbing a broken branch from the ground, he shoved it inside the dark cavern and twisted it from side to side. Convinced that no creature resided within, he squirmed through the narrow opening as far down as he could push himself.

The smell of damp rotting wood filled Tavin's nostrils. Time ticked to the maddening cadence of heavy rain. Waiting. Listening. He dared not move. Fear held him in its raw tenacious grip, just as tightly as the hollow log held his cramped body. His mind seemed unable to comprehend the events that had so suddenly changed the course of his life. The instinct to survive harnessed his being, rational logic was beyond him.

After an amount of time, of which he had no grasp, Tavin slowly wiggled himself back through the log opening. The cold rain had stopped, and a ghostlike mist hung close to the wet, leaf covered forest floor. He stood. Glancing quickly around, he was alone. Slumping down alongside the mossy log, he wrapped his arms around his knees, dropped his head and wept. Dripping leaves clinging precariously from barren branches seemed to mock his tears. Shame consumed him, as he imagined the fate of his family. The family he was supposed to protect.

With the savage howl of the warrior ringing in his ears, Tavin accused himself, "*You sniffling coward!*" wiping his nose on his wet, dirty sleeve. He had acquired enough French from neighboring friendly Indians in trade deals to understand what "*peureux*" meant and it cut him to the heart. Jumping to his feet, he began navigating his way back along the ravine, cautiously angling up the steep incline, pausing behind wide tree trunks and boulders, listening for any indications of painted raiders.

Reaching the top, black smoke rolled high above the distant tree line. Crouching low, he moved slowly across the clearing, easing closer to the cabin. Monstrous tentacles of smoke seeped between cracks in the siding of the barn, stretching for the sky. Finally reaching the side of an outbuilding, he pressed his back tightly against the rough planks. Inching his way to the corner, he whispered to himself, "*You have to look. If warriors are still here, so be it, but you have to look.*"

Sweat rolled down his forehead and smoke filled his nostrils. Closing his eyes, he took a deep breath and stepped into view, expecting a savage shriek and a tomahawk blow. Silence. Only the crackling of the flames lapping at weathered barn wood. His mother lay motionless across the threshold of the cabin doorway. He could see, even at that distance, that she was dead, her auburn hair stained a deep scarlet. He turned and vomited.

Hearing a moan, Tavin jerked back again against the side of the outbuilding, his heart pounding in his ears. Another moan and a choking cough. Cautiously peering around the corner, the barn door was flung wide open, feeding the hungry flames with fresh air. Smoke curled and rolled as if it were a living, breathing thing. Squinting his burning eyes, he could see Jakob crumpled in the dirt just beyond the door, the bludgeoned cow laying lifeless behind him. Covering his mouth and nose with his shirt sleeve, Tavin sprinted across the muddy ground and entered the barn, stumbling over his clumsy feet, through suffocating smoke.

Finding Jakob, he quickly wrapped his arms around his brother's waist and dragged him out, laying him down a safe distance away. Jakob, dazed and unaware, reached for his head. Tavin firmly held his arms down. *"It's alright, Jakob. It's alright. You are alive. Don't touch your head. We'll get help. You'll be fine. Don't touch your head,"* he firmly stated, with tears rolling down his soot covered face.

Looking up, Henryk seemed to appear from nowhere, standing like a statue over their mother, a bucket of water in his hands. *"Henryk!!",* Tavin screamed, rushing to his little brother, he dropped to his knees. *"Where were you?!"*

Henryk's wiry body shook, his clear blue eyes glazed in confusion. With a trembling voice, he answered, *"I went to the spring for water and then I saw a big fish and tried to catch it. But I didn't. Catch it, I mean. I didn't catch it. I'm all wet because I fell in, but I didn't catch it."* In shock, Henryk had put more words together than Tavin had ever heard him speak. Turning away from the sight of their mothers' lifeless body, Tavin stood and grabbed Henryk's hand, more roughly than he meant, and nearly dragged him over to where Jakob lay unmoving on the ground, the bucket of water splashing behind them.

"Henryk, did you see anything? Did you see Katherine or Berta?" Henryk shook his head, *"No,"* and buried his face in his hands as Tavin ripped the bottom of his shirt into strips and clumsily wrapped the deep wound that stretched in a perfect circle from Jakob's brow to the top of his head. Cupping his hands into the pail, he gently dribbled water into Jakob's dry mouth, most of it running off his lips and onto his shirt. *"Henryk, I need you to be brave and stay with Jakob, while I go to Fincher's Mill for help. Can you do that?"* Henryk violently shook his head. *"No!"* Tavin's mind was spiraling. He glanced at the barn and knew there was nothing he could do to stop the fire, silently hoping that the rain would douse the flames.

Running back the cabin, he slowed his frantic pace to reverently step past the body of his once bright and bold mother. No time to mourn. The cabin door was broken and hanging off one hinge. He entered the dark room. Furniture and belongings had been scattered, smashed. Smoldering logs were pulled from the hearth but had failed to ignite. He called, "*Katherine?! Berta?!*" hoping to hear a response. There was no answer. He called again. Silence. His eyes darted to the fireplace mantle; the musket was gone. He quickly stripped two blankets off the corner beds. His mother's green woolen shawl was still hanging on the wooden peg behind the busted door. He grabbed it.

Gently laying the shawl over his mother's serene, bloodstained face, he could find no words to pray, pausing only a moment, until the sense of urgency returned and shook him to attention. His mind was tumbling as the white-water of a river, rolling, and swerving, unsure of its end. Rushing back to Jakob and Henryk he knelt, wrapping one blanket around Henryk's shivering shoulders and laying the other across Jakob. Jakob moaned again and opened his eyes. "*Jakob, I'm going for help. Henryk will stay here with you. The raiders are gone. They must be moving fast. They didn't take much. The warrior, the one with a tattooed turtle on his neck, chased me, but no further than the hill. I think it would have taken too much time for him to hunt for me. They are gone. You are safe. I will be back with help as quick as I can,*" Tavin rattled, in a jerky cadence.

Jakob attempted to stand, crying out, "*Don't leave me here! I can walk. Henryk and I will not be left here. I can walk!*" his voice shaking with pain. Henryk sat with a blank stare, as if in a trance, his blond hair still dripping with creek water.

"*I have to go. We need help!*" bellowed Tavin. Looking around once more, Tavin leaped to his feet and began to run toward the muddy pathway. Suddenly Henryk let out a blood-curdling howl, "*Don't leave us!!!*" Tavin stopped, spun around, and bolted back to where Henryk had collapsed beside Jakob. "*Alright!*" dropping to his knees to comfort the sobbing boy. "*We will figure something out. I won't go without you.*" His eyes focused on the cabin. "*The door,*" he said out loud. Running back, once more, he solemnly passed his mother's still body, and entered the house. Forcefully pulling the heavy door off the remaining hinge, he awkwardly slid it to the ground and dragged it where Jakob lay.

Panting heavily, he rasped, "*Jakob, we'll make a travois and I'll pull you as far as Fincher's mill.*" Scanning the darkening sky, he added, "*Hopefully we can get there before nightfall.*" Jakob nodded weakly, his eyes watery and bloodshot with agony.

Working as quickly as he could, Tavin breathed a sigh of relief to find his father's old hatchet driven into a log in the woodpile. *"They missed this! It's rusty but it will do."* Thin, tall saplings stood near the ridge, easily felled with a few swift chops. Stripping off the brittle branches, two eight-foot raw poles remained. Using rope that hung on the side of the house, he strapped them to the door, each on a side.

Keenly aware that daylight was slipping away, Tavin's voice held a nervous edge. *"We need to hurry. I won't be able to follow the trail in the dark."* And added, with a twinge of hope, *"Maybe we'll intercept Mr. Schaffer on his way back along Swatara Creek."* Flipping the travois over, it landed with a loud thud, splashing mud and water. Rain continued to drizzle from the menacing sky.

Carefully sliding Jakob onto the door Tavin used the blue and gray bed blanket to cradle his bleeding head. With excess rope he secured his brother, pinning his arms down, so that he was unable to flail or reach his head with his hands. Tavin lifted the heavy travois with the poles, and began pulling, his back muscles pumping and straining like a horse at plow.

Henryk followed behind, while Jakob returned to a world of painful delirium, moaning with each bounce along the rough terrain. *"Fincher's Mill is two miles, as the crow flies, but we'll take the Swatara Creek path. I can't pull this over rocky hills and gullies. Henryk, you must stay close and be watchful. We will be fine,",* Tavin boldly pronounced, feeling much less confident than his tone implied. He suddenly thought to add, *"With God's help,"* as his mother would have him, albeit God seemed extremely far away. Images of Katherine and Berta continually wheeled around his grieving mind, yet he dare not imagine the fate of his little sisters. Reaching Fincher's Mill was paramount.

The murky path, shadowed by high pine trees swaying above, seemed to whisper ominous threats. Henryk walked behind, his eyes flashing fear, as if demons hung overhead. Concentrating on the uneven and rutted ground before him, Tavin's shoulders and arms shook with each painful exertion. His legs buckled and his lungs burned like fire. The threatening black clouds moved slowly on to the east and an orange glow ringed the tops of scraggly cedars. Sunset. Darkness prevailed. In the near distance, he could hear the tumbling of a waterfall on Swatara Creek and the dull, unvarying turning of the water wheel in the black current. A light flickered through the seams of the wall inside the wooden grist mill and Tavin began shouting for help.

CHAPTER

4

A pewter sky spit remaining raindrops from a few low hanging clouds, even as solemn thunder rumbled to the south. The morning felt dismal and bleak. Agnes helped her mother load the final belongings deemed too fragile to be haphazardly tossed onto the wagon and too precious to leave behind. *"This was my mother's porcelain bowl. Notice how beautifully delicate and translucent,"* said Agnes's mother, turning the hand painted blue landscape over in her hands. *"My mother wasn't wealthy, but she loved beautiful things. This bowl was a special gift, given to her by her well-to-do aunt...."*

"Yes mother. I remember," Agnes interrupted her mother who once again reminisced a story she'd heard so many times before. With an edge of regret in her voice she added, *"We'll wrap it in this cotton bedding and tuck it securely inside the trunk."*

Mathias and Thomas hitched the horse to the cart. Thomas grabbed the reigns and jumped onto the seat. *"We are ready! I will drive father."* he called out. Mathias waved his approval and smiled, *"The Terrence watch house should be less than two days, if we move at a good swift pace. It's late in the day, but we can get a jump on the miles."*

Agnes and her mother scurried through the door; their woolen wraps draped tightly around their shoulders against the chill of the cold wind. Tears welled up in Agnes's eyes and she silently wondered if she'd ever return to their cozy little farm on the frontier, as she walked wearily behind the horse and wagon plodding slowly down the narrow, heavily wooded lane.

"This doesn't feel like a 'swift pace", mused Agnes. Mud from the nights rain made travel tedious and difficult. Glancing back at the house, she took a deep breath.

Her emotions surprised her. Venturing into this undeveloped and wild land was not something she had wanted. The only consolation was knowing that she would soon marry and join Renz in Reading. She was betrothed. She smiled at the thought. And yet, walking away from the farm that she, her brother, and their parents had worked so hard to make a reality, felt sad. While at the same time, the thought of returning to a population center excited her.

She had enjoyed a certain amount of attention and admiration by several suitors in Reading and the Tulpehocken settlement before moving so deep into the wilderness. It had been flattering, but it was Renz who had most vigorously pursued her since the first day they'd met. Others readily stepped back once Renz had designs on Agnes. Coming from a prominent, well-established family, no one wished to enter into a dispute with him. Agnes's father approved of the match. Renz was educated, ambitious and handsome, bringing the promise of a bright future. Agnes felt drawn to him and dutifully accepted the proposal of marriage, setting aside the few uninvited hesitations that followed her. With a deep sense of loyalty and natural agreeableness, Agnes easily yielded in submission to the opinions of others, especially her fathers.

Her resolve to marry Renz observed social expectations. It made sense. Agnes would marry and move to Reading, where the Provincial militia's base of operations was located, and Renz was building a career and a house for his future bride. It was decided.

Sauntering slowly behind the wagon, happily caught up in these notions, she fell further behind. Occasionally jumping from one side of the rutted tracks to the other, avoiding the deeper mud puddles, oblivious to her surroundings, she hummed a favorite folk ballad she'd heard before leaving Reading. Suddenly a loud whoop came from the woods on her left and a strong hand grasped her hair from behind, throwing her to the ground.

CHAPTER

5

Waking to the rhythmic sound of churning water and a rooster crowing morning greetings, Tavin stretched. Hazy sunlight shone through the cracks of the wooden walls. Laying on a straw pallet, the cobwebs of sleep slowly disappeared, and when his mind became alert, anguish returned. It seemed that he had been transported into a lurid nightmare. Shaking off emotions he didn't have time to indulge, he sat up. Henryk lay next to him, his back pressed up as close as he could get. Tavin reached out and stroked his little brother's blond head. *"Henryk, wake up. I am going to talk to Mr. Fincher and then I am leaving. I cannot allow mother to lay there, unburied. And I must try to find Katherine and Berta."*

Stepping to the edge of the turbulent creek, he scooped water over his head and vigorously scrubbed his face with his hands. After relieving himself, he stepped around the corner of the mill house just as Mr. Fincher was walking across the clearing from his cabin several yards away, his hair shining in the sun like white cotton, deep creases crisscrossed his haggard face. A crippled old grey dog followed. Carrying two steaming wooden bowls, he called out, *"Mrs. Fincher has seen to your breakfast."*

"How's Jakob?" Tavin nervously questioned.

"Your brother is in a bad way. My wife attended him throughout the night. He sleeps now. I think the sooner we can get him to a doctor the better. I've heard that a Dr. Boyle has had experience with scalping victims, in Bethlehem. My wife believes that Jakob is too fragile to survive the trip. We should wait and see if he gains strength and give that wound time to heal some if he lives. Here's porridge for you and Henryk," handing the meager meal to Tavin.

"I thank you for your kindness and for your frankness, as well."

"Tavin, I need hear the details of what happened. I've heard rumors of Indian attacks, but this is the first time…."

Tavin stopped him, *"Wait. Didn't Johann Schaffer come by here yesterday with the news?"*

"No. I haven't seen Johann. Not since he last brought in his grain for grinding several weeks back."

Tavin went on to explain the massacre at Penn's Creek, ending with, *"I can't let my mother lay without going back to bury her and I need to find my sisters. May Jakob and Henryk remain with you and your wife? I can pay you later."*

"God would have us help. Go. Henryk will be well cared for, and we will pray for Jakob, while doing all in our earthy power to help him survive. But you must go. See to your mother and sisters."

When the sun was high, Tavin was equipped with a clean linen shirt, an old matchcoat, an ancient musket, and ammunition, provided selflessly by the Fincher's. Dropping to one knee he held Henryk firmly by the shoulders. *"You do whatever you need to do to stay safe. Remain with the Fincher's. We owe them a huge debt of gratitude. Help them with chores and be on the watch. If Jakob survives, they will take him for medical attention as soon as he is strong enough to travel. Go with them."* His voice was firm and strong.

Henryk straightened his twelve-year-old slumped body and with determination in his voice he replied, *"I will Tavin. And I will leave a sign, so you know where we are, so you can find us."*

Turning to Mr. Fincher Tavin vigorously shook his hand. *"Your selfless generosity will not go unrewarded or forgotten."*

Mr. Fincher smiled, ignoring Tavin's proclamation. *"Since our daughter, Hannah and her children have gone and moved back to Bethlehem, over in Northampton County with her new husband, Mrs. Fincher has been aching to make a fuss over young'uns again. Believe me, these two brothers of yours are in the best of hands.*" Bending down to pat the head of his old dog, he went on to say, "*When you are ready to find us, we will be in Bethlehem. Our prayers go with you. May God's gracious hand guide and protect you and bring success in recovering your precious sisters. If you meet Johann on his return trip, inform him of our situation here.*"

Tavin nodded and walked away with determination in his stride and nagging uncertainty haunting his every step. The borrowed musket slung over his shoulder with a worn leather strap felt uncomfortable and bulky. Only his boots felt familiar as the dark forest loomed before him. Doubts circled like vultures. "*Mother lies unburied, while every minute counts if there is any hope of finding my sisters before they are beyond reach. If I go back to bury mother, I will lose valuable time and any hope of finding Katherine and Berta.*"

Questions unnerved his swirling mind like sinister ghouls. "*Who do I think I am? How would I even go about looking? Even if I did find them, what would I do then? Singlehandedly take on experienced warriors? I could be killed.*"

Apprehensions grew with each stride, soon turning to anger and accusation, as the image of his godly mother lying dead across the threshold of their family home seared as deeply as a hot branding iron into his brain. "*And what about God? He wasn't there yesterday. My mother lay dead. My brother is dying, and my sisters are lost. Where was God?*" Without confidence or faith, he continued to move forward as if he had both, taking one dubious step at a time.

The path widened as it forked away from the Swatara and approached the Tulpehocken Path. Rays of late sunshine pulsed through the broad clearing ahead. Barren trees gently swayed against the brilliant sky, casting thin quivering shadows across the well-trodden trail. Rainwater from the night before shimmered in perfect stillness outlining deep wagon tracks, cutting through sticky mud like slithering snakes. Tavin stopped, debating which way to go. "*South. To the Terrence watch house,*" he assertively pronounced, his reasoning clear for the first time. "*God, if you hear me, ask my mother to forgive me. I must leave her lay and find help for my sisters. I cannot do this alone.*" His confidence in God's dependability remained uncertain, yet his mother's unflappable faith had planted too many seeds to ignore.

Breaking off into the forest, Tavin forged through the damp, thick undergrowth, ducking beneath low hanging limbs, keeping close enough to see the trail, but far enough away should he need to take cover. Pushing all else aside, the miles slipped past, as he trained his thoughts on his sisters, forcing himself forward. Clawing branches slapped at his face and briars grappled at his arms and legs. Climbing long, steep, slippery hills and scrambling down rocky embankments, the only sound he heard was his own heavy breathing. His lungs felt torched. *"Katherine, Berta."* Their faces rang across his memories like a funeral song.

Panting as he leaned against a tree to catch his breath. *"There's no time to rest. Keep moving,"* loudly scolding himself. Running his hand through his dirty, sweaty hair, he was suddenly aware of how his voice seemed to carry through the brimming silence. Bleak and oppressive stillness followed as he continued on.

Shifting his musket off his shoulder, to his hand, he stopped cold in his tracks. Squinting through the tangled brush he saw a dark shape laying across the trail in the distance. Quickly jumping behind a fallen oak for barricade, he waited, pressing his back firmly against the rotting bark. A bird sang a repetitive melody overhead, as Tavin strained his ears to hear any sounds of trouble. Gradually peering over the tree, he could make out the grim contour of a man's body.

His thoughts whirled and conflicted, *"He is not my concern. He is most likely dead. Indians may be hiding behind these trees ready to attack should I show myself. I need to keep moving to find help."*

"Peureux!" That piercing voice challenged his courage once again, *"Coward!"* Crouching low, he crept forward, continuing to skirt the trail, moving closer until his view was clear. Mathias Bowen lay stretched out on his back; eyes open wide, blank in death.

The carnage was complete. Further along the trail, Mrs. Bowen lay face down and next to her, Agnes's older brother, Thomas. Tavin checked the three lifeless bodies. Hastily scanning the surrounding area, Agnes was nowhere. A deep desperation overwhelmed him, rushing in like a flood cascading down a mountain side. He slumped to the ground and wrapped his arms around his head, as if to bury himself away from the horrors of the past two days. *"Agnes?!"* he cried, his mind a blur of anguish.

Finally wiping his eyes with his sleeve, he exhaled, *"God, what is happening?"* and stood, wrestling with what to do. He had to reach the watch house for help. Turning to hurry back toward the sanctuary of the woods, a muffled cry stopped him. Reeling around, he slowed his breathing and listened. *"There it is again."* Turning his head from side to side, his blue eyes shifting, searching back and forth, he finally knelt next to Mrs. Bowen's body. Taking ahold of her cold arm, he gently rolled her over onto her side to discover a newborn underneath, wrapped snuggly inside a green blanket. *"Well, who are you?"* he quietly choked out.

Quickly unwrapping the infant, she let out a loud howl. With renewed sense of urgency, he pulled the blood-stained woolen shawl out from around Mrs. Bowen's shoulders and untangled the wet blanket from under the infant. Grabbing a finely embroidered ivory kerchief, tossed aside next to an old trunk, he shook out shards of broken glass and blue pottery to swaddle her, remembering how he had done the same seven years earlier for his little sister Berta. Then, rewrapping the woolen shawl around the infant for warmth, he picked her up, pressing her against his chest and began to run along the steep rocky path. Darkness was falling. It was cold and the baby was silent. He softly repeated in whispered tones, *"Hold on little one. Hold on. Don't die,"* with a renewed sense of urgency and purpose. His breaths were short, and quick. The crisp mountain air nipped relentlessly at his sweat covered body, sending shivers down his spine.

Ignoring the foreboding he had of travelling directly on the trail, Tavin held the infant tight and ran like a rabbit chased by a fox, stumbling over rocks and roots, yet never falling, always aware of the hushed tiny bundle he carried. Coming up over the last rise, a faint light flickered through the darkness. The Terrance watch house. *"Help! Help! I need help!"* Tavin hollered madly. A man stepped outside holding a lantern high above his head with one hand, and a musket aimed in Tavin's direction in his other hand. His body appeared as a bulky dark shadow against the light of the open cabin door behind him, and he yelled, *"Who goes there?!"*

"Tavin Shire! My father is Josef Shire. We settled just over the barrier ridge. My family has been attacked by Huron or Lenape. I need help!" The man set the lantern down and leveled his gun, calling back, *"Walk forward slowly, into the light, so I can see your face."*

"I am alone, sir, except for this infant I found along the trail. She is weak and I fear will die without attention. A family, the Bowens, are dead. Mr. and Mrs. as well as their son Thomas lay on the trail. There was no sign of anyone else. I don't know whose baby this is." Tavin's words stumbled over each other, competing to be understood, as he stepped closer to the light.

"Come in. Quickly!"

Tavin immediately felt the warmth of the fire that blazed on one side of the crowded room. He shuttered and glanced around. A dozen or more men, women, and children, were huddled tightly together, their eyes glassy and suspicious. Suddenly, a woman screamed, *"My child!"* and lunged toward Tavin. Startled, he instinctively stepped back and clutched the tiny bundle tightly in his arms. The woman's eyes displayed a kind of crazed madness, as a man leaped up and wrapped his arms around her waist, holding her back, yelling her name, *"Elizabeth!"*

His wife struggled to free herself, and the man spewed, *"Sir, we were traveling over the mountain when we intercepted the Bowen family. Mrs. Bowen offered to help by carrying the infant, as my wife remained weak from the delivery. I believe that you now hold our child in your arms."*

Tavin loosened his grip and held the quiet bundle out for the woman. Calmer now, her eyes softened. She slowly stepped forward and gently took the child, her hands shaking. An elderly woman stood from an old rocking chair in the corner near the fire and offered it to her. She sat down and with the baby in her lap, began to unwrap her.

The room filled with silent eagerness and prayer, except for a soft lullaby the mother hummed. Tavin stood in nervous dread. The mother began to firmly rub the newborns head, arms, and legs in her rough hands. The baby's small body convulsed slightly, and she opened her eyes. The silence of the room was suddenly shattered by the loud wailing cries of the hungry child. Tavin breathed a sigh of relief as the crowded room erupted in guarded celebration.

"Well done boy! Well done," a stranger said slapping Tavin on the back. *"A miracle indeed. The good Lord knows we need good news in this dark*

time! Praise God!" Tavin briefly shared the circumstances of finding the infant, as well as the attack upon his family. Yet as he sat cordially accepting the many verbal expressions of praise, he felt numb. With a warm plate of venison and corn stew in front of him, he grievously listened to the many stories of escape and was stunned to learn that hordes of people were abandoning their farms and flooding down the Tulpehocken Path seeking refuge.

Adam Terrence was a big, intimidating man. He verbosely espoused on how his trading post and farm had become a stopping point and a watch house, a refuge for those seeking shelter and supplies. Tavin politely sat listening, however suspicious that Terrence was more interested in his own financial gain at the expense of suffering pioneers, than offering true selfless sanctuary. Nonetheless, Terrence boasted relentlessly over his own generous heroism, at least as he saw it.

Anxious to seek an answer to the question that burned within him. *"Where is Agnes?"* Tavin finally interrupted Terrence to redirect the conversation to Mr. Grover, who stood by his wife as she nursed their newborn daughter, now safely back in her arms. Tavin felt joyous over the small life he had saved, however the fate of his sisters and Agnes weighed as heavily on his chest as an iron anvil making it hard to breathe. Katherine and Berta so young and innocent. Agnes so beautiful and spirited, his heart knitted tightly around every thought of her.

Charles Grover explained that he and his family had settled land along Lorberry Creek two months earlier. He was an amiable man, with kind brown eyes. Tavin liked him. *"Sir, may I inquire as to the details of the attack you survived. I have reason to believe that perhaps a girl was taken captive. Agnes Rose Bowen. Was she with her family on the trail?"*

"Yes. She was traveling with her parents. I did not see what happened. As I mentioned, we were further ahead. When we heard the whoops and gunfire, the only thing we could do was run. We have three other young ones," he said, motioning toward the small golden heads huddled together in the corner. *"We had no other choice. We had to get them to safety."* Tavin identified with the sound of rationale mixed with guilt. They were familiar companions.

Probing for more information, Tavin asked, *"Could you see how many Indians? Did you notice any captives with them? My sisters were taken. They are ages nine and seven. They both have blond hair. Did you see them?"*

Just then a middle-aged man with a fleshy face, weak chin and long greasy black hair straggling out from under a dirty black felt hat, spoke up from near the door. *"I think I may have seen 'em. A couple days back, three injun's came sauntering up to my door, all painted up. At first, they seemed friendly, asking for rum or whiskey. I offered 'em none and then they wanted tobacco, which I gave 'em. They smoked, all nice like, while I waited. They didn't know that my three boys, here, were hidin' with their muskets ready and aimed at their black hearts."* Taking a step closer to Tavin, he continued, his breath stale with alcohol. *"My boys are crack shots."* He paused like a theatrical performer. *"Then, the leader said, 'We are your enemy. You must die.' Just like that he said it. He was all tattooed up and ornery as a snake. That's when my boys stepped out from behind the cabin door and that put an end to their evil intent. They backed off real quick like."*

Tavin was growing impatient. *"You said that you may have seen two girls. Did you? Did you see two young girls? And the tattooed warrior…was it a turtle? Was there a turtle design on his neck?"*

"I'm gettin' to it. Hold on," the man indignantly replied, obviously enjoying the center of attention. *"Just let me think on it a bit more. Yep. It was a turtle, for sure. Darndest thing I've ever seen. And his arms was covered with zigzags and all sorts of fancy do-dads."*

Tavin interrupted again. *"Did you see the girls? Did you see my sisters?"*

"Well, as they was leavin', I was watchin' real close. Those sneaky brutes might just spin around for an attack. That's when I saw yellow hair movin' along the tree line. Just a glimpse, but plain as day I saw it. It could have been two of 'em, too."

Tavin's shoulders slumped. *"That warrior scalped my brother. My mother now lays unburied on the stoop of our cabin and my sisters are carried off."*

Mr. Grover now stood next to Tavin and quietly commented, *"I wish I could tell you if those were the same Indians who took Agnes Bowen. I just did not see. I cannot help on that regard, nonetheless, I owe you a debt of gratitude for the life of our child."* Extending his hand to Tavin, he continued, *"I volunteer to go back and bury your mother and see to the Bowen's burial as well. Go to Berks County with a clear conscience and find the help you need.*

Locate and return your sisters. Trade for them. Do what you need to do." Tavin fervently shook Mr. Grover's hand and thanked him, turning his head quickly so that the tears welling up in his tired eyes were not seen.

Mrs. Grover exclaimed from the other side of the room, shaking her head in fear. *"Charles, no! It is too dangerous."*

"Elizabeth, we owe this young man! I will go." he vehemently stated. At that, three other robust appearing men stepped forward and volunteered to help. Charles Grover thanked them in his subdued demeanor. *"We shall depart at morning's light."*

CHAPTER

6

Agnes pulled at the taut leather leash around her throat with her fingers. Her wrists, raw and bleeding, the binding cutting into her skin. Katherine leaned in snugly against her. Berta curled at her feet. They had followed the snaking line of Lenape warriors through the dismal shadowy forest at a brutal pace throughout the day without stopping. Climbing a steep embankment, they finally sheltered under low hanging cedars and pines, as a cold wet rain began. A tall, lithe young bowman, with several eagle feathers protruding from the back of his shaved head, huddled with the oldest warrior on a nearby rock, conversing in quiet animated tones. Agnes assumed that the seasoned, grey-haired man was the leader. He held an air of authority. The sullen face of a muscular warrior sat nearby, staring at Agnes with intense black eyes, his neck muscles flexing under a distinctive black etching, a turtle.

Whispering to Katherine, *"Don't worry sweet girl, someone will find us. But until then, you must stay strong. Don't stumble or cause reason for them to think that you can't keep up."* Her words felt cold and empty.

Katherine turned to face Agnes; shivering, her dirty cheeks streaked with tears, the leather noose cutting into her small neck. *"Why have they taken us?"*

"*Shhhh…*" uttered Agnes, glancing toward the men. "*I can't answer that, but God is….*" Suddenly the line snapped, jerking her violently forward causing her to tumble headfirst, landing with her face in the scratchy leaves and muddy ground. The shorter, stocky bowman on the other end gave a muffled laugh, covering his mouth with his blue painted hand. A deep, fresh cut traced from his ear to his chin. The others joined in muted snickers. Agnes struggled to right herself and the line snapped again; this time there was no laughter, only a message of power. She was theirs and she was at their mercy.

After a short discussion among themselves, the line jerked once again, and Agnes stumbled to her feet. Continuing to pull at the choking noose to protect her throat with her bound hands, she kept her eyes on the two little girls in front of her, quietly coaxing them to keep pace. The overcast sky gave way to the setting sun, and Agnes knew that they were moving northwest. Further and deeper into the mountainous wilderness.

The Lenape were uneasy and watchful as they twisted along the barely distinguishable forest path in single file. Katherine, Berta and Agnes, prodded with venomous eyes and murderous motions when they stumbled or groped for balance, remained obedient, though near collapse. Their lungs burned and their leg muscles throbbed. The grey hair led the way. The powerful warrior displaying the neck tattoo tracked intently behind him, while the two younger bowmen, one tall and slender, the other squatty and clinching the rawhide rope in his wrathful blue painted hand, brought up the rear.

Soon a fifth bowman appeared, his round face exaggerating his large nose and close-set eyes. Agnes watched as he waved and pointed, obviously reporting what he had observed as he had returned from scouting behind them. Their sour moods became rattled and flustered. Continuing westward, the pace quickened. Agnes prodded Katherine and Berta forward with breathy whispers of encouragement, fearful that they stumble or fall.

Carefully covering tracks and erasing any indication that they had passed, there was nothing but the silence of the forest, the occasional rustling of the wind in the pines and terrifying tension. No one spoke. Any crack of a twig or stumble of the feet brought scowls and menacing glares, of which could not be misunderstood. Aggravated expressions, sullen eyes and never ending marching deeper into the wilds of an untouched wilderness gradually began to erode thoughts of rescue from Agnes.

The only confidence she felt was to observe that her captors continued to worry that they were being followed. One or more would often disappear into the dark woods, returning hours later with their reconnaissance. After several days, they finally seemed satisfied that there was no immediate danger. At that, all hope for Agnes evaporated into the cold mountain air. Her captor's demeanor relaxed, and conversation became less subdued, although their sober mood remained. The excitement of their attack had worn off, they were now left cold, hungry, and wet. Despair and misery crept upon Agnes, even as she continued to urge the two little girls with whispered shreds of what felt like cruel promise.

CHAPTER

7

Brilliant morning sun blazed through the wide-open door. The rain had given way to sunshine and icy temperatures, as Tavin felt cold air drift in from outside. He rubbed his heavy eyes and yawned. A dog barked frantically somewhere in the distance. People were already up and moving about, worn, and weary. The room, so crowded the night before, was now empty except for two older women idly stoking the fire under a steaming cauldron. Hazy smoke battled against the stream of sunlight cast across the room. Tavin blinked hard. Suddenly there was commotion in the yard. He quickly tossed off the frayed blanket, and pulling on his black cavalier boots, he jumped up from the hardwood floor on which he had slept and ran for the narrow stoop.

His boots always made him feel taller and somehow stronger. Every time he pulled them on, almost to his knees, he thought of his late grandfather, Gustav Shire, who came to possess them shortly after arriving from the Palatinate, so many years before. They had been his grandfather's prize possession and Tavin was proud to inherit them. It was never quite clear how his grandfather came to own such a pair of boots, but rumors included a rife tale of thievery involving one of New York's naval stores and an arrogant British sailor. The story grew in lurid details and the embellished tale always made Tavin smile.

He could see his breath, like steam from a kettle, as he stepped out from the long porch to join the excited crowd. Twenty or thirty men rode wildly in, stirring up mud and emotions. *"Go find them savages and teach 'em a lesson!"* someone hollered from in front of the trading post, his strong German brogue filling the air.

A booming voice responded, *"The provincial army will be on the advance soon enough. We come from Berks County and our intentions are to bury the dead at Penns Creek."* Tavin recognized Frederick Weiser, the son of Conrad Weiser, from the Tulpehocken Valley, as he confidently dismounted. John Harris, a well-known tradesman and frontiersman, reined in his spirited horse and with a frown added, *"God-fearing people have lost their lives. Retribution will come later; you can be sure."*

An impassioned cry came from the crowd, *"Retribution?! The British and the provincial army have done nothing to protect us and now you speak of retribution. After Braddock's defeat, we all knew this was comin' and instead of buildin' blockhouses for defense, they've been lickin' their wounds, while the frontier burns."*

"Make no mistake, plans are underway for protection. But at this moment we will see to the burial of the poor souls murdered at Penns Creek. Reports have arrived implicating Lenape warriors from the Allegheny Valley. The government is offering two shillings a day, two loaves of bread, two pounds of beef and a gill of rum, as well as powder and lead, to any man volunteering as scout or guard. You must have your own weapon." Weiser spoke with the confidence of a man who understood the importance of authority.

"You can count on me," a hardy voice rose from the crowd. *"Count me in too,"* came another. Someone from the back hollered, *"The wages are a trifle! I'll not risk my life, leaving my family vulnerable for a pittance."*

"Do what you must do! No one is here to judge you the worse," Weiser loudly declared.

"Sir!" Tavin hollered, working his way to where Weiser had dismounted, *"My family was attacked several days past. My brother is severely wounded and in need of medical attention. My mother is dead. My two young sisters have been taken captive. And there is another family, the Bowens, who have been killed along the Tulpehoken Path. Their daughter is also carried off. I would like to...."*

Suddenly a familiar voice rose from among the ranks of horseman, *"Tavin Shire, is that you?! It's me, Renz Millar!"* Leaping off his horse, with a certain heir of superiority, he decidedly strode to where Tavin stood, *"Agnes?! Did you say Agnes was taken?!"*

"Yes. Yes," Tavin stuttered, *"it looks to be the case, although there is no witness. The fact remains, she is not among the dead of her family."* He was aware that his words sounded blunt and cold, lacking the passion that his heart felt. Renz became emphatic, grabbing Tavin by the shoulders, his dark eyes blazing with anger, *"Where? Where exactly did this happen?"*

Charles Grover quickly stepped forward and with a calming manner offered, *"I can lead you to the spot. I was there with my family at the time of the attack. I will be in heading that direction as soon as I gather some provisions."* Tavin gave Mr. Grover a grateful nod. Renz gave Tavin a disgusted look and remounted his feisty charger. Directing his attention to Mr. Grover with a most condescending air, he proudly stated, *"I am riding to Penns Creek as a lieutenant for the Provincial Militia. I thank you to see to the Bowen's burial. As for Agnes, my deep affection for her remains, while I doubt that she is within reach. May God have His will. If she is taken to Quebec she may be traded or purchased, but with her family gone, I doubt that anyone else has the wealth to reclaim her."* At that he feigned grief with a wipe of a false tear and spun his horse around, rejoining the Penns Creek contingent.

He looked dashing, mounted on his spirited horse, his grey wig tied in a neat queue at the back of his neck and his strong square chin held high. Tavin noted the way Renz sat in the saddle, his back ramrod straight with brass buttons on the cuffs of his clean dark brown coat sparkling in the sunlight. He looked down at the dirty, oversized white linen shirt and the worn woolen matchcoat that Mr. Fincher had loaned to him. He had no hat, no wig, no possessions of his own at all, except for his breeches and his boots. Everything else had come through the charity of others, even the worn black belt that snuggly cinched his thin matchcoat closed.

Tavin stood stunned at Renz's words. Straightening his demoralized posture, he turned to Mr. Grover with new resolve and determination, *"May the arrogant be ashamed, for they subvert me with a lie, it says in Psalms."* surprising himself with the quote that so quickly came to remembrance. *"Renz has relegated himself to a position of haughty falsehoods, stepping back from his duty to Agnes. How can he say that he loves her and not fight for her life?"* There was bitter bewilderment in Tavin's voice.

"God will be his judge," mumbled Mr. Grover, shaking his head and walking toward his horse.

Displaced homesteaders milled about the yard, unsure and fearful, eyeing the three Iroquois scouts who had ridden in with Weiser and Harris. Some bought additional supplies from the Terrence Trading Post, preparing to continue further east, while others merely appeared to have no purpose, no direction, their faces as a blank canvas. Poor and destitute. New families continued to arrive periodically from over the mountains with lurid stories of escape. Even young faces appeared hauntingly grey and aged.

Frederick Weiser watered his horse and barked orders to the riders. Tavin, with newfound courage, approached him again. *"Mr. Weiser, I wish to borrow a horse. My father, Josef Shire, was with General Braddock, as a waggoneer, and has not returned. He has with him our gelding. As I said, my sisters were carried off, as well as a friend, and if there is a chance that I can find them; I will do whatever it takes."*

Weiser took off his black cocked hat and rubbed his forehead. *"I admire your fortitude, albeit, unfortunate. Without a horse, I can see no opportunity for you. I have no horse to spare."* Turning to tighten his saddle, Weiser casually added, as if speaking to the air, *"The only possibility I can see, is you join up with the Indian scouts. They are Iroquois, Seneca, from the Ohio Country, across the mountains. They know the land and understand the mindset of those invaders who have pillaged, murdered and burned."*

Tavin quickly responded, *"I beg your pardon, sir, but I am confused. Are they not scouting ahead of you? Heading for Penn's Creek?"*

"No. They have refused; returning home to see to the safety of their relatives. But you can be sure they'll have a sharp eye on the trail for any Lenape, Shawnee or Huron in the area. If God be with you, you might come upon your sister's tracks, although chances are slim to none," said Weiser with a final gesture toward the reclining Indians.

"Thank you, sir." Tavin nervously glanced over at the Seneca contingent of three men. *"Do I just go ask them?"* Weiser chuckled, *"Yes. You just go ask them."*

Tavin, assuming a false confidence, abruptly waved as he approached the men reclining on the ground under a barren red maple tree. A man of middle age and stature, with a dark olive complexion and a slight smirk on his severely pock marked and ornately tattooed face, stood as Tavin approached. Another, younger, remained seated and hesitantly gave an almost imperceptible wave back. A painted trade musket rested across his lap and silver ear ornaments lined both ears. He appeared sullen and suspicious, his features chiseled and weathered. A beautifully beaded pouch, hung prominently at his hip, displaying an emblem resembling the red cross of Saint George on the British flag. Tavin felt regret, fearing that he had crossed some improper line with his wave. His nerves were getting the best of him. These Indians looked remarkably like those who had attacked his family.

He halted his approach several feet away and stammered, *"I wish to accompany you on your journey west. In particular, I am hoping to find my two sisters. The girls are young, and I hope to rescue them before they are taken too deep into the wilderness or reach an Indian town."*

A much taller man now stood as well, dignified and stalwart. His head was shaved except for a single scalp-lock, with an eagle feather tied at the base of the crown. He wore handsome indigo leggings, a black loincloth, and a white linen trade shirt, with sleeves rolled up. Blue-black tattoos adorned his strong forearms, like the tips of arrows and spearheads. Multiple piercings lined the rim of both ears. His face was smooth, and a thick line of black paint ran across his nose from ear to ear. Tattoo markings lined his jawline. A shiny silver British gorget hung around his neck. The red and black Hudson Bay trade blanket slung over one shoulder was muted and worn. Tavin waited.

The man, Tavin surmised, looked to be a bit older than his father. His presence was imposing as he stared quizzically into Tavin's eyes, unblinking. He finally spoke, *"What do they call you?"* With only the slightest variance in tone and inflection, his English was perfect. *"I am Tavin Shire,"* feeling embarrassed that he did not think to first introduce himself. He had a lot to learn. *"I have no horse and Mr. Weiser suggested that I could travel with you, as your pace would be slower, allowing me to follow on foot. It would save valuable time if I did not have to travel into Berks County to find help."* His voice was breathy and even in the cold he was sweating. Large snowflakes gently drifted through the air.

The tall Seneca, eyed Tavin in puzzlement and firmly answered, *"I am Ga:da's. Called 'Drake' by Weiser. Weiser knows that I will not allow you to join us. We take no orders from the provincial army or the British. We have no time to oversee a naïve cub."* And with a finality of dismissal, he turned his back on Tavin, ending the conversation.

Tavin found himself respecting this man's countenance as well as his use of English, although bristling at being referred to in such a derogatory manner. A *"cub"*. Ignoring the slight, he persisted, *"I know how to shoot. I can follow behind and watch the rear. I will not be any trouble and if I prove to be a bother, you can leave me. Please, I beg of you. My sisters are so small. I have to find them!"* pleaded Tavin.

"Go back to Weiser. You are on a fool's journey. We cannot take you. Remain here. You will be safe," Drake stated with a definite edge of irritation in his voice. An edge that Tavin did not want to feel the greater sharpness of. Yet he continued, *"My safety is not my primary concern. I must find my sisters."* Drake ignored him. Turning to walk sullenly back toward the trading post, Tavin momentarily wondered at Drake's peculiar comment concerning his well-being.

Leaning against a broken-down hitching post, Tavin watched Frederick Weiser and John Harris lead the mounted riders northwest toward Penn's Creek. Pushing his hair back off his face, he paced back and forth, alone, contemplating what he should do next. It seemed everyone had purpose and direction. Right or wrong, they had plans to match their motivation. All but him.

Renz rode by on his majestic horse, frowning, giving Tavin an especially sick feeling. Mrs. Grover and her three young children clung tearfully to Mr. Grover, saying their goodbyes, while the baby, still wrapped in Mrs. Bowen's green woolen shawl, slept peacefully in her arms. *"Even she, an infant, knows what her role is and how to accomplish it,"* thought Tavin.

Mr. Grover and the three additional volunteers mounted their horses. Tavin recognized that Mr. Grover, as a good man, would honor his word in finding and burying his mother. That, at least, gave him some comfort in his distress.

As the Swatara Creek burying detail plodded past, Mr. Grover tipped his hat to Tavin. *"We will see to your mother and to the Bowens. God be with you in your endeavors, and may He grant you the grace to recover your sisters, and God willing, Agnes will be with them."*

Tavin nodded haplessly.

Drake and the two unnamed Seneca warriors, whom Tavin had privately designated as *'Pock'* and *'Flag'*, were packing supplies. Drake glanced in Tavin's direction with a perplexed look on his handsome etched face, speaking in low tones to Flag. Snow flurries were now dancing freely through the air and sticking to the ground. The temperature had continued to drop and Tavin thought of Berta, dressed only in her thin stockings, blue cotton dress and homespun petticoat. *"She must be cold,"* he sadly thought.

His mind wandered back, reliving three days before, Katherine's blond hair tied in a new yellow ribbon, her white linen apron bouncing to the rhythm of a childish song that she and Berta sang, as they spun in joyous circles across the yard. And then their screams rang through his memories once again.

"I ran. I ran," he flatly repeated out loud, guilt holding his heart for ransom.

The Seneca's rode away from the trading post without looking back. Their horses trudged slowly, their multi-colored blankets flapping lightly in the icy breeze. *"I have to go,"* he pronounced to himself. Bounding onto the porch of the house and rushing inside, he hadn't noticed Mrs. Grover peacefully rocking her baby in the corner. Hastily rolling up his rough woolen blanket, he stuffed it inside his pack. Slinging it over his shoulder he grabbed Fincher's old musket and bolted for the door. *"God bless you Tavin Shire,"* called a soft voice in a thick German brogue.

Startled, he turned and adjusted his eyes, *"I haven't seen much of God's blessing of late Mrs. Grover. I expect I am on my own,"* he cynically replied.

"Don't be too quick to dismiss God, Tavin. Just when you think He has abandoned you, He will show Himself ever faithful, even through the worse of circumstance. As the Psalmist says, 'God is our refuge and strength, a very present help in trouble'. Tavin solemnly smiled and left the house.

CHAPTER

8

Amber-colored leaves lay as a noisy carpet under a delicate blanket of white snow. The ground crunched loudly as he walked. Tavin slowed his pace, remaining far back, fearful of being detected. The tracks were easy to pursue. Following directly on the path of the unshod horse's hoof prints in the snow, he paused occasionally to listen. The silence felt icy and ominous.

As darkness fell, he quickly realized that his preparation for trailing the Iroquois through the wilderness was greatly lacking. In his desperation, he had been unwisely impetuous. He shivered with cold and hunger. Having traveled only five miles or so, he was already aware of his grim situation. The nighttime temperatures promised to be brutal and without adequate clothing, food, or knowledge of survival in the wilderness, the odds were against him. He unrolled his blanket and snorted to himself, *"Well, at least I have a blanket, such as it is."*

With his fingers red and stiff, he scooped out a small hole close to a gnarly tree. Laying down, he curled himself into a tight ball, pulling leaves across the blanket. The added weight and insulation did little to help. Shivering through the night, his toes grew painful and then numb. Pulling off his boots he vigorously rubbed his feet, until feeling returned. Rolling back into his blanket he forced himself to be still.

Sleep eluded him. In the rawness of morning, frost covered his back and shoulders. Splashes of gold and orange streams of light melded gaily together in the eastern sky, shifting above a stand of birch trees. Finally rays of sunshine streaked through tangled fallow limbs, providing a hint of warmth.

Rediscovering the Iroquois' tracks, he heedlessly pressed on, a stabbing wind stinging his watery eyes. By mid-day, the sun brilliantly glistened, thawing the remaining remnants of snowy patches. The mountain path was steep, sidling, stony, and slippery. Barely discernible. Stumbling, Tavin plunged down a craggy embankment, ripping his breeches, his knee bleeding. Gathering himself up, he studied the ground and realized that he was unsure whether the tracks he followed were tracks at all. Crouching down on his bloodied knee, he ran his hand across what he thought to be a hoof print. At that moment he fully understood that he was indeed ignorant of this thorny wilderness and its ways.

Suddenly a strong arm was around his neck and the point of a knife at his back. *"Tavin Shire, what you lack in wisdom, you settle with boldness. It will get you killed."* Tavin recognized the deep fluctuating tones of Drake. *"Are you going to kill me?"*, Tavin asked, his voice choking under the grip. Drake relaxed his arm, *"Maybe. But not today."*

"That's fair, I guess," rubbing his neck. *"So, what are you going to do with me?"*.

"Blood leaves tracks." said Drake, motioning to Tavin's knee. Tavin sat down, blotting his knee with the edge of his linen shirt, until the bleeding stopped. Drake stood nearby for a moment and then abruptly began walking, saying nothing more. Tavin jumped up, scrambling to grab his blanket and musket, he followed.

Drake moved deftly through heavy brush and deadfall. Tavin's single-minded resolve drove him, even as he struggled to keep up. Observing how the experienced warrior stepped purposely, avoiding snapping branches as he went, Tavin tried to imitate. Covering several miles, they finally dropped halfway down into a steep ravine. Drake raised his hand, signaling quiet. He crouched, cupped his mouth, giving a birdlike call. A short high-pitched bark answered, and they proceeded down the hill. Pock and Flag sat squatting close to a smokeless fire, wrapped in pelt capes and trade blankets, warming their hands. Another Indian had joined them. He was young, about Tavin's age. The three horses stood tethered close by and Tavin could hear a stream gently gurgling off to his right.

He eyed the fire. His body shook at the thought of warmth. *"Sit"*, Drake quietly said, motioning. Tavin timidly hunched down and sat between the silent men. They gave him no greeting or acknowledgement. The heat on his face felt as warm as a summer sun. His ears ached as numbness gave way to feeling. He wiggled his rigid fingers over the flames. The young Indian glanced up; his piercing gray eyes shimmered with flecks of gold in the firelight. Tavin brought his hands down and tucked them between his legs, unsure of himself.

The companions chatted with each other in low tones in their own language. Tavin listened closely. He could not decipher any understanding, nonetheless, it was obvious that they shared deep friendship and close connection. After a while, they tossed a larger log on the fire and fell silent, drifting off into sleep. Tavin scooted closer to the hot embers, using his arm for a pillow; his eyes grew heavy, and he wondered if his sisters had a fire to warm them.

He slept soundly and woke to heavy low clouds blotting out the morning sun. Watching the four friends eat sparingly from their food pouches, Tavin's mouth watered with hunger. When the younger man offered a handful of beech nuts and small strip of dried meat, Tavin responded with a quick nod of his head and said, *"Thank you."*, barely chewing before he swallowed. *"Nya:wëh sgë:nö'"*, came the pleasant reply and a half smile. Tavin felt grateful and confused. Why were they treating him with such kindness? He was an intruder. He had been told that he wasn't welcome and yet, Drake had come back for him, he slept next to a warm fire, and now he was offered food.

Tavin watched as all four then knelt by the cold mountain stream and washed themselves, in what appeared to be an almost reverent manner. No one seemed in a hurry. Once again unsure of his place, he anxiously rolled his course blanket and checked his musket.

Returning from the stream, Drake, Pock and Flag opened small, leather pouches and mixed rancid bear grease with charcoal in the palm of their hands. Delicately, they applied paint to their faces. When they were satisfied, they worked to camouflage the campsite. Flag carefully buried the black coals left from the fire and spread leaves over the top, concealing any indication that they had been there. Pock swept the area where they had slept with a pine branch, carefully lifting leaves and twigs.

Drake turned to Tavin, *"The enemy is sloppy and weak. They have left a trail through the forest as wide as the white man's roads. We'll follow. Horses are of no use to us now. Too easy to track. We go on foot from here."*

Tavin excitedly responded, *"My family's farm is not far from here, near Swatara Creek. These could be the tracks of the warriors who took my sisters. Can we overtake them?"*

Ignoring Tavin's question, Drake responded, *"Tavin Shire, you do not know the ways of survival. You do not know the enemy. You, like our horses, are of no use."*

"But I tracked you from the watch house. Doesn't that prove that I am capable?"

Drake smiled wryly, red war paint crinkling around his dark eyes, *"Tavin Shire, we remained on the well-travelled Indian path, allowing you to follow close behind to understand your determination. You are strong-willed. When you did not return to Adam Terrance at the trading post, as we expected you would, we conversed. It was decided that to leave you would be as to leave a wounded buck. A wolf would soon find a meal. I cannot let you die."*

"You mean you knew that I was following?"

Drake shook his head in disgust, ignoring the rhetorical question. *"It has been decided that you will go with us. You may be useful in one regard."*

Tavin's voice grew excitedly loud. *"Thank you! I will do whatever you say! I can be useful! I can! I promise...."*

Drake firmly held his hand up, indicating silence and spoke in a husky whisper, *"Your zeal is as fat as a farmer's pig, while your skill is slender and shapeless. The first lesson in hunting is that you do not warn the prey of your arrival. You have much to learn. You use too many words, and your voice carries as rattling thunder across the sky."* Tavin felt sheepish. In attempting to assure Drake that he would be no trouble and could help, he only made matters worse.

After a short pause, Drake added, *"You will come. You will obey every direction that I give. There is no talk. There are no questions. I will keep you safe."*

Tavin gratefully agreed, baffled again at the continued reference to his well-being.

By mid-morning, they began walking. The younger Indian newcomer with the unusual grey eyes traveled in a different direction with the horses. Tavin wondered who he was. His blue-black hair was not shaved like the others, rather it was parted in the middle, hanging long, and sleek to his shoulders. His face was smooth and handsome. He was as tall as Drake, but more slender. His teeth were as white as shells and his mouth almost always seemed to hold a subtle smile. Nevertheless, Tavin held his curiosity in check, remembering Drake's mandates, recalling that his role was to listen and obey, not to inquire.

The pace felt painfully slow, as the three occasionally stopped to squat close together on the cold ground, speaking in low tones, observing a broken twig or a disturbance on the otherwise undisturbed landscape. Tavin concentrated on isolating their words, deciphering their meaning, with little success.

The colder weather brought with it a sticky snow, as two more days passed. Tavin easily surmised that his lack of experience and preparation put them all in potential danger, slowing them down. Although sickness quickly became the real issue. Tavin's lungs throbbed in pain and a persistent cough reverberated through the threatening still forest. Every raspy hack announced their coming, every knee-buckling stumble betrayed their position.

Shivering with chills by the end of the third day, he huddled close to the small fire, his eyes bloodshot with fever. Voices seemed to float in sing-song melodies, intermingling overhead, dancing with the flames. Blackness followed.

★　★　★　★　★

Waking, Tavin's head pounded. His arms and legs felt stiff and useless. His stomach empty and hollow. He was alone. Disoriented, he weakly pushed himself to sit. A faded black and red trade blanket covered him. He recognized it. It was Drake's. Shifting his body, he focused on his surroundings. Branches arched over him in a tight crisscross pattern, like a warm cocoon. Through a small opening, he could see the flickering of a fire. Heat wafted in on a light breeze. A twig snapped and Tavin ducked back down.

"Do not fear, Tavin Shire, you are protected." Drake squatted down and peered inside the makeshift hut. *"You have been very sick, but now you gain strength."*

Sliding out from inside the warm shelter, Tavin's breath billowed like steam in the open crisp air. Returning from relieving himself he asked, *"How long have I been out?"*, eyeing the skinned squirrel, pierced through by a thick stick, and hanging over the hot coals. The aroma caused Tavin's mouth to water, as it sizzled and popped.

"Two days. You moaned and thrashed about in your dreams, calling out a name, Agnes," Drake commented, pulling the charcoaled meat up and blowing on it. *"Here. Eat."* He handed it to Tavin.

Devouring the tough meat, his mouth dripped with grease that caught in the stubble of his chin. Tavin sheepishly replied, *"Yes, Agnes. She is spoken for and will marry another man. She was captured by the Lenape. I am hopeful that she was taken by the same raiding party who took my sisters, and I can find them all together."*

"Why is it that you search for the girl? Where is her man?"

Tavin's jaw tightened, *"He assumes that she is gone and beyond help."*

"And yet you search for her and your sisters."

A sudden panic overwhelmed Tavin, *"My sisters! I've lost time! How will I find them now?!"*

"My Onödowá'ga:' brother's will not lose the tracks we follow. If they are the ones who took your sisters, they will not escape."

Tavin stood, his legs wobbly, *"I can travel. I can't sit here like a wounded bird any longer. Please let's go now."*

Drake nodded his head, *"Áédwahdë:di'. We go, but first, eat more. You will need strength. Your grit does not limp, but your body stumbles."*

It was late morning before they gathered their supplies and weapons. Slinging the heavy packs across their backs they began walking. Struggling for balance, Tavin drove himself forward, across miles of rough terrain and swampy ravines. Drake set a steady, swift pace, following the faint signs of the murky, narrow path before him. The further Tavin walked, the stronger he felt. His cough disappeared, and his lungs felt free and clear. *"God are you with me?"* he found himself hopefully questioning.

When darkness came, they silently continued, keeping the north star on their right shoulder. Stars twinkled between snow-lined branches which appeared as brooms sweeping the black sky. Finally stopping to rest, Drake handed Tavin his pouch of dried beans and berries.

Sitting against a large tree trunk, with a small, warming fire set between them, Tavin mustered his courage and asked, *"Why have you helped me? You could have gone on. You should have left me behind."*

"You are evidence of our good intention. White men are hot headed and do not always discern between an enemy Indian and an ally. If they see a white man, they may not be so hasty."

Tavin waited, and then pressed, feeling like there was something Drake was keeping from him, *"But you first refused to take me with you and now you have saved my life and continue to keep me safe. Earlier, you told me that you could not let me die. Why?"*

Drake's liquid dark eyes grew soft and thoughtful as the fire's orange glow danced shadows across his sullen face. He finally spoke, *"As a boy I went into the wilderness in search of my Manitou…my guardian spirit. On the fifth day of fasting and waiting for the Great Mystery to reveal His divine message to me, I had a dream. A sunburst appeared from thunderous clouds and in the midst was a black bird. The bird tumbled and fell to earth, weak and injured. A young man appeared, his face clear and white. He picked up the bird. In the young man's hands, its wings were healed, and it soared strong and brave. The young man then continued his journey and the bird followed, in gratitude, determined to protect the young man from danger. Tavin Shire, you were the one in my dream so many summers ago. I have watched patiently for your face to appear."*

Stunned, Tavin had no reply. Sitting in silence he soaked in the story. Finally, he spoke, *"I am greatly humbled before God. It gives me courage and yet causes me to wonder. You have protected me, but I haven't saved you from anything, as your vision told you."* Feeling bolder, Tavin asked, *"What does it mean?"*

"Hojë:nō'kda'öh, Creator, will reveal that in time. For now, I must obey the message of the vision. You are under my protection, as my son, my brother, and my friend. Enough talk. We sleep now."

Perplexed and amazed at the same time, Tavin pondered these circumstances. Could God have used this man of the wild to send a message? Was this God's way of providing safety for him and a rescue for his sisters? He laid on his back with his arms wrapped comfortably around the back of his head. Staring up through barren treetops, the cold brilliant sky blaring its majesty in boundless stars. The fog of his mind seemed to wash away. He felt clear-headed and focused for the first time since the attack. An unexplained peace came to him, and he remembered his mother's words, *"Alles ist gut"*. All is well. Closing his eyes, he wanted to pray, but again no words came, only images of the past and a newly discovered hope for the future.

The next morning, feeling oddly rested and at ease, Tavin rolled his blanket and asked, *"What do you call your companions? Are there English names? I mean, Weiser calls you by 'Drake'. My parents call me 'Tavin', even though my given name is 'Gustav', like my grandfather."*

Drake rolled his eyes and shook his head in amusement, smiling, he explained, *"Do:hsetweh had what the whites call 'smallpox' as a younger man. His face is severely scarred, bringing great sorrow and shame. You may call him Job. His body is scarred, but his heart is strong."*

"Job", Tavin repeated. *"I like that. It makes sense. But how did he get such a Biblical name?"*

"A young white man came to Shamokin Village, named Alexander Riegel. He saw Do:hsetweh's scars and heard of the suffering that belongs to Do:hsetweh, as his wife had died and his only son drowned. Riegel said Do:hsetweh was as the man called Job, in God's book."

Tavin was curious to hear more of the story of Riegel but knew Drake's tolerance for lengthy conversation was minimal, so rather than press it he asked, *"What about the other, the one with the beaded bag that resembles the British flag?"*

"Call him Kaendae," said Drake, with a hint of impatience in his voice.

Tavin's curiosity was heightened. *"Cane-die. I can remember that. What does it mean?"*

Drake waved him off; finished talking.

"Job and Kaendae. Good. I am happy to have their names." Tavin thoughtfully commented to himself and asked, *"What is the plan? Will we catch up to them today?"*

"We already have," said Drake with a slight smile on his face, just as Job and Kaendae appeared, like ghosts rising from a low white mist steaming up from the damp forest floor. The three friends spoke in quick animated gestures, while Tavin stood back and waited. The two warriors then turned and sprinted off in the direction from which they had come. *"Is there a problem?"* Tavin asked Drake, shuffling his feet to keep them warm. *"A Lenape raiding party is just over the next ridge. Four or five warriors. No captives. We will flank them and catch them by surprise."*

Moving as cautiously as a cat stalking a bird, Drake crept stealthily up the steep incline. At the top, he stretched out flat on his stomach, peering through the brush at the Lenape below, who lounged casually unaware. Tavin counted four of them, as he lowered himself carefully next to Drake, who firmly stated, *"Remain here. Do not raise your head or make a sound."*

Watching as Drake crouched low and slowly angled his way down the hill, Tavin's heart pounded out a steady, pulsing beat, like a drummer boy in the British army; so loud, he was sure that the Lenape could hear it. Suddenly there was a shrill whoop and the Seneca crashed into the Lenape camp, from three different sides. Tomahawks blazed in rapid brutality. War clubs collided with painted skulls, while scalping knives flashed in violent, quick succession. It was over in a matter of minutes. Tavin did not move.

"Tavin Shire, ga:jih! Come here!" Drake motioned with his scarlet hand, as he called up the hill. Clamoring down, Tavin cut his hand on a thorny branch. Blood pooled in his palm. He stared at it, and then looked again at the carnage of the scene before him. Stunned by the brutality that he had witnessed, he wiped his hand along his thigh, staining his ripped, tan breeches. He sank to the ground in dismay. The Seneca had easily over-powered the unsuspecting Lenape.

Ignoring Tavin, they quickly gathered supplies that could be useful, along with two large bundles of beaver coat pelts and furs, ready for trade. Drake picked up a pewter mug from the ground and sniffed. *"Rum. Fools!"* he said shaking his head in disgust.

A horse stood tethered to a tree. A black gelding. Tavin recognized it. It was Johann Schaffer's. He stuttered, *"What…What about the horse? I know the man who owns this horse. He came to my family on the day of the attack to warn us."* Drake stooped down and slid his crimson scalping knife across a pile of dry leaves, his face and arms splattered, *"We will take the horse with us as far as the river. Load the pelt bundles and supplies onto his back."*

"But the horse belongs to Johann Schaffer. We have to get it back to him," Tavin reasoned.

"If the Lenape have the horse, the man is dead," Drake bluntly pointed out.

"Of course," Tavin sadly mumbled, feeling naïve and sick to his stomach.

CHAPTER

9

Warily observing her captors huddled in their Hudson Bay trade blankets near the small fire, Agnes shivered and tucked her bound hands between her knees. Deer-tail headpieces on painted skulls appeared as living creatures, breathing and bobbing in the shadows of firelight. Flintlocks, bows, and arrow quivers laid close by. Feathers and torn strips of gaudy trade cloth fluttered from weapons and war bags, while fat wet snowflakes drifted across the dark sky. Nighttime temperatures dropped, sending trembling chills through her body. Sleep was illusive.

The grueling pace continued the next morning. Agnes slowly began to differentiate personality traits among her abductors, understanding who she could depend on for mercy and who not. Falling into a cautious balance of attempting to develop a foundation of rapport while staving off angry consequences, she singled out the taller, youngest bowman, whose mood appeared less foul than the others.

Agnes's throat burned with thirst and her empty stomach ached for food when they finally stopped. Dusk. The mood felt eerie, ghostly, as the hazy orange ball tipped over the horizon and disappeared. Darkness again prevailed. She slumped against a large, decayed stump. Katherine and Berta snuggled close against her. Watching the firelight shifting across the five relaxed Lenape faces as they warmed themselves, seemingly unconcerned, she, Katherine and Berta shivered in damp clothes. Waiting to catch the young bowman's attention, she stared in his direction. Finally, his dark, wolf-like eyes caught hers. She motioned that she was hungry. He quickly turned his back.

The next morning, she woke to find a handful of nuts and a small strip of jerky. Carefully scooping it into her bound hands with her fingers she nudged the sleeping girls awake and dropped the nourishment into their eager mouths like baby birds. The squatty bowman scowled as he watched. Later that morning, wading into a nearby stream, Agnes fell onto her knees along the bank and drank deeply, lapping like a dog. Katherine and Berta did the same. No one stopped them.

Days melted into each other until Agnes lost track of how many. Further and further, they traveled. Clear cloudless afternoons gave way to chilling wind whipping snow through blinding air. Climbing steep inclines and sliding down rocky hills, crossing fast moving rivers and soggy, muddy swamps. Her captors were gradually feeling bolder and less agitated the deeper they journeyed into the unknown wilds. Agnes, her teeth chattering with cold, watched as her captors ate delicately from their food pouches, their buoyant voices louder and more animated.

She offered a kind smile in their direction and nodded toward the dried beans and cornmeal hoping for a taste and gingerly gestured toward a nearby stream for water. They smirked and scowled, except for the youngest. Leaning down close to the seasoned grey-haired leader's ear, he whispered something. Nodding, the older leader began angrily chiding the mockery of the others, indicating that the prisoners should be fed.

Abruptly standing, he lunged toward Agnes, with a knife in his hand. She cowered, as he tersely cut the leather straps off her wrists, motioning for her to gather wood." As he walked away, he tossed a scrap of food back in her direction. Katherine and Berta began to cry. Agnes's fingers tingled as the circulation returned, bristling with pain and relief at the same time. She quickly gathered the crumbs from the ground and handed them to Katherine.

"It's alright. Don't worry. I am fine. Here, share this with Berta. Shhh…" she said, as she loosened the noose from her neck and slipped it over her head. *"I am going to gather wood for the fire. Stay still."*

That night the temperatures once again dropped. Wolves howled in the distance. A fox yapped and three more Lenape strode into camp, proud and brash, with another captive in tow. A girl, about Agnes's age, tattered and dirty. They pushed her down to the ground and she remained motionless, her eyes cast down. Deer roaches quivered on their red painted heads; tattered, gaudy, trade cloth flapped in the breeze and scalps hung from their belts. Agnes snuggled close to Katherine and Berta, wrapping them up as tightly as she could in her arms throughout the night, glancing occasionally at the girl curled on the ground, unmoving, and silent a few feet away.

Cheerful greetings and boisterous stories were shared among the reunited warriors. Agnes listened to what sounded like a contest of whose atrocity was greatest or whose tale of conquest brought the most laughter. The Lenape finally slept. As the night wore on, Berta continued to cough and the grey-haired leader woke glaring angrily at Berta as firelight danced daggers in his eyes. Agnes quietly coached Berta to cough into the crook of her arm, praying the muffled sound would pacify the painted, feathered men.

In the morning, they again pressed on, continuing west, until coming to a fork in the path. The tall young bowman lifted Berta onto his back. Motioning to Katherine, she fell obediently in line. Without pausing he followed directly behind the older grey-haired warrior on the path leading to the right, along with the three new colorful arrivals.

Agnes anxiously watched the five of them take Katherine and Berta, as her wrists were again tied with leather rawhide and rope tautly secured around her throat. The gruff warrior with the turtle etched along his neck yanked roughly on her tether leading along the indiscernible path to the left, with the remaining two bowmen shadowing in submissive silence. *"No!"* Agnes screamed. *"No!"* as she watched the two girls drop out of sight. The line jerked and she sprawled to the ground clutching at her throat.

Berta and Katherine's cries resonated like the clang of a church bell slowly fading into silence. A hand gently caught her arm, helping her to regain her footing. *"The Lord is our refuge and shield. Keep walking,"* the whispered breath of the captive girl spoke. They locked eyes and Agnes thought she'd never seen eyes so green.

CHAPTER

10

Clouds drifted gracefully over the face of the moon. Staring up, Tavin sat mesmerized as one followed the other in rhythmic succession, like a flock of shapeless, mindless sheep. He shivered and yanked the tanned hide tightly around his shoulders. Holding a scrawny rabbit over the hot flames of a smokeless fire, a sense of satisfaction came to him. He hadn't used Fincher's old musket to secure this meager meal, rather, he had used the bow. The attack on the Lenape raiding party had provided a windfall of supplies and necessary weaponry, including bows, arrows, and war clubs. *"If you wish to survive, you will learn to use a bow,"* Drake had said, handing Tavin the unfamiliar weapon. *"Long gun's boom and answer themselves through the forest, announcing their presence to every corner."*

Several days had passed since they had fallen upon the Lenape camp and Tavin was growing anxious. Turning the rabbit over and over, he cautiously commented, *"The enemy is going deeper into this wilderness with my sisters, and it seems we are no closer to catching them."*

"We do not track to catch them. We determine their direction, know their plans and move to get ahead of them," said Drake, as he adjusted a log on the fire that was beginning to give off dense smoke. *"The tracks we found today are fresh. There are captives. No horses. Once they reach the river, they will*

retrieve the canoes hidden and head for Chinklacamoose. It is a Lenape town, north by northwest along a branch of the Susquehanna."

"Do you think my sisters are alright?" asked Tavin.

"Captives ease the pain of those grieving. A raiding party will return prisoners to a family who has seen death. It is decided by the mourning family whether the captive is to be put to death, adopted, or traded north, maybe to Quebec. Atonement must occur, one way or another. It is the path to appeasing grief. No bad deed goes unpunished."

"My sisters didn't commit any bad deeds!" yelled Tavin, horrified.

"Quiet Tavin Shire!" demanded Drake, his voice elastic and deep. *"Your sisters are young. If they are healthy and do not cause trouble, they will may be adopted as tribal members or sold to the north. Maybe we will find them first. Maybe we will trade for them,"* nodding toward the bundles of furs and supplies. *"Ready yourself for morning, we are close. But remember, swallow your thundering voice down deep within your belly. You continue to forget the hushed ways. Sleep now."*

Kaendae shook Tavin's shoulder and held his finger to his lips, indicating silence. Rubbing sleep from his eyes, Tavin slowly sat up, confused and groggy. Looking around, it was pre-dawn, a thin sliver of grey hazy light stretched across the frigid eastern sky, and he was alone. Kaendae was gone. Drake and Job were nowhere to be seen. The air was filled with a deadly quiet. Something was very wrong.

Slowly he reached for the flintlock next to him. With his finger firmly on the trigger, he sat perfectly still. Waiting. He was glad he had primed and rammed down the cartridge the night before. It was half-cocked and ready to fire. His ears tuned to every drop of dew, every chirp of a bird. A branch snapped and leaves crunched. A primeval scream echoed across the forest and a body slammed into Tavin from behind. An iron hatchet came violently down. Tavin threw himself to the side, avoiding the blow. The sharp blade sunk deep into the ground, narrowly missing his head. He rolled hard throwing his assailant off balance. Suddenly the deadly warrior wilted, limp and lifeless, two arrows in his back, crumpling onto Tavin. Pushing him off Tavin caught a glimpse of Job.

Another war whoop sounded. Job barreled through the brush like a charging bear and vaulted through the air, his feet slamming into the legs of a tall young warrior ready with bow and arrow aimed at Tavin. Instantly flipping around with his axe, Job caught the back of the attacker's neck. From the dark underbrush, another warrior ran at Job, seasoned with age, his face filled with rage and his arm raised high above his shaved head. In his hand a decorated war club, poised for death. Tavin scrambled for his musket, his muscles limp, his arms heavy, as he set it to his shoulder, aimed and pulled the trigger, hitting his mark.

Time became a blur of fluid flashes and frozen images of violent battle. Drake and Kaendae sprang from concealment and besieged upon two heavily painted warriors in hand-to hand combat. Fringes of bright colored fabric and shining paint swirled and collided in a whirlwind of fierce struggle. Tavin quickly poured black powder, inserted a lead ball, and rammed paper wadding into the hot barrel of his flintlock. He waited for a clear shot, as Drake continued to battle. The short burly warrior slashed his knife through the air in vicious, swift thrusts, catching Drake's side. Job dropped to one knee from a few yards away and dispatched a rapid succession of deadly arrows. The raider crumbled to the ground.

Kaendae twisted and coiled, writhing in merciless combat, the enemy overpowering him. Drake pulled his scalping knife just as the looming attacker brought his war club down in brutal strength over Kaendae's head. Kaendae jerked to the side, but not before the edge smashed against his ear. Drake's knife spun through the air and the enemy slumped in death.

Catching his breath, Tavin sat stunned and dropped his musket from his shoulder. In a matter of minutes, five enemy attackers lay dead. Kaendae and Drake wounded. Tavin, reeling from the surreal explosion of violence, came to his senses, jumped to his feet and ran to where Drake stood holding his hand to his bleeding side. *"How bad is it? Let me see."*

Drake fell to his knees, dropping his hand. Tavin lifted his crimson stained shirt. The knife had sliced a path from under his ribcage, extending midway around his left side. *"It doesn't look too deep, but we have to stop the bleeding."* Tavin firmly stated, surprised at the authority in his own voice. *"Hold your hand against it tightly. I'll get strips of cloth and water. We'll bandage it."*

Once Drake's gash was wrapped and the bleeding seemed to subside, Tavin turned to Kaendae who leaned against a tree catching his breath. Job had given him a rag to hold against his ear and disappeared from the camp like a banshee through the morning mist. Kaendae flinched as Tavin removed the dirty rag. His looped silver earrings had pulled away and ripped the top of the lobe almost completely off. *"Well, you won't be wearing ear silver anymore, but at least you still have an ear."* Kaendae gave a short painful laugh. Tavin looked puzzled and wondered to himself if Kaendae understood more English than he had let on. *"Let me get more water,"* said Tavin. He grabbed an old kettle that they had confiscated from the Lenape camp they had attacked earlier and headed for the stream that ran just over the hill.

Squatting next to the clear cold spring, Tavin stared at his own reflection, immersed in despairing gloom. *"What am I doing here?! Agnes is out of my reach. I am no closer to Katherine and Berta than I was weeks ago and now I have shot and killed a man. Savagery consumes each day, and my heart feels as rigid and stony as these mountain boulders."* Lifting his eyes skyward, he confessed, *"I have no more hope and no words to pray."* His heart felt as cold and lifeless as the aged warrior he had shot saving Job's life.

Listening to the familiar sounds of early morning and the serene rippling of the cascading stream, his tense muscles slowly began to relax. Bending down, he drank, like his old dog, Georg, lapping greedily. Dunking his head into the icy cold water he held it there until his ears numbed and he was out of breath. Throwing his head back he smoothed his sand-colored, wet hair flat with both hands, wringing it out. It hung to his shoulders, dripping down his back. He glanced up again. Dawn. Bold streaks of light beamed in every direction above the tops of dark, jagged evergreens.

He closed his eyes and for a fleeting moment felt God's presence, as the words of Jesus came flooding to mind, *"Whoever drinketh of this water shall thirst again. But whosoever drinketh of the water that I shall give him shall never thirst; but the water that I shall give him shall be in him a well of water springing into eternal life."* Tavin smiled. The scripture resounded in his memory with his mother's sweet German brogue.

"Lord God, you are still using her to teach me. I have yet to learn what it means to never thirst, but I long for it now in this bleak and dismal time," surprised that he had found enough faith to express his need for God's presence. Dismissing the moment, he filled the kettle and stood.

Climbing back up the hill, and approaching the camp, two girls sat huddled together with their backs to him, their blond curls matted and dirty. *"Katherine! Berta!"* Stumbling to reach them, he fell on their necks and sobbed, *"It's you! You're both alive! You're here!"* Hugging them and stroking their hollow, ashen faces he finally released them and wiped their tears with the tail of his dirty shirt. *"How?!"* he implored, looking at Drake.

Drake motioned toward Job. *"The raiders came at us, leaving their captives bound, confident of their success. Job found them tied to a tree by their necklines."* Tavin looked at his sisters; a ribbon of raw, swollen streaks ringed both of their throats, like the girdling of a tree. The rawhide towlines lay on the ground at their feet. Their eyes were sunken. Their skin, grey and thin. Their clothes ragged and torn. *"When was the last time you ate?"* Tavin tenderly asked Katherine. *"A long time ago,"* she answered, her voice flat and frail.

Berta curled up tightly and nestled as close to Katherine as she could get. Tavin grabbed his trade blanket and heavy beaver pelt, wrapping both around the quivering girls. He pulled out dried fish and chestnuts to give them. Berta refused food. Tipping water from an old pewter mug to their lips, they sipped. Tavin was careful that they not drink too much too fast.

Turning to Job, he frantically asked, *"Were there other captives? Are there more?"* Job answered in his Iroquois tongue. Drake interpreted, wincing in pain, his hand pressed against his wounded side. *"There were no more."*

Tavin shuttered. *"God's sovereign mercy was in this,"* he admitted out loud. Drake half smiled. Job nodded as if to agree. Kaendae frowned, still holding his bleeding ear.

Katherine spoke up, *"I want to see mother! I want to go home!"* Dark circles rimmed her bloodshot blue eyes. Tavin paused, *"Let's not worry about that right now. Once you're healthy and strong we can talk.*" Berta coughed. Tavin worried at the raspy sound of her lungs. Katherine tenderly pulled her little sister tighter and whispered warm, consoling words, *"Tavin's here now Berta. He will protect us."* Tavin's legs trembled at her certainty, as he remembered the day of the attack on their family. He silently determined, *"I won't fail them this time."*

Knowing what to expect, Tavin knelt next to the girls, shielding their eyes as Kaendae, Job and Drake finished their morbid tasks with the lifeless Lenape attackers. Drake's white shirt hung in tatters, his indigo leggings dirty and bloodstained and his tattooed face twisted in agony. *"Too many dangers here. We move quickly to Shamokin."*

"My sisters need food and shelter. We need to take them back south, over the mountains."

"Tavin Shire, we will continue to Shamokin Village. There is food and shelter, and it is close," coughed Drake.

With force in his shaky voice, Tavin uttered, *"I won't take them to an Indian village. My sisters require the safety of a white settlement. And you can't trust that there are not warriors there ready to burn us and you as well!"*

"There are Onōdowá'ga:' and Gayōgwe:onö' (Cayuga) from the north at Shamokin. Mingo. We will find aid. You would be wise to come with us, but I know your stubborn way. Stay off the main trail and follow what I have taught you as you go back to the white settlements. We go to Shamokin." Drake coughed again, holding his wounded side.

Frustrated, Tavin pleaded, *"It was you who told me that the Shamokin village holds many different loyalties. Shawnee and Lenape also live there. They are incensed with whites, and you have helped the whites by acting as a scout and have killed many Lenape warriors. Don't go there!"* He was surprised at his genuine concern for Drake's life.

Calming himself, Tavin continued, *"You are injured, and Kaendae is hurt as well. Wouldn't it be best if you traveled south with us? You can give a report of what you have discovered, seek treatment for your injuries at Conrad Weiser's homestead and then go back to Shamokin, if that is what you want."*

Drake thought for a moment. Motioning to his friends, Job and Kaendae crouched down next to him and after a terse conversation, Drake spoke. *"My brothers are of the opinion that your words are naive. In their rage, the whites make no distinction between Indians. They are paid for scalps. We will find our own people to heal the wounds inflicted upon us by the spineless Lenape."*

Pushing himself up painfully from the ground to stand, he continued, gesturing toward Kaendae and Job. *"They say that I am soft and that I have led them into treacherous waters because of you, yet you have proven yourself loyal, and more useful than expected. The vision told me to protect you, but we will not go back over the mountains to the south. We will continue to Shamokin to learn what the Ohio-Seneca do there."*

Drake's voice dropped to a whisper, fervent and forceful, *"Tavin Shire, I am forever your brother, as my dream foretold. I will honor you with my protection, yet my wounds direct me in the opposite path you travel. Hojë:nō'kda'öh is not finished. I will see you again."*

Tavin nodded his head in resignation, *"I thank you for everything that you have done for me. May God protect you on your journey."* He then somberly added, *"My prayer now is that Agnes has somehow found safety."*

"Agnes was with us," Katherine flatly stated.

Berta wiped her nose with her sleeve and sadly added, *"We cried when they took her away."*

"When?! When did they take her away? What do you mean!? Who took her?" Tavin's voice quivered.

"Three Indians. One of them with a funny tattoo that looks like a turtle."

"Lenape, turtle clan," Drake commented.

Katherine continued, her eyes glazed and unblinking, *"He was mean. And there was a short one with a blue painted hand. He pulled Agnes with the rope and made her fall a lot."*

Berta spoke up, excited to add to the conversation, *"Don't forget the man with the large nose. He was strong and quiet but scowled at me and liked to spit. They took Agnes away. I don't know where they went. When she was with us, we weren't so scared, but they took her away."*

Katherine's voice cracked with emotion, *"Agnes kept us alive."*

Drake interrupted, pressing his hand firmly against the bandaging of his wound. *"It is common to split up captives and travel in a smaller party, especially when being tracked. They will most likely continue to Chinklacamoose. When they discover that their brothers are dead, and the young girls are gone, their anger will be great."* Drake glanced at the five lifeless Lenape lying scattered about them. *"At Chinklacamoose her fate will be decided by the grieving families."*

"I remember," Tavin blankly said, his thoughts spinning.

Tavin was torn inside. Knowing that his first duty to Katherine and Berta remained, his stomached churned with despair at the thought of leaving Agnes while she was in grave danger and potentially within reach.

CHAPTER

11

December 1755

Breaking camp, the sun was high. An easy breeze merrily rustled dry leaves across a thin layer of white snow, while the clear crisp air contended with the desperate decay pressing heavily on Tavin's weary heart. A cavernous dread lay upon him. He watched as Job, Kaendae, and Drake followed an almost invisible path north toward Shamokin Village. Drake limped in pain as Job led. Kaendae turned to look back and give a quick wave before they dropped from sight. Tavin grinned, recalling that first day they had met. He waved back and was tempted to change his mind and head to Shamokin village with the men he had come to trust as brothers.

Loading the final packs onto Johann's black gelding, he turned to the girls. *"There is no need to worry. God, in his mercy, has provided this horse. You can ride all the way home!"* Tavin forced cheerfulness into his voice, while the secret anxiety held him like a rabbit in the jaws of a fox. Following the path in the opposite direction of his Indian friends, doubts haunted him, and he continued to question his decision to travel without them. Nonetheless, this was their lot.

The girls were frail and sickly, especially Berta, whose ragged cough persisted. Cold wind cut like a knife, as Tavin cautiously led the spirited animal down rocky, steep bluffs and up slippery, leaf-covered slopes, his sisters clinging to each other and the thick black mane. The iron-faced mountains loomed relentlessly in front of them. A wild knotted country offering no resolution, but to keep moving up and over.

"We'll camp here for the night," said Tavin. *"Let's get you both down from your chariot and see if we can get some food in you."* Katherine laughed, *"I've never heard of a chariot with four legs and a tail."* It was good to hear her laugh.

Tavin opened his pouch and pulled out some dried meat and handed it to the girls. *"I'll scrounge around to find some nuts. There were plenty of chestnut trees back along the path."*

"No!" screamed Katherine, *"Don't leave us!"*

"It's alright, don't worry, I won't leave," whispered Tavin, dropping to his knees to hold her tightly and reaching out to enfold Berta in his muscular arms. *"You feel different. Your hug is hard, not so soft like it used to be."* Berta had a pointed and direct way about her.

That night, Tavin lit no fire. Clearing a wet layer of snow to create a dry patch he spread three beaver pelts down and stretched his long body across them. His sisters snuggled securely against him, one on each side, as he pulled trade blankets over them all. Lying flat on his back, he folded his arms under his head and listened to his sisters soft breathing. Watching as stars moved soundlessly, peacefully, through the sky, he wondered how they could shine night after night as if nothing had changed. He had changed. His world had changed, but the constant ebb and flow of the universe remained stable and sure, bringing an unsettled comfort. There was something bigger than himself. A design. A plan. He felt it. Yet, he had no answers. Agnes. God was in control and as much as he tried to take the reins, he knew that the end belonged to a Sovereign will that was greater than his own. Could he trust a God that allowed fear, brutality, and death? Agnes. A bottomless despair pushed his heart deeper into darkness, while stars soothed his mind back toward the Creator.

"God, will you protect her?" Tavin silently asked, with the greater question remaining, *"If you don't, can I still believe what my mother taught*

me? Are you my God? Are you to be trusted? Are you good?" His mind whirled with the events of the past few weeks. His mother's death, Jakob, the kindness of strangers, the Grover baby, Drake's dream, bloodshed, cruelty, Johann's horse, the miraculous recovery of Katherine and Berta. Tavin saw them for the first time, not as singular threads, but strands intertwined into a larger tapestry of purpose. But where was it all going? His two sisters squirmed next to him, seeming to echo his brewing emotions, nestling closer, seeking the warmth and comfort which eluded them all.

After two long days, they reached the broader Tulpehocken Path. Tavin was hesitant to remain directly on the well-traveled thoroughfare, as Drake warned, nonetheless urgency overpowered fear. Berta was growing still weaker, and Katherine had now developed a hacking cough as well. *"I need to get you both under shelter and soon. Just hold on and we should find a farm near Mahantango Creek,"* said Tavin, with an uplifting, sing-song quality in his tone to encourage his suffering sisters.

"Let's name this horse. I'm sure Johann had a name for him, but I don't know it," quipped Tavin.

"Knight," said Berta.

"That was fast. Is that what Johann called him, or have you been thinking about a name?"

"I've just been thinking. Knight is a good name. He isn't royalty like a king, but he is honorable and brave, like a knight."

Abruptly Knight reared, his front legs thrashing, his eyes wild. Berta flipped backwards off the fur pelts and tumbled from the big black to the ground. Katherine gripped the mane, her legs flailing through the air. Tavin pulled down hard on the reins to bring the horse under control, but it was no use. All sinew and muscle, Tavin could not hold him. Breaking free, he bolted into the forest, crashing through thorny bushes and over tangled deadfall. Katherine finally let go and rolled four or five times before striking a boulder. A rattlesnake slithered to the other side of the path and curled up, rattling its threats.

Tavin pulled his hatchet from his belt and without thought flung it, catching the side of the menacing rattler. It spun around, slipping away between two large rocks. Berta promptly sat up with surprising vigor. Tavin crouched down to check her over. No broken bones. *"Stay* here!" Retrieving his hatchet, he sprinted through prickly briar bushes. Finding Katherine unconscious, her breathing shallow, he glanced quickly around, the horse was gone. Katherine moaned as he carried her limp body to where Berta sat cross-legged on the path and gently laid her down. *"Berta, stay here with Katherine. Don't move!"* he emphatically stated.

His only thought was to find the horse. Bounding catlike through the forest, the broken trail was easy to follow. Cracked branches and bloodied prickly bushes drove a clear path. A few yards ahead he heard a loud whinny. Knight stood throwing his head back and forth, the reins caught around the low hanging branches and vines of a scraggly tree. Whispering calmly, Tavin slowly approached the agitated and wild-eyed black. Reaching out, he untangled the reins and cautiously led him back toward his sisters.

Berta sat in the same position, perfectly still, exactly as Tavin had told her. Katherine groaned. Tavin felt the back of her head. Underneath her matted hair was a large swollen knot. *"We need shelter."* Carefully gathering Katherine in his arms, while holding a tight grip on the horse's leather leads, he barked, *"Berta, walk close behind me."* Turning off the path, pushing their way warily through the quiet forest, Tavin settled on a small indentation next to a large stand of hemlocks. A thin stream trickled nearby.

Looping the reins around one of the trees, he gently laid Katherine down and ripped open one of the fur bundles. Laying several pelts across the damp ground he arranged Katherine comfortably on the warm dry beaver blankets. *"Berta, sit next to your sister and wait here."* Berta firmly nodded her head, her sky-blue eyes huge with apprehension.

Tavin quickly collected long broken branches and bending them in an arch, built a makeshift lean-to, just as Drake had done for him. As he laid pelts on top of the tiny rickety hut, an icy wind picked up. Dropping to his knees he hurriedly dug out a deep hole in the black dirt, in front of the small entrance and deposited dry twigs. Sweat dripping from his forehead, he used a flint and steel, striking it several times before the kindling finally offered up dancing sparks fluttering like fireflies on a dark night. Blowing gently, tentative orange flames took hold. Feeding it with small sticks, Tavin relished the heat and briskly rubbed his hands together over the small blaze.

Bending low, he crept inside the small, covered dome, laying extra beaver blankets on the cold ground. Glorious warmth was already seeping in, as he gently lifted Katherine and slid her inside, Berta eagerly crawling in behind them. *"Berta, I have to go back and conceal our tracks. Again, I need you to wait here with Katherine. Can you do that?"* Berta nodded, this time her eyes were tranquil, and she gave Tavin a nervous smile. *"It's warm in here,"* she exclaimed. Tavin smiled in return.

Setting a small pile of dry twigs just inside the lean-to entrance, he explained, *"Slowly feed these into the fire, to keep it going. But not too fast, we cannot have smoke. Smoke will reveal our secret hideout."* Berta laughed. She liked secrets and hiding places.

Cautiously retracing their steps, Tavin inched his way back toward the trail, lifting crushed leaves, checking for snapped twigs, boot scuffs, and blood traces left behind from the deeply etched scratches on Knight's flanks. Once reaching the path, he felt satisfied that their tracks were erased, camouflaged. He had just begun to move cautiously back toward his sisters when something caught his attention. He slowly crouched down and listened.

"Wundchenneu!" a loud voice echoed from down the trail. Tavin leaped into thick brush along the rocky embankment and flattened himself out. Concealed from sight and perfectly still he prayed that his sisters remain quiet. Soon seven Lenape warriors appeared with six captives in tow, their necklines strung together, like baby ducks following their mother. Tavin's eyes, level with the path, watched as beaded moccasin feet gingerly filed by. Men's worn boots and women's dirty skirts followed in limping, agonizing succession.

Three warriors suddenly stopped in front of Tavin, and excited conversation flared. Tavin slowed his breathing and remained motionless, amazed at the noisy, boisterous banter. He found himself thinking of Drake and his constant admonition for reticence. The leaders continued their steady pace up the path with their captives following in compulsory obedience, while the three garishly painted warriors remained back, squatting down, studying the ground. Finally standing, they spread out and dropped down over the embankment on the other side of the trail, where Johann's horse had crashed through. The warriors were searching in the wrong direction.

The sun dipped into the tangled limbs above, carrying twisted, shifting shadows across the stony path. Tavin sustained himself in unmoving tension, the ground cold and prickly. Waiting. He could hear their voices; sullen warriors pushing noisily through the thorny blackberry bushes. Soon, all three emerged back on the path. Their faces angry and confused. The tall one extended his arm for the other two to see. Deep scratches oozed red. Thorny bushes had clawed with a vengeance. They kicked the ground and grunted words of complaint for a few more minutes and then turned to trudge up the path and out of sight.

Tavin breathed a sigh of relief as he warily slid out from his hiding place and back to the makeshift lean-to. The fire was burning brightly inside the deep hole, hidden from sight. The two girls were tucked snuggly within the cozy cocoon, and Katherine was awake. Warm flames brought comfort and a reminder of home and what life once was. *"We are safe,"* assured Tavin, *"Get some sleep. Tomorrow will be another day."*

Katherine grimaced and rubbed her head. *"It hurts."*

Tavin put his hand to her forehead. It was warm. *"You have a fever. But I imagine that by tomorrow you'll be good as new. You gave us quite a scare."*

"Won't you please pray that Katherine can hold onto Knight better, Tavin?" Berta meekly asked.

Tavin and Katherine both laughed. *"I can do that I guess,"* Tavin answered. He uttered a short, cursory prayer concerning Katherine's grip on the horse, and after the girls were asleep, he found himself staring at their peaceful faces and wondered at their fate had they remained on the path and come face to face with that raiding party. *"What was a rattlesnake doing out here? They hibernate this time of year. If God used a snake to save us, at what cost will it be?"* Tavin questioned to himself, as he reached over to feel Katherine's feverish head once more.

Katherine tossed and turned in restlessness most of the dark night. By early morning she woke groggy and disoriented. Vomiting what little food was in her stomach, she slept until the sun was high, finally waking and asking for food. Tavin sat outside the lean-to with the long bow watching for a rabbit, squirrel or even a chipmunk. Fresh meat would provide needed strength. He smiled, remembering the meager hare that he had shot the morning of the attack on his family. *"I was so angry with that scrawny little hare. Now, I would give anything if one would come hopping gleefully past."*

"Tavin!" Berta called out from inside the snug shelter.

"Quiet...remember the rules; no loud voices," corrected Tavin as he stuck his head through the narrow opening. Berta wrinkled her innocent face and scrunched up her mouth for a loud whisper, *"I have to go wee."* Katherine laughed.

Tavin grunted, *"Again?! Well, the privy we use today is that tree over there. Go behind it, but no further."* Berta wriggled out of the opening like a new-born baby, headfirst, full of spunk and vinegar. The trauma of the previous weeks had rolled off her as quickly as it had entangled her. She nearly skipped across the leaf-covered ground, disappearing behind an old maple to do her duties.

Just then a squirrel scampered down a tree, his claws bringing a familiar scratching sound on the rough bark. Tavin stood, took aim, and shot. The iron tipped arrow pierced the creature directly through the side. He smiled to himself, as he walked over to retrieve what would be a hot meal. *"I'm getting pretty good at this."* Reaching down for the small, limp carcass, a pair of black boots stepped into view.

CHAPTER

12

Morning sun washed over Agnes as a warm blanket, shining through the low languid mist that followed the narrow expanse of cold river. Paddles splashed in uniform cadence, almost musical to Agnes's ears. The bark canoe rocked in rhythmic smoothness. Agnes lay curled on the wet bottom of the flimsy instrument, while the harsh tattooed warrior paddled in front, his back stiff and muscles flexing with each melodic stroke. The bowman with the close-set eyes and pronounced nose knelt behind her, dipping his paddle deep and pulling with power. He was quiet and Agnes had noted that he held a gentler, kinder demeanor. The river tapered, and low hanging limbs scraped the sides. Dew-covered leaves showered over her, smearing the newly applied red paint across her forehead.

The girl with the green eyes was forced to row in the second canoe, in front of the stocky, irritable bowman. He bellowed a loud complaint when the girl ducked to avoid a branch as it snapped back and struck him. Agnes tentatively lifted her eyes over the edge to see what was happening. The bowman sitting in the stern caught her attention and shook his head in warning. She dropped down and pulled her knees up, curling as tightly as she could, like a cat warm and content. She closed her eyes and strained to imagine that she was safe in the comfort and love of her family. Agnes did not know where they were going, but with each stroke she was taken further from home, out of reach. Praying, she asked that God allow her to die in that moment and spare her whatever was to come next.

Smelling smoke, her fingers slowly inched over the birch bark edge and raising her head, she peered out to see a village in the distance. Trembling with fear, her arms and legs shook wildly. She pushed herself back into a snug ball, attempting to calm her body. Her captors proudly straightened their backs and in unison repeated three high yips as they approached the riverbank. The canoe slid noiselessly into the black icy mud and stopped abruptly. Grabbing Agnes by the hair, she was forced out of the canoe and onto the gravely muck, stumbling to her knees.

The second canoe glided to a stop and Agnes saw the green-eyed girl violently yanked out and shoved to the ground. There had been no opportunity for the two of them to talk, other than to murmur names. Liza Schell. Agnes Bowen.

A large expanse of field spread between the river and the Indian village which was encircled with a tall wooden palisade. As Agnes adjusted her eyes, she watched as men, women, and children seemed to pour through an opening like angry bees from a hive. The tattooed warrior ceremoniously pulled his prisoner to her feet and pushed her forward, calling out in loud, dramatic fashion as he roughly prodded her. Agnes could not understand the words he thundered, but it was obvious that he was proud, and she was despised.

The host of excitement swarmed toward the shoreline shouting taunts toward the new prisoners. Women hissed and spat at them. Children threw stones. Men chanted in low tones, their black eyes shining with pride and satisfaction.

CHAPTER

13

Stumbling backwards, Tavin fell and frantically flailed about, like a desperate beetle on its back, frantic to regain his footing and locate the bow which he had dropped in his panic. A friendly voice boomed, *"No need to get your breeches in a knot laddie. I mean you no harm."*

"Who are you!?" Tavin yelled. Berta, who was now standing directly behind the stranger, reprimanded, *"Shhhh…"* Tavin glanced at her and tipped his head, his icy blue eyes telling her to step back. Katherine's head popped out from the lean-to to see what was happening, still feeling dizzy but stronger, holding Tavin's musket in her hands, pointed at the stranger. *"Wait now, little missy. I am no danger to you. I followed the scent of your fire. Thought maybe you was some of those revenge filled raiders who've been causing all the fuss. My name's Casper Wolfe. I trap around here."*

Tavin silently reprimanded himself. He'd become too slack. He had not paid close enough attention to the fire's smoke or to his surroundings. After a long pause, he finally offered, *"Mr. Wolfe, as you can see, we are not any kind of Indian. Now, kindly, be on your way."*

"What are you three doing out here?" asked Wolfe, his rough red face smiling in curiosity, as he eyed the pelts and furs. He stood tall and lean, with long, stringy dark hair hanging out from under a dirty raccoon

skin hat. His reddish beard was peppered in gray and when he smiled, his rosy cheeks rounded beneath intense grey eyes.

Tavin felt suspicious, but answered, *"We are traveling back over the mountain. Heading to the Terrance Trading Post and then to Bethel, and finally Bethlehem, where my two brothers are."*

"I don't know if Terrence and his family are still there, but I can tell you that Bethel, on the other side of Blue Mountain is all but evacuated. Screaming warriors have been murdering and burning all through the country." Rubbing his stubbly greying beard, Wolfe then added, *"I have a cabin near the Mahantango, not three miles east from here. My woman is there, and she can cook up some food for you and these little girls real quick. Don't see no sense in you stayin' out here to freeze or be carried off."*

Wolfe tossed his flintlock over his shoulder, ignoring Katherine who continued to confidently aim the musket directly at him. *"Don't make me no never mind. You do what you want, but it seems to me that these little girls need more help than you can give them."* Tavin bristled at the comment, yet he knew it to be true. Katherine was regaining her faculties, nonetheless she complained of a headache, dizziness and nausea. Berta was skin and bone. She needed real food. More than a squirrel.

"I will agree to go with you. Albeit I do not know you and I shall be on my watch should you be deceitful in your intentions. My sisters are under my protection, and I will do what need be in seeing to their safe return to civilization," said Tavin, with a confidence that he did not feel, but was getting used to. Turning, he quickly covered the fire, dismantled and scattered the branches of the shelter, bundled the pelts and furs, and lifted both girls onto Knight, while Wolfe waited patiently, leaning against a tree chewing on a piece of jerky.

"Follow me, you'll be warm and cozy in no time," said Wolfe with a tip of his head and a shrug as he stood. He started off at a quick pace. Tavin, with the girls balanced again on Knight, followed.

As they walked, Tavin's eyes burrowed suspiciously into Wolfe's back, holding a tight grip on the reins with one hand and his musket with the other. The trail branched off onto a shrouded path. The sun shone brightly, warming against the cold wind, as dark, heavy clouds remained well to the south. Nevertheless, Tavin felt an ominous chill. There was something about this man he did not fully trust.

A small cabin came into view and Tavin could see a woman standing outside scraping pelts, stretched across wooden frames, a sharp metal knife in her hand. She wore a dark blue skirt, leggings, and a long brown tunic with decorative beadwork along the bottom. Her shiny black hair held streaks of white and was plaited down the middle in a perfect line. One long, thick braid fell across her back. Looking up as they approached, Tavin could see that she was middle-aged, with a lovely smooth oval face and bright dark eyes. She greeted them with a warm *"Sge:no"*. Her smile was broad and sincere.

"This is my wife. You may call her Mary. She'll get you some food and you can settle in for the night," said Wolfe. Turning to Mary he spoke in her native language, which Tavin derived was Seneca. Mary nodded and walked with short quick steps toward the cabin. Wolfe pulled the pelt bundles off the horse's back. *"You get your sisters inside. I'll feed and water this animal with the others."*

"His name is Knight," declared Berta, smiling happily, as she patted the horse's haunch affectionately.

Lifting Katherine and Berta down, Tavin noted again how thin each had become. A solid meal was a welcome thought. Stepping through the cabin door, the room was clean, small, and sparse. The smell of cornbread permeated the air and a fire blazed under a hanging iron kettle. Mary motioned for them to sit at the roughhewn table, her face tranquil and pleasant. Tavin settled Katherine and Berta tightly together on the long, worn bench and watched as Mary pulled steaming bread from the stone hearth. His stomach rumbled.

She ladled a hot broth filled with boiled meat and a few potatoes into pewter bowls and handed each of them silver spoons to eat with. *"I don't think I've ever tasted anything so good in my whole life!"* Katherine exclaimed. Berta giggled, with soup dripping down her chin, her face flushed with warmth and color. Tavin sat spellbound watching his sisters slurp up the thick meaty soup. It seemed with each delightful bite their eyes brightened, and vitality grew. Mary handed him a bowl. He took it; *"Thank you."*

Wolfe ducked to get through the low beam of the doorway. As he hung his hat on a peg and his flintlock on a rusted nail over the fireplace, Tavin's eyes settled on his powder horn, suspended by a thick leather strap across Wolfe's chest. A crude etching, "Psalm 27:1", was clearly visible. Tavin began to quietly recite it from memory, *"The Lord is my light and my salvation; whom shall I fear? The Lord is the strength of my life; of whom shall I be afraid?"* Taking a deep breath, a rage overcame him as he'd never felt before. *"Where did you get that?!"*, he shouted and leapt through the air, tackling Wolfe to the floor. *"Where did you get it!!"*, pounding his fists into the startled man's belly.

Wolfe grabbed Tavin's arm and rolled, pinning him on his back. *"Are you stark raving mad?! What are you hollering about?!"*

"That's my father's powder horn! How did you get it!? Did you kill him?!"

The bigger man slowly loosened his grip on Tavin. *"I didn't kill him. I am gonna let you up, but you need to calm down. I can explain."* His glassy eyes glanced sadly up at the terrified girls and Mary. Mary nodded and lovingly wrapped her arms around the girls' shoulders.

"Let me up and explain now!" Tavin thrashed about and howled. *"My mother scratched 'Psalm 27:1' onto my father's powder horn. She told him to always remember where his strength came from. How do you have it?!"*. Feeling sick to his stomach as Wolfe released him, Tavin quickly gathered himself and stood, his body shaking, his face red with fury and accusation.

Wolfe, leaning on one elbow, ran his hand through his beard, *"I take it that your father is Josef Shire?"*

"Yes! What did you do to him?!"

Wolfe began, *"Your father was my friend. He was the best waggoneer I ever met. He knew where he needed to be and how to get there. He was no nonsense and stiff backbone. The sheer force of his loyalty kept many a man in check, including me,"* he chuckled.

Pushing himself up from the floor, Wolfe stood and continued to reminisce as if no one were listening. His eyes drifted off into the distance as his memories unfolded. *"General Braddock's confounded ignorance of Indian warfare led to the annihilation of his army. He looked on Indians, as he would dogs to be kicked around until they cowered in the shadow of his mighty ego. Offending so many that they left him and would not submit under his command. They were the smart ones. They warned him of the danger he was in with his army. He wouldn't listen. Captain Washington warned him too, but, to Braddock, Washington was nothing more than a colonial child."*

Mary walked to Wolfe's side and put her hand on his arm. He smiled down at her and continued. *"It looked like we had the upper-hand, fighting Braddock's way, as 'gentlemen',"* Wolfe said with bitterness in his voice.

"Cannon blasts ripped through the trees, tearing down branches and sounding like thunder coming up from the pits of hades, scared off the French and their Indian allies, at first. Thinking they had the enemy on the run, the British advanced quick as could be. Then, the French encircled them into a mass of hand-to-hand combat. French allies, Huron, Shawnee, Lenape and more sniped from behind trees, picking off British soldiers one by one. Militiamen accompanying the British army took cover and began fighting from the woods." Wolfe took a deep breath.

"Your father joined them, encouraging other waggoneers. 'God is with us, men. Let us do our duty!' he shouted. Just as he spoke those words a British regular, in panic, mistook him for the enemy and shot." Wolfe paused and looked around the small room at the sullen faces before him.

"It was hours before I got to him. By then, it was too late. Shire was dead, Braddock was shot off his horse and Washington organized a rear guard. We were movin' fast to disengage and get out of there with our lives. I grabbed your father's powder horn...," Wolfe held it high in the air, *"and ran."*

With tears brimming in his heavy eyes, Wolfe added, *"I won't describe the horror of the scene, the way my mind's eye recalls. Of fourteen-hundred British regulars, militia, and Indian allies, 500 more or less died on that battlefield, and close to as many wounded. General Braddock died on the retreat. Those regular soldiers, straight off the boat from England and Scotland, behaved in such cowardice fear that I can barely conceive of it to this day. The thought of being captured, tortured, and scalped just took them to flight, like a flock of birds chased by a mountain lion. I guess I can't blame them."*

Tavin sat down on the bench, his mind spinning with the revelation, although it came as no real surprise. His father was dead. *"Finest man God ever set on this earth, but for Jesus Himself,"* added Wolfe, and leaned against the wall. Katherine and Berta quietly cried. Mary ran to them, wrapping both tightly in her arms. Wolfe excused himself, *"I have to tend to the horses. Stay here, get some rest."*

The next morning, clouds appeared, low, heavy and threatening. Tavin loaded the pelt bundles across the back of Johann's horse and called to the girls. *"Katherine, Berta! Say your goodbyes. The day is wasting, and it looks like the weather is turning."* Wolfe stepped out of the makeshift barn with three eggs in his ruddy hands. *"That chicken is scrawny as all get out, but she can lay eggs like nobody's business,"* handing them to Tavin.

"Thank You. Thank you for the food and shelter and for the clothes that your wife insisted that I take. I'm not used to the breechcloth and leggings, but my clothes and boots were pretty torn up, not to mention the stench!" said Tavin, laughing. Continuing, he looked down at his feet. *"My grandfather would understand. The boots couldn't last forever, and I think I can get used to wearing moccasins. Comfortable!"* He laughed, wrapping his matchcoat around the clean linen shirt that Mary had also given to him.

Berta spoke up, *"You look like an Indian, Tavin."*

"Well, it's still me under these buckskins. Just a warmer me."

Turning to Wolfe, Tavin confessed, *"I owe you an apology. I was a poor judge of character. I thought the worst of you, and I regret that,"* tucking the eggs inside the bundles, where they would hopefully be cushioned enough not to break.

Wolfe stared at the ground and kicked a stone, *"Honest truth, you were wise to suspect me. I was greatly tempted to take your beaver blankets and furs for myself. Those…."* he nodded toward the bundles, *"are worth a small fortune. They are coveted coat beaver pelts. You be careful on the trail. Both Indian and white trapper will kill you for those as much as look at you."*

"I thank you for your honesty and for the care that you and your wife have given to us." Katherine and Berta walked from the cabin, each holding one of Mary's hands. *"The girls have grown strangely attached to Mary in such a short time. It seems odd to say, but they will miss her,"* Tavin added.

"Mary has that way with people." Wolfe smiled. Slipping the leather strap holding the powder horn off his shoulder and over his head, he handed it to Tavin. *"This belongs to you."* Tavin took it and extended his hand. Shaking it firmly, he said, *"Casper Wolfe, I'm glad to have you as a friend and not a foe!"*

Wolfe nodded and gave a short chuckle.

CHAPTER

14

Dense, wet snow began to fall. Tavin wrapped each girl tightly in blankets. Swaying steadily atop the thorn scarred black they trudged over steep, slippery slopes, their eyes drooped in sleepiness. Progress was slow and the day was long, although Knight behaved less agitated and more compliant, allowing Tavin to maintain a steady enough pace.

"I cannot wait to see mother again!" Berta loudly exclaimed.

"I am going to run to her and wrap my arms around her neck and never let go," said Katherine, her voice quivering, as she swayed in lightheadedness, staring blankly into the distance.

"Girls! You cannot talk! You must remain silent as we travel!" Tavin reprimanded, his teeth clenched in an angry loud whisper. Berta's face dropped in sadness. Katherine closed her eyes in fatigue. Feeling guilty for his outburst, he added in a calmer tone, *"I'm sorry that I was harsh with you."*

"We should remember to be quiet," whispered Berta.

"I am sorry." Katherine's voice was weak and barely discernable.

Tavin felt hollow and regretted allowing his temper to ignite so quickly. He knew the true reason behind his anger. It came from deep within his core. Their mother. Soon he would have to tell the girls that their mother was dead. Although they had proven to be stronger and more resilient than he had ever imagined, he simply had not been willing to give them that news. It weighed heavily on him.

By late afternoon the snow subsided. Tavin's anticipation grew, as they approached the last ridge. The thought of a hot meal and warm shelter put extra vigor in his steps. The girls would be safe at last. Clouds dispersed, the setting sun shot its splendid warm beams across the land and Tavin's heart sank like a stone. The Terrence watch house lay in a pile of ashes. The skeletal remains of blackened buildings rested starkly cold against a row of tall cedars, their branches weighted down with heavy snow, glistened with gold and orange hues. A glorious backdrop to somber destruction. Stillness echoed across the clearing until crows began their incessant cawing.

Leading Knight around the burned-out property Tavin stopped and bent down to pick up a handful of ashes, releasing them to the wind. Black soot swirled up like a dark thundercloud and scattered thinly through the crisp air. *"It's been a while. No smoke. No hot embers,"* Tavin mumbled to himself.

Turning to the girls, he said, *"We'll keep moving on the Tulpehocken Path. Once we get on the other side of Blue Mountain, we will have a better idea of what to do. If Bethel is deserted, like Wolfe said, we'll follow the roads until we reach safety."*

Making their camp that night, Tavin knew he could delay it no longer. He solemnly began, *"Katherine, Berta, I have something to tell you about mother. It's a hard thing for you to know, but…."* his voice choked.

"Our mother has left this world for a better place," Katherine softly interrupted.

"Yes," responded Tavin, surprised. *"She is in God's presence in the heavenlies. She has joined father."*

The small fire cast a golden glow on Katherine's somber young face. *"Heaven is warm,"* she reflected. *"It is the gate of joy, free from this earth's coldness and sorrow."*

"Yes," answered Tavin, curiously eyeing Katherine, while Berta openly sobbed. Feeling unsure of how to continue the conversation he simply said, *"Let's rest now. We can talk more tomorrow."*

A fitful night's sleep brought sore muscles and a sluggish start for Tavin the next day. A cloudless sky welcomed the morning sun, warming his face. He sat up, rubbed his eyes, blinked hard and stretched his arms like a feral barn cat. He turned to Berta. She opened her eyes, grinning at him. He grinned back, *"Good morning. Today should be a better day."*

He turned to Katherine. She lay on her back, her face white as snow, a soft smile on her ashen lips. Tavin shook her. *"Katherine!"* Scooping her up in his arms, he buried his face in her neck and wept uncontrollably, her limp body icy cold. Berta wrapped her small arms around Tavin's shaking shoulders, *"Is Katherine gone? Is she gone to Heaven too?"*

Without looking up, Tavin sobbed, *"Yes. She's gone."*

Silence hung in the air between them. Finally, Betta responded. *"Alles ist gut. All is well. Katherine is with Jesus. Warm. In heaven with mother."*

Stunned at the calm demeanor of his seven-year-old sister, Tavin lifted his head and turned to stare into Berta's soft eyes. *"Berta, do you understand? Katherine is dead!"*

"I do understand. I know that Jesus holds her now. I will miss her. I miss mother and father, but I know where they are and I will see them again one day, with Jesus," Berta said with a confidence beyond her years and tears freely flowing down her rosy cheeks. Death had become such a natural part of life that its sting came as no surprise, and even more, it always loomed expectant. It besieged them as a constant companion. Not a friend. It hovered unwelcome over the tenuous life they lived. Now death had come for Katherine, and Berta accepted its cruel finality while embracing the eternal truths. Her faith was astounding.

Tavin's faith faltered. He hadn't kept his promise. He had failed Katherine. As he wrapped and tied beaver skins around her small body, he berated himself, heavy with guilt and sorrow. Berta watched, intuitively understanding Tavin's thoughts. *"It's not your fault. This burden, heavy as lead, is not yours to carry. You have been so brave to rescue Katherine and me from capture and possible death."*

"Then whose fault is it? What good did it do that I 'rescued' you? Katherine is dead. God teased me with success, only to pull the rug out from me. I had every opportunity and I failed. He failed," said Tavin, with venom in his voice.

Berta sheepishly replied, *"Mother always said, 'We might not understand God's plans, but we know who He is.' He is God. He is good."*

"Just when I was beginning to think I knew Him to be good," he paused and shook his head, *"I'm not so sure now."*

"God is God. Just because He does not do what you think is best, doesn't mean that He isn't good," Berta argued, tentative and gentle.

"Katherine is laying wrapped in beaver blankets. Dead. How is that good?!" Tavin yelled.

Berta put her finger to her lips, *"Quiet...."* glancing nervously around.

Tavin half smiled. *"You have a lot of wisdom for your age. I guess spending so much time with mother has paid off."*

"During our chores she would have us memorize scripture. Do you remember that?"

"Yes."

Berta proudly recited, *"Thus saith the Lord, He that created the heavens, and stretched them out; He that spread forth the earth, and that which cometh out of it; He that giveth breath unto people upon it, and spirit to them that walk therein.... I am the Lord; that is my name.' And in Job, it says, 'the Lord gave, and the Lord hath taken away; blessed be the name of the Lord.'*

She paused for a moment and then added, *"God gives us breath and God takes it away. He is God. You cannot take that away from Him, Tavin. It's not yours."*

Shaking his head in wonderment, Tavin lifted Berta onto the back of Knight and gently laid Katherine's body across the withers. *"Hold your sister tight, Berta,"* with a tremor in his voice. The pelts and furs were fastened behind and Tavin began once again leading the precious cargo toward civilization.

The sun rose high. Warmth embraced them. Snow melted, wet and clear, as water dripped from tree branches and the ground became wet and mushy. Bethel was soon in their sights coming down off the Blue Mountain. Cleared farmland looked as if a patchwork quilt had been laid across the landscape. The Tulpehocken Path led toward established homesteads and fertile fields recovering from the summer's severe drought.

Tavin felt safe, yet he knew that they were not out of danger. The renegade Lenape had flooded over the mountain attacking, burning, and pillaging throughout Berks County. *"It looks like Wolfe was correct when he told us that Bethel would be deserted,"* Tavin sadly commented to Berta. *"We'll keep following along this road. We might find someone who can help us."*

Coming upon a burned-out homestead, Tavin stopped. *"Let's rest here for a while. There must be a stream nearby. Maybe I can catch a fish for dinner."*

Berta laughed, *"You can't catch a fish. Henryk is the only one who catches fish."*

Tavin's mind raced back to the morning of the attack and the image of Henryk, soaking wet, standing over their mother. *"Well, that may be true. But I can always learn!"*

"I like fish, they...."

"Hush!" Tavin cut her off, motioning frantically for her silence. Quickly, he slid her off the horse. *"Follow me."* Grabbing the reigns, he pulled hard and led Knight behind the tarnished remains of the blackened building.

The thunderous sound of horses beating down the road grew in reverberation. Tavin and Berta ducked down and peered through the charred logs, as Knight threw his head in agitation. Soon, over fifty-men, mounted and armed, rode into view. Tavin stepped out and began waving his arms.

Half of the bedlam rode on, while the other half, twenty or so, turned in response to Tavin's excited waving. *"What are you doing here?"* hollered a gruff-faced man riding on what Tavin concluded was a plow horse.

"I am in need of assistance. My family was attacked. I am seeking to reach Bethlehem, with my sister." Tavin wrapped his arm around Berta. *"Our brothers are residing there with a family; the miller named Fincher, and his wife, from the other side of the mountain."*

"Bethlehem is a long way off. Regardless, refugees have been pouring into that township by the droves," offered another man, with seeming more authority. Horses jostled against each other in a chaos of confusion and eagerness. *"May I ask about the body laid across your horse?"* he directly inquired.

"*Our sister, Katherine, succumbed to a head injury in this night past. I had hoped to find an undertaker to see to her burial in a proper way,*" Tavin dropped his head to hide tears welling up in his eyes.

Dropping down from his horse, the man stood stout and strong with a ragged scar cutting downward across his forehead, above his left eye to his ear. His thick brown beard bristled like a porcupine. Looking more closely at his face, Tavin was surprised to realize that he was not as old as first appearance suggested. Maybe forty at best. His demeanor was calm, calculated, and confident. He wore tan knee-breeches, a belted brown cape, black leather buckled boots and a black tri-corner hat. A leather pouch hung at his side, beautifully beaded, reminding Tavin of the bag that Kaendae carried.

There was something rigid in his close-set brown eyes, even as he smiled. He seemed trustworthy enough, a likable man, while at the same time, a man capable of violence. "*Name's Adoniram Leeds. First things first. There is no undertaker within fifty miles of here. If you are amiable to it, I would like to help you bury your sister and accompany you into Bethlehem. I can see that you have suffered in great ways and could use the assistance. My own family waits there for my return, so I would be grateful as well.*"

Turning to the mass of riders, Leeds shouted, "*You men, go along now. Keep to the west side of the Schuylkill and take possession of any homesteads that have not seen attack! You'll give those raiders a surprise they won't soon forget if they come back through this way!*" Hoots and hollers resounded. Fierce kicks to the sides of spirited stallions, spavined geldings, and sad, old nags, set them spinning in loud commotion. Frenzy permeated the air. Volunteer farmers, merchants, shoemakers, and blacksmiths, all assembled for one resounding cause: to protect and defend. And wherever possible, to take revenge on any Indian who had the misfortune of being caught.

In the midst of the mayhem, another voice began shouting orders. Tavin caught a glimpse of a familiar figure. "*Renz?!*" hollered Tavin through the din of noise and jostling horses. "*Renz!!*" he yelled again. Renz spun around and finally recognized Tavin. Kicking his horse forward, free from the commotion, he jumped down and boldly strode toward Tavin. "*Tavin Shire? You look like you've been in a bear fight and the bear won. I didn't recognize you.*" Glancing at Berta and then the small body wrapped in beaver blankets laying across Knight, he added with a smirk, *"I see that you have recovered your sisters, without total success."*

Tavin's jaw tightened, and his fists clenched. *"My sisters are of no concern to you. Is there any word of Agnes?"*

"No. No. I am afraid that she is gone forever. I must swallow my grief and move on with my life."

"When you had opportunity to track her abductors you chose to look the other way and leave her in their hands, caring little or nothing!"

"You know naught of my feelings for Agnes! My duty is now as an officer in the Provincial Militia, and it takes priority over any personal objectives. These untrained, raucous men require my leadership. Agnes would not expect that I should chase after her, as much as my grieving heart calls for it."

"You speak of your grieving heart?! Agnes is a captive. If she is still alive, she is held as a slave in an Indian village, or traded north, well beyond reach and you have made it about yourself!"

"Now settle down," Adoniram Leeds interrupted. *"I don't know what's going on here but let's take it slow and attend to the immediate. Bury this poor girl."*

Ignoring Leeds, Tavin's pent-up emotions erupted. His blood boiled in fury, *"You didn't even try to find her! Coward!"* and lunged at Renz. Leeds stepped in between and holding Tavin back, wildly reasoned, *"If we dig right now, we may be able to see to your sister's burial before the sun goes down! The ground's frozen less than a foot at most. Let's not get distracted."*

Renz stepped back, his eyes hard, his handsome face red and glaring at Tavin. *"I will ignore your slanderous words, as you are nothing more than a poor useless farm boy who suffers from naive infatuation!"* Spitting on the ground he continued, *"You are pathetic."*

"I am going back. I will find her." Tavin seethed, his eyes flashing.

"If you think you can put on the clothes of a frontier mountain man or an Indian and save Agnes, you are a fool. You should not waste your time or risk your pitiful neck. I quickly realized that she is a ruined woman. I couldn't bring myself to return her to civilization with that kind of shame. I am only thinking of her," said Renz, with an air of superiority.

Tavin stepped closer to Renz, his breath steaming, *"You were only thinking of yourself! She is too good for you. You arrogant snake!"*

Brushing the dust from his uniform, Renz directed his haughty words to Leeds, *"Please inform Mr. Shire, that my duties are great. Agnes is gone. I do not wish to die in the wilderness on a wild goose chase."* Leaping with graceful ease into the saddle, he sat for a moment and added, *"Shire, I know when to count my losses. You should do the same."*

"I understand my losses better than you will ever know," fumed Tavin.

Renz huffed and kicked his feisty mount into motion. Tavin watched as he galloped away, appearing every bit the fine gallant soldier. Yet all Tavin saw was ambition, ego and pride plunging as deep as an ocean.

CHAPTER

15

Languid music could be heard in muffled shades within the impressive limestone walls of a three-story building as they passed by. Glass-paned windows reverberated in chorus. Tavin turned to Berta, who sat atop Knight, her eyes wide with excitement, *"This is Bethlehem Berta."*

"Jesus was born here!" she squealed.

Tavin laughed, *"No. Jesus was born in Bethlehem, but not here."* Muted voices raised familiar hymns of praise in Germanic sweetness and Tavin felt his heart warmed.

Bethlehem was a growing industrial center, as sawmills, soap-mills, and grist mills lined Monocacy Creek and the Lehigh River. Continuing along the streets they came upon wash houses, bakeries, tailors, cobblers, and a butchery. People of all ages scurried around or sauntered with no apparent purpose but to enjoy the day. Overwhelmed at seeing such a lively town with so much activity, Tavin stood in wonder. *"The beauty and serenity of this place is astounding. I suppose after having been issued to the forest for so long, the appearance of such novel and unexpected transition is bound to shock one's system,"* he laughed.

Leeds coldly grunted, *"It is a village. Just a village like any other."*

Leading Knight along the busy streets brought stares with expressions of sympathy and understanding. A refugee family sat on a corner; their meager belongings gathered around them. Faces dirty and eyes waiting. Waiting for what? Tavin had no idea, yet it was apparent that their lives had been uprooted and their futures uncertain. Only one thing was sure, they were alive. Tavin knew the feeling and nodded as they passed.

Leeds held the reins as Tavin slid Berta down off the top of Knight. Taking Berta's hand, they stepped inside a tinsmith shop. The door was propped open even as a cold wind blew dusts of loose snow through the sunny air. An older man with gentle eyes and a white beard looked up from polishing a fine pewter pitcher. Tavin inquired, *"Sir, I am looking for a family by the name of Fincher. They would have arrived from over the mountain, to join their daughter. Her name, I do not know."*

Noticing Berta, the tinker put down his cloth and slapping his hand to his wrinkled cheek, breathed in sorrowful despair, *"Oh! My dear girl!"* Tavin, having forgotten how disheveled Berta was in her torn and tattered dress, with dirt and grime covering her thin arms and legs, quickly explained, *"This is my sister. She was carried off by renegade Indians and recently recovered. We are seeking the whereabouts of our brothers who have traveled here with the afore mentioned Finchers, a kind and Godly family, refugees themselves."*

"Many a refugee has seen their way here, although not all kind and Godly I fear." The tinker sadly sighed. *"Walk north. The widow, Sister Huber, has received and assisted families fleeing the Indian uprising. She might know of where the Fincher's are located."*

"I thank you for your kindness."

Reaching inside his vest, the tinker pulled out two coins, *"Young man, if you'd like to purchase a fresh loaf of bread for this poor child, it'd be my honor to provide it. There is a fine bakehouse just across the way. I can see that your sufferings have been great."*

"Thank you. Indeed, we have suffered greatly. Your generosity is unexpected and appreciated."

The tinker smiled down at Berta, *"And may God continue to bless you both."*

Berta returned the smile, *"You are a very nice man."*

Stepping back onto the street, Leeds appeared edgy. Quickly handing the reins to Tavin, he flatly stated, *"I'll be going on to Philadelphia now."*

"What about your family?"

"Oh. Yes, of course I will see to them first before I leave. Then, I have business in Philadelphia," Leeds said, shuffling his feet and looking tensely at the ground, his eyes narrow and nervous.

After thanking Leeds, Tavin and Berta set out to the north of the village. A large wooden barn loomed in front of them with a neatly situated two-story limestone house set off the road. The fields were a patchwork of withered straw-colored cornstalks, bent and beaten, with a fresh layer of white snow neatly lining the path of shadowed narrow rows. Tavin's hands felt cold and numb, as he kept a tight-fisted grip on Knight's reins. Approaching the impressive house, Berta sat firmly atop the black, snuggly wrapped in a beaver cape and trade blanket.

There was no answer as Tavin rapped on the blue painted front door. Smoke rolled from the tops of two large chimneys. A dog barked from inside. Stepping off the stoop and feeling discouraged, he took up Knight's reins and led him slowly back toward the village along the peaceful roadway. Berta hummed a tuneless melody atop the horse as it plodded in surprising rhythm. A cart approached. The driver pulled in his lively pony with a loud, *"Whoa!"*. He was a black man and wore a plain cotton cap, fitted tightly to his head, with the bottom turned up to form a brim all the way around. His green frock was accented with a bright red knitted scarf tied around his neck, the tails hanging smartly across his back. He smiled broadly, *"Greetings. Were you up to see Sister Huber? She's ailing today."*

"Yes. I was. No one answered the door. I am looking for information regarding a refugee family named Fincher. They are caring for my two brothers. Their daughter and family live here."

"Don't know that name, but Sister Vogt welcomed her parents a while back. They had two boys in tow with them, escaping the wrath of the savages burning and murdering the frontier settlers. Maybe that's who you are looking for. Their farm is down the road, no more than a mile. You'll know it. Funniest thing, it has a gray and blue blanket flapping around a fence post, with what looks like blood stains on it."

Tavin smiled and shook his head in amusement, *"That would be my little brother Henryk's doing. He told me he'd leave a sign for me to find him. That must be it. Thank you, sir. You've been a great help!"*

The driver nodded, *"God bless you. We have a saying here, "In essentials, unity; in non-essentials liberty; in all things, love,"* and continued down the road.

Clouds cleared and the sun's rays beat down. The sudden warmth gave Tavin a quick shiver. As he walked, he commented, as much to himself as to Berta, *"This is a unique place. I can't really put my finger on it, but there is a sameness among everyone we've met. They are kind, generous."*

"I liked the music coming from that building. It's been a long time since hearing music."

"Yes," agreed Tavin.

Coming over a rise in the road, Tavin spotted Mr. Fincher in the distance chopping wood behind a small, pristine log farmhouse. His eyes filled with tears, yelling, *"Mr. Fincher!"* Tavin began to run, and Knight dropped easily into a lively trot as he quickened his pace, Berta happily bouncing on top. Mr. Fincher looked up, covering his eyes against the brightness of the sun to see who was hollering and waved when he recognized Tavin.

"Good to see you, young man! We were not sure that this day would ever come. God be praised!" Mr. Fincher exclaimed shaking Tavin's hand with firmness and vigor. *"And who do we have here?"* he asked, smiling up at Berta who continued to sit atop Knight.

"I'm Berta. I was carried off by Indians with my sister, Katherine. But God took Katherine to be with mother and father in Heaven."

"Well, my dear, I'm glad you are here," Mr. Fincher said as a sadness crossed his face. Bending down he picked up an armload of wood. *"Come in! Come in! Mrs. Fincher will fix you up with a hearty meal and you can warm yourselves by the fire."*

"Thank you. Are Jakob and Henryk here?" Tavin asked, lifting Berta down and looping Knights reins around a nearby hitching post.

"They are in school, just up the road. Not far. They'll be busting in here real soon, happy as jack rabbits."

Mrs. Fincher burst into tears at the sight of Tavin and Berta, rushing to wrap Berta up in a tight squeeze against her ample figure. *"Oh, you sweet girl! You're nothing but skin and bone! Such an ordeal you have experienced, but you are safe now! Let me feed you!".*

Mr. Fincher laughed, *"Let her go Mother, before you crush the tiny thing."*

Tavin handed Mr. Fincher his old musket. *"This has saved my life more than once. I thank you for its use."*

"Keep it. You'll have need of it again, I have no doubt."

"Once again, I am in your debt. Please, tell me of Jakob and Henryk. Are they well? I am of course most anxious to hear of Jakob's wounds."

"They are well. Jakob had a rough go of it in the beginning. That scalping is a cruel business. Mrs. Fincher cared for him for another week at the mill after you left. We were testing fate at meeting the wrath of those looking to destroy life and property. After Jakob assured us that he was strong enough, we pulled up and headed over the mountain. It was no small thing, but Jakob is as stalwart as any grown man. Never complained a lick, although he has a tart way about him. Likes to argue a mite." Mr. Fincher stopped to light a pipe. Tavin understood. Jakob was still Jakob.

"And Henryk?" asked Tavin.

Mr. Fincher chuckled. *"With some folks, waters run deep. That's Henryk. Doesn't say much, but when he does, we all listen up."*

Mrs. Fincher fussed and stewed over Berta, washing her face and hands, and combing out the tangles of her dirty blond hair, adding a bright red ribbon. Bringing out a dress that her nine-year-old granddaughter had outgrown, she exclaimed, *"Now that's better!"* Slipping off Berta's worn and muddy shoes, she vigorously rubbed her icy feet. *"These little toes are freezing!"* Berta giggled.

A thick corn soup boiled in a cauldron over a hot fire. The smell permeated the room with aromas that Tavin had almost forgotten. His mouth watered with anticipation. Finally sitting down at the long well sanded table, they bowed their heads as Mr. Fincher prayed, *"Vater unser im Himmel geheiligt werde dein Name…"*

Hearing the Lord's Prayer recited in German brought emotions to Tavin that he had pushed down for a very long time. He could see his father's calloused hands folded as he prayed those very same words. He could hear his mothers, *"Amen."* Images of his family gathered around the table, talking, and laughing, with energetic banter winging back and forth over silly things overwhelmed Tavin. He excused himself. Stepping outside, his hands covered his face and he wept.

Returning inside, he sat down at the table and Berta shouted, *"Tavin! You'll never guess, but this tastes as good as Mrs. Mary Wolfe's stew and Mrs. Fincher is just as nice!"* Soup dripped off her chin and Tavin laughed. *"That's good to hear, but let's mind our manners."* Berta was a free and energetic soul.

An hour later, Jakob and Henryk bolted through the door. *"Tavin! Berta!"* they both shouted and rushed to embrace them. Tears and laughter were shared as stories recounting the past months bounced between them in a bedlam of noise. Sharing the news of Katherines' death was especially difficult, while tales of adventure and daring were exaggerated and reveled in.

Finally, all was quiet. The fire crackled and Tavin marveled as he looked into his brothers faces, glowing in the golden flickering brightness. Jakob sat on the wood plank floor, leaning against the hearth, wearing a cap similar the one the kind black man wore on the road earlier in the day. It covered the top of his head, coming down close to his ears, like a nightcap, with strands of his reddish-blond hair escaping in the back. He looked older than his sixteen years. His freckles appeared less pronounced, and his round face had slimmed. He was less agitated, calmer, yet that same factious attitude loomed underneath.

Henryk's blond hair was shaggy and tousled and knobby knees poked through the holes in his breeches. His eyes danced back and forth between Tavin and Berta as if to absorb their presence, like a sponge soaking up drops of fresh water from a dry basin. His twelve-year-old legs had stretched long and Tavin was surprised that Henryk was almost as tall as Jakob. Had Henryk grown that much in the weeks since the attack, or had he simply never noticed?

Gathering his courage, Tavin spoke, explaining more than he needed to explain in nervous energy. *"As you may have already guessed, Father is not coming back. He was killed while bravely serving with Braddock's army last summer."* The boys sadly nodded, as if they already knew.

Taking a moment for that unsurprising news to sink in, Tavin then continued, *"I have spoken with Mr. and Mrs. Fincher. This house is available for their use for as long as they wish to remain. As you know, their daughter and her family, the Vogts live here in the Moravian way of life, caring for each other as one community. They have opened their hearts and arms to you, Jakob and Henryk, with schooling and seeing to your needs. We owe them a great gratitude."*

Glancing over at Mr. and Mrs. Fincher and nodding, Tavin looked back at his siblings with stern intensity, *"You three will remain here by the gracious kindness of these fine people, until I return. I go back over the mountains within the week. Agnes remains lost and I must seek to find her."*

Jakob interrupted, *"If you leave, I go with you."* Henryk and Berta clamored the same sentiment.

"No. Jakob, I need you to remain here. Where I go is dangerous. I have an idea of where she may be held, and it is a treacherous venture. But I go alone. I cannot be worried for your safety. I will sell the pelts and furs that I have, purchase the equipment needed for my journey, and give a stipend to the Fincher's to carry on with your care. Then I will be on my way."

Jakob continued to plead his case day after day, in bitter, verbose defenses, but to no gain. Tavin's mind was set. Henryk would occasionally simply announce that he was going, in his straightforward, quiet way. No great dramatic directives. Just a statement, *"I'm going with you."* Nonetheless, this was something Tavin had to do without them. Berta took no more convincing. She had decided that she would rather remain with the Fincher's, who doted on her hand and foot. At the tender age of seven, she had already experienced enough of what the wilderness offered, feeling more than content to remain in Mrs. Fincher's sufficient loving arms.

Three days later, Tavin went into town. Entering the tawery he quickly settled on a fair price for the pelts. Crossing the street to the general store, he was intrigued with the uniformity of dress. Women's hair was all but out of sight under a close cambric cap tied with a single pink ribbon under the chin; blue if the woman was married. Wearing dark colored skirts, with short waistcoats and white handkerchiefs pinned modestly down around shoulders and necks, they emerged in contented consistency. Muslin aprons flounced merrily around as if sails in a shipyard and the atmosphere was one of gracious congeniality. Not until he focused on the pleasant faces, did he begin to see them as individuals.

Finding Sister Hannah Vogt, the Fincher's married daughter, working in the back of the mercantile, cleaning off shelving, he introduced himself and thanked her for her kindness to Jakob and Henryk. *"They are fine boys,"* she said, her ruddy cheeks almost covering her squinty eyes when she smiled. Handing her the list of the provisions he needed, she enthusiastically walked him around the well-stocked store collecting enough in the way of supplies to subsist for several weeks. Dried beans, nuts, meats, woolen blankets, a fur hat, a pewter mug, a kettle, an axe, and a spade as well as a large, sturdy pack with wide leather straps.

Satisfied that he had everything, he loaded his goods onto Knight and began walking back toward the Fincher's. Suddenly a voice called from behind him, *"Tavin Shire!"*. Adoniram Leeds approached him at a quick pace. *"I thought maybe you'd still be here. I am heading back over the mountains to my cabin. Looks like you're loading up to travel that way, looking for that missing girl. Agnes, is it? If you are, I would be obliged if I could tag along, at least for a while."*

"I leave in two days and welcome the company."

CHAPTER

16

January 1756

Tavin vigorously rubbed his hands together. *"It's a cold night."* He tugged at his blanket, pulling it tightly around his shoulders. Leeds tossed another log on the fire and sat back. Reaching into his beaded bag, he checked its contents. *"Only a few balls left. This musket won't do me much good if I don't have ammunition."*

"I have extra if you need it," replied Tavin.

"I'd appreciate that," and shifting his weight he added, *"Brrrr! It's as cold as the grave!"*

Tavin flinched, as he stared into the benign flames flickering softly into his blue eyes and idly repeated, *"Cold as the grave."*

Glancing over at Tavin, Leeds commented, *"Death is a final thing. Not easy."*

"It's been weeks and I still cannot come to terms with it. My parents. But especially Katherine. I hear her sweet voice in my dreams. The only joy I have is knowing that Berta is safe in Bethlehem with Jakob and Henryk. The Fincher's are Godly people. Berta took to Mrs. Fincher right off. And Henryk…" Tavin laughed, *"I'd not be surprised if he weren't secretly tracking us! That twelve-year-old might be quiet, but he's got grit!"*

"*They will be fine.*"

"*Yes,*" answered Tavin. "*They are well cared for. Selling those beaver coat pelts allowed me to see to it. The Finchers tried to refuse the money, but it was only right that I provide for their expenses. Berta eats like a bird, but Henryk's stomach is never satisfied. Jakob will need further medical attention. He's as sour as vinegar right now, although he tries to hide it somewhat.*"

"*You've done well by them. But you could have sold that black for a good amount of money as well,*" Leeds casually noted.

"*Johann Shaeffer would have wanted the horse returned to his family. When I discovered they had fled to Bethlehem, I knew it was the right thing to do. I continue to be amazed at God's hand of provision. That horse got us to safety and now he is back with his rightful owners.*"

"*I suppose.*"

Ignoring Leeds nonchalant response, Tavin continued, "*Now if only God will grant me favor once again, I will find Agnes.*" He rubbed his stubbled chin, realizing how his faith wavered up one hill and down the next in unsettled familiarity, never securing level ground. Rolling to his side, his head cupped in the crook of his arm, he closed his eyes and fell into a restless sleep.

Icy rain fell for days, stretching time into an endless haze of monotony, as they walked mile after mile across dangerous territory. Approaching Mahantango Creek, Tavin recognized the little-used path veering into a tangled hollow. "*Wolfe and his wife live down this way. They helped me and my sisters. He's a trapper who was with my father at Braddock's defeat. We can spend a night, dry our wet clothes and get a hearty meal.*" Tavin's pace quickened in eager anticipation.

Leeds hesitated and complained, "*There's plenty of daylight. We should keep moving.*"

"*We are wet, cold and hungry. Wolfe and his wife, Mary, know me. She gave me these buckskin leggings, these moccasins, and this shirt. We'll be welcomed,*" explained Tavin and continued down the less-traveled path. Leeds grimly followed.

Coming up over the last ridge, the cabin came into sight. A thin column of gray smoke curled from the top of the short stone chimney. "*Who goes there!*" came a familiar shout.

"Tavin Shire. I bring with me a friend, named Leeds. We seek shelter for a night!"

"Come closer. Let me see your face," called Wolfe.

Tavin and Leeds trudged heavily down the steep path, until they were within Wolf's sight. *"I'm a might surprised to see you Tavin. Thought you'd be settled back into civilization by now,"* Wolfe happily shouted, waving them forward. Mary stepped from inside the cabin, wiping her hands on a white linen apron, greeting Tavin with a broad smile, *"Hae'tsih!" Hello, friend!"*

"What brings you this way Tavin? How is it with your sisters?" Casper Wolfe inquired.

"Berta is safe with a good family in Bethlehem. Katherine, I am grieved to say, died on our journey. She is buried over the mountain at Bethel. I am now in search of my friend, Agnes, who was carried away on the same day as my sisters. Adoniram Leeds," Tavin motioned toward his companion, *"has agreed to accompany me as far north as Mahanoy Creek, where he and his family had settled before the raids began."*

Wolfe eyed Leeds suspiciously. *"Come in out of the rain. We'll talk."*

Tavin stepped inside and adjusted his eyes to the hazy smokiness of the room. Sitting at the table with his hands wrapped around a steaming pewter mug was a young man. His long, sleek black hair hung loose. He looked up with cat-like gray eyes, and Tavin immediately recognized him. He had been with Job and Kaendae sitting at the fire, so many weeks before. He was the nameless young man who remained back with the horses.

"Tavin, this is my son. His mother calls him 'Heyōnöhsoödahdöh'. It means 'the night has disappeared!' Wolfe said with flair and drama. *"She was afraid that she would never bare a child, so when she finally did, he brought the brightness of day and the darkness was no more!"* He proudly laughed and continued, *"Now that name's a mouthful for me, so I call him Asch, on account of his grey eyes, like the ash of a burnt-up fire. He got those from me."* Tavin recognized the German pronunciation, *"Asch"*. His mother's accent had offered the same. The young man sat seemingly amused at his father's verbose explanation, a tight-lipped smile crossed his serene and handsome face.

"I know you," said Tavin to Asch. *"You helped Drake and the others with their horses. I wondered where you would go. It makes sense now."*

Asch nodded his head. *"Ë:h. Yes."*

"You speak English? I didn't know that," Tavin thoughtfully reflected.

"Better to keep secrets from strangers," said Asch, eyeing Leeds.

"I can understand that. Has Drake come for the horses yet? He was injured a while back. Have you seen him or Job and Kaendae?" asked Tavin, excited at this new turn of events and anxious to hear news.

"No one has returned."

Mary interrupted and addressed Leeds with suspicion. *"Are you not the trader I have seen with the French at Shamokin village?"*

"No ma'am. I am a farmer, a settler, with my family near Mahanoy Creek. I have not traded at Shamokin," Leeds emphatically replied.

"You lie," Mary bluntly stated. *"I know your face. You are sided with the French, the Lenape and the Huron. You trade with them for profit, selling muskets and ammunition. Tell the truth. What are your intentions here?"*

Wolfe cautiously lifted his musket off the mantle. Asch stood, his arms lean and flexed, his hands clinched. *"Hold on. I can explain,"* said Leeds, nervously glancing around like a trapped animal, his flintlock poised in his right hand. He lifted it and aimed at Wolfe.

Tavin, confused, spoke up to defend Leeds, *"This man has helped me. Why would he remain a week in the British settlements if he were sympathetic to the French cause? He's English. And he wouldn't have assisted in securing my safety to Bethlehem with Berta if he were sided with the French."*

"He would if he were looking for information to pass along to the French at Fort Duquesne. A spy. You and Berta made a fine cover. Who would suspect a kind man helping poor destitute victims of Indian raids?"

Leeds roared, *"I am no spy. I have a wife and children removed to Bethlehem for safety. I go to my place near the Mahanoy to see what destruction there may be. Ask Tavin. He'll tell you!"*

Wolfe bent his head toward Tavin, while keeping his musket aimed at Leeds. *"Tavin, did you see this man's family? Did you see a wife and children in Bethlehem?"*

"Well, not actually," said Tavin, pausing to reflect back, *"He accompanied me with Berta to Bethlehem and then I didn't see him again until two weeks later."* Shifting his weight, he continued, as if thinking out

loud. *"He told me that he was going to Philadelphia. When I next saw him, he was ready to go back to his property. He said he was leaving his family in Bethlehem and offered to travel with me as far as Mahanoy Creek."*

"So, he conveniently offered to trek with you back into the hostile wilderness and you never actually saw any family? Tavin, you were his goodwill alibi against British and provincial forces until he got deeper into French occupation. He used you should he run into troops or militia, or anyone who may know him. If we recognized him, then you can be sure others would as well. He was covering his bets and he most likely plans to kill you when you are of no further use," Wolfe surmised, glaring at Leeds.

"This is a bunch of foolishness!" yelled Leeds, his eyes flashing.

The room stood still, and quiet, with only the crackle of the fire and rain gently pattering on the cabin roof. Tensions grew. Finally, Asch pointedly spoke, *"You trade for years with the French at Shamokin. I have seen you with my own eyes trade muskets, ammunition, and iron knives to the Lenape in return for rich beaver pelt and furs. You are not a farmer."*

Leeds jumped to the side and fired. The musket clicked and jammed. Tavin heard Mary scream, *"Sayá'dën! Get down!"* Wolfe fired at Leeds. The deafening boom rang through Tavin's ears, orange flame shot from the barrel and the smell of gun powder filled the air. Clearing his eyes of the steely sulfur smoke, he stared at Wolfe, who calmly stated, *"My powder was dry, but my aim not so good."* Leeds had bolted out the door, a thin trail of blood left behind. He'd been hit.

Asch looked at his mother, who was standing with a knife still clutched in her shaking hand. *"Nó'yëh,"* he said, getting her attention. Mary's eyes drifted to her son, and she said, in her unflappable way, *"I didn't expect to have gun fire inside my home."*

"Do you want to track him?" asked Wolfe, looking at Tavin.

Tavin thought for a moment, *"Let him go. Time is too valuable. My loyalty to my country is undercut by my resolve to find Agnes. If I am to find her, I cannot be diverted by the likes of a man as Leeds. He's wounded. He may not even survive to return to the French with his reconnaissance. Agnes has been in captivity for far too long already. As God is my guide, I will not be sidetracked for love of king and country."*

Tavin stepped outside after a satisfying meal. An icy wet wind blew across his face. He couldn't help but yearn for the fresh smells of spring. The cold dregs of winter seemed to cling as tightly as a guilty conscience. Asch stepped out into the night air and standing next to Tavin, commented, *"You trusted Leeds. Bad judgment."*

Tavin chuckled and nodded, *"Yep. Bad judgment. I thought he was a good man. I guess all of us have a certain amount of good and bad in us. We appear to do good things and say what is right, while our motives are hidden, and our hearts find sin to be easy. Maybe Leeds wasn't all bad. Maybe he just let the bad have its way and discarded the good that God made available to him."*

"Leeds had a secret agenda. It was to help you so that he could hide behind you. He traded guns and ammunition to the French and to the Lenape for raiding, burning, and murdering white settlements. He tried to kill my father. He is a bad man," said Asch.

"I guess. But I know one thing for sure, I was once again naïve in my understanding of life out here. I don't know when I will ever learn. I go rushing off in one direction or the other only to find myself as much a castaway as Robinson Crusoe."

Ashe scrunched his face in confusion. *"Who is he?"*

"Robinson Crusoe is a book. It's the story of a man on a desert island with no way to escape. I am simply saying that I seem to find myself as lost and caught in dangerous circumstances as he was."

Asch smiled, *"You have a strange way about you, Tavin Shire."*

Tavin laughed, *"Probably true, but hopefully God will direct my path."*

CHAPTER

17

Agnes laid on the hard, cold dirt floor lined with withered grasses and wilted cattail rushes. Her body hampered with painful cuts and bruises, made every movement scream in anguish. A torn, worn shawl wrapped around her thin shoulders. Adjusting her eyes to the smokey light, she bit her dry lips and watched as the old woman slept soundly on a low pole bed lashed to the inside framework of the long lodge. Sunshine angled sharply in from a smoke hole cut directly above smoldering embers. The fire had gone out in the night and the chill of morning set her teeth chattering.

Unfamiliar smells filled her nostrils. Bark baskets bursting with various types of dried herbs, berries and nuts were bundled together and hanging from leather thongs attached across the ribs of the lodge. Curing venison hung in strips over her head. The air was close and dry. She sniffed and rubbed the sleep from her eyes, gathering her wits about her. *"Lord, I am still alive,"* she whispered. Beginning to cry, she stopped herself. *"I have to be strong. They can't see me weak."*

It had been almost a week since arriving at Chinklacamoose, or at least that's what she thought. Time was a deceitful thing. The bruises on her face, arms and legs were slowly fading. Her sides hurt, and she worried that her ribs were broken, but she had survived. The old woman had spared her life. Agnes understood that it was not from sympathy or kindness, but from a practical concern. Agnes was young and strong; she could work hard. Peering through the smoky haze, she waited in silence. The old woman snored loudly. Agnes still waited. Waited for the shrill barking of indiscernible orders.

Rubbing her burning throat, she felt the scars around her neck, not as defined anymore. The rawhide noose was no longer there, but the faint thin line of scar remained. Her stomach rumbled with hunger. As she slowly sat up, a commotion stirred outside. The old woman bolted up at the noise and shrieked in her high-pitched way, angrily motioning toward the dwindling fire. Agnes quickly scrambled to her feet and exited the lodge. Trudging through newly fallen wind-blown snow, she hurried through the gate and headed for the wooded area that edged the fields outside the palisade. No one was concerned that she escape. An immeasurable wilderness lay between Chinklacamoose and the white world. No one watched, it was not necessary.

Returning with arms full of kindling, she spotted the source of the excitement and stopped to watch. A ruddy faced Frenchman wearing a bright red felt hat was surrounded by chattering, excited villagers. He greeted the chief warmly and under his bristling black beard, he laughed heartily. Turning to the growing crowd around him, he shoved his hand deep inside the large pack that was fastened to a droopy mule. Pulling out pots, kettles, ribbons, shells and various trinkets. Enthusiasm spread. The old woman was there as well as most of the village women and children, happily clamoring for gifts and valuable products to make their lives easier and gain superiority.

Liza Schell, standing back from the throng, caught Agnes's eye and offered a forlorn smile, casting her eyes quickly to the ground. Agnes had found only brief encounters with Liza since arriving at Chinklacamoose. They were kept separate for the most part. Yet Agnes became quickly aware that Liza was an intriguing and curious girl. A profoundly joyful countenance clashed in a baffling way with the suffering which was her circumstance. Peace radiated from Liza. She appeared impervious to the misery that she was enduring. Her captors recognize it as well. Village children flocked to her and the women, who regularly had beaten Liza with rods, whether they were irritated or not, stopped. There was an unexplainable reverence given to Liza. A mystery to Agnes. Yet in this brief exchange, as the barrel-chested Frenchman boisterously delivered gifts, Liza appeared lost in sadness, absorbing a pain that was not her own.

The Frenchman loudly shouted a cheerful finality, his hands high in the air, indicating that the presents were gone. The crowd moaned in disappointment. Agnes wanted to call to him, but fear held her as tightly as leather straps. She knew a few words of French. Maybe he would help her. Yet just as quickly as the thought crossed her mind, it melted away. Her hope could not be encouraged by the presence of this energetic, obese Frenchman. The truth was, she rightly feared the French more than the Lenape or the Shawnee. Her chances of freedom were better as she remain in the village. Although freedom in general was a hope long gone.

Taking a deep breath, the cold morning air stinging her lungs and her arms burning with the weight of kindling and heavy logs for the fire, her attention shifted to the continued chanting among the animated crowd. Squinting against the hazy, rising sun, she suddenly realized the focus of Liza's distress. A man stood tightly bound to a stake, in the center of the village, his face painted black, his eyes savage and glaring defiantly at the jeering crowd who had quickly turned their interest away from the now empty-handed Frenchman to focus on him.

Hurriedly she reentered the lodge, dropping the wood near the smoldering embers, her heart pounding as she vigorously snapped twigs and small branches. Her mind a blur, she fed the eager fire until its warmth leapt into the air. *"Lord, where did he come from? What will be his end?"* she silently asked, knowing the awful answers. Tears rolled down her cold, red cheeks. A deep chill shook her frail body. The flames grew higher.

Peering through the slats of the elm bark wall, she eyed the Frenchman who jubilantly sang a lively French tune, as he pulled a beaver blanket from the mule, wrapping it around his shoulders against the frigid morning air and proudly strode toward the joyous crowd. Children danced, played games, and threw rocks at the trussed prisoner. Their normal morning routine had been transformed into a frenzied celebration. Torture. Agnes felt sick as she scrutinized the captive man.

"Lord, don't let them burn him," she prayed, feeling a horror creep inside, while at the same time a disturbing relief. She was not the one to face a tortuous death.

Agnes had reasoned weeks earlier that the old woman had suffered a great grief. A beloved son had died in battle. She was thankful to have been spared, even as a despised slave. Stepping out into the fresh cold air, she cautiously walked toward the crowd. Standing back, afraid to see too much, yet held captivated by the scene.

A disheveled old trapper sauntered through the narrow gate at mid-morning with two large barrels strapped to the sides of his plodding donkey. Waving, he too greeted the chief in friendly expressions. The Frenchman bellowed a happy welcome. The arrival of the trapper created even more jubilation among the people and the old woman bolted to where Agnes stood and sternly thrust her back inside the lodge, motioning for her to remain hidden. Agnes marveled at the almost giddy mood the old woman was in as she briefly warmed her hands at the fire and rejoined the enthusiastic crowd. This was obviously a grand and special day.

A sudden impulse overcame Agnes, her mind racing with thoughts of rescue. Pushing past her mistress she burst from the bark lodge and began yelling for the trader who stood negotiating with the chieftain and the Frenchman. *"My name is Agnes Bowen! I am a captive from the east! Help me! My name is Agnes!"* A firm hand grabbed her hair and pulled down hard, yanking her head back violently. Off balance, she fell backward, and the old woman wrenched her fist tighter into the tangle of brown hair, dragging Agnes through the opening and into the dark, smoky shelter, but not before the trapper saw her and callously waved his hand, dismissing her calls for help. A calculating expression crossed the greedy Frenchman's face before he turned to continue the negotiations for the rum.

Remaining inside throughout the ongoing boisterous celebration, she continued to peer through the slats. Suddenly Agnes caught the whites of his eyes. The prisoner, staked and beaten, gazed unblinking in her direction, as if he knew she was there.

CHAPTER

18

Waterless clouds stretched across the cobalt sky in thin, long, wispy streaks. Light shimmered and sparkled down through high dripping branches and across the spongy leaf covered ground. It felt like spring, yet it was still just January. The fickle weather teased between icy snow, rain, and sunlit days. Thin, tall, trees stood straight and smooth, appearing as though a thousand arrows, reaching for the blue heavens in a wooded maze.

Asch and Tavin, carrying their weapons and heavy packs with supplies and trade goods, worked their way silently through deep ravines and muddy meadows, along rough ridges and up steep bluffs. The terrain had been treacherously difficult and now the wide Susquehanna was before them. They scoured the shoreline looking for hidden canoes stashed along the river. Eventually finding an old dug out with two short paddles buried in the mud nearby, they waited and crossed to the other side under the cover of darkness. By mid-day, moving fast, they found themselves well beyond the river. Any possible assistance from stalwart settlers, British military, or Provincial militia was well behind them now, entrenched within a treacherous wilderness.

Deeply tanned with a short scratchy beard, Tavin's straw-colored hair hung to just past his broad shoulders. His body had hardened into muscle and grown in strength; his blue eyes held unambiguous clarity. The tragic experiences of the previous months had brought a keen sense of alertness to his surroundings, an awareness that he had previously lacked. His skills as a survivor, hunter and tracker were emerging like a pup gradually becoming a wolf.

Tavin was no longer a sulky boy, feeding his selfish sorrows and questioning God's wisdom. He was a man who had finally settled his differences with the Almighty, no longer questioning, no longer filled with anger. The days of seeking Agnes had evolved into a quiet, earnest search for God, and God was found faithful.

Questions and grief remained, they always would, but he understood his purpose for the first time. *"And be not conformed to this world but be ye transformed by the renewing of your mind, that ye may prove what is that good, and acceptable and perfect will of God."* The verse reverberated across his mind, and he embraced it. What was once complex and bewildering, was now clear and effortless. Asking the 'why' was replaced with knowing the 'Who'. He lived in the moment God had provided. Each day was its own. Each day led to a point of resolution. His mission was clear. Honor the Lord with his life and find Agnes.

An hour before sunset, Asch and Tavin made camp. *"I'll see what I can scrounge up for food,"* said Tavin.

"Ka'go:wa:h"

"What do you mean, 'it is pointless'? I'm getting good with this bow," Tavin laughed.

"Maybe you are getting good with the Onōdowá'ga:', language, but you bring only a scrawny squirrel or a bony hare with your bow."

"Well, maybe today I will surprise you!", Tavin said in a forced whisper, as he walked away, once again grateful for Asch's companionship. Turning back around he lifted his bow over his head like a victor over a defeated opponent. Asch shook his head in amusement and wondered how he ever found himself in this situation, traveling with someone who did not really know where he was going or what he was going to do when he got there. Tavin had a way about him. A stubborn way. He would elbow himself deep into hostile French and Indian territory, with no information and no direction, to find a girl who did not want him.

As irrational as it was, Asch somehow admired the persistence, even though Tavin's convictions pushed him toward certain defeat.

A few minutes later Tavin appeared with two black squirrels. *"See, I told you I'd surprise you. TWO! One for you and one for me."*

"You have outdone yourself," Asch mocked, giving a quick bow of his head.

Later as they sat together, each with a skinned squirrel sizzling on a stick, Tavin said, *"I know why you agreed to accompany me. It's because of Drake, isn't it? Because of Drake's dream."*

"Drake's vision is his own. It is true, Drake is a powerful, brave and respected leader. I wish to honor him but choosing to guide you to Chinklacamoose is my choice alone. I am here because you would be dead by now if I weren't."

"True enough. But again, why would you even care if I died?" Tavin asked, always curious to understand.

"I don't," said Asch, a huge smile stretched across his statuesque face.

Tavin nodded, *"Glad that's clear,"* knocking Asch's squirrel off the stick and into the hot ashes. Sparks flew into the air like a thousand fireflies. *"I'll share mine with you. Wouldn't want you to die of starvation."* They both laughed quietly.

After a few minutes, Tavin reflected, *"I used to worry about being brave. But I don't even think about that anymore, 'Fear not, for I am with you; be not dismayed, for I am your God. I will strengthen you, yes, I will help you, I will uphold you with my righteous hand.' With God, I overcome my fears. I can't do it on my own."* He rubbed his hands together over the warm flames.

"Bravery is proven only when tested," said Asch, his gray eyes reflecting specks of gold.

"I suppose you're right. The question is, do I take credit for it, or do I give God the glory? I can say, from my experience and what it says in God's Holy Word…my courage alone is weak. I've proven that. But God has been true and in His Almighty hand I trust. Even in the face of death, I trust Him."

"You speak of your God in ways that I do not understand," Asch sighed.

"Well, I don't understand it myself sometimes," Tavin chuckled and scooted closer to the fire. *"Let's get some sleep. Maybe we can make good time tomorrow if this unpredictable weather holds."*

After a long pause, Asch added, *"You talk too much."*

"E:h. I know." Tavin chuckled and closed his eyes.

A week later, winter returned with howling winds and blinding snow. The two companions pulled beaver capes tightly around their shoulders and drudged sluggishly forward. Their progress had slowed, but Chinklacamoose was only a day's walk if the weather would cooperate. Tavin was getting anxious. There was no real plan once they reached the Indian town. *"Do you think we have enough to trade for Agnes, if she's there?"* asked Tavin.

"Depends on how valuable they say she is if they are even willing to trade at all. Or they may just kill us first and take the goods." Asch responded in low, hushed tones, adding, *"We will conceal ourselves along the Chinklacamoose path and watch for our opportunity."*

"What opportunity? asked Tavin.

"I don't know. We'll know it when we see it," Asch said, his breathing heavy, as he scrambled up a steep embankment, with Tavin on his heels.

"Opportunity. We can't just wait for opportunity and how many Indians use the word 'opportunity' anyway?" Tavin mumbled.

Coming to the path, the two companions crouched down on a high hill that rose from the path. *"We'll find cover here."* Asch whispered. Walking along the ridge, Tavin spotted a large, uprooted pine tree. They settled behind it. Tavin leaned against the tree and pulled out a strip of dried venison. *"This seems like a waste of time."*

"Quiet. Be patient," Asch reprimanded, as he peered over the wet, frozen trunk. *"A fox stalks his prey carefully before he pounces. If not, he misses the mark or worse, loses his life."*

Tavin understood. Asch was a child of the wilderness. He knew how to measure it, how to process it and how to endure through it. Tavin trusted him. *"Wi:yo:h. Good. It's good,"* He conceded, relaxing to wait.

The morning waned into afternoon. Nothing. *"Brrrrr..."* Tavin shivered. *"A warm fire sounds nice about now. It's close to sundown. Maybe we should make camp."*

Just then jingling could be heard coming from a distance down the path from the west, from Chinklacamoose. Asch and Tavin leveled their muskets across the ice covered log aimed toward the road below. Soon, a lone white trapper, riding an old mule, came sauntering along singing an undiscernible tune.

Motioning to Tavin, Asch slid down the embankment and circled behind the oblivious traveler. Tavin bolted straight down the side of the hill, and called out, *"You There! Stop!"*, his musket aimed at the ready.

The startled old trapper's arms tangled in a tightly wrapped heavy blanket, as he flailed about atop the mule. Losing his balance, he tumbled off and hit the frozen ground with a loud thud. Freshly fallen snow kicked up in a flurry, as if a windstorm swept through. Dirt and dust from the beefy man's clothes floated in the air like a rippling murky cloud as he rolled about. Thrashing in desperation to recover his rusty musket he howled obscenities, until Tavin's foot pinned his arm firmly to the ground and he saw the barrel of a long gun inches from his head. His sallow face contorted into an ill-tempered scowl. *"I don't have any money! I only have a few pelts. Been a wasted trip,"* he said, looking nervously up at Tavin, his bushy eyebrows nearly concealing his beady eyes. Tavin could smell his foul breath.

"I'm not here to rob you, but I am curious about a few things," said Tavin, slowing relaxing the pressure and releasing the trapper's arm. *"Who are you?"*

"Names Bender. If you are not going to rob me, what do you want? I've done nothing wrong. I'm just a free trapper trying to make a living. I'm beholden' to no one," he said as he rubbed his sore bicep, untangled himself and sat up.

Tavin dropped the gun easily to his side and asked, *"What were you trading at Chinklacamoose?"*

Bender eyed his musket, which was just within reach, his voice calm, yet nervous, *"Trinkets, wampum, blankets.... the usual,"* he said. Suddenly he lunged for his gun and just as suddenly a strong arm was around his filthy neck and the point of a sharp knife was at his hairy throat.

"There's no cause to act rashly Mr. Bender. My friend will release you, but you must behave like a civilized human being and tell me the truth," said Tavin. Asch looked up, grinning, his black hair shining in the sun with his knife poised and ready.

"Alright. Just tell him to loosen his grip," Bender choked out.

"I'm afraid that I don't tell him to do anything. But you can ask him yourself if you want."

Asch removed the knife and slipped it back alongside his belt and stood. His deeply sculptured cheekbones, long sleek hair, fierce eyes and formidable stature reminded Tavin of etchings he had seen of European nobility. Asch's good nature almost seemed a contradiction to his stalwart appearance. With his bow in his hand and a quiver of arrows slung across his back, Tavin found himself thankful that Asch was a friend and not a foe.

"What did you trade at Chinklacamoose?" Tavin asked again.

Obviously scared, Bender stuttered, *"Rum. Mostly rum. Some ammunition, beads and trinkets too, but mostly rum."*

"Tell me how many are in the camp and if there are captives," Tavin demanded.

"Most of the warriors are off raiding to the south. It wasn't a good trading day. That old chief is unreasonable and greedy, especially when drunk. And that Frenchman, he is devious. Cheated in gambling, too. He took my goods and gave me barely enough for my trouble. But none of them is in a mood to be crossed, so I let it be and went on my way. They've got a bee in their bonnet for sure."

"There are French at Chinklacamoose?" Asch asked.

"Just one."

"Captives! Are there white captives?!" Tavin yelled with his teeth clinched.

"They usually hide any captives when I come around. But chances are that they has captives. Hard to say for sure."

Tavin grabbed the man by his grimy shirt collar and with an intensity that was unfamiliar to him, he questioned, *"Are you telling the truth?! Did you see any captives?"*

"No! I didn't see anyone. Well maybe one. A girl. She was a long way off and I can't say for sure. God's honest truth: that's all I know!" Bender was breathing heavy, and sweat was pouring off his wrinkled, dirt-lined face, creating a muddy stream.

"Don't move," Tavin ordered, his eyes flashing. Turning to Asch, *"What do you think? It could be Agnes."*

"Could be."

"What do we do with him?" Tavin pointed to Bender.

"*We have had opportunity to learn who is at Chinklacamoose. Let him go. He is of no more use to us,*" said Asch giving Tavin a knowing glance, cutting the tension.

"*Yes, opportunity. Waiting for opportunity was a good idea. We now know that most of the warriors are gone, and Agnes may be in the village. Patience proved better than charging in like a mad bull. I need to remember that,*" Tavin quietly laughed and took a deep breath.

CHAPTER

19

An hour after darkness had fallen Chinklacamoose was in view. From the top of a distant hill, Tavin pulled out his brass eyeglass and peered through it. *"Here, look,"* he whispered to Asch. Taking it from Tavin, Asch put his eye to it and quietly replied, *"I see now how this is a useful thing,"* and handed it back.

By the glow of a huge fire burning in the center of a large open area, Tavin could clearly see fifteen to twenty lodges silhouetted against the dark forest, like flickering globes with narrow streams of bluish smoke billowing from the centers. Several longhouses sat to the far left where children ran energetically in and out. A high stockade surrounded the village, and the land was totally cleared around it. Tavin assumed fields were ready to be planted in the spring. Forest stretched beyond it all.

Focusing again, figures came into view. *"They appear drunk,"* said Tavin. He could see forms sprawled in drunken stupor or asleep in clusters around the fire. Others danced and swayed, unsteady, staggering. Methodically Tavin moved his vision from one corner of the village to the other and then settled back on the fire once more.

"Do you see captives?" breathed Asch.

"No. Wait, yes. A man. I think a warrior. His face is blackened with paint or soot. He is standing, bound. Bender didn't mention an Indian captive," said

Tavin, pressing the looking glass tightly to his eye. *"What will they do with him?"*

"Bender is a lying snake. They will burn him," answered Asch in a matter-of-fact tone.

Distant high-pitched pulses drifted up the hillside, like a chorus of buzzing bees. Tambourine drums and turtle rattles beat out a sinister rhythm, heralding the death of an enemy warrior. Taking his time, Tavin silently studied the bound prisoner, mesmerized by the scene playing out before him. *"He must be Iroquois. He appears strong and defiant in the face of the torture he is enduring."*

"It is an honor to prove courage in such a way. He will not cry out; he will not beg for mercy." There was pride in Asch's voice.

Hours passed and the village became quiet. *"Maybe we can save him. They are drunk from the rum Bender gave them and most of their warriors are gone, if we can believe that monger,"* said Tavin.

"We wait. If they are too drunk to burn him tonight, we will see what might be possible. Watch for your woman." Asch turned to lean his back against the log and added, *"I will sleep."*

Tavin settled in, adjusting his eyeglass to one section of the village and then the other, always returning to the constrained warrior. The center fire burned lower, dimmer, making it harder to see as clearly, while a full moon continued to provide hazy winter light. The tall timbers of the blaze finally collapsed into hot embers and glowing ash. The shadowed, restrained figure continued to stand immovable and aberrant.

The village remained still and silent, with only the occasional yap of a dog. *"Asch. Wake up. I see no sign of Agnes, but we have to go down there. No one would suspect that we would waltz into that village and steal their prisoner."*

Asch sat up, looking over the log; he scrutinized the village below. *"Why? He is of no concern to you. If you did not see your woman, then we keep moving. Maybe your woman is traded to the north. Maybe at Kittanning Village, on the Allegheny or Logstown."*

"You don't know that for certain. I need to be sure. We can free that warrior. He might have information. The village is asleep, and their brains are soggy with drink. It would not be that difficult to sneak in and cut him loose. I have

weighed the consequences. I am willing to take the risk for myself. And maybe he…" Tavin motioned toward the warrior prisoner, *"…maybe he has even seen Agnes. AND, by the way, she is not 'my woman', she is betrothed to someone else,"* Tavin stated quietly, but firmly.

"O:h!" Asch mocked with a skeptical grin and raised eyebrows.

Tavin shook his head and quietly chuckled, adding in defense, *"Do:ges! It's true! She is not my woman, and maybe it is YOU who talks too much."*

Asch smiled, his strong white teeth glowing in the moonlight. After a few minutes, he shifted in the thin layer of snow. *"We must consider something else. That warrior may be too far gone, too weak from hunger, thirst and whatever torture he has already endured."*

Tavin answered, *"Let's take it one step at a time. Let's go down there. I see a way in under the palisade on the south side, closest to us. It looks like it was damaged at some point, and we can slip under it. We can then skirt around the inside and angle toward the post where he is tied."*

"What about the dogs?" Asch asked. *"Do you have an answer for the dogs?"*

"E:h!" Tavin said, smiling.

The full-moon shone through the denseness of pines and wind-stripped elms, as the two companions slinked down the hill and crept across the barren field toward the village. A gaping hole in the palisade wall allowed them entrance, just as Tavin had said. All was silence as they watched their own crouching shadows sculk along the inside wall. Slipping between lodges, Asch whispered, *"Let me talk to him. There is no time to wonder if he understands your English tongue."*

Suddenly a dog began frantically barking and dashing toward them, sounding the alarm, drawing his lips back and showing his fangs. Tavin reach into his pouch and pulled out a long piece of venison. He threw it. The meat sailed over the dog's head, landing behind him. Spinning in confusion, the mutt raced back to investigate, picked it up in his drooling jaws and pranced happily off.

"Huh, that worked," Asch quietly mused.

"I had a dog once, Georg, if anyone gave him food, he was their friend for life."

Crouching low, they ran across the dancing ground. Smoldering embers curled heavy, dense smoke from the once hot burning fire. Two bodies lay perfectly still off to one side. *"Dead?"* Tavin asked with hand motions. *"Drunk,"* Asch replied. Gingerly stepping past them, they cautiously approached the post where the warrior stood, his hands and feet tightly secured.

"Tsih. Egoywaya'dage:ha," Asch hoarsely whispered. His breath steamed against the frosty air.

The warrior lifted his blackened face. Recognizing Asch and Tavin, he hissed in his Onōdowá'ga:' tongue, *"Go. I do not need your help. I will die here with honor and courage. I am ready to meet my God. These lice will see how a true warrior of the Hodínöhšö:ni: comes to the end."*

"Job?" rasped Tavin, knowing his friends rooted voice and the inflections of his dire words. *"We will get you out of here!"* Tavin loudly whispered.

"Go. You are on a fool's errand," Asch translated Job's contention.

"No. Hë'ëh!" Tavin firmly stated, as he began cutting the leather straps from the wooden pole.

"Leave me!" exclaimed Job. *"I am finished."*

"You're not finished until God takes your final breath," Tavin quietly muttered, lifting Job's arm around his neck, they crept back across the wide expanse of ground. Panting in the cold night air, Job's legs wobbled and limped to keep pace as they again skirted around the inside palisade, toward the hole in the wall. The mangy dog sat gnawing on his prize, glanced up and then returned to his digression, unconcerned.

Asch followed, his eyes darting back and forth, his musket and hatchet ready. Reaching the gap in the barrier wall, Tavin lowered himself and slid through first. Job ducked down and squirmed painfully under, his wounds tearing open on the rough ground. Asch was close behind.

"How fast can you move?" Asch whispered to Job.

"I can keep up. Find the creek. The blood trail that I leave will be too easy to follow." Job's voice was strong, infused with new energy and purpose. Silently crossing the moonlit field, they quickly reached the steep wooded hillside and followed along the snowy base. The creek could be heard; water rolling and gurgling over rocks and under fallen logs toward the wider, deeper river behind them.

Stepping into the icy water, Tavin sucked in his breath to keep from calling out in pain. Flashing beads of light showered against the blackness of large boulders, with patches of fresh snow outlining the creek bank. A ribbon of graceful white turbulence glowed in the moon's beam. *"Is this current too strong for you to hold your balance?"* Tavin called back to Job over the roar of tumbling water, his teeth chattering. *"He'eh"* answered Job. He stepped in, as if walking a smooth path on a summer's day.

Pushing their legs against the gushing current while keeping their packs and weapons over their heads, Asch and Tavin steadied themselves against every slippery rock and uneven foothold threatening to take them under, until they could no longer bear the burning cold. Struggling up the slick embankment, the three collapsed on the frozen ground breathing heavily. The sun was beginning to rise over the tops of jagged evergreens. Morning mist moved ghostlike across the stream as it widened and meandered on.

"Daylight. They will easily follow our trail from the village, but hopefully once they reach the creek, they won't know which way to follow. It will give us time," said Asch, pulling himself up to stand. Tavin leaned over the embankment and sucked in the clear icy water. Turning to Job, who sat rubbing life back into his frozen feet, his wet buckskin moccasins lying next to him, Tavin asked, and Asch translated, *"What happened? How did they capture you?"*

"Drake knew that you would come to Chinklacamoose for your woman." Job explained, desperately sucking in air, *"Your stubborn heart was too lovesick, and you would get killed."*

Tavin shrugged, *"Well, I'm not dead yet and if I'm not mistaken, you would be, if we hadn't come along."*

Job grinned, *"You remain a determined and a bold man."*

"Maybe so, but I have yet to find Agnes and she's not my woman; she remains betrothed to another." Tavin said, with a defensiveness he could not seem to avoid.

Asch smiled and turned back to Job, who continued to explain. *"I agreed to come with Drake to find you. Two days ago, where the trail splits, he took one and I took another. I was careless and the Lenape surrounded me. I killed one of their warriors. A life for a life is the way. I was to burn last night, but the old trader, Bender, came with his barrels of rum and the night turned into a drunken frolic. My time never came. They were too far gone and slept."*

"Where's Drake now?" asked Asch.

"Somewhere nearby. He would not leave," explained Job, pulling his moccasins on his numb feet. *"There is something else,"* he added, looking at Tavin. *"Your woman was living at Chinklacamoose. She was given to a grieving old widow. She is alive. When she saw the trader, Bender, she began screaming that her name was Agnes, begging for help. I watched as he waved her away and she was kicked by her mistress and dragged off."*

"You saw her there?"

"E:h. She is gone now."

"Where is she!?"

"A Frenchman visiting at Chinklacamoose; he gambled throughout the day with the old drunk chief and then left with your woman and another captive. Two warriors went with him. After that, the trader loaded his mule and rode away, while the village continued to drink themselves foolish," explained Job, staring at Asch, his blackened face streaked with water and sweat, as Asch translated his words.

Tavin raised his angry voice, *"Bender. He saw Agnes! He saw that Frenchman leave with her. Let's go!"*

Asch grabbed Tavin's arm firmly, *"Remember, if you rush about with no thought or preparation, you will die and you will most likely get your woman…"* he paused, and corrected himself, *"…Agnes, killed. First, we cover our tracks which announce us as clearly as the squawking of a crow. Then we circle back around to Chinklacamoose to pick up the Frenchman's trail. Maybe we find Drake along the way."*

Breathing deeply, Tavin replied, *"Alright. Yes. My impulsiveness is not always sensible. Thankfully, God has had His hand on me, or I'd be dead, sure as anything."*

"We move," said Job, wracked with pain as he stood.

Setting a steady quick pace, the three men climbed, breathing heavy white puffs of steam from their warm breath, their lungs burning. Tavin never felt so alive. This was the first information he had of Agnes. She lived. Thoughts of her rescue invigorated him. His legs seemed to move as swift and light as a deer, his muscles pumping as smooth as a languid river, unobstructed and established.

With loud hollow bark, a startled bull elk bounded across the steep path in front of Tavin. The animal snorted, threw his head and bolted, crashing wild-eyed through the dense forest. Tavin dropped to his knees as Asch pulled his bow. An arrow sailed unwavering through the air, over Tavin's head, penetrating deep into the elk's neck. It dropped with a thud and began a death roll, thrashing back and forth in pain. When Asch reached it, he pulled back another arrow and put the bull out of its misery with a merciful shot to the heart.

"We camp here," smiled Asch.

Tavin offered, *"I'll snake back to see if we are followed, even though I doubt those Lenape have much of a stomach for trailing us very far. They had filled themselves with so much of that poison drink last night, I'd be surprised that they can even walk straight let alone track us past the creek."*

Job sat down next to the sprawled elk, motioning for Tavin's knife. Tavin was reluctant in handing it over. He felt incomplete without it tucked snuggly against his hip. Resting his right hand on the handle as he walked was a well engrained habit. But the thought of satisfying his deep hunger with a meal of roasted flank easily outweighed his hesitations. He slipped it out and relinquished it to Job, *"I'll be back before dark,"* he said, turning to amble back downhill.

"Watch and listen," Asch reminded Tavin.

Careful to conceal traces of his footsteps, Tavin moved cautiously, his eyes, and ears alert. Reaching the brink of a steep gully, he stopped, listening. Silence surrounded him. He felt something was wrong, a wild instinct that was new and exhilarating. Crouching low, he sniffed the air and waited. Nothing. Slowly moving down the hill, ducking under low hanging branches, his knuckles white, he gripped his musket with a sweaty hand.

Stopping again, squinting, he studied the wooded slope on the other side of the boulder strewn ravine. Fixing his eyes on a dark point in the shadows of a large, uprooted hemlock just below the ridge line above him, he could make out the shape of what looked to be an arm. A subtle shifting proved his suspicion. A man.

Suddenly he caught another movement to the left, above the hidden, crouching figure. The shadow of a Lenape warrior crept slowly down, a sharpened hatchet in one hand and a war club in the other. Pulling out his brass eyeglass, Tavin found the dark figure behind the muddy roots. Focusing, the blurry image slowly came into clarity as the man's head shifted into view. Drake. Tavin could see that his friend was unaware of the approaching attack. Covering his mouth, he yapped like a she-fox to give warning. At that, the attacker gave a loud whoop and ran at Drake, who had already turned at the warning signal.

Seizing his attacker by the arm Drake pulled down hard, avoiding the sharp edge of the blade, as the Lenape lost his grip, and the weapon spun violently through the air, disappearing into the dry leaves. The two tumbled downhill locked together in bitter struggle, finally striking a rock. Drake appeared dazed and off balance. The Lenape jumped to his feet, his knife drawn and leapt toward Drake for a final death blow.

Tavin had scurried the rest of the way down the embankment and halfway up the other side before dropping behind a boulder to level his gun up the hill. Pulling the trigger, a blast of orange flared from the muzzle and the boom rang in his ears. The attacker's arms flailed back, like a hawk floating on the winds, holding momentarily, as the impact of the musket ball halted his forward momentum. Tavin recognized him. He was the warrior with the turtle etched on his neck. His surprised eyes caught Tavin's, and he dropped backwards with a hard thump. Drake quickly pulled himself up from the slick leaf covered ground and stumbled behind the rock for shield. "Gya:soh Ga:da's!" he called out.

"I know who you are!" Tavin called back.

Drake stood and stepped out from behind the boulder. *"Tavin Shire?"*

"E:h" said Tavin.

"You have become a warrior," Drake said, stepping down the hillside, holding the old, yet painful wound on his side and checking the Lenape of the Turtle Clan for life. There was none.

"I don't know that I am a warrior. It just looked like you could use a little help," he answered, frowning as he glanced over at the crumpled body lying face up on the hillside. *"This is the man who killed my mother and the Bowen's. He scalped Jakob, took my sisters and Agnes."* Tavin was surprised that there was no satisfaction in killing the man who had caused so much pain. It felt a hollow, empty conquest. *"Maybe this is justice. But somehow it feels less and now there is little chance in finding Agnes. He,"* Tavin pointed to the dead warrior, *"can give us no answers."*

Pushing down the revulsion that swept over his stomach, he turned to Drake. *"It is good to see you again my friend. Do you recover from your injuries of the past?"* noticing the grimace on Drake's face as he bent to collect his weapons.

"E:h. I am healing. It is good you are well," as the two grasped each other's shoulders in welcome greeting. *"Now we move. That musket boomed like a British cannon blast,"* Drake flatly stated. Turning abruptly, he clamored back up the hill using his hands and feet for balance.

"Wait. I am with Job. The other direction," called Tavin.

Drake stopped and turned to look at Tavin, a broad smile crossed his painted face. *"I have Agnes. This direction."*

Suddenly a woman's head appeared from behind the gnarled, soil dripping roots of the fallen tree from which Tavin had first spotted Drake. *"Tavin? Tavin!"* Agnes faintly cried.

"Agnes!" Tavin hollered. Drake scowled. Tavin understood the look. He was once again, too loud for the silent deadly forest, but at that moment it didn't matter. Tavin bolted up the side of the bluff, hands and feet slipping on snow-covered leaves and clamoring over gray boulders which appeared to be dropped randomly from heaven itself.

Reaching Agnes, Tavin barely recognized her. Her once full, oval face was narrow and ashen, her cheeks sunken and dirty. She fell into his arms, her thin body clinging to him, clawing at his back for fear he was not real. She buried her face against his chest and wept. Tavin closed his eyes and soaked in the feel of her, enveloping her tightly in his arms with the musty smell of earth and sweat filling his nostrils. After a few minutes, he pulled her back and took hold of her shoulders, looking intently into her liquid dark eyes. *"God has answered my prayer."*

Agnes stood staring probingly up at him, *"Is it really you?* she weakly laughed. *"How did this happen? How did you find me?"* her voice flat and unsure.

"We can talk later. Right now, we need to go," said Tavin, noticing for the first time a thin figure standing next to Drake. Drake bent down, picking his pack up from the ground, *"This is Liza Schell. We go, now."*

Tavin's mind was plummeted with questions, but there was no time. There was no way to know if the enemy was close at hand. The musket blast put them at greater risk. *"Are you able to keep a swift pace?"* asked

Tavin. *"Yes. Yes. We will follow."* Agnes readily answered, wincing in pain as she held her bruised side.

The day was closing in. Long shadows cut across the uneven terrain. Agnes and Liza were weak and jittery, their strength waning through their ordeal, yet thoughts of being re-captured prompted a determined pace. They moved in silence, climbing, stumbling, striding toward warmth, nourishment, and safety, teetering, and falling, but always pressing forward.

Tavin took the lead, retracing his way back to Job and Asch, remaining off any obvious path. Drake followed behind the two women, removing trail evidence, lifting branches that had bent, removing fabric that had been caught and smoothing snowy ground that had been trampled. Thorny briars grabbed at their clothes and a maze of deadfall slowed them down. Coming to a wide shallow creek, a stand of birch trees glistened in the sunlight, their long white trunks catching the setting sun with golds and pinks reflecting in wavy imperfection across the slow-moving current. Drake and Tavin knelt and spoke in murmured tones. *"We follow this until we reach a steep incline, cross the creek at that point and skirt along the base. Job and Asch are not far,"* said Tavin. Drake nodded.

Standing, he turned to Agnes and Liza and whispered, *"Drink here. It's not much further. There will be meat. Elk. You can rest once we arrive."*

Tavin studied Agnes as she bent down and sucked up the clear cold water. Cupping her hands, she splashed and rubbed her face over and over, as if washing memories away. Her blue shirtwaist was stained and smudged, her brown skirt torn and hanging in shreds and her petticoat was rimmed in black dirt. Glancing up at Tavin, her expression appeared vacant and heavy. She stood and shivered, wrapping her arms tightly around herself. Tavin pulled his trade blanket off his shoulder and handed it to her, ashamed that he hadn't realized how cold she must be. *"Thank you,"* she said, a slight smile crossing her chapped lips.

Liza eagerly scooped water into her mouth with her hand. Losing her balance, she caught herself before toppling in, and laughed. Her eyes were hauntingly wide and green. Pushing herself up, she adjusted a thin woolen blanket tightly around her neck, just under her ears and tucked it snuggly back into the waistband of her frayed gray linen skirt.

Tavin noticed red and wrinkled scarring across her neck before she hid it from view.

"I have blankets, once we reach camp," he sheepishly said, not sure if she had noticed him staring.

"Please, do not worry about me. I am fine with this ragged old thing. Actually, I've grown rather attached to it." Liza had a light, almost musical German accent and an unusual, yet genuine way about her. Tavin was eager to hear how she ended up with Agnes. But it had to wait.

Drake huffed, indicating that time was wasting. *"If we reach Do:hsetweh and 'Heyōnöhsoödahdöh' before nightfall we eat and rest for a short time and then keep moving."*

"E:h," replied Tavin.

Agnes and Liza stepped in behind Tavin as he meticulously worked his way along the edge of the creek, cautious not to leave impressions in the soft bank soil, carefully pulling back overhanging branches and sliding over fallen tree trunks. Drake stayed close, watchful, and wary. Finally crossing over the creek to the other side, they climbed a short rocky hill and stopped. Tavin squatted to the ground, cupped his hands, and gave a high-pitched guttural yap. The low trembling cry of a hoot owl echoed back through the trees. Agnes watched in astonishment, perplexed and curious.

Smiling, Tavin motioned forward. Coming over the top of the hill, Asch stood, leaning on his long musket, the glow of a small fire reflected on his strong shiny arms. The smell of roasting meat permeated the air. Agnes felt faint with hunger. Her stomach growled. Liza stumbled as she hurried down the embankment, her arms flapping about like a bird taking flight.

Resting against a tree, Job sat with his legs curled in front of him, his scarred face twisted in pain. The wind blew harder. Dusk. Sparks peppered the air above the flames and white curls of smoke lifted high and drifted across the deep forest. Job scooted to the blaze and pulled off two logs. *"Too much smoke."* He then spotted Drake. *"Hae'tsih!"* he greeted, coughing quietly.

"Nya:wëh sgë:nö" Drake greeted in return. Concerned at Job's condition, he turned to Tavin, *"What happened?"*

"Captured and taken to Chinklacamoose two days past. He was set to burn last night, after he ran the gauntlet, but an old trapper named Bender showed up with barrels of rum. The party ended in a drunken frenzy and most everyone fell over in a stupor. Their bellies and brains set afire! Asch and I easily snuck in and cut him loose."

Crouching down, Drake spoke with Job in deep reticence. The two friends sat together talking for a time, while Tavin pulled pelts and a trade blanket from his pack. *"Sit here,"* he motioned to Agnes and Liza, as he spread the furs onto the hard, cold ground. Sitting close together with fear in their eyes, they stared nervously at Job, whose face remained smudged in black grease paint. *"You have nothing to fear from my friend,"* Tavin explained, *"Job saved my life several weeks ago. He was captured looking for me. You saw him tied to the stake at Chinklacamoose. He is a good man."*

Both Agnes and Liza nodded in recognition, while Liza softly said, *"I was praying for you."*

"You have met Drake." Tavin smiled, shaking his head, while recalling his relationship with Drake. *"God has used him in miraculous ways. He has taught me how to survive. I would not be here if it were not for him."*

Asch stooped over the fire feeding the blaze with dry wood and turning the elk haunch on the makeshift spit. Satisfied, he stood and walked to where Tavin was sorting through his pack and quizzically asked, *"How did you end up with two women?"*

Tavin lowered his head and mumbled, *"Di'gwas:h."*

"You don't know?" Asch quietly laughed and rolled his eyes.

"I'll explain later. Right now, they are hungry, cold, and scared, so do what you can to help." Tavin sounded more impatient than he felt. It had been an exhausting and unexpected day, although a day that had brought him much happiness. A day that had brought him Agnes.

CHAPTER

20

A trace of snow filled the steely sky. *"God was with us,"* Tavin whispered to Agnes, as he handed her a hot piece of meat drenched with fat. The fire sizzled with greasy drippings. A thick thong suspended between two green saplings sagged by the weight. Asch sliced off a piece off the large smoldering hindquarter. He pushed it toward Liza on the tip of his knife. She flinched and scooted back, at the sudden gesture. Her eyes filled with terror, as if a momentary nightmare had gripped her mind.

Tavin reached out and gently squeezed her arm, *"Liza! It's alright. This is Heyonosodahoh. You may call him Asch. He is as trusted as a brother."* Liza nodded and looked directly at Asch, tentatively reaching out with quivering fingers to slide the flank off the blade, repeating his name, *"Asch."*

"*E:h. Yes,*" Asch quietly replied, dropping his gaze, and feeling a little queasy at the way she made him feel. Her eyes, so green, flashing in the firelight. Her face, so full of warmth. Tavin smiled to himself as he watched. Asch gathered his wits quickly and standing abruptly he moved to the other side of the fire, near Drake and Job, who raised their eyebrows knowingly. Asch rolled to his side in a huff, unused to such unwanted attention.

Darkness came. *"We will rest until the moon is high. Then we travel. Waiting is a bad idea,"* said Drake with definitive authority. No one questioned. Rolling up inside pelt capes and blankets they each laid down near the warm orange glow of the fire, their stomachs satisfied and their spirits cautiously optimistic. All except for Drake, who sat against a tree, tense and alert, listening for any undo noise creeping across the forest floor.

"I keep thinking that you cannot be Tavin. Tavin is dead," whispered Agnes, firelight reflected in her shining brown eyes peering out from underneath a blanket.

Propping himself on one elbow, Tavin thought for a moment. Glancing around, everyone appeared asleep. Finally, he quietly answered, *"Maybe Tavin is dead. At least the Tavin who used to be."*

"The Tavin I knew was kind and thoughtful, but younger, a bit gloomy and less sure," said Agnes, pulling the heavy cover tighter around her neck. The fires faint glow danced shadows across her serene face, as she stared unseeingly into the heart of the embers. She softly continued, *"When I saw the flash from your musket and you saved the life of your friend, it was as if I were seeing a ghost. Your sister, Katherine, had told me that you were dead. She was sure of it."*

"God has done his work. My life was spared, Katherines was not." Tavin sadly continued, *"There is much I need to tell you, but sleep. We can talk when you are rested, and we have found safety."*

"I have so many questions," Agnes dismally sighed.

"Rest now," said Tavin.

Drake nudged Tavin with his foot. *"Wake up. Enough sleep."* There was no rim of light in the eastern sky and the forest remained black and still. Thin columns of white smoke curled wistfully from the ash covering the orange embers of the nights fire. *"No need to mask the firepit. Even the worst tracker will know that we were here,"* he said, motioning toward the elk carcass lying not far off.

"How many follow us?" asked Tavin. *"I saw you talking with Job; I know that you have concerns."*

"The women were with two Lenape and one Frenchman when I surprised them. My arrow ended the life of one. The French coward escaped at my first shot. The remaining warrior fled only to track us and attack on the hill. Your musket

ended his life." Drake crouched and cut strips of meat off the remaining elk haunch hanging over the dying embers. *"If the weak-willed Frenchman finds his way back to the Lenape, they will come. Captives are valuable. They will come looking."*

Job grunted in agreement.

Feeling their way through the blackness of the forest, Tavin followed the white billows of misty steam coming from heavy breathing. They moved slowly, keeping the north star over their left shoulder as it sparkled through clawing branches above. As daylight began to peek over the horizon, bitter cold seemed to borough through their coats and blankets. Drake led the way. Job kept pace, nonetheless, his injuries causing obvious discomfort. Agnes and Liza, trailed behind, keeping their eyes to the ground, cautious in their steps. Tavin and Asch remained in the rear, covering any indications of their passing. It was something that Tavin had grown accustomed to, and it gave him the only sense of control he had in this unpredictable wilderness.

Coming to the west branch of the Susquehanna River, Drake stopped and motioned for silence. A wolf howled. Asch sank down, motioning for the women to do the same. They waited, listening. Job painfully inched forward to where Drake squatted on the ground. They conferred and Job motioned for Asch to move forward. Ducking low, he scrambled past the two women to reach Drake and Job. Tavin slid up to the women who sat clinging to each other in nervous fear. *"Crossing the river can be dangerous, especially in daylight. It may be watched."*

"I have seen what happens to captives who try to escape. Torture and burning. Do not let me be re-captured, no matter what it takes," Agnes murmured with tears in her eyes. Brushing her matted hair from her wind-whipped face she firmly added, *"Promise. No matter what. I will happily meet my Savior in Heaven this day, before going back to die in torment."*

Tavin hesitated. *"I will not let them take you again,"* he finally assured, silently praying that he would never be forced to make such a desperate decision.

Drake crept back to Tavin and whispered, *"We split up and scour the bank for hidden canoes. Signal if you find something. You take your woman, and Job. Asch and I will take the other."*

Tavin began to correct the *"your woman"* comment but, sighing, thought better of it. It seemed a fruitless effort. *"We will search south. God be with us all,"* said Tavin. Drake nodded. Job stood, bending low, and led the way close to the river's edge, his eyes glued to the muddy shoreline looking for signs of canoes, paddles or a cache of supplies concealed in thick brush. His breathing was heavy and Tavin could hear a rattle coming from his lungs. Tavin stretched out his arm and put his hand on Job's shoulder. *"Sano:kda:nih?"* he asked.

"Do:ges," Job answered, suppressing a cough, looking at Tavin, his black eyes narrow and dim.

"What did you ask him? What did he say?" Agnes anxiously inquired.

"I asked him if he was sick. He is," Tavin sadly answered, as they continued to search along the tangled bank.

"Do you think he will be ok? He suffered great abuse in that village. I watched. I didn't want to, but I had to see what was happening. My heart burned with sorrow for him."

"Sayá'dën!' Job violently whispered.

Tavin grabbed Agnes by the shoulders and shoved her forcefully to the hard ground. *"Quiet!"* he rasped. Agnes laid flat on her stomach, while Tavin kept his arm securely across her back and warily raised his head. On the other side of the wide river a party of ten to fifteen warriors paced along the rocky edge. *"They look for their canoes,"* Tavin whispered. Job nodded, *"Shawnee and Lenape,"* and signed for them to remain while he tracked back to where they had left Drake, Asch, and Liza. Tavin put his mouth close to Agnes' ear and uttered, *"Let me get you hidden. Crawl that way,"* he pointed. *"Be careful not to rustle any branches,"* his hot breath sending shivers down her spine.

Time seemed to move into a drifting space of hovering anticipation. Slithering across the rooted snow-covered ground on their bellies, deeper into the tangle of forest, Tavin spotted a dead tree intertwined with a thick maze of clinging vines. Images of having been chased by the warrior with the distinct turtle etching, flashed across his mind with the bellowing, *"Peureux!"* echoing once again. Quickly dismissing the memory, he pulled aside enough of the jumbled creepers to create a small opening.

Holding her scratched arms as she slid herself backwards through the narrow opening, Tavin thought to himself, *"Her arms feel as thin as these vines."* Her dark watery eyes gazed up at him in fear as she curled up inside the dark cocoon, pressing against the rotted tree, hidden by choking climbers. She said nothing. Tavin mouthed, *"I'll be back,"* and held his hand up, indicating that she remain still. Gathering extra deadfall, he leaned tangled branches up against the gap and cleared any tracks.

Suddenly a musket fired in the distance. Hearing loud howls and war whoops, Tavin ran toward the sounds, ducking low, his bow across his back and his musket in hand. Coming closer he dropped down in high grass. Through the brush he saw Job, lying motionless, a stout warrior stooping down to pull his scalp. Tavin averted his eyes in despair and waited. Thin rippling V-shaped wakes crisscrossed each other as three more canoes silently glided across the river toward the rocky shore. The river glinted gray and dull as pewter. Feathery mist hung close to smooth cold water. Canoes scraped along the shallow riverbed and were dragged onto the beach.

Coming ashore, the raiding party quietly joked and teased each other in good-natured comradeship, while cautiously spreading out to secure the area. Tavin noticed Drakes pack lying near Job's body. *"He must have left it there while searching the bank,"* he silently thought. Holding his breath, moccasin covered feet came close, with hatchets swinging back and forth to flush out any would-be danger. Tavin held his breath. Finally satisfied that there was no threat, the warriors worked together casually pulling supplies from canoes, while carrying paddles ashore to conceal until the later return. Telling animated stories, as Job lay lifeless in their midst, a rage filled Tavin.

A warrior mocked, *"Howënöih!"* pointing toward Job's body, and a voice, in English replied, *"Yes! He must have been possessed. Did he think the ball of a musket could not touch him?"* There was a malicious triumph ring to his voice. Tavin recognized the gravelly tones. Adoniram Leeds stood over Job, priming his hot long gun.

Two things became quickly clear. Job had sacrificed himself; a single diversion to draw fire, allowing the rest time to hide. And Leeds was alive. He had found his way back to the French and their Indian allies, carrying the reconnaissance from Bethlehem and Philadelphia. Now he accompanied warriors routing the frontier. He killed Job. Looking more closely he could see that Leeds limped severely as he strode along the riverbank, waiting for his companions to bury their cache and hide the canoes. *"Wolfe's musket shot must have caught his leg,"* Tavin surmised, remembering that day inside Wolfe's cabin, regretting his decision to let Leeds go. Job was dead, as Leeds stood over his lifeless body in gloating satisfaction. Tavin shook with rage.

Laying perfectly motionless a prayer flooded his troubled mind. Unsure of where it came from, it flowed freely and unobstructed. *"Father God, death has surrounded me once again and I grieve. Job was a sad soul and a friend. A slave to the wilderness and free to live with valor. A violent man and a savior. A complicated man, who lived simply. You, O mighty God, have the rights of life and death in your hands. You alone offer salvation from the bondage of death through your son, Jesus. May I not be afraid to shout your good news, for indeed, I am the 'Peureux!' I have always been and without your power I am voiceless. Forgive me in Jesus' name alone."* The words surged across his mind, like a fresh spring, washing over him in unexplainable comfort.

After several hours, Tavin's legs and arms were numb with cold, as he continued prone on the cold ground unmoving, watching. Eight warriors took hold of the four canoes and carried them along the bank, hiding them under brush along the shoreline. The others continued their banter and eventually gave attention to Job's body, stripping off weapons, clothing and rummaging through Drake's pack.

Pulling out what appeared to be a book, a squatty man with silver crucifixes dangling from his ears and a colorful woolen trade blanket wrapped loosely around his fleshy shoulders, turned it over in his hands. A thin string held a piece of dark leather over the small package, like a gift ready to be opened. Tossing it aside with a disgusted *"humph"*, the man dug deeper into the pack. Finding only a few items of any real worth, he dropped it and kicked Job's body. Anger once again swelled inside of Tavin.

Leeds barked an order and two young warriors, their forearms lined with black and red tattoos, grabbed Job by each arm and leg and carried him to the river, casting him into the languid current. Job's body floated downstream, like a log slowly drifting to an unknown end.

The raiding party moved on and still Tavin waited. He wondered where Drake, Asch and Liza were hiding and if they saw what had happened to Job. He flinched in anxiousness to get back to where Agnes was securely hidden. Finally, when he felt it was safe, he lifted his stiff body and cautiously stood.

Stepping into the narrow clearing on the riverbank, he squatted at the water's edge, and pulled the eyeglass out of his pack, scanning the river for Job's body. He saw nothing. Job was gone. A twig snapped behind him. Spinning around, Drake stood, his eyes dark with fury and sorrow. *"I lay hidden while they took the soul of my friend,"* he rasped, his teeth grit together and his fists clenched.

"Job gave himself for us. He did it on purpose. He wanted us to live," said Tavin. Fearful of what Drake was thinking, he continued, *"To avenge Job's death and risk the lives he saved, would not be what he wished to happen. He distracted them and gave us time to hide. We must honor his sacrifice."*

Drake looked at Tavin, his face expressionless and walked away. Tavin dropped his head in resigned sadness and took a deep breath. Asch squatted down and picked up the discarded package. *"What is it?"* Tavin quietly called to Asch. Holding it in one hand, Asch answered, *"A book. Maybe."*

"Why did Drake drop his pack here?" asked Tavin, picking up the scattered contents.

"He wanted relief from the weight. The cut in his side has not healed. I saw the blood on his shirt, around his waist."

Tavin reached out for the package and Asch handed it to him, asking, *"You read?"*

"Yes," said Tavin, and tucked the package into his pack.

"Where is Agnes?" came a soft, hesitant voice from behind them.

Tavin snapped his head around, as if suddenly remembering, *"Liza. Yes. Agnes is hiding. I'll get her,"* he called back, already running toward the frozen swampy ground where Agnes hid.

Squatting down next the decayed, camouflaged tree, Tavin whispered, *"Agnes?"*

"Tavin! I thought you'd never come back for me," came Agnes' jittery muffled answer.

"I've come this far to find you; do you think I'd abandon you now?" the sound of his own chuckle grating on his nerves.

"Do not even make fun. I could hear their voices and laughter. I feared that you had perished." she sobbed. Tavin said nothing, yanking the remaining vines aside. Holding both of her hands he pulled, sliding her out from the dark sanctuary. Attempting to stand, her legs numb and unsteady, she stumbled. Tavin reached out to catch her and as she fell into his arms, he involuntarily laughed. *"Tavin Shire, you are insufferable."*

Releasing her, Tavin looked into her eyes and wondered at how she could make him feel happiness, even amid such tragedy. It was then that she saw the conflict. *"What is wrong? Is Liza safe? What has happened?"*

"Liza is not in any danger. She is with Drake and Asch. Job was killed. He created a diversion with his own life."

"I am sorry. I know that he was a friend," said Agnes, reaching out and wrapping her arms around him.

Her tender embrace shook Tavin to his core. He closed his eyes, enveloping her gaunt body in his long arms, her head resting on his chest. His heart, cloaked in a passion he could not ignore, rattled in dispute. She was betrothed to marry another, unaware of Renz's betrayal. Tavin had no rights to claim her as his own. He desperately wanted to spew the words, *"You don't know who Renz really is!"* Regaining his senses, he pushed her back, and choked out, *"Agnes, there is much I need to tell you."* Just then Tavin heard the hoot of an owl. Asch stepped from the high brush.

"There is much I need to tell you as well," Agnes softly replied.

"God will give us time. Later. Now, we go. There are canoes to cross the river. We watched as the Lenape hid them."

Drake had slipped one of the hidden canoes from the brush and slid it into the icy water. Standing knee deep in the river holding it against the current, his high beaded moccasins submerged, and his rich indigo leggings wet to his thighs, Tavin knew that he was not going with them. Pushing the bulky weight of the dugout deep into the muddy shoreline, Drake secured it solidly, and stepped out of the water, lifted his shaved head to Tavin and said, *"Remain here, concealed, until the sun is gone, and darkness hides your movement. Travel the river one night, maybe two. Although it flows to the main body of the Susquehanna, it meanders like a coiled snake and will draw your days. Stay clear of the banks and keep silent."*

"You cannot avenge Job's sacrifice," said Tavin.

"He'eh. No. Job chose his way, yet a greater evil must be dealt with. I know the white man with the raiders. Leeds. He has no honor and many more will die at his hand," offered Drake. He said no more. Tavin stood dumbfounded. How did Drake know Leeds? His curiosity compelled him to ask, yet caution obliged his silence.

Knowing not to push his friend further, Tavin walked back toward the clearing, scratching his head in bewilderment, grief following him like a menacing darkness. Agnes, Liza and Asch sat on the ground, waiting. The scene brought a slight smile to Tavin's face. Such a miscellaneous crew of wanderers. Agnes, with her tattered, dirty clothing, and disheveled hair, rested against a tree, her legs curled beneath her, running her finger along the ground making varied designs and impressions. Liza, her gray dress, thread bare, burrowed inside her sentimental faded woolen blanket, sat with her legs stretched out in front of her like a child playing with toys, staring up at clouds as they drifted by. Asch, ever watchful, a half-breed trapper/warrior, who befriended a reckless, determined German colonial for no good reason at all. Tavin shook his head in wonder and silently prayed, *"Lord, my heart is torn between anguish and joy. How can it be, but with Your mysterious hand?"*

Squatting down, he opened his pack. Retrieving the package, he stood and handed it to Drake. *"The Lenape discarded this. It came from your pack. Why do you have a book?"*

"I have carried it a long while. I believed that you would like it," Drake replied, handing it back to Tavin.

"Should I open it?"

"E:h."

Hastily snapping off the string, and peeling back the stiff leather, Tavin held a German Bible in his hands. A faint whiff of wood smoke filled Tavin's nostrils as he rubbed his thumb against the soft cover, for a moment entranced by the beauty. Visions of his mother sitting near the hearth of a warm fire with her open Bible, reading aloud in her German tongue overwhelmed him. Tears welled up in his eyes and he wiped them away with his sleeve. He couldn't remember the last time he'd held a Bible. It felt a lifetime ago.

"*Where did you find this?*" choked Tavin.

"*A burned-out cabin, north of the first ridge of the Blue Mountain. Years ago, when the young white minister, Alexander Riegel came to live at Shamokin village, he shared many things with Job and others. Job believed the words of the book, calling it 'God's Truth'. He told me that it would mean a great deal to you,*" explained Drake.

Tavin had been waiting to hear more of Alexander Riegel and eagerly asked, "*What happened to Riegel? Does he remain at Shamokin?*"

"*He lived among us for a year and then moved back over the mountain. He described how there were too few ministers of the gospel to serve his own people. He returned to the Tulpehocken settlement.*"

Questions swirled across Tavin's mind, as Drake continued to speak, "*Job lived with the disgrace of his hated scars. Smallpox. When his wife and son died, and the sickness covered his body he did not wish to live any longer. Shame and sorrow stalked him. Many of our people could not endure the misery of disfiguring pockmarks, choosing to die by their own hand, rather than suffer as Job. Riegel showed Job a hope found in the book. A man, named Jesus. Hojë:nō'kda'öh; the Creator's love and mercy allowed him to find peace. Job explained this to me many times.*"

Tavin thoughtfully replied, "*Some talk of truth. Others walk in it.*" A boundless hope rose inside of him, and he smiled as he continued to stare at the worn Bible. "*God's Word brought light and life to a suffering soul. To Job,*" he solemnly reflected. The mystery of God at work provided another brick in the foundation of Tavin's own faith, another thread in the tapestry of God's work in his life and gave him a deep peace.

Drake nodded and staring unblinking into Tavin's eyes, he solemnly began, "*We have traveled together and experienced much Tavin Shire. Hoje:no'kda'oh has been with you. I have seen many miraculous things and I will consider the words that you and my brother Job tell me about the truth you say is in the book. If it is Jesus who brings life to those who are lifeless, that is a great power. I have much to ponder.*" He then turned to walk away.

"*Where are you going?*" Tavin asked, panic and concern in his voice. "*You cannot seek revenge alone.*"

"I return north to the Ohio-Seneca."

Seeing Tavin's worried face, Drake added, *"Leeds is not a stranger. He traded with us. Befriended us. Betrayed us and ran. I go to find Kaendae, who holds deep hatred against Leeds. Together we will find Leeds and end him. He has caused much grief and now he will pay for Job's death."*

As Drake began to walk away, Tavin stepped forward, and stretched out his arm to place his hand on Drake's shoulder. Drake turned, his dark eyes cheerless, *"You saved me from death, as my vision predicted, and I have remained your friend. We will meet again."*

Tavin's throat choked with emotion. *"I believe that there is deeper meaning to your vision."* Drake tipped his head, curious. Tavin continued, *"God has given us a rare and rich blessing. I have given this much thought. You were the black bird tumbling to earth, amid the thunderclouds, weak and injured and I was the face in your dream. It is true, you were the bird, but I was never meant to be perceived as your Savior. I was there to point the way. There is only one who truly saves. You will soar strong and brave, just as your vision foretold, not because of me, but because Jesus saves. I pray you find Him. I will revere you always and hold you in my heart. May God be with you."*

Drake took hold of Tavin's shoulders, embraced him firmly and was gone.

CHAPTER

21

They had paddled most of the night. Beams of sunlight danced through barren oaks while shadowy pine branches waved coldly overhead, reflecting across the silver weaving river. Steep dark hills reached down to trace the shoreline. A shallow cove offered seclusion just as light tipped over the eastern sky. A new day. The canoe slid across the water finally skidding noisily on the rocky bottom. Moss-covered rocks and icy weather-beaten evergreens disguised the boat and they clamored, exhausted, to higher ground, leaving the marshy riverbank. Making camp they slept throughout the day.

Rolling himself out from his blanket, Tavin stood and stretched, glancing over at Agnes. Her eyes wide open, she stared directly at him. *"It's hard to sleep with the sun so bright."*

"I'll see if I can find something for us to eat," he awkwardly mumbled, and quickly sprinted off, wondering at the power she held over him, feeling foolish for his abrupt response. She made him uncomfortable. There was so much that he wanted to say to her but couldn't. She was pledged to Renz. Until she understood who and what Renz was, Tavin held his thoughts and feelings to himself.

The squawking of a crow resonated through unmoving trees directly above. Tavin found himself wishing that Drake had not turned back. He was unfamiliar with this part of the country and Asch was just as uneasy. Returning to camp, Asch had stoked a small fire and the women had ventured down the embankment. At the river's edge, they eagerly drank the clear cold water and washed themselves.

"We should leave the river and head south," said Asch.

"I agree. We start on foot."

Walking slowly together back up the hill, toward the camp, Agnes and Liza chatted happily in low tones, stopping every few feet to catch their breath and soak in the warmth of the dipping sun. Stepping close to the fire, Liza shivered and rubbed her rough hands together over the welcoming flames. *"As difficult as events have proven, I must admit that there is a part of me that has reveled in the beauty and freedom of this vast wilderness."*

Agnes appeared confused. *"Beauty be sure, but Liza, does not the separation from our loved ones so greatly outweigh any beauty we witness in this desolate land as to make it void? We were carried off. The savage treatment and degrading dealings we have endured robbed us of our freedom and stripped any opportunity for revelry. We cannot declare any part of our circumstance as worthy of admiration in the least."*

Liza gently responded, her green eyes soft and consoling, *"God's purposes are beyond our understanding. Finding the good that He intends amid tragedy affords the steppingstones for increased faith, hope and love. I have learned that lesson through the burns and welts that cover my neck and back. My future may not be what I had dreamed as a girl but my faith in the one who holds my future remains sure. If I view my capture solely through the eyes of calamity, my life is in ruin, and I am then held captive to the sorrow. I know God's love for me, and I will seek His peace and discover beauty no matter the outcome."*

Agnes dropped her head in despair. *"I believe that God loves me. It is through the sacrifice, death and resurrection of Jesus that my faith is held in place, yet I find it difficult to see Him or His good purpose when the future is fraught with uncertainty and constant peril."*

"That's exactly when you can see Him!" Liza replied, with a wistful optimism that was beyond Agnes' ability to comprehend.

Tavin had been standing nearby. Hearing the conversation, he recalled the same turmoil of doubt and grief in his own experience. *"If you cannot see God along the way, He will find you in the end, Agnes. Watch and wait. You are called according to His purpose."*

Lifting her watery eyes, Agnes asked. *"Tavin, won't you tell me of the events of that awful day? Tell me of my family and of Renz. I am ready to hear."*

Clearing his throat Tavin looked over at Asch, who leaned solemnly against a tree, his musket held in the crook of his folded arms, his face somber. Tavin hesitantly began, *"My mother was slain the day my sisters were carried off. Jakob was scalped and Henryk was in shock. After taking them to Fincher's Mill on the Swatara, I started for the Terrence blockhouse. I needed help to find Berta and Katherine. Along the trail, I came upon your family. Your father, mother and brother, Thomas, were dead. I did not know where you were. Underneath your mother was a newborn. She had protected the baby with her own body."*

"I remember." Agnes's eyes drifted off as if watching a scene play out in her mind. *"We came upon a family named Grover on the trail. Mother offered to carry the infant so that Mrs. Grover could have a respite while climbing the steep path. The attack was sudden. I was lagging behind, daydreaming of my future, like some silly girl, when strong arms wrapped tightly around me and threw me to the ground. There were shots fired. I could not see clearly."* Turning her moist eyes to Tavin, she concluded, *"I had hoped that my family survived but, in my heart, I knew they had not. Thank you for telling me. I needed to hear the words. Did the infant live?"*

"Yes. A baby girl," Tavin quietly answered.

"Do you know anything of Renz? Is he safe? Have you seen him?"

"I haven't seen Renz in a very long while." Tavin honestly answered and then quickly added, *"We should go. We need to put as many miles behind us while still a few hours of light."*

Slogging through a wide expanse of wet marsh, along the river's edge, the soft swampy ground and ragged evergreens finally gave way to higher rocky ground. An open hardwood forest was before them. Heavy boughs whispered above in the chilly breeze. The gold of the sun began to slowly sink over the horizon, cooling to soft pinks and lavender. Breathing sighs of relief, walking was easier, and their spirits lifted, even as they now ascended steep wind-swept ridges.

Asch sidled up to Tavin as they climbed and whispered in a hoarse voice, *"Why did you not tell Agnes that her man is a coward who speaks falsely and does not search for her or seek to raise money for trade?"*

"She loves him. If I am to tell her who Renz really is, her love for him will not diminish, she will only find me a jealous suitor, who would tarnish the name of the man she is to marry. It is better that she discover the truth on her own."

"I will never understand your way of thinking."

Tavin laughed, *"Maybe that's not such a bad thing!"*

That evening Agnes and Liza built a fire, digging a pit and using only dry kindling, feeding it slowly, just as they had been shown. The flames popped as the smokeless blaze warmed them. Asch felled a doe. The thought of fresh meat lifted their spirits. Cutting sharp skewers, the women sliced small chunks of flank and waited until the dripping venison sizzled and smoked. The smell of roasted meat permeated the air.

With their stomachs full, they wrapped snuggly into their blankets to sleep. The sounds of night came with a serenade of remote hoots and distant wolf howls. Contemplating the events of his life, Tavin smiled, and an inscrutable harmony swept over him. There was no other place on earth he would rather be. The troubles and tragedies that had defined his path felt warmly satisfied by God's grace. A single flame in the dying fire reflected on his serene expression. Agnes saw it. *"Tavin, what is it that has changed you? You are not the same."* Agnes's soft voice seemed to meld with the forest's regale in natural rhythm.

Rolling onto this back, Tavin began. *"God has blessed me with trials and testing. When all hope was lost, He gave me the grace to endure. Do you see those stars overhead? They are not seen in the sunshine of day. Hope is like those stars. It is not apparent in the light of prosperity or well-being. But like those stars, it is discovered in the night of adversity. My hope remains. Faith endures. Peace perseveres."*

Agnes slid closer and Tavin could feel her warm breath on his face. She whispered, *"I have doubted my faith. I believed it to be strong, but these weeks of captivity and hardship, death and destruction, have weakened my trust. The woman I was given to in the village resented me. Her son had been killed and I was the painful reminder. She chose to allow my survival, while using a switch whenever she felt I was not working fast enough or well enough. I alternated between hope and despair, doubting that I would ever be free again or that God was with me."*

"I understand that. My mother often quoted a verse, I think it was in Proverbs, 'The fining pot is for silver and the furnace is for gold, but the Lord trieth the heart.' God took my parents and my sister, Katherine. And now here I am. I forge through streams, swim rivers, and climb mountains with a heavy pack of sorrow across my back, while God contends with my weak faith. And yet, His grace has never looked so grand. He is my hope. If I have changed, I pray it be for the better, by God's mercy."

Agnes began to cry. *"When you found me, I thanked God for the miracle it was, yet I remain full of grief, guilt and uncertainty."* Tavin reached for her. Curling close, her body shaking with sobs, she finally fell asleep in his arms.

Morning brought a new hope. In the distance a blur of blue smoke drifted beneath storm clouds. *"Looks like a cabin ahead,"* said Asch, as he picked up the pace. Creeping to the top of the stony bluff, a log structure sat along a wide meadow. Crouching low, Tavin pulled his brass eyeglass from his pack and stretching out flat, scanned the area. *"I don't see anyone. Let me go down alone. If he is white, he might be more amiable to receiving me than you,"* Tavin said to Asch.

"Good idea. White men like to shoot an Indian first and ask questions later."

Tavin huffed, *"And sometimes they just shoot and forget the asking altogether."*

Skidding down the steep embankment, Tavin kept his musket in a ready position. Suddenly a shot rang out and a man yelled, *"Get yourself right back up that hill! I don't want any of your trouble coming my way!"*

"We are white and your generosity in allowing us shelter for a night would be compensated for. We have two women with us. They have been through an ordeal."

Tavin could see the man now, hiding around the corner of his cabin. The barrel of his gun flashed again, *"Like I told you! Be on your way! There's no shelter or food or anything else for you here! The next time I'll shoot clean through you, so you'd better get!"*

Frustrated, Tavin turned and scrambled back to where Asch, Agnes and Liza waited. As he approached, his heart sank. Liza laid in Asch's arms; eyes closed. *"What happened?"* he shouted.

Tears streamed down Agnes's cheeks, *"She was shot."*

Asch looked up, *"Stray bullet from that madman's musket down there. It's not bad. Grazed her shoulder. The ball went straight through."*

Liza opened her tear-filled eyes. Looking up at Asch, she forced a painful smile, *"I'll be fine. Really. It knocked me down, but it's just a scratch."*

"It's a little more than a scratch. We need to get some pressure on that to stop the bleeding," stated Agnes, as she gently unwrapped the old-worn blanket from around Liza's neck and shoulders. Liza shuddered, squeezing her eyes tightly shut.

"I'm sorry. I will try not to hurt you."

"It doesn't hurt."

Watching, Tavin understood. It wasn't pain that had caused her to flinch. She had taken great care to hide the scars and red welts that marked her shoulders and neck. Her face flushed with embarrassment.

Asch did not move. Holding Liza brought feelings that he had been unaware of. Agnes squatted down next to Liza, tending to the wound, as Asch gently stroked Liza's hair. Agnes stood, wiping her dirty hands on her skirt, *"We'll need water to clean it, but if you hold it tightly that should slow the bleeding."*

"I can do that," Liza firmly replied. Asch helped her to stand, gingerly wrapping his arm around her shoulders, supporting her until he was certain that she was steady on her feet. Liza's arm slipped around his waist as she warily took several steps. *"I'm not feeling dizzy. I can walk,"* keeping her gaze to the ground. *"Thank you,"* she softly added.

Quickly glancing at Agnes, she asked, *"Could you wrap my blanket around my neck?"* averting her eyes back to the ground.

"Yes, of course."

Asch removed his arm and walked to where his pack lay on the ground, sliding it across his back. Agnes tucked the blanket around Liza the way she always wore it, whispering, *"You have nothing to be ashamed of Liza. Your scars do not confuse the beauty of who you are."*

Traveling only a few more miles, certain they were clear of the crazed man at the cabin, they made an early camp near a crisp snow-fed creek. Agnes checked Liza's shoulder. It was bleeding heavily. Unwrapping the soaked cotton strips, Liza cringed with pain. Scarlet stains covered her shirtwaist and Agnes's hands became stiff with blood as she gently removed the bandaging.

"The bleeding should stop once we clean it well and wrap it properly. Hold pressure on it while I get water to clean it," said Agnes, her face smudged,

as she swiped her hair back from her face with the back of her hand, tracing a trail of red across her forehead.

Tavin marveled at how collected Agnes was, noting to Asch, *"Agnes is not prone to hysteria. Her compassion and kindness outweigh any sensitivities. A woman of lesser fiber may have fainted or become squeamish. She is delicate in one way, yet unabashed in another."*

"You consider a woman who is not yours to consider. It is you yourself who has exclaimed that she is not your woman."

Tavin gave a short laugh, *"Ne:'. It is true. I freely admit she will never be mine, while I am also destined to languish over my defeat and, as you put it, to 'consider' her. The duration of my lament is only known by God Himself."*

Asch leaned his musket against a tree and slipped his bow off his shoulder. *"It is strange to me that you are as persistent as a dog with a bone in any other matter, yet in this matter, you so easily roll over."*

Tavin watched him walk away, wondering at the complexities of his own emotions. *"I can't make her love me! Better to admit my loss!"* he silently exclaimed and turned to collect wood for the fire, his mind wandering in turmoil like the complicated vines on a picket fence.

Agnes sat on her knees and plunged her hands deep into the ice cold, crystal-clear stream. Vigorously rubbing them together, the caked on reddish pigment dissolved and floated away in pink transparent clouds. Splashing her face, she trembled and cupped her hands to drink in the freezing water. Lifting her skirt, she stripped another length from her shift and dunked it in, scrubbing it harshly of dirt and grime, before squeezing out the excess moisture.

Returning to Liza, she gently washed the wound. *"Does it hurt?"* she asked.

Liza squirmed. *"A bit."*

"You are ever the brave one. It looks like the bleeding has finally stopped. God spared you. The bullet could have been more direct."

"E:h," said Liza.

Agnes's head jerked up, *"What did you say?!"*

"It means 'Yes.' I've heard Tavin and Asch use it."

"Liza, you must be careful. We are civilized women, returning to our families. Do not mistake this wilderness for your home."

Liza's nostrils flared and her eyes momentarily flashed dark with anger, "*Maybe your home is one that brings memories of love and laughter. I return to a life of servitude. On our voyage from Rotterdam, after fleeing the Palatinate, my father died unexpectedly. He had signed an indenture to work off the cost of the passage once we arrived. My mother was frail and unable to work. She could barely care for my younger siblings. It fell to me. I was auctioned off from Philadelphia to work as a chamber maid in an inn near Reading, The Red Owl. Two years remain before the balance is satisfied. Please do not lecture me on propriety. If I am not worn and bent by the time that I am twenty, I will continue as a burned and scarred woman. No good man will want me as his wife. And now,*" she paused, and in a calmer, factual manner continued, "*and now, I return, a woman sullied, to be gossiped over and pitied as having lived with the savages. I am not naïve to my plight nor am I misguided concerning my future. My only hope is in Jesus, who restores my soul and lifts me from the pit. He is where I find my joy. He is the reason I find peace whether in the civilized world or in the darkness of the wilderness. He is my home! I have no other.*"

"*My words were insensitive, and I seek your forgiveness,*" Agnes sadly replied. Dropping her head, she continued, "*I cannot defend my reprimand. I can only say, my own perceptions are selfish. I envy your faith. You have suffered and endured so much more than I and yet, I am the one who is afraid. My future is uncertain, although I am betrothed. Questions haunt my heart. Will Renz still want me even after the humiliation and prattle my captivity is sure to bring? He is a man of position and ambition, warm and kind. I fear I would be too much a burden.*"

Tavin silently listened as Agnes and Liza continue to softly share doubts and worries with each other. Cringing inside, he wanted to comfort Agnes and explain that her high opinion of Renz was misguided. He wanted to shout, "*Renz is absorbed in the perception of his own grandeur, in the public personae of his own heroism, in the selfish ambition of his own ego!*" He wanted to tell her that Renz did not deserve her and that she had nothing to fear. He wanted to tell her that he loved her.

Darkness fell. Asch leaned on one elbow near the fire and gave Tavin a knowing look. Tavin shrugged, turned his back, and closed his eyes. But sleep would not come.

CHAPTER

22

January 1756

When Bethlehem came into view, they each breathed a sigh of relief. Liza was growing weaker. *"There will be a doctor here, Liza,"* Tavin assured.

"There is no need. I simply need a bath and a bed," she laughed, and then cringed in pain.

The unique Moravian community was just as Tavin had described. Monocracy Creek flowed into the Lehigh River and idealistic dreams abounded within the structures built and the people who built them. As Agnes walked among the crowds of people, she commented, *"It's much larger than I expected."*

Tavin nodded, saying nothing.

The bustling village on the colonial frontier had quickly transformed from a tranquil hamlet into a haven for displaced, disheartened, and deprived people. Tavin was surprised by the changes even since he had first arrived with Berta. Looking into the faces of those passing by it was clear that Indian assaults ravaging the countryside had imposed great suffering and deep poverty on the already impoverished.

Refugees from the surrounding settlements huddled closely together on street corners and alongside the roadway, their forlorn appearance testifying to the horrors they had witnessed and the dismal futures they expected. Bethlehem was overwhelmed and did it's best to ease the misery. Moravian women mingled cheerily, wearing their uniform style of dress, ankle length shifts with clean white half-aprons. The haube head covering, or sister cap distinguished them, as they offered water and comfort.

Sunken eyes and blank expressions followed as Agnes, Liza, Tavin and Asch walked slowly through the town, passing the log-hewn shops lined side by side in a neat row on either side of the street. The heart of town itself was a formidable fortress, built along a limestone bluff, with five story buildings, prepared with heavy stones placed along the window ledges, ready to drop on the heads of would-be attackers. Tavin hadn't really taken notice of the details of Bethlehem on his previous visit, although it was all reminiscent in general.

Asch tensed at so many white men with flintlocks and knives, their glassy eyes trailing with suspicion. Tavin later learned of the Indian uprising in the Moravian farming settlement, established for Christian Indian converts to the north at Gnadenhutten. This attack signaled that no whites were safe, not even fervent Moravians devoted to helping the Indians. It was at that time a strong militia was called for and Bethlehem secured a bold posture of defense, while welcoming white and Indian refugees, along with blacks and immigrants from countries far and wide. Times were changing rapidly, and no one knew how it would end.

A caldron of steaming corn soup boiled over a flaming fire next to the butchery. An elderly woman, with countless dainty wrinkles framing her gentle eyes, attended the pot with a large wooden spoon. *"Oh, dear children!"* she cried, motioning briefly to Liza's arm in a tattered sling and her scarlet-soaked shirtwaist. A wide white ribbon was neatly tied under her chin and Tavin recalled to himself that a white ribbon indicated that she was a widow. *"Come near. Please, sit, here, on the bench. The soup will warm your insides and fresh bread will be here in a moment from the bakehouse. You have just arrived, yes?"* she asked, in her heavy German brogue. Her round, red face and narrow eyes filled with warmth and concern.

At that moment Agnes realized how utterly downtrodden she also appeared. Smoothing her dirty brown hair with her hand, she averted her eyes and replied, *"Yes madame, we have come over the mountain, having escaped the wrath of natives who have assaulted the settlements in such ruinous terms."*

"Please call me Sister Bain. You must be exhausted. And dear girl, it looks to me like you need to see a doctor," she said to Liza, as she poured piping hot soup into worn pewter bowls.

"It has indeed been a long and arduous journey. My appearance may suggest a more serious injury than is reality, yet, in time, I do believe that a doctor will be required," Liza replied as she carefully sipped the thick broth and pulled her dirty blanket higher upon her neck. *"This is delicious. Thank you."*

Sitting tightly together on the narrow bench with steaming bowls and chunks of fresh warm bread in their hands, Tavin reflected, *"It hardly seems three months since the initial attacks occurred. By the will of God, I pray our calamity is over."*

"What will you do now Tavin?" Agnes softly asked.

Taking a moment to think, Tavin gave a short laugh. *"I have not even considered what my future holds. I will first see to my brothers and sister, of course. After that, I cannot tell."*

Tears filled Agnes's eyes and her thoughts shifted. *"These poor people. They are without the means to build a future for themselves or their children,"* she quietly reflected to Tavin, glancing up and down the crowded street, seemingly unaware of her similar destitute situation.

"The displaced people you see sadly clustered together have lost their homes and their livelihoods, not to mention loved ones. They are angry and filled with vengeful thoughts and deep sorrow." Turning to Asch, Tavin added, *"Watch your back brother. I fear many here may simply see you as an Indian to satisfy their rancorous emotions."*

Liza lifted her soft eyes to Asch. *"I'm glad that you are here with us. Thank you."*

Tavin looked at Agnes. Agnes sadly smiled.

Seeming to ignore Liza's gratitude, Asch commented, *"I see many converted Lenape and even Mohican here in this town mingling peaceably with these Christian white Moravians. Yet I agree, the refugees from the settlements do not feel the same goodwill. An Indian is an Indian."* A group of gruff looking men strolled past eyeing Asch suspiciously. *"I think I will not remain long,"* he added, his wary gray eyes glaring in their direction.

Tavin stood, holding his musket in his hand, indicating that the men should move along. Walking off complaining quietly to each other they slowly strolled sluggishly down the street and entered the mercantile. Tavin gave Asch a calculating look and Asch nodded. They would be alert.

Recognizing the concerned look on Liza's face Tavin shared encouraging news he had gleaned from an elderly man along the roadside in a brief conversation. *"Commissioner Benjamin Franklin was granted the authority to assemble a militia by Governor Morris. The breech of Lehigh Pass finally stunned the provincial authorities into action. Franklin supplied guns, ammunition, and appointed militia officers. From here in Bethlehem, over five-hundred troops assembled into companies and marched a detachment to plug the pass on January 7th."*

"So, all of this will be over soon?" Agnes asked with hope in her voice.

Asch explained, *"The fury raging over the mountain will not cease in light of a militia. Warriors see white settlers, volunteer militia or British troops as one enemy. There is no distinction. They will continue to attack up and down the frontier settlements until there is some agreed upon treaty."*

Tavin sourly added, *"Blind hatred runs just as fully on both sides. Unfortunately, white settlers and militia, as well as British troops, do not always distinguish between an enemy warrior and a friendly half-breed traveling with a white man and two white women."*

Asch smiled and nodded in agreement.

Sister Kiehl approached, again radiating kindness and patient care. *"I will notify Dr. Schwarz and he will be expecting you, young lady!"* she cheerfully exclaimed to Liza. *"In the meantime, it looks to me like you could all use a bath and a change of clothes. We have separate accommodations for men and women who have become evacuees through this terrible time."*

Tavin answered, *"Thank you. My friend and I will be well cared for at the Fincher's cabin north of town, although both Miss Bowen and Miss Schell, I'm certain, would be pleased to accept your gracious offer."*

"Oh Yes! Pleased indeed! I cannot thank you enough for your liberal generosity," cried Agnes, her eyes gleaming with gratitude, while Liza used the corner of her filthy blanket to wipe her tear-stained cheeks. *"I am so very grateful for your kindness!"* she choked out.

"So, it is good-bye," said Tavin, forcing a jovial air.

"How will we find you? You aren't going to leave us, are you?" Agnes exclaimed, with a hint of panic in her voice.

"No, I won't leave. I will be only a mile or so north. I'll take Asch with me before one of these settlers decides to remove his scalp as a trophy."

Asch nodded, *"There is truth to that."*

As Tavin walked away, Agnes stared after him. She noted his broad, square shoulders, and the way he carried his musket across his arm, as he effortlessly strode up the road bearing the heavy pack as if it were no weight at all. She shivered and felt a powerful urge to call after him, to run to him. Shaking her feelings aside, she turned to Liza, *"We will find our place. God has us in His loving hands."*

"Yes Agnes. I remind myself continually that my confidence resides in God alone, my maker and my redeemer, through whatever trials or hardships may come."

Agnes thoughtfully added, *"It appears the cross we bear is prepared for us and appointed by God's divine love, for His good purpose. Jesus promises that His yoke is easy and His burden light,"* as she glanced back over her shoulder and down the street to catch one last glimpse of Tavin.

"To trample the yoke in sulkiness or fall under it in despair or run from it in fear only leads to a thorny path of sorrow. Jesus took up His cross and we shall do the same!" Liza gaily pronounced, as she and Agnes followed Sister Bain to a three-story, stone building specified for women only. *"This is not to say that I do not weep and beg God for His mercies, especially for you, Tavin and Asch. I will continue to pray,"* added Liza. Agnes understood Liza's concern. The earlier conversation and threatening stares from armed men had caused her to worry for Asch.

★ ★ ★ ★ ★

The sky frowned in anger, echoing Tavin's emotions. Agnes was all he wanted. Walking away and leaving her standing on the street threatened to break him. They had only spoken of Renz once and now that she was returned, Tavin held down his urges to spew the truth. He recalled the blithe words Renz used when debating over whether Agnes should be liberated from her captors, *"She is a ruined woman,"* Renz had coldly stated. Tavin gripped the butt of his musket tighter and prayed, *"Lord, help me bow to your Spirit and go forth trusting Your purposes."*

"I won't be going with you," Asch interrupted Tavin's thoughts. *"I need to see to my family. My father and mother. You are as close as a brother, I will not forget you."* His blunt and abrupt words caught Tavin by surprise.

"Your friendship is as a brother. I will see you again. Once Jakob, Henryk and Berta's future is permanently settled, I will decide what to do next, but my intent is to go back over the mountain. There is nothing here for me. Tell Wolfe and Mary that I pray for them in these unsettled times. God be with you."

"And you," Asch replied, clutching Tavin firmly by the shoulders.

★ ★ ★ ★ ★

The fury of a dark storm quickly spent itself out, giving way to low, grim clouds, that rested heavily overhead in dismal overcast grayness. Inside the cabin, the mood was as a warm blanket, comfortable and relaxed. Sitting at the Fincher's table with his siblings, exchanging news and sharing personal antics, Tavin reveled in the cheery conversation. Faces reflected laughter, surprise and banter as stories were swapped in the flutter of firelight. Henryk and Berta were growing and thriving with energy and health. Jakob was in love. The Fincher's sixteen-year-old granddaughter had caught his eye. While his antagonistic nature remained, his overall demeanor had softened, and his faith had strengthened. Tavin was astounded at a joy seen in Jakob, a joy that had not been there before.

Later that evening, when all was quiet, Mr. Fincher inquired, *"So how is it with you, Tavin? You have experienced the wildness of nature and the trauma of violence. Now you return to a quiet life."*

Tavin's elbows rested on the table, and he thought for a moment. With his face deeply bronzed from the sun, his hair long and shaggy, he looked more like a fierce mountain trapper in his buckskin leggings and shirt, than a young German farmer. *"I cannot predict my future. God has brought me through a trial by fire, so to speak. I can say that my faith has settled, and my doubts have decreased. I have witnessed His goodness amid the horrors. I have seen His hand move in miraculous ways."*

"Though your parents and Katherine have seen an end to this earthly life, you believe that God is good and merciful?" Mr. Fincher prodded.

"Indeed. God is God. Night after night in the darkness of the wilderness I gazed up at the stars and observed His handiwork. In those moments, when all appeared only sorrow, I felt His presence reminding me that it is He who sits upon the circle of the earth and as the book of Isaiah tells us, 'The inhabitants thereof are as grasshoppers'. God stretched out the heavens as a curtain. He holds it all together and His word stands forever. What shall I cry against Him?"

Mr. Fincher smiled a knowing smile, his white hair shining in the firelight.

Tavin stood and walked to where his pack lay. Pulling out the worn German Bible, he held it up. *"My brother, Job, some would call a savage, understood the meaning of this book. He was far less a savage than many 'godly' men who claim Jesus as their Savior yet walk in hypocrisy and pride. I judged Job as a sinner requiring God's pardon, while all along it was me. I was lost. I rebelled and struggled against God. Time and time again The Lord probed the secrets of my stubborn heart, until I finally bent under His loving pursuit amid the most dire time of my life."*

"What happened to Job?"

"He gave his life to save his friends. He saved me, Agnes, all of us. I have no real assurance of Job's faith in Jesus, but when Drake gave me this Bible and explained Job's encounter with a missionary, I must wonder. Job was a quiet, strong man who had suffered greatly, and my hope is that he found his peace in Christ. Drake seemed to think it so."

Mr. Fincher took a moment to contemplate. *"God's ways are indeed mysterious. And what of you, Tavin? What are your plans?"*

"I've just now been giving it thought. Our grandparents and other family are living in Germantown, near Philadelphia. I will see that the children join them. I have not shared this with anyone before, but I believe that God is impressing upon me to join in this war, although on my own terms. I have nothing holding me here and if I can be of use, I am willing. The farm holds nothing any longer."

Jakob spoke up from a shadowy corner of the cabin. *"I will not go to Germantown. I wish to continue here. I have found friendship and acceptance. I have no desire to remove to the city and receive the gawking curiosity of strangers."* Jakob removed his cap and rubbed the blotchy, patchy scarring on the top of his head.

"I will not argue with you Jakob. Your circumstance dictates a different path. But Henryk and Berta have a right to return to family, at least for now."

In the following days, Tavin slept as if he was of the dead. Having bathed and tumbled onto a soft bed, one dream followed another like duck's swimming circles on a smooth pond. Mrs. Fincher cheerfully remarked, *"The poor boy has become so deprived, sleeping on the cold hard ground these many weeks. That down filled mattress has taken ahold of his senses and swallowed him whole."* To which Berta's bright blue eyes became huge with concern. *"There, there, child,"* she continued, consoling the girl's fears. *"No need to fuss. He will awake. Just give him time."*

A day later Tavin sat up, swinging his long legs over the edge of the short bed. A linen curtain hung at a small window and a thin slit in the fabric cast a narrow stream of sunlight across the floor. Particles of dust danced across the beam in hazy glory. Breathing deeply, he tossed the patchwork quilt to the side and stood, his nightshirt hanging past his knees. Stretching, he pulled on clean breeches and ambled barefoot across the cabin to the table near the hearth, feeling oddly out of place without his dirty buckskins. *"How long have I slept?* he asked Mrs. Fincher.

"A long while. I'll fetch some water from the well and fill the washbasin for you. You know where the privy is. You must be half-starved. There is porridge in the kettle." Her apron barely fit around her plentiful figure as she grabbed the brass bucket and marched for the door humming a pitchy tune. Tavin marveled at her ever-present cheery disposition.

Finishing his breakfast, he heard a cart coming along the road. *"Now who could that be?"* Mrs. Fincher chirped. *"I don't expect Mr. Fincher back from the market this soon."* Wiping her hands on her apron she scurried out the door. Waving her flabby arms in the air, she hollered, *"Oh gracious me! Aren't you simply lovely? You must be Tavin's friend. He has spoken of you."* At hearing this, Tavin choked on a piece of bread and quickly poured a mug of water from the pitcher to wash it down.

Composing himself, he calmly stepped through the doorway. Agnes sat on the bench of the cart with a huge smile. *"Sister Kiehl allowed me the use of her buggy!"* Agnes exclaimed; the morning sun encircling her in shimmering rays. She looked like an angel. Tavin stood dumbfounded. Gathering his senses, he gruffed, *"It is dangerous for you to be alone out here."*

"Isn't she as pretty as a flower?!" Mrs. Fincher crooned. Berta came rushing from the cabin, pushing herself past Tavin and yelling, *"Agnes! Agnes!"* Running toward the buggy she scrambled up and threw herself across Agnes's lap. Cupping her hands around Berta's sweet face, Agnes exclaimed, *"Oh dear little one, I can't tell you how my heart soars at seeing you so well! You've filled out and the sparkle has returned to those eyes!"*

"I am perfect!"

Tavin interrupted, *"Well now, I don't think we can go that far!"*

Agnes laughed, *"Tavin, she is as perfect as any seven-year-old I have ever met!"* A white muslin scarf framed her tanned face perfectly. She wore a dark blue skirt, a short white waistcoat, and a black cape draped around her shoulders. A small cambric cap, lay on the seat next to her, with a red ribbon lightly flapping in the breeze. *"Sister Kiehl helped to provide me with these clothes. I took the cap off though. I've never been one for bonnets or caps."*

"Your hair is so beautiful; it'd be a shame to hide it. I like the way it twists on the top of your head!" shouted Berta.

Agnes smiled warmly. *"Thank you. I value your opinion,"* she cheerfully responded, helping Berta slide down from her lap to the ground. As Agnes stood to turn and step down herself, Mrs. Fincher firmly punched Tavin's arm and whispered, *"Help the lady from the cart!"*

Tavin sauntered over to offer his hand, too late. Agnes jumped from the step to the ground, *"I believe I have forgotten how a lady is supposed to behave! I have evidently been too long in the wild,"* she laughed. Tavin found himself wishing that she weren't so likable. In his attempts to keep her at a distance, protecting his own heart, she was making it difficult.

"Have you located Renz?" Tavin coldly asked.

"Possibly. I spoke with a militiaman who remained in town recovering from an illness. He believed that Renz was selected as one of the militia officers, leading troops north to Lehigh Pass. Of course, I was not surprised. It is in Renz's good spirit to serve. Once the provincial government in Philadelphia finally decided on a permanent military force, mustered in at Bethlehem, he would naturally volunteer to do whatever he could to assist. His leadership abilities are extraordinary."

"Citizen soldiers are generally disorganized, ill-trained and led by inexperienced officers," said Tavin. Flinching as he recognized his own

bitter prejudice against Renz, he quickly added, *"Renz will undoubtedly rise to the occasion."*

"Do you not believe that the militia can effectively sway the tide and bring peace?"

"Stealth, speed, and the element of surprise gives experienced warriors an advantage. They seek targets of opportunity, not an open battle against a militia force. I see no immediate relief for the frontier settlements."

Agnes wrung her hands together. A troubled expression crossed her face. *"My heart aches for the poor evacuees who fled their homes with nothing more than the clothes on their backs. I met an eighty-year-old woman just this morning before traveling to see you."* Tears welled up in Agnes's dark-brown eyes. *"She is alone and destitute. She wept bitterly as she recounted fleeing in terror from her home. Her advanced age only offers greater adversity. She told me that the Word of God is her only comfort."*

Mrs. Fincher interrupted, *"Come now. You must be freezing standing out here conversing. I have a pot of hot tea to warm your insides."* It was only then that Tavin realized that he was barefoot on the frozen ground.

Sitting at the rough wooden table, Berta pushed tightly against Agnes, her head leaning on Agnes's shoulder. Tavin sat across from them, after he had hurriedly finished dressing in an appropriate manner, shoes and all. Appearing the epidemy of social decorum, he felt uncomfortable in the grey linen breeches, the high-necked white shirt, stockings, and the black leather shoes that Mr. Fincher had provided for him. A white ruffled cravat was neatly shoved inside his buff-colored knee length buttoned waistcoat. He had tucked in his shirt and although the sleeves were loose and long, it all felt tight and imposing.

After a few minutes of benign chatter, Agnes asked, *"Where is Asch?"*

"He is gone. Back to see to his family. His father and mother."

"He didn't even say goodbye," said Agnes, arching her eyebrows in disappointment.

"Asch is not one to linger over farewells."

"But what of Liza? She will be heartbroken. She has never said the words, yet I know that she longs to be with Asch!" Agnes exclaimed. Smoothing her dress, she calmed her voice, and added, *"And yet, maybe it is for the best. I am sure that with her indentured position, she has dismissed all thoughts of marriage. Liza is determined to return to her service. It will be two more years*

before the debt of passage across the ocean from Europe is paid. And then there is the much larger fact that Asch is not of the Christian faith. Yet they do make a superb couple!"

"How does your mind come to such conclusions regarding Liza's feelings? And how did you ever reach the notion of Asch and Liza marrying?!"

"Well, I don't know what you saw while we were in the wilderness, but I was very aware of a bond forming between them. I believe that I am correct in stating that Asch too has feelings for Liza. Perhaps that is why he left without even an explanation. Perhaps he is scared."

Knowing that there was some truth behind Agnes's words, Tavin fidgeted in his seat. *"I have never known Asch to be scared of anything."*

"You do not know what is in his heart," Agnes retorted, her eyes leveled directly at him, unblinking.

Tavin pulled at his collar, suddenly feeling sweaty and uncomfortable, and pausing for a moment, he wisely changed the subject, *"Has Liza healed from her gunshot wound?*

"She has." Agnes tartly answered.

Recognizing her irritation, he ignored her tone, and asked another question, *"Has she shared what happened to her? Her scars, I mean. What happened?"*

Agnes sighed, temporarily accepting that Tavin had no intention of pursuing further conversation concerning Asch, she answered, *"When Liza was nine years old her little brother held a stick in the hearth fire and began swinging the flame about in playfulness. It caught in Liza's hair, which was hanging loose, un-braided. The flames quickly spread, burning her neck and back. She spent many months lying in painful agony on her stomach until the wounds finally healed yet leaving their deep marks."*

Tavin mused, "Liza has seen profound tragedy. Suffering such painful burns, her father's death on the voyage to Philadelphia, fulfilling the indenture for herself, her mother, and siblings, and then captivity. I wonder at her expressed happiness. It is truly a great marvel."

"Yes. Liza has discovered joy in all things, as the scriptures say. Yet, her heart is lonely and her love and concern for Asch is evident. Do you believe that Asch is repulsed by the scars on Liza? Liza believes that no man could ever love her, because of her 'mutilation', as she puts it." Somehow Agnes had delicately shifted the discussion back to Asch.

Tavin responded with impatience in his voice, *"What does it matter? As you said, they could never be together. Asch has indicated little interest in the God of the Bible, although he holds reverence and respect. And then of course his Indian blood may indeed be a stumbling block to any union. Leave it be, Agnes."*

Agnes bristled. *"I will not let it be. Have you shared the gospel message with Asch? Has he heard the good news of God's forgiveness of sin and free offer of love and grace?"*

"I began many times. His concept of the creator God is much different than the God of the Bible. It is of little use."

"Really? I do not see it that way. All you need do is share the truth; God does the rest. Explain that the Creator is separate from the creation. God is not dwelling within or around or through any inanimate object. He alone is God, one God. He is the "I AM" and He has provided a wonderful plan of redemption for lost people, through Jesus.

Feeling an even greater discomfort with Agnes's fervent perspective, although causing him to reconsider his own assumptions, he responded, *"Where is Liza now? If she is so enamored with Asch, why didn't she come out here with you, thinking she could see him? She could then explain God and they can ride off together forever,"* challenged Tavin.

Exasperated, she stiffened her back, and snapped, *"Tavin Shire, I do not appreciate your sarcasm or your hard-hearted criticisms. Liza and Asch deserve a chance to be together if it is God's will."*

Tavin immediately thought of his relationship with Agnes, and shoved down the temptation to holler, *"We deserve the same chance!"*

Agnes took a sip of tea and answered Tavin's question in a calmer voice, *"Liza is leaving. A patron of the inn where Liza serves recognized her yesterday. She has agreed to return to the Red Owl Inn with him. He did not even use her name or inquire as to her health. He just called her 'girl', like she was a thing and there was rum on his breath. I fear for her safety, although she assured me that the man is harmless."*

"It is not our affair. Liza is bound by the indebtedness incurred by herself and her family."

"She is indeed bound! But should social dictates hold the right to strip a woman of individual alternatives? Should not compassion override her duties to servitude? Should the law determine her future prospects, but rather, should it not speak on her behalf? Where is the kindheartedness?"

Tavin was impressed with the passion in which Agnes spoke, although completely outside the norm of provincial thinking. *"You make valid points. But the fact remains, Liza is indebted. Money is the only language that will ever free her. The law backs it up. It is not our place to pass judgment or to intervene into these affairs. Perhaps we need pray that the holders of her indentureship become softened to Liza's plight and forgive her obligation."*

"Pray, yes. But my heart knows that Asch is hurting as much as Liza is right now. I can hardly bare to see the two of them suffer this way. I will not only pray that Liza is released from her requirements, but that Asch will come to a knowledge of our Lord and pursue Liza in marriage."

Tavin chuckled. *"You are asking a lot!"*

"Our God is BIG and GOOD, Tavin!" exclaimed Agnes, finally smiling away the tension between them.

From that point forward, benevolent conversation waned back and forth between the current Indian crisis, government action and the weather. There was no more mention of Renz, Liza, or Asch. Finally, Agnes rose, *"I must be going. I promised Sister Hannah that I would help her in the mercantile this afternoon."*

"You are welcome anytime!" Mrs. Fincher gushed.

"Thank you for your hospitality. And Berta, it was wonderful to see you!"

Berta beamed from ear to ear.

Tavin walked Agnes to her carriage, aware again of how uncomfortable his clothes and shoes felt. His mind flashed back to when Mary Wolfe had traded buckskins and moccasins for his grandfather's boots, and he smiled to himself. *"Let me ride along with you back to town,"* he offered Agnes, interrupting his quick daydream.

"It's only a mile. I will be safe. You do not need to worry about me anymore, Tavin."

She hadn't meant for that statement to sound so final, but it did. Watching her slap the reigns against the horses back and turn down the road, Tavin made a hasty decision. He would take the children and leave for Germantown tomorrow.

CHAPTER

23

March 1756

Tavin pulled the sinew of his cottonwood bow back and the steel-tipped arrow hit its mark. The comfort he had lacked in the colonies had returned with the beauty of the woodlands and mountains. Crossing the lush meadow, surrounded by budding hardwood trees, he wondered at the serenity that swept over him, until, just as quickly, recollections of the past months returned. The circumstances of treachery, violence and the ongoing war with the French interrupted the momentary tranquility. Pushing uninvited memories aside, he approached the big buck. A clean shot. Pulling the arrow from the heart, he slung the heavy carcass around his shoulders, carrying it back to the burned-out cabin.

Two eagles soared overhead, while crows cawed in agitation. The blurry morning sun felt warm. The air was calm. White mist hung low on wet, melting snow. Plodding through high dense grass, his eyes lifted to the sound of a woodpecker hammering on a hollow tree. He smiled and thought of Berta. Her observant nature had so often led her to acts of mercy in the animal kingdom, at least by her definition. She would scamper up a tree to feed baby birds she insisted were abandoned or gather newborn rabbits from a nest as pets. The sound of a woodpecker often caused her great concern. *"All that pecking must hurt!"*

He hadn't seen Henryk or Berta since he had taken them to Germantown, two months earlier. Their Grandmother Shire had embraced them in her loving arms exclaiming in German, *"God is merciful! To Him be praise!"* With that, Tavin was assured that Henryk and Berta would be welcomed and cared for. Jakob remained in Bethlehem with thoughts of the Fincher's granddaughter consuming him. Tavin wondered if this was a Shire trait or maybe a curse.

Musing over the circumstances that led him back into the wilderness, he recounted again his conversations and chance encounters in Philadelphia. He had heard rumors that Benjamin Franklin was recruiting additional volunteers to serve as militia to protect the settlements from further Indian raids, securing a string of guard stations and forts along the mountain ridges. Borrowing his deceased grandfather's broken-down nag, he had sauntered down Water Street along the Delaware River and eventually the boardwalk leading to Carpenters Wharf. The Tun Tavern was bursting with men crowded along the long, narrow covered porch. A low, melodious, persuasive voice could be heard expounding from inside.

"Who's speaking?" asked Tavin. *"Benjamin Franklin is making his case for the militia,"* a gruff old man explained, a mug of brown beer in his hand. Glancing around, men's faces were attentive. Heads were nodding in agreement and as the oratory concluded, a rousing applause followed. *"We'll send those savages back to the gates of hades!"* one man shouted.

Tavin cringed. The anger felt justifiable and Tavin could relate. After all, his family had suffered more than most, and yet, he owed a great debt of gratitude to his Indian friends. He feared that there would be made no distinction with Indian allies, as had been pointed out to him on numerous occasions. Tavin understood what was happening in the counties south of the Blue Mountain and along the Susquehanna. There were bloodthirsty renegades who terrorized, murdered, captured, and burned. There were also Indian allies, although most of whom functioned with a fluidity toward alliance, depending on who could provide the better trade standards at any given moment. This made it difficult to know who to trust and often caused innocents to suffer.

As Tavin silently observed the rancor, mixed with frustration and fear pouring from the tavern that day, he spotted a familiar face. Charles Grover. Pushing his way along the crowded veranda, the strong smell of sweat and beer caused him to feel so sick that he held his breath as he hollered, *"Mr. Grover!"* Grover turned with a huge smile, *"Tavin Shire! It is good to see you!"* Vigorously shaking Tavin's hand, he quickly asked in his heavy German brogue, *"Please, did you find your precious sisters?"* The two exchanged news and recounted the past months. Mr. Grover told of finding Tavin's mother and her burial. He went on to explain that his family had settled off Germantown Avenue and the baby girl Tavin had rescued was thriving and named Gustava, after Tavin. Tavin told of his experiences in the wilderness and God's hand of goodness, even beyond the death of Katherine.

As their conversation was concluding Mr. Grover, scratched his beard and thoughtfully said, *"There is someone I'd like you to meet."* Motioning toward a pristine, middle aged British officer, he explained, *"This is Colonel William Clapham. He is assisting Benjamin Franklin, Conrad Weiser and Governor Morris in establishing a series of forts to protect the frontier."* After Mr. Grover made his initial introductions, Colonel Clapham promptly and directly inquired, *"Mr. Shire, will you serve the Crown? I could use eyes and ears west, as far as Fort Duquesne. Your experience with the Indians and your knowledge of the wilderness, would be most valuable in acquiring important information as to the enemy's strength, plans and movements."*

Tavin did not really like Colonel Clapham's haughty tone and verbose countenance. Adjusting the weight of the buck on his shoulders, Tavin smiled as he walked back toward Wolfe's cabin, recalling the response he'd given to Clapham on that afternoon in Philadelphia, *"I have nothing better to do at this moment. I will happily serve the immigrate people of Pennsylvania who simply seek to live their lives free from Indian attack, due to the incompetent, greedy and deceitful treaties which displaced the Lenape in the first place."*

Colonel Clapham's lips had curled in mocking retort, *"Your opinion is duly noted."* Pausing for dramatic sake he continued, *"I assume you reference the 1737 Walking Purchase. If that be the case, perhaps you should bring your accusations against the Iroquois Confederacy who refused to intervene on behalf of their hapless southern neighbors, the Lenape."* Clapham rubbed his bristly beard and pronounced his next sentence for the benefit of anyone standing within hearing distance, *"Or conceivably you should turn your eye to the lackless French who encroach upon us like rabid dogs ready to be shot."* Several men laughed.

Tavin smiled again at the memory. He had gotten under Colonel Clapham's skin.

Stepping from the immeasurable expanse of virgin forest behind him and into the small clearing where the dismal cabin sat, Tavin hollered, *"A buck has offered himself up."*

Asch stood in the broken doorway, *"It is a good thing!"*

"I agree. God has provided for us this day," he said, dropping the heavy carcass on the ground, and stepping inside.

"You never cease to speak of God as if He is with you." Asch commented.

"He is."

Asch grinned and soberly changed the subject. His clear, mournful grey eyes scanned two fresh graves under a nearby oak. *"I often wonder where God was while my mother lay dying on the floor in front of the hearth. My father outside, with Leeds beaded bag wrapped around his neck. Murdered. My heart remains heavy with sorrow and my blood burns for revenge."*

"Leeds wanted us to know that he did this. He murdered your parents," Tavin bitterly stated.

"E:h."

"I am sorry that I brought Leeds here. I mourn with you. Your no'yeh, had a special gentleness about her. I will be forever grateful for her kindness toward Berta and Katherine. And your ha'nih, although his original intent was to steal from me, he was an honorable, good man," said Tavin, feeling a deep sadness.

Regaining his composure, Asch took a deep breath, *"I will go with you on this mission, but for one purpose. Leeds is most likely back with the French. I will find him. Where do we meet with the provincial troops once we have the information they request?"*

"After we've determined French movements and numbers at Fort Duquesne, on the forks of the Ohio River, we will go back east and find Colonel Clapham at Fort Augusta."

"Fort Augusta. It looks to be well situated at the east and west branches of the Susquehanna."

"You've seen it?" Tavin asked, surprised.

"E:h. After I buried my parents, I went north to Shamokin village, seeking help in finding Leeds. My mother had Seneca family there." Tossing another log on the fire, Asch continued, *"By the time I arrived, the village was deserted and burned. I found no help in tracking the murderer, Leeds. It was during this time I discovered the British building their Fort Augusta."*

"What about your Seneca relatives?"

"They are gone, back to Kanandarque, far to the north. I have no family but you, Tavin Shire."

Tavin moved closer to the hearth rubbing his hands together over golden hot flames. Stepping back from the heat, he thoughtfully noted, *"We share a common grief. Our families have suffered atrocities and death at the hands of others. We are as brothers now."*

Several contented moments of silence passed between them, as the fire crackled, and venison sizzled. Asch finally spoke, *"They liked you. They didn't even blame you for bringing that French spy into their home."*

"Adoniram Leeds." Tavin spewed the name with venom. *"Mary and Wolfe may still be alive had I not let him go. Drake is also hunting him, with Kaendae. Leeds has made many enemies."*

"Justice will be mine."

Tavin rubbed his prickly chin, in contemplation, *"This is difficult."*

"E:h. He runs and hides, but he will be found."

"He will be hard to locate, but I wasn't referring to that. The scriptures say, "Vengeance is mine, I will repay, saith the Lord'. I pray God will show it to us, in the way that is His and not ours."

"Leeds killed my parents and Job. I will not wait for God. It is mine," Asch seethed.

"Eternity rights the wrongs of time. God is true. He will not fail. Trusting Him has never been easy for me and it's not easy now, but I am learning to follow His lead and it is the best." At that, the conversation was dropped and Tavin silently prayed that God's hand would guide them both.

Two days later, they packed their supplies and began walking. Crossing the Susquehanna well south of Fort Augusta, they pressed west, toward Fort Duquesne, some two-hundred miles. Maintaining a steady pace over mountainous terrain on foot, the fort was within sight at ten days.

As Tavin stood high on a bluff, an icy wind whipped through his hair. With his eyeglass, overlooking the formidable Fort Duquesne in the distance he could not help but reflect on General Braddock and the hundreds of British soldiers and officers killed in the heat of the past summer. That ill-fated campaign had also taken his father's life. *"Braddock's Defeat"*, as it had become known. A defeat that allowed the French continued control of the Ohio Valley and the resources it provided. Having access to the fur and supply routes stretching all the way to Canada, France now laid claim on the territory as solely theirs.

"It looks like there may be but two-hundred French regular troops within the fort," said Tavin.

"I count several hundred Lenape, Shawnee and Huron camped outside the walls. No sign of Leeds."

The weather turned colder as they cautiously skirted well outside the cleared perimeter of the fort. Temperatures dropped and snow filled the air, covering the forest floor. Snaking their way down a hillside and working their way along the edge of the Allegheny, they decided to cross and move upriver, hoping for a better view of the fort's structure. The reconnaissance they gathered would prove invaluable to British operations and readiness.

The once frozen river had begun to melt, and the flowing water held large chunks of shifting ice. *"We cannot walk across,"* stated Asch.

"A raft. We might cross with setting poles maneuvering between the ice flow."

"E:h, *a raft,*" Asch agreed, pulling his hatchet from his pack.

As they labored throughout the day, their conversation eventually wandered to the question that Asch had dodged, *"What of Agnes and Liza?"*

Stripping prickly limbs from slender trees, Tavin scratched his beard, *"I wondered when you would ask. I've thought a lot about how to answer."*

"And how do you answer?"

Tavin laughed. *"If I knew that, I'd have mentioned it myself a couple of weeks back."*

He then continued, *"As far as Liza. I will be honest. I am not certain. According to Agnes, her shoulder healed well, and she has returned to her work somewhere east of Reading, in the Schuylkill Valley. She has a strong sense of duty, even in the face of those who view her with disdain and pity her."*

"Pity her?"

"She is marked both physically and in status. She lived among 'savages' and her scars are the subject of cruel speculation as well as sympathy. She is viewed as spoiled goods. A woman no man would marry. She is seen as blemished, damaged, a marred woman."

"I will kill them."

Smiling, Tavin responded, *"I don't believe that is the answer, although I'm sure that your intentions are well-meaning, aimed to restore her honor."* Chopping vigorously at a stubborn branch, he continued, breathing heavily with the exertion. *"Agnes explained that Liza survives, despite the adversities, as though her life is complete and satisfying. One would not guess that she is the target of cruelty or condescending kindness. She lives with a countenance of joy about her that is not contrived, but genuine. Those who know her soon see beyond the scars and appear captivated."*

"Why do you believe this is? Is she a sorcerer or a witch?"

Tavin laughed, *"Asch, no. She is indeed a contradiction to her circumstances, but it is the Lord who provides her joy and comfort."*

"Once again you mention your God."

"He's not MY God. He is everybody's God. There is no other and He is good," replied Tavin, as he recalled his conversation with Agnes before he left Bethlehem, challenging him to simply tell Asch the gospel news.

"Why do you follow this spirit God?" asked Asch.

"God is as limitless space, true, faithful, and as bright as a thousand suns. My decisions are smoke and vapor and my mind spins deceit and delusion. I have learned the hard way to quiet myself and wait on Him. My heart was as swollen as a river after a heavy rain with wounded pride. The false god of ego carried me in its strong current from bank to bank. No end was in sight. Now I am carried by the one true God."

"This does not make sense," said Asch, as he cut barren vines into long lengths for rope.

"I know. God's ways are not our ways. God gave us His plan in the scriptures, the book that Drake saved for me. The same book that provided Job the courage to live his life despite the rejection and sadness that losing his family and disfiguring smallpox offered."

"E:h. The book you read each evening. You trust this God, even though your mother, father and sister have died? You watch as the one you love marries another and you continue to say that God is good, and you are joyful with no fear?"

"I cannot say that I have no fear or that I do not grieve. I grieve. I mourn. My mind is often perplexed and divided. I doubt. But my faith is sustained not through my own might. God hears my broken cries and knows who I am. If my faith were dependent on me, I would be lost and never found. I am as a withered leaf that the wind tosses away. But God reached down with His merciful hand and scooped me into His loving hands through the life, death and resurrection of Jesus. My weakness, my sin, is forgiven and I am declared free. Now I pray that He grants me grace to bear His will."

"I have seen the evidence of this God in you, in Liza and Agnes. It has baffled me a great amount."

"Well, while you stand there baffled, I'm going to strap these trees together and get this raft finished to cross that river tonight," laughed Tavin, pointing at the ice-covered water.

The sun set like an orange ball slowly sinking into the windswept treetops. Stars quickly appeared, twinkling brightly across the clear, frosty night sky. White ice packs gently rose and fell in the languid current as if breathing; cracking and creaking against each other in a symphony of frozen turmoil.

Tavin shuddered. The river appeared ghostly, with menacing black water narrowly defining the path forward. Using the setting poles, he pushed off the bank. Asch lay balanced on the front of the raft, pushing thick ice packs out of the way with his hands, the muscles in his arms aching with tension and cold, his hands frigid and stiff. Slowly inching their way toward the middle of the river, they suddenly stopped. Jammed between formidable ice walls, the raft would not budge. Tavin sat down next to Asch, using their legs they pushed with all their might. It was no use. The ice would not release them.

Struggling for hours, numb and exhausted, Asch conceded, *"We'll have to leave the raft here. We rest a while, regain our strength, then we walk or swim."*

Tavin fell back against the raft and sighed, *"Can you swim?"*

"E:h. But I do not think drowning will be our problem. It's the cold. We will probably freeze to death before we reach the shore."

"Yeah, probably." Chuckling at Asch's obvious attempt at humor, Tavin added, *"We'll have to move quickly to keep our muscles from seizing*

up. It looks to be maybe 25 yards. Once we climb over this ice pack, we can slide into the water and wade from here."

"*The current is strong, but the water is not deep.*" Asch's teeth were chattering as he spoke.

For several more hours they waited until finally ready to face the icy river. Asch was first to climb off the raft and slide on his belly across a wide expanse of solid ice, before dropping into the freezing river. Tavin followed. Dark water rose chest high. Holding their packs and muskets over their heads, they fought their way through the maze of floating barriers. Pushing against the swirling flux, and laboring for balance on the rocky river bottom, their bodies shivering violently. Chunks of ice drifted across their path, slowing progress, and adding precious time. "*We are almost there. Keep moving,*" said Tavin, his words came slurred and breathy from behind Asch.

Finally, Asch stumbled, teeth chattering, across the shoreline and collapsed. As if in a drunken stupor, confused and clumsy, he lay numb with cold. A sliver of light shone in the eastern sky. Lifting his head, he stared back at the river, squinting his eyes searching for Tavin. All was quiet and serene. Awkwardly sitting up, fear gripped him. He yelled, "*Tavin!*"

From the corner of his eye, Asch saw movement in the forest to his left, just as a war party burst from hiding. Yaps and war whoops echoed in wild excitement. Quickly surrounding him, their muskets primed, and arrows poised, Asch was helpless to respond. Before he understood what was happening a single warrior shed his woolen matchcoat and sprinted into the frigid river. Diving under the black water, he disappeared for what seemed too long. Suddenly a monstrous splash disrupted the calm of the river, dividing ice floats in all directions.

Pulling Tavin to the bank and rolling him roughly onto his stomach, the warrior began to pound on Tavin's back. Choking and spitting up water, Tavin coughed several times, uncontrollably sucking air into his deprived lungs. The warrior sat back, with one arm supporting his weight, panting to catch his own breath, waiting as Tavin lay on the frozen ground heaving for breath.

Asch watched in confusion as the warrior stood and gathered his trade blanket to drape it over Tavin. He wiped the indigo war paint from his eyes with the back of his hand as it streaked down his dark face. He was muscular, and so lean that his ribs showed beneath the ruffled linen shirt which clung tightly to his wet trembling body. His dyed deer roach hung drenched with icy water and sagged across the back of his shaved head. He wore a breechcloth decorated with zigzag lines over his buckskin breeches. Silver earrings lined the top of both ears. A red and blue beaded pouch hung loosely around his neck. The warrior sat down again next to Tavin; his legs curled. Asch then recognized who this savior was.

Coughing and spitting, Tavin attempted to push himself up, only to fall onto his back, his coordination and strength gone. Finally, he focused on the warrior sitting next to him. *"Kaendae, I see your ear has healed,"* smiled Tavin, slurring his words in a weak voice.

"E:h," Kaendae smiled back.

Time blurred, casting shadows and suspicions all about. Tavin shook violently, his mind a tangled maze of chaos. Reality and delusion blended as to obscure one from the other. A large fire roared near his head. Wrapped tightly in a heavy bear blanket, he drifted in and out of consciousness, with images of painted Indians in decorative animal skins and colorful leggings intermingled with visions of his father's outstretched arm, waving goodbye, atop his muscled brown gelding, off to war. His mother's soft crying.

A hand shook him vigorously. Tavin opened his eyes. He jerked and tried to sit up, but collapsed back, his head spinning with dizziness. *"Slow. You have seen the shore of death and returned,"* came the familiar voice. Asch sat down; his legs folded under him.

Tavin began to haltingly recount and sort his memories, *"We were crossing the river in the raft. It became jammed and we had to walk. I was under the water and when I tried to come up, ice held me down. I couldn't find an opening."*

"E:h. Yes. You sank. You should not be alive. Kaendae saved you."

"Kaendae. Yes, I remember now. I thought it was a dream." Tavin rubbed his head attempting to center his thoughts. *"He was sitting next to me. How was it that he was here? Where is he now?"* Questions swirled in panoramic blends of colors and images, as he glanced around at the empty dark forest and languid river. His arms and legs felt like heavy

weights pinning him to the ground. He forcefully pushed himself up once again, breathing hard. *"Tell me,"* he said, hunched over and massaging his lifeless legs.

"Kaendae is leading a war party of Lenape and Shawnee. They are meeting French troops at Fort Duquesne. They seek to destroy the British Fort Augusta."

"How can this be true? He was supportive of the English cause, or at least neutral. He is Iroquois, Onōdowá'ga:'...Seneca. Why is he raiding with the Lenape and the French?"

"His mother was Lenape, at Kittanning. His father, Seneca, and brother to Drake. Kaendae was eight years old when his mother and father died of smallpox. He was raised by his mother's sister, known for her beadwork." Asch paused. *"She was married to Adoniram Leeds."*

"Leeds is Kaendae's uncle? And Drake is also his uncle?" Tavin's mind spun to connect the story.

Taking a breath, Asch continued, *"Yes. Both. Leeds was cruel. Kaendae ran away while a young boy and was embraced by Drake and his Iroquois relatives in the Ohio Valley. A few years later, his beloved aunt died and Kaendae blames Leeds."*

"Where is Drake now?"

Silence sat between them. Asch hung his head. His black hair covered his face, shining in the firelight, as he breathed the words, *"While they tracked the murderer Leeds, Drake was mistaken for Huron. He was killed by British troops on the Tulpehocken Path two moons past."*

"Drake is dead?" Tavin exclaimed in dismay and sorrow.

"E:h." Waiting several minutes, allowing the news to sink in, Asch resumed, *"A spark has ignited, and the embers of revenge burn in Kaendae's heart against English. He has returned to the Lenape and Shawnee village at Kittanning, reuniting with his mother's people, quickly establishing himself with honor and hoping to also discover Leeds among the French and Lenape there. Many of the eager Lenape trust him. Hating the English and the treaties that take more and more land, pushing them further and further west, they are impatient to fight. Kaendae leads many."*

"So, he was here with a war party?" asked Tavin, feeling bewildered.

"E:h."

"Why are we still alive?"

"Your God is a mystery. Maybe more powerful than hate and vengeance," Asch mused.

"Yes. He is. God's purposes are beyond our understanding."

"Drake would not let you die, and neither would Kaendae. To honor Drake, he risked his own life for yours in the icy water of the river. Drake's vision, received so many years ago, has followed you and allowed you to remain alive. This is very much a mystery to me and causes me to consider the nature of your God."

Tavin stretched his legs and thoughtfully said, *"It is truly a miracle by God's grace alone. But remember, the Lord, the one true God, has also spared your life through all of this. We are the enemy in this wilderness. We came here as spies, to return valuable information for the British and ..."* Tavin pointed across the river, *"... they let us, both of us, go free."*

A rumbling cold shuddered through Tavin's body. Feeling weak and woozy once again, he fell back into a fitful sleep. Vivid dreams danced like illusive butterflies. Drake, Job, Kaendae, Wolfe, Leeds, and his mother. But habitually it was Agnes, sitting on a pristine stone wall, the sun framing her body in blinding light. A brick rowhouse stood behind her. A child ran in happy circles, his grey eyes flashing delight. By late afternoon he woke covered in sweat. Cold air filled his lungs, feeling prickly and heavy. The river shimmered with brilliant sunlight and the ice floats had disappeared, leaving only a wide expanse of radiant open water.

Asch squatted next to the fire. *"We should go. I looked through your eyeglass. The walls of the fort are impressive, as are the numbers of French troops and Indian allies. I also spotted many white captives among them. No sign of Leeds. We need to move, especially since there are several Lenape and Shawnee warriors over there who know exactly where we are. I doubt that they will remain as friendly and protective as Kaendae."*

"You found my pack?"

"E:h. I found it not far from shore. But your musket is in the river. Lost." Asch lifted an immaculate looking long gun over his head and smiling announced, *"Your musket is gone, yet your God somehow sees that you have another. Kaendae has given this to you as a gift."*

"God is indeed good." Tavin thoughtfully pondered, once again amazed.

"It seems He is. Now we need to move."

"Yes, we should go. I apologize for the delay."

"I will forgive you. But the next time you drown don't take so long to recover." Asch laughed. Tavin was pleased to hear Asch truly laugh. It had been a long time.

"Nyoh! Amen!" Tavin responded as he stood, feeling wobbly. Gradually regaining his senses, he could feel strength returning to his unsteady muscles. As he and Asch rolled their packs and slung them over their shoulders, a high-pitched yap of a fox came from the forest behind them. Quickly hoisting their long guns in unison, they stood back-to-back and slowly circled, their eyes as sharp as hawks, scanning the tree line. Another yap and a cluck and Kaendae stepped out.

Dropping their muskets to their sides, Kaendae strode toward them, a rolling gate of confidence, his face freshly painted indigo blue with a thick black stripe tracing across his dark eyes. Two hawk feathers and red porcupine quills protruded from the deer roach attached to the back of his head and the silver rings that lined his ears glittered in the sunlight. A British officer's gorget, beautifully etched and ornately enameled, hung around his neck. Tavin recognized it. It was Drake's. The familiar blue and red beaded pouch dangled from his hip. His leggings and breech cloth were now dry, having been drenched in the icy river the day before. As he walked toward them a smile crossed his face and his teeth shone white against the blue paint surrounding his red lips. Tavin couldn't help but think how truly majestic and splendid he appeared.

"Haksa'go:wa:h" said Kaendae.

"E:h. Do:ges," Asch replied.

Tavin answered, *"Yes, I am well. I thank you, Kaendae. You risked your life to save mine. I have no gift to give you and yet you have presented me with this fine musket. You are a brave and honorable man."* Tavin paused for a moment, *"I share the sorrow of Drake's death and grieve alongside you."*

Kaendae nodded in acknowledgment of Tavin's gratitude and sympathies. Turning to Asch he spoke in long animated sentences too rapidly for Tavin to catch the meaning. Asch responded, *"Wi:yo:h"*.

"Good? What's good?" Tavin asked, frustrated.

"French soldiers advance toward Fort Augusta tomorrow along the Susquehanna. They have a large contingent of warriors with them. Kaendae says that if we wish to remain alive, we should travel south and then turn east. We will be out of the path of the French advancement," Asch responded.

Just as suddenly as he had arrived, Kaendae melted back into the dark forest. Tavin and Asch quietly discussed their plans and easily decided to trust the advice and travel south. They walked in silence the rest of the day. The sun was high in a bright blue sky. Birds floated across the warming air in effortless freedom. Trees were slowly beginning to show signs of budding and the smell of an early spring filled Tavin's nostrils. Climbing steep, rocky embankments, avoiding any obvious trails, his ears and eyes remained alert to any approaching danger, and yet, there was a raw wonder that enveloped him, a joy that wasn't easy to explain, nor did it need to be.

The tragic circumstances of Tavin's life felt like steppingstones to where God wanted him. Not so much a place, but a position. Not so much behavior, but a boldness of heart. Not so much self-motivation but motivated for the sake of others and ultimately to honor the God who justified him from his sin and saved him to new life. Tavin felt clean.

He marveled as Asch led the way, occasionally stopping to listen to forest sounds around them, before moving forward. Shaking his head, Tavin mumbled a prayer, *"God, who could ever have imagined that I would be here in this untamed wilderness with a friend who is closer than a brother. Thank you."*

CHAPTER

24

The fidgety gray pranced and threw his head. Lt. Renz Millar sat regally in the saddle, relishing in the reckless nature of his spirited charger and the attention he was gleaning. Wearing a white waistcoat under a dark blue jacket with red facing, he paraded the grounds with authority and influence. His black tricorn hat framed his grey powdered wig and handsome features. Gold tassels hung from his Hessian boots, rising just below his knees. A slender sheathed saber was attached to his left side and a second ceremonial sword lay affixed on his other side, flashing the sun's light. A brown holster held a flintlock pistol, looped securely over the saddle horn with a leather thong. His musket tucked just behind his right hip, fastened to the saddle. With bravado and swagger he appeared the ideal mystic warrior ready to conquer the devils who scourged the land.

Shouting orders as if he were scolding children, Renz spun his gelding around and leaning down, slapped a young militia volunteer alongside the head with his open hand. *"If you cannot manage a straight line in full gear while standing at attention during inspection, how do you expect to survive in battle? The savages are primitive and without sense, but your incompetence sickens me even more."*

At that moment he caught sight of Tavin and Asch casually leaning on their muskets watching. *"Dismissed!"* he yelled to the motley company of men who happily dropped their hefty packs of equipment and sank to the ground.

"Renz, you expect to model these men after British soldiers? They are farmers and merchants, not pack animals. Marching into a battle with hundred-pound bags on their backs is a mistake," hollered Tavin.

Renz bristled with anger, *"Shire! You are the last person to give advice on how to defeat savages. Your mother was murdered, your brother scalped, and your sisters captured. Where were you?"*

Tavin had come to terms with what had happened to his family. Once upon a time, those words would have cut him as a knife to his heart, but no longer. Ignoring the implied accusation of cowardice, Tavin gave a half smile, *"I have seen combat against seasoned warriors, and I can tell you that if you have no respect for them, they will see you dead and buried."*

Renz laughed in disgust, *"They have no taste for a real fight. Their lack of aptitude shared with their laziness causes them to lay around their villages, smoking pipes, while their women serve them."*

Asch held a sneer of contempt on his face, gripping his musket so hard that his knuckles turned white. Tavin put his hand on Asch's arm. An unspoken word to calm him. Renz shifted anxiously in his saddle, unnerved by the fire in Asch's steel-grey eyes. Tavin changed the subject, *"We bring reconnaissance from Fort Duquesne. Where can we find Colonel Clapham?"*

"You can give me your information. I doubt that it is anything worth the Colonel's time, but I will pass it along," Renz said with an air of superiority.

"Lt. Millar!" came a stern voice from behind Renz. *"Please escort these gentlemen to the mess and see to it they receive a meal and the opportunity to clean up. When they are ready, I will be waiting in my office to receive their report."* Turning briefly to Tavin, he nodded in stony recognition, *"Shire,"* and walked away.

Renz dismounted and handed the reigns to a young boy who stood timidly nearby. Perplexed at the Colonel's familiarity with Tavin and embarrassed that he hadn't been aware that the Colonel had walked up behind him, Renz reluctantly said, *"Yes sir."* Then turning back to Tavin and Asch he scowled and demanded, *"This way."*

Tavin gave Asch a friendly punch in the shoulder as they followed Renz. They both laughed. The *"mess"* was nothing more than two firepits with a hanging cauldron over one and a spit with blackened beef over the other, yet it tasted like a banquet to Tavin and Asch. Beef, beans, and rough brown bread. It'd been a long time since they had enjoyed anything other than wild game. A mug of brown beer washed it down.

The fort was under varying degrees of construction since the arrival of Colonel Clapham and his four-hundred troops of the Third Battalion. Frustration levels were running high with supplies limited and slow progress. Clapham's discontent had been heightened when he discovered upon arrival that the large Shamokin Indian village, which was located near this sight, had been abandoned, and burned to the ground. Clapham was eager to move on to more glorious exploits. With varying degrees of military success, combined with a blotch on his record regarding the death of a prisoner, of whom Clapham had gagged too tightly, he was impatient to see the fort finished and eager to restore his tarnished reputation.

"What news do you bring of the French movements and their Indian allies?" demanded Clapham, without cursory conversation. He sat at a mahogany desk, impeccably dressed in an unseasonably lightweight uniform. His red flowing overcoat was perfectly cut with gold frills and braids adorning the shoulders. His hat lay on a chair set off to the side, also trimmed in fancy trappings. He wore no choking collar as Tavin had observed with the regular troops. A silver gorget hung around his neck, to which Tavin could see no real purpose.

"Several hundred French march from Duquesne, Kittanning, Venango, and Le Boeuf to the Susquehanna along the Shamokin Path. The passage down the river on bateaux and rafts will be slow. They carry with them two small cannon," Tavin reported.

"And what is your assessment of our defense against such an attack?" asked Clapham, not looking up from the paperwork strewn across his desk.

"The distance is too great for their guns to reach the fort from the surrounding hills opposite the fort. The forts position should easily withstand any siege."

"Thank you. You are dismissed."

Tavin felt frustrated. *"Colonel, if I might add. We witnessed many captives held at Fort Duquesne."*

"I understand your concern. Nonetheless, captives are not my prerogative. My orders are to build and secure this fort. Nothing more. Again, you are dismissed."

Asch reached out and grabbed Tavin's arm, shaking his head. There was no use in arguing. The colonel had his orders and was not to be challenged. No one doubted the crucial importance of Fort Augusta. It stood at the junction of the north and west branches of the Susquehanna, linking travel and communication to the pioneer settlements downstream. It also offered a significant defense against further Indian and French attacks along the frontier, with easy access to the Kittanning Path. Attempts at recovering women and children carried off into slavery would be of secondary importance. Albeit Tavin's blood boiled that no military exploits or treaty negotiations were underway for the recovery of hundreds of captives.

Stepping out into the filtered light of dusk, it seemed the world had descended into a chaos of shifting crimson turmoil. The golden glow of sunset illuminated hundreds of scarlet British uniforms as aimless, walking flames. Soldiers sullenly meandered in heavy woolen greatcoats. The restrictive sleeves, tight as stockings. Perspiration rolled from their sour, exhausted faces.

Nationalistic fervor demanded that their uniforms consistently bring respect to The Crown no matter the physical labor or weather. Col. Clapham agreed. And so, with picks and shovels they ended the day covered in sweat and dirt with high stiff collars and tight breeches. Wide leather belts rested heavily over their shoulders and across their chests, supporting a cartridge box for powder and shot. A bayonet scabbard hung at the waist. Ever at the ready.

"How these men cut, trim and haul pine trees, dig holes for vertical posts and excavate a ditch all the way around the fort, while wearing those heavy, uncomfortable uniforms baffles me. Perspiration rolls off them in this sun, even as cold as it is," said Tavin.

"They hold to their duty. Is it not honorable?" reflected Asch.

"*They haven't a choice. Insubordination is a serious offense. I simply see no reason for soldiers to suffer in full uniform while digging ditches. Honor be sure, yet protocol seems to exceed wisdom here.*"

Suddenly a gravelly voice called from behind them, "*And what would you know of honor or wisdom Tavin Shire?*" Leaning against the door frame, a pipe in one hand, Renz's gaze was clear and brash. Tavin noted the smirk on his perfect face and replied, "*I only claim what the scriptures tell us, 'He that followeth after righteousness and mercy findeth life, righteousness, and honor.'*"

"*I am sure that Agnes would indeed swoon to your sanctimonious quoting, but you can leave it be. I am not impressed.*"

His curiosity overcoming his pride, Tavin held his breath for fear of the answer as he asked, "*And what of Agnes? I assume that you found her in Bethlehem and broke off your engagement. As you said, "she is ruined."*"

Renz sneered, "*Her reputation is sullied, but once the matter of her dowry and inheritance is settled, I shall marry her. She pines after me like an excited child over a shiny new toy. Her heart beats with passion to be my wife!*" he laughed. "*She is a lovely girl, simple and easily swayed, indeed ruined by rumor, albeit with time her position in society will be restored. Her holdings remain intact. She's worth a fair amount. We will marry soon.*"

"*You need speak of her in a respectful manner or you will answer to me!*" Tavin spewed through gritted teeth and flared nostrils.

Glaring at Tavin, the sun catching his dark, liquid eyes, as if the angel of death dwelt behind them, Renz twisted his lips and raised his eyebrows, "*You still have feelings for her, don't you!? Your ridiculous infatua...*" just then Colonel Clapham opened the door. Renz side-stepped, "*Sir!*"

"*Why do you block my doorway Millar? Move along.*" Renz quickly spun around and walked toward a group of militia men huddled together over a cook fire, his handsome chin held high.

Colonel Clapham lifted his gaze to look the much taller Tavin in the eye, "*I couldn't help but overhear your exchange with Lt. Millar. I will not have a contest over the honor of a woman or any other reason in this fort. There is too much work to be done. Distractions and conflicts between soldiers, militia, scouts or Indian allies...*" Clapham looked at Asch, "*will not be tolerated.*"

"*I understand sir,*" Tavin answered.

"Now, I have drafted new orders for you and your Indian companion. You will scout north to surmise French strength along the Allegheny Trail as far as…."

Tavin interrupted, *"With all due respect Colonel, we are not your scouts. We voluntarily offered to do reconnaissance on Fort Duquesne, but we are free men, assigned to no post. We will not take orders."*

Clapham became flustered. *"My understanding is that you serve the Crown. It is for King George II that your loyalties lie. Do you shirk your duty?"*

"My loyalties lie with God alone. As for King George II, he is the British king, but make no mistake, he is not my sovereign. My friend can speak for himself," said Tavin, nodding toward Asch, *"But I can assure you that King George II is not his sovereign either. Our duty, at this moment, remains 'sovereignly' exempt from British military authority."* Tavin glanced at Asch. The left corner of Asch's mouth curled slightly up, into the half smile that Tavin knew well.

Composing himself Clapham, sighed, *"Of course. In a way, I envy you. Thank you for the report of Fort Duquesne. It is invaluable. Go in peace."* And then as an afterthought, he turned to Tavin and added with a sour look, *"I wouldn't have known that you were white. You should be careful."*

Clapham's seemingly demure response, along with his further assessment of Tavin, came as a bewilderment. Tavin and Asch walked in silence toward the east gate. *"Do you trust him?"* Asch finally asked. *"I don't know. We'll be on the watch."*

Tavin's fringed buckskin breeches were dirty and worn. His white linen shirt hung loosely just above his knees, almost covering the black breechcloth. A red finger-woven woolen sash was tied around his narrow waist. His father's powder horn hung from it. The leather strap of his musket crossed his chest, as another strap holding a quiver with arrows crisscrossed it. He carried a heavy pack holding supplies across his back, wore high moccasins and carried a bow. He was chiseled and squared by the wilderness and his appearance reflected it.

Tavin noted the way he looked as they sauntered toward sentries at the gate and thought to himself, *"Colonel Clapham judges the outward façade of a person, God looks at the heart."*

Asch stopped, *"I can see that your thoughts drift away. What is it?"*

Tavin laughed, smoothing his greasy shoulder length blond hair to the back of his head. *"I was just remembering what the Bible says in I Samuel,*

'For the Lord does not see as man sees; for man looks at the outward appearance, but the Lord looks at the heart."

Suddenly a familiar voice called out from across the parade grounds. "Tavin Shire! Should we meet again, I assure you, it will not be so pleasant. I advise you to forget Agnes. She will be my wife. And tell your Indian friend, that he should forget that scarred and damaged strumpet he fancies as well. Yes!" Renz laughed, "Agnes told me of the pathetic desires between two misfit creatures. A half-breed and a sullied maid who is indentured to the whims of her masters. A woman of ill fame at the Red Owl! Ready for the advances of any man who comes along." Laughing louder, Renz spun ceremoniously around and marched away with arrogance hovering over him like a vile cloud.

CHAPTER

25

Intentions and direction can shift, sometimes within a moment. Asch had built a wall around himself, protecting his focus of vengeance against Leeds. The walls had cracked several weeks before with Tavin's description of Liza's position and status in the eyes of others, *'spoiled goods. A woman no man would marry. She is seen as blemished, a damaged woman'*, Tavin had told him. Asch had allowed Liza a small, guarded corner into his heart. Now, Renz had unwittingly flung open the gates and unleashed a lion. Once those vindictive words were spewed, Asch was fiercely on the move. Liza. Leeds would have to wait.

Rocky, steep mountains loomed before them, as they crossed Shamokin Creek toward Tulhoo Gap. Tavin kept silent, uncertain of Asch's objectives, while perceiving his fury. He waited for Asch to speak, asking no questions. Climbing the first mountain range, Tavin could see the tension pulsing through Asch's body. His muscles, taut and flexed, rippled across his back like the flank of a running horse. His pace grueling and swift. His long black hair dripped with sweat in the cold mountain air.

Breathing heavily, Asch finally stopped. His eyes dimmed mimicking the darkening sky above, *"Renz Millar deserves my vengeance, though I will not kill him. No. Coming to my senses, I only see Liza. If she suffers dishonor* and mistreatment, I will take her from it." Sitting on the cold ground, he pulled a stained leather bag of rancid bear fat and began mixing blue and black color. Carefully outlining his eyes in blue paint and running black lines down his cheeks, he slowly stood. *"I am the son of my mother of the Onodowa'ga, and I have chosen."*

"Wait," said Tavin, perplexed, *"What have you chosen? You can't just decide to take Liza."*

"Tavin Shire, you have waited in proper ways for Agnes, and you have lost her. She will marry a spineless man, while you say nothing. I am Onodowa'ga, my mother is dead, no one has arranged a marriage for me. I must follow my own path. I will not force Liza to come with me as my wife, but she will know my intentions."

"This isn't about Agnes or me. This is about what you are about to do. If Liza should agree, where will you go? How will you live? This is not a good plan." Tavin felt panicked.

"My white father and my Onodowa'ga mother lived together, worked together and made a life in the wilderness. So shall we."

"Asch, they also died together. The wilderness is shrinking. Soon, civilization, settlers, farmers, and families will encroach further and deeper into the frontier. You will never be free to live in peace with Liza."

Asch looked at Tavin with a sorrowful expression, *"Tavin Shire, is it not you who had taught me that God brings freedom. It does not matter what surrounds us, in Christ we are free. That is what you have said. 'It is for freedom that Christ has set us free.' Liza knows this too. Together we will be free."*

Tavin paused, surprised that Asch had grasped so much. He gathered his thoughts before responding to some misconstrued understanding. *"God's promise of freedom through Christ involves being rescued from the law of sin and death to live freely in right relationship with Him through forgiveness of sin. Whether you and Liza find a life together is a separate issue from God's offer of freedom. While it is true that with the promise comes God's mercy in circumstances, it does not promise protection from those circumstances. In other words, we will always face trials and hardship, but with Christ, we are free from fear and abiding sorrows, to live without hindrance through difficulty, not without difficulty."*

"I am willing to trust in your God, in Liza's God. I know He is to be feared. I have seen great things."

Tavin gently reflected, *"Your faith encourages me. My own coldness of heart too often forgets God's converting grace. I become too easily indifferent or hardened. But I see His power at work in you and I praise Him for it."* Looking up as a million stars sparkled across the night sky, he quoted from Psalms, *"For as far as the heaven is high above the earth, so great is His mercy toward them that fear Him. As far as the east is from the west, so hath he removed our transgressions from us."*

"Good. I am ready. How do we find this 'Red Owl'?"

"Well, that is 'good', but may I suggest that we rest for the night? My legs cannot keep this harsh pace any longer. And I think the Red Owl Inn is northeast of Reading, in the Schuylkill Valley along the Kings Highway from Easton."

"We rest, but only until you have strength. I can see that you are weak and tired," jabbed Asch, with that all too familiar smile on his blue and black painted face.

★ ★ ★ ★ ★

Blue smoke rolled from the brick chimney of the Red Owl protruding from the gable roof of the two-story stone structure. The center door was painted red with two small windows flanking either side. Three square windows evenly spaced above, reflected orange light from the setting sun, their wooden frames painted red as the door.

Tavin's eye strained as he peered through his eyeglass from a nearby hillside. Patrons buzzed about like bees to the honeycomb. Soldiers and militia, farmers, and merchants, all eager for the news of the day, a good meal and ready to toss back rum, brown beer, or fine wine. There was no sign of Liza. *"Wait here. I will go down and see what I can find out."*

"I don't think you are going to blend in very well down there," Asch commented.

"Better than you," Tavin replied, laughing, while tossing the eyeglass to Asch.

The inn was filled with rowdy noise and smoke. Several dining tables sat along one side of the spacious room with a long bar stretching across the far wall. A billiards table on the opposite side was surrounded by well-dressed men in powdered wigs, wagering on the winner. As Tavin entered, suspicious eyes scowled, and he felt out of place. As casually as he could, he sauntered to the bar and stood next to an elderly patron with mistrusting eyes, wearing wire spectacles and a crooked grey wig. With wariness in his wobbly voice the man casually commented, *"You look like you've come a long way. Been trapping up north?"*

"Something like that," Tavin answered, shifting his body and attention toward the rosy cheeked matron who stood smiling behind the bar; he nervously smiled in return. Rotund and cheery, she asked, *"What will you have this evening? Rum or brown beer?"* Her disheveled gray hair was tucked haphazardly inside her white mop-cap, which was too small for her large head. She tugged at her snug corset and expectantly waited for his response.

Realizing that he had no coin, he ignored the question and straightforwardly inquired, *"I am looking for a friend. She may have begun working here recently. Her name is Liza Schell."*

The matron's tone changed as her suspicions rose. *"Liza. Yes, what do you want with her? I don't know who you are, but Liza has seen enough trouble. It would be best if you left. She is a good domestic. The gentlemen like her and drudging up any past that you bring with you might only disrupt her current situation."*

"My name is Tavin Shire. You judge me as someone detrimental to Liza's welfare. I assure you, I am not a threat or a danger to Liza or her work here. She will welcome my presence. I come as a friend."

"Friend or not, Liza is here to work off a debt. Mr. Demerest purchased Liza's contract at auction and the duty remains. We thought we'd never see her again after she was carried off by Indians. Mr. Demerest is a miserly man, and he will see to it that she remains this time until the debt is paid in full." Scrutinizing Tavin warily, she continued, *"To be honest you don't look like anyone who's seen this side of civilization in a long time. What do you want from Liza?"*

"As I mentioned, I am a friend and I wish to see her. My business with her is a private matter."

The toothy matron smiled shrewdly, as if her clever wits had exposed a mystery. *"She's in the barn. I sent her out there a while ago to milk the cow. Butter's running low. But don't you go carrying her off. Mr. Demerest would be mighty put out."*

The sky had darkened and light from the waning moon was slowly masked by dense clouds drifting lazily to the east. The night was still, and wolves could be heard howling in the far distance. Tavin shuddered and adjusted his musket across his shoulder, as he strolled toward the barn. Glancing back at the bright, crowded tavern he couldn't help but to imagine how wonderful a soft feather bed would feel, rather than the hard ground he had become so accustomed to. The inn offered two rooms upstairs for travelers and they were tempting. Dismissing the thought, he turned his attention once again toward finding Liza. The barn, privy and sheds were set off some distance from the tavern itself. A short walk uphill.

Ahead, a lantern could be seen hanging on a peg through the wide-open barn door, illuminating the dark interior just enough for him to see bits of dust and straw floating haphazardly through the otherwise stagnant interior. An old, dappled cow raised its head. The subdued sound of a bell jangled briefly around its thick neck.

A muffled cry came from inside. Tavin crossed the remaining distance quickly and paused before entering, breathing heavily, and clutching his musket. Crouching low, he cautiously stepped inside. Liza stood in the hazy light, her petite body wrapped in the arms of Asch, her face pressed firmly against his chest, sobbing quietly. A man laid crumpled on the straw-covered floor at their feet. Tavin rubbed his eyes of floating dust with his sleeve and coughed. *"What happened?",* he anxiously questioned as he swiftly closed the barn door behind him.

Liza answered, turning her head slightly toward Tavin, her face taut with anguish, *"I was milking the cow and suddenly a hand slapped across my mouth. That man…"* she pointed to the motionless body sprawled on the barn floor, *"…whispered his evil intention in my ear. His breath filled with alcohol. He threw me down and began clawing at my clothes. It was God who saved me by bringing Asch."* She turned her face again against Asch and wrapping her arms around his waist, she clung to him.

Asch held Liza with an iron grip, his steel-grey eyes shining with rage, as he glared down at the man. *"I watched, through your looking glass as Liza entered the barn. I waited, thinking you would find her. Instead, this man came from the shadows and entered. I could not wait any longer. She was in danger."* Blue and black paint dripped from his sweat covered face.

"Do you know who he is?" Tavin asked, putting his hand on Liza's shoulder, tugging slightly, encouraging her to release Asch. She dropped

her arms and stepped back, looking sheepishly up into Asch's eyes, *"I apologize. You must think me terribly forward."* Asch nodded and smiled, knowing that her mind was befuddled and dazed by the sudden violent events.

Shaking, Liza nervously smoothed her striped cotton dress down over her white thread stockings and adjusted her linen kerchief around her shoulders, pulling at the torn shoulder seam of her dress. Beneath her gown, her waist was tightly cinched by a stiff corset, giving her an attractive shapely appearance. *"No. I don't know his name."* she answered, her voice strained and unsteady. *"A local merchant. He comes to the tavern several times a week and has always been kind in his manner and words. I hadn't expected anything more."*

Looking down at the crumpled, motionless man on the ground, a six-inch flintlock pistol rested in his limp right hand. Tavin kicked it away. The man laid sprawled on his stomach. His curled powdered wig sat cockeyed and was blotted crimson red at the back of his neck, laying twisted across the collar of his white ruffled shirt. His sleeves were adorned with gold cuff buttons, linked with narrow gold chains. His obvious bulging belly suggested that he ate well and was most likely a man of means.

Unsure of what to do, Tavin probed, *"So that I understand, this man was attempting to ravish you. Asch arrived and killed him?"*

"He'eh. No. He is not dead. Unconscious," Asch firmly responded, not looking up, continuing to scowl down at the unmoving man.

Liza quickly added, *"I struck him with the back of Asch's hatchet. I hit him hard at the base of his head. You and Asch need to go. Go now."* Her voice rose in short, panicked sentences, *"I will admit to this! The man was attacking me. Asch wrestled with him. His hatchet came loose. I picked it up. The man pulled his pistol."*

Glancing at Asch, she continued, calming her nerves, *"But he paused, gloating with insults, saying terrible things about money and scalps, laughing. He had forgotten about me. I was behind him. He lifted the gun and took direct aim. I couldn't stand by and watch Asch die. I hit the man with all my might."*

Asch bent to pick his hatchet up off the ground and held it up, his eyes blazing with rage. Lisa recognized Asch's intention. *"You and Tavin need to go. Go now. I will explain this. The man attacked me."*

Tavin squatted down next the heavy-set man. *"This is a gentleman of substance and most likely wealth. His word will hold weight and he is not apt to admit that he attacked a tavern girl. No, he will make another claim, protecting his reputation. Liza, he will lie and label you a liar or worse. You could possibly be prosecuted for his injuries. We hide his body, and we leave, taking you with us."*

Catching his breath, Tavin huffed as he helped Asch drag the heavy man, pulling his body inside an empty clean stall. Rope hung on a peg. They quickly bound his arms and legs and covered him with straw. Closing the stall door, Asch stared coldly back at the man's body and said nothing. Tavin brushed bits of hay off his buckskin leggings and observed, *"Between the bump on his head and the alcohol on his breath, I'd say he'll be out for a while. Long enough for us to get far enough away."*

Liza stood sobbing near the barn door, using her dirty white apron to wipe her eyes and nose. *He's still bleeding. Should we wrap the wound?"*

"Liza, you needn't be concerned for an injury sustained to a man who intended you harm. He was a man who acted out his evil desires. He reaped what he sowed. He was going to kill Asch and may have killed you," Tavin gently, but firmly stated. Taking a deep breath and exhaling, *"He is a wolf in sheep's clothing, and we let him lay as he is."*

"Quickly. We go," Asch whispered, wrapping his arm around Liza's shoulders. He gently guided her to the edge of the door and pushed it open. Leaning out he saw no one. The moon's bright glow was reduced to a pale ghostlike sphere behind the increasing heaviness of clouds. Music and merriment drifted from the Red Owl. *"I see no one,"* he whispered back to Tavin.

Picking up his musket, bow and pack, Tavin slung them over his shoulder. *"Liza, you must be quiet. Once we are away from this place and back to the safety of the mountain, we will talk more."* As she nodded her head, the frays on her lopsided mop cap flopped and long strands of her brown hair hung freely across her face. Her hauntingly green eyes wide and tear filled. She scooped up the black woolen cape she had worn to the barn and breathed a prayer, *"God guide our steps."*

Moving swiftly, they crossed the creek on the west end of the property and began to head north. No one spoke. The air was fresh and cool, as the clouds of night floated slowly east. A light breeze sighed sadly through the trees, as they walked without stopping until the brim of daylight inched above the distant horizon. Golden rays stretched up and outward. The rich blue sky brightened. Birds sang their various tunes and squirrels chattered their jumpy annoyance. Morning dew brought the fresh smell of herbs and glistened like drops of sparkling diamonds across the ground.

Liza limped and struggled to keep pace, without complaint. Once the sun tilted over the treetops, Asch finally spoke, *"We can rest there for a while,"* pointing to a protected meadow at the bottom of a steep ravine. A wide shallow stream gurgled peacefully. The ground was soft. Liza sat down heavily on the large branch of a fallen old maple tree. Black scorch marks crept across and over its jagged end like it had been brushed in tar. The work of lightning. She slipped her black leather shoes off. Her stockings were ripped and thread bare. Her feet, chapped and red, bleeding sore blisters. She grimaced, *"These shoes are hand-me-downs."*

Asch leaned his musket against a tree, dropped his pack and resolutely walked to where Liza sat. Scooping her up in his arms he carried her to the stream. Clutching Asch's neck, she dropped her head onto his shoulder until he set her down on a moss-covered boulder. Flinching slightly when her feet submerged into the cold water, she tugged at her neck scarf, pulling it snugly, as was her habit, hiding her pinkish scars.

Standing silently next to her, Asch waited. Finally, she looked up, her sage eyes glassy, *"You risked your life to save me. First in the wilderness from my Indian abductors and now from an evil white man. I am not worthy of your kindness. I have put you in danger over and over. Yet, God has seen fit to bless me with your courage."*

"Your God is a great mystery," Asch quietly responded. Squatting down at the stream, he shoved both hands into the rocky bottom. Digging up sandy, wet gravel he rubbed his face vigorously. Black and blue paint swirled and evaporated with the languid current. When he finished, his skin was smooth, clear, and flushed with the rich copper color of his natural tone. He smiled and held her firmly in the frank gaze of his gray eyes.

Liza embraced his stare and with curiosity, asked, *"How does it happen that you were at the Red Owl?"*

"*My blood boiled at hearing that you were owned and forced to labor in a place where you were not respected or protected.*"

"*Asch, the Demerests are good to me. The attack that occurred last night was an anomaly. I am not abused or a slave, yet I am bound in my duty to reimburse my indebtedness. My father had no money to pay for our family's passage across the Atlantic. When he died, it fell to me.*"

"*You are not safe there,*" Asch flatly stated.

Liza smiled and reached for his hand. "*I am safe. The Lord had you ready and waiting at just the right moment. My heart is full knowing that you sought me, concerned for my safety.*"

Asch crouched down next to her, "*I am of my mother's people. Onodowa'ga. The war paint that washed away in the stream was for you. I came to take you, to fight for you.*"

"*You prepared yourself to fight for me? Why? I am damaged goods. Scarred,*" cried Liza, her voice shaking and emotions swelling.

With tenderness in his voice explained, "*Tavin has told me of your God. He told me of how your God seeks out people. How he sacrificed His son to seek the lost. I was lost. The Creator of all did battle for me. He found me and now I have found you.*"

"*What does this mean? You have found me?*" she cried, stunned and trembling.

Asch looked tensely over at Tavin, who quickly glanced away. Turning back to Liza, he finally said, "*Tavin Shire is my brother. He has not yet discovered his own path, but he has shown me the truth of the book and guided me to you. And now, I wish to become your husband.*" extending his hand to Liza. She clutched it and stood, finding her balance on the smooth stony bottom of the icy stream, her feet unsteady and numb.

In a whisper, she studied his face, and struggled to find her answer. "*I had resolved in my heart that I would most assuredly remain unmarried. It seemed at every turn my circumstance dictated it to be so. Who could want me? The Lord has been my all and in Him I found the peace to live alone.*"

"*My life has been torn. Two worlds collide inside of me. For the first time, I am sure of who I am, with you, with God.*"

Liza smiled and with joyful resolve replied, "*You are not only Heyonohsodahoh or Asch Wolfe. You are not only Seneca, or white, but you are a man of God's own choosing. I accept a life devoted to you as your wife. But I must first fulfill my duty to pay my family's debt. I am the only one who can. Mr. and Mrs. Demerest were not cruel. They were kind and defended me whenever men overstepped their bounds. I cannot leave them before making things right. God would have me honor my responsibility. Please understand."*

Dropping her hand, Asch shook his head in wonder, *"You would return to washing bedding, scrubbing floors, emptying pots and being subjected to the stares, vile disrespect and dangers offered by drunken men, because God would have you do so? You were attacked just last night. What would have happened if Tavin and I hadn't arrived?"*

"I do not worry. The Lord is my defender. Do you believe that it was merely a coincidence that you were there at just the right time? But even more importantly, if you hadn't been there, my life would still be in God's hands. He is the one who saves through whatever the circumstance."

Asch took a step back, feeling frustrated, turning his head away he watched the sun slowly rising higher. Liza reached out and took his hand again, *"Asch, when I make a commitment, a promise, it is binding. My heart soars at the thought of pledging myself to you as your wife, if you are willing to wait for me to be free."*

Looking back down at her, Asch felt as if he were falling helplessly into the green abyss of her eyes. Grasping her around her waist, he lifted her from the stream, her feet dangling freely, spinning her in a joyous circle. Liza's arms clung to his neck, and she laughed, as her toes skimmed along the surface spraying glistening water in a joyous arch. *"I do not understand your ways, but I will wait."*

Tavin shook his head as he watched, grinning, *"God works in the most unlikely of ways!"*

CHAPTER

26

April 1756

The following week brought the kind of uncertainty that accompanies grand amounts of unexpected news. Tavin ventured alone into the heart of Reading, the county seat of Berks. Soldiers milled about the streets in various stages of duty, waiting for orders to be passed down. Reading supported a military base of operations supporting the chain of forts being built along the Blue Mountain.

The Schuylkill River flowed in languid beauty, its banks holding back high water from the snow melt of winter. A new road had been completed from Reading reaching as far as Easton. Travel was easier and its use was increasing with merchant carts, military supply wagons and various sojourners from all walks of life. It was called The King's Highway, as all roads were called, and it offered no bridges for crossing the many rivers and creeks that came across its path, yet it remained a vast improvement from the rough, wilderness roads of the past. Although, fording on foot or horseback was still required unless a random ferry was accessible on a rare occasion.

Tavin felt lost. A stray dog, a vagrant, with no aim but the immediate. Wandering the pristine streets of the carefully plotted town of Reading, his dirty buckskins were out of place. At the same time his two-fold purpose was heightened. Captives and Leeds.

The captives he had seen while spying with Asch clung to his thoughts, as tar on shingles, refusing to give way. Frustrated by Captain Clapham's response at hearing the news of white captives seen at Fort Duquesne, Tavin decided to attempt to gather information from the British and militia command at Reading. He needed to hear if there were plans to take military action or if a treaty was underway that included terms for freeing those carried off.

And always, the dark cloud of Leeds loomed overhead. If Tavin could warn them of the murderous spy, Adoniram Leeds, the military powers that be may perhaps find him and dispatch him, removing the ever-present darkness of unsettled justice. The blight of Leeds was not going to go away until he was discovered and dealt with. Tavin knew that until it was settled, Asch would not surrender his need for retribution, even for love of Liza.

Finding himself in the heart of the shopping district, two upstanding ladies approached, dressed in brocade and fine embroidered shawls too warm for a humid April morning. Upon noticing Tavin before them, one turned to the other and blandly whispered, *"A wild beast. One cannot discover whether he belongs to this world or some other undiscovered land."* They giggled. All the while the teenage girl strolling behind them offered her batting eyes and coy smile.

Suddenly a firm hand grabbed the leather strap to the musket that lay across his back, stopping him abruptly. *"Should you truly be charming young women with a bounty on your head Tavin Shire?"* came the melodious and familiar voice. Agnes stood with her hands on her hips, eyebrows raised and a half-smile on her face.

"And what would you be referring to, Agnes Bowen? I charm no one and I can think of no reason a bounty be issued in reference to me."

"We cannot talk here. Follow me." Her tone humorless, as she marched off. He followed.

Tavin was confused and curious, not to mention extremely happy to have Agnes in his presence. They walked silently a few blocks and turned up Penn Street stopping at a modest two-story limestone residence. Entering, Agnes quickly closed the door and released the heavy curtains from their ties, covering the large glass window in the small parlor.

"*What is going on? Why all the secrecy?*" asked Tavin.

Agnes put her hands once again on her slender hips. "*First of all, I need a few answers from you.*"

"*I know. You are probably upset that I left Bethlehem without saying goodbye back in February. I had my reasons for leaving so suddenly. Reasons that I am not at liberty to share. Although, there was truth in the fact that I needed to move Henryk and Berta to our family in Germantown. Our grandmother Shire….*"

"*I don't care about that right now!*" interrupted Agnes, her brown eyes flashing.

"*Then what is this about?!*"

"*Did you attack a man at the Red Owl Inn?*"

"*Of course not!*" shouted Tavin.

"*A prominent man of some wealth was severely injured in a barn on the premises of the Red Owl. He claims that he was innocently speaking with a chamber maid when someone struck him over the head from behind. When he woke, the maid, whose name was Liza Schell,*" Agnes raised her eyebrows knowingly, "*was gone. A woman, Mrs. Demerest, the wife of the tavern owner, provided a name and a detailed description of a disheveled young man in buckskin who came looking for Liza. She had directed him to the barn. The gentleman has placed a bounty on the head of his attacker, Tavin Shire, with additional charges of kidnapping.*"

"*So that's his story, I should have known he'd place the blame to me,*" Tavin cynically laughed, "*…and he's no gentleman. He is seeking to save his own reputation. Accusing me, rather than admitting that he attacked Liza.*"

"*You could be arrested and imprisoned!*"

"*Agnes, there are details that you are unaware of. Yes, I was at the Red Owl asking for Liza. Asch was with me. We had come from Fort Augusta to find Liza and see to her situation, having heard rumors that she was being abused. As it turned out, we arrived at the very moment the 'prominent man' seized her. Asch stopped him and they fought. The man pulled a gun and was about to shoot Asch when Liza struck him over the head, knocking him out.*" Tavin smiled. "*She's stronger than she looks! Anyway, we pulled him into a stall and took Liza, knowing that he would make up a story to save his own neck, making a liar of Liza and tarnishing her reputation, or worse, have her arrested for his injuries."*

"Where is Liza now? Is she safe?" Agnes asked, with concern in her voice.

"She is with Asch but determined to return to her duties at the tavern. She holds that God would have her honor the contract, settling the travel debt she and her family incurred."

"Yes, I remember. She is bound to labor under that contract for two more years. It is just like her to put herself back there and refuse the freedom she now has!" There was exasperation in Agnes's voice. She smoothed the front of her linen apron and shook her head. *"Her selfless qualities and loyal fortitude continue to bewilder me."*

"She is not free until her debt is paid."

Agnes frowned and thought for a moment. *"And what of Asch?"* she finally asked.

"He took Liza over the mountain to wait. I came back alone to explain to the Demerests what happened that night. Once the truth is known, I will see to it that Liza is again a chamber maid at the Red Owl, as is her wish."

"And yet you came to Reading? Why? You could have simply gone directly to the proprietors of the Red Owl and gone back into the wild. That's all that you want, isn't it? To live in the wild?" Her words sounded accusatory and harsh.

Tavin bristled. *"You oversimplify and diminish my intentions. Hundreds of white captives are held by Lenape, Shawnee, Huron, and French. I came here, before talking with the Demerests, to surmise if any plans be underway for their recovery. I also thought to bring Leeds to the attention of the military base here."*

Ashamed of her stinging charge, Agnes tempered her tone and pleaded, *"Your mission is valiant, but you mustn't reveal yourself! The man who has set a bounty on your head is very influential. If no one shoots you first, you will certainly be arrested. You must promise me that you will leave Reading and not speak to anyone."*

"I promise. But you must remember, with God's help, I have become fairly adept at avoiding those who seek me harm," he said, with a playful gleam in his eye.

"This is not a light matter, Tavin Shire."

He laughed and changing the subject to the question that had weighed him down since stepping through the door, asked, *"Tell me now, what is this house?"*

Agnes confidently raised her head, to look Tavin square in the eyes, *"This is the home of Mr. Gehman. I am governess to his two children. His wife sadly died in childbirth along with the infant several months past. He is set to remarry soon, and I will then find other accommodations. Mr. Gehman has been kind and considerate of my unfortunate circumstances."*

A hint of bitterness resonated in Tavin's voice, as he surmised, *"Waiting for Renz to return from his duties with the militia must be difficult for you. It is an unfortunate circumstance."* Turning his head he feigned interest in a glass figurine on the pristine mantle, not wanting her to see his disgust at mentioning Renz by name, wishing that he could explain the true nature of who Renz was.

"My difficult circumstances have nothing to do with my engagement to Renz. How can you not know that gossip abounds at my expense? I am the subject of gross speculation."

"I only supposed that being separated from the man you love and forced to postpone your marriage is a challenging course," Tavin retorted.

Agnes tipped her head and with a glint in her eye she said, *"I am ashamed to say I am no longer betrothed."*

Tavin's heart leaped. Nervously he replied, *"I saw Renz at Fort Augusta. He plans to marry you."*

"His plans are not mine. Once he realized that I was returned, the lure of my dowry and inheritance overcame his disgust of my capture." Agnes snapped back. Smoothing her apron, she added, *"My dowry is but a meager portion, yet my father was a shrewd and suspicious businessman, accepting only sterling and gold for his portion of the mill sold to his old business partner. Assuming that I can return to our farm after this war is settled, it is buried in a metal box under a tree near the house. Renz is aware of this 'treasure' although knows not where to find it. And as you well know, in the eyes of the law I am merged to my husband and my property is thus transferred by virtue of this legal binding to him. Renz is indeed eager for our marriage."*

Tavin reached out and touched her hand. *"If you have ended your engagement, why does he remain convinced that you will marry?"*

"His ego cannot conceive that I will not wilt in wonder at his glorious presence, while his greed forces his insistence." With a whiff of contempt in her voice, she continued, *"Renz clarified his great courage and valor as he searched for me after I was taken. He then conveyed that my captivity sadly cast disparaging light on his own reputation, jeopardizing his future. Regardless, he would honor his commitment to marriage and of course see to the property and belongings of my deceased parents. I was to be eternally grateful for his great sacrifice in making me his wife. His words oozed with fabricated warmth."* The last sentence hung in the air.

Tavin was surprised. *"I have longed for you to see Renz for who he really is."*

Agnes laughed, *"Tavin, I'm not as naïve as you might think me to be. Renz's arrogant pride showed itself in ugly, unsavory ways well before I was carried off. I just hadn't wanted to admit it. When I returned, I quickly determined that I could not marry. When he rode off to Fort Augusta his last words were, 'You will change your mind. No one else would want you.' I smiled and told him,' I believe there is someone who will."*

Tavin prodded, *"So am I to understand that you are not a heartbroken, lovesick girl sulking over your lost love?"*

"Well, maybe. It depends on what you are planning to say next," she teased, raising her eyebrows, her dark eyes shining.

Tavin straightened and gathered his thoughts. Stumbling over his words, in nervous uncertainty he began, *"If you are saying what I think you are saying, I will dare to tell you,"* Tavin took a deep breath. *"Agnes Bowen, I cannot remember a time when I have not loved you."* Looking down, he fumbled with the strap of his musket and brushed his hair behind his ear with his hand. Shifting his weight and staring at the floral beige and ochre rug on the floor, he added, *"I do have one question. You said that you felt ashamed that you are no longer betrothed to Renz. Why? Why should you feel ashamed?"*

"My shame comes from the fact that I had ignored the prompting and direction that I knew God was giving me. I should never have been in a position where a man like Renz manipulated and wooed me into believing a lie. I allowed myself to be deceived and to enter an engagement of falsehood. There is my shame." Tears rolled down her cheeks.

Tavin took a step closer. *"Agnes."* She peered up at him, eyes shimmering. He breathed in slowly, *"I judge you for nothing. Evil will always lie close at hand, waging war against us, but thanks be to God through our Lord, Jesus Christ, who alone is our salvation."*

"How grateful I am!"

Tavin cleared his throat and haltingly began, *"My life has been thrown about as a leaf on the wind. I have no real direction, no certain future, no plans and now I am apparently a wanted man. But God has shown me many things over these long cold months. I cannot make promises to you on my own strength, but with God's help, I can pledge to hold you high, look to your needs, defend you against all aggressors and lead you in love and faith. If you will have me."*

Agnes did not hesitate. *"Tavin Shire, I will have you. God has brought me down a grim path of loss,"* she took a shuddering breath, remembering, *"only to find you patiently waiting and trusting."*

He reached down and took her hands. She lifted her chin and he kissed her lightly. The tension that had held them separated from each other for so long suddenly vanished and Tavin wrapped her firmly in his arms, whispering, *"Thank you Father God for your love and mercy!"*

CHAPTER

27

Tavin stood soberly near Agnes as she explained to Mr. Gehman, in lengthy detail, why this unkempt, buckskinned man was standing in his parlor. Mr. Gehman listened thoughtfully as he sat rocking in his chair, his hands folded in his lap. He was a man of faith, with a brilliant mind, although a bit eccentric. His weakness was his belief that evil had boundaries. It took some convincing of the truth concerning the attack on Liza and the lies surrounding Tavin. Mr. Gehman had believed the notable gentleman, by the name of Mr. Hoch, to be a man of integrity and initially found it incomprehensible that he should rather instead be such a flagrant, unrepentant evildoer.

Agnes added, *"I know the name. My father had some dealings with him a few years ago. He is a conniving man."*

"My instincts tell me, Agnes, that you are sincere and accurate in your assessment of Mr. Hoch and his wrongful intentions toward your friend. I have always felt a certain caution regarding him," mused Mr. Gehman, reaching for an unlit pipe on the table next to him. Turning to Tavin, his attentive eyes squinting against streams of dusty light escaping the edges of the heavy curtain, he continued, *"I should surmise by your appearance that you are a man of action, Mr. Shire."*

Tavin stood tall and confident. *"Action is often a necessity, although impetuous and imprudent encounters are wisely avoided. My friend, whom I trust as a brother, and I made a conscious choice concerning Liza and her safety. We took her away. It was neither impetuous nor imprudent. Leaving Mr. Hoch alive was also a conscious choice."*

Mr. Gehman grimaced, *"Granted, allowing him to live speaks well to your character, yet you remain in a predicament. I am surprised that you were not apprehended in the forest on your passage through the Tulpehocken Valley before reaching Reading. Local watches have been established forming a loose defensive perimeter against Indian attacks. They range the woods up and down the frontier and will surely also be alert to your apprehension, especially with a bounty on your head."*

Stepping forward, Tavin's hand rested on the butt of the knife strapped across his hip, as was his natural tendency. He responded, *"I aim to employ added precaution on my return north, after I have spoken with the Demerests. You have been most kind, Mr. Gehman. My intentions were never to bring trouble to your door. My deepest apologies to you and your family."*

Mr. Gehman adjusted his grey wig, replying tartly, *"Darkness is falling. You may find fresh hay in the stable behind the house. Sleep tonight and be gone by morning."*

"I am grateful."

As Tavin opened the back door to leave, Agnes grasped his arm. *"I am sorry Mr. Gehman spoke to you in that tone of voice."*

"He is nervous and rightly so. He is harboring a wanted man."

"Tavin, I have been thinking of the bounty placed on you. You cannot go alone to see Mr. and Mrs. Demerest. You are a stranger whose words will ring empty. They will not believe you and even if they did, the bounty is a great temptation. I fear you will be arrested. If it is true that they are fond of Liza, bring her back. Let her explain. I know that you did not think it safe for her to return with you, but the situation calls for her testimony. Go. Bring her back."

Tavin thought for a moment. *"You may be right. Now that I know Hoch has laid the blame solely on me and left Liza out of his story, I think she is safe to return, at least until Hoch denies everything."* Resting his hand on her waist, in an easy gesture of tenderness, his face close to hers, he whispered, *"In the morning, before light, come to the stable. We will talk more. There is something I have not told you concerning Asch and Liza."*

"*What is it?!*" she excitedly questioned.

He grinned at her, "*In the morning we will talk.*" He kissed her cheek and walked across the dark yard toward the stable, his heart soaring.

★ ★ ★ ★ ★

The familiar smells of the forest flooded Tavin's nostrils. Gigantic trees of black walnut, ash, beech, and maple loomed overhead with buds of spring ready to burst forth. The weather turned warm with heavy rains soaking the earth. Mist, fog, and an abundance of rich mud made travel difficult and yet Tavin never felt more alive. Wild turkey, white-tailed deer, elk, beaver, wolves, otter, and bear appeared in profusion as if celebrating new life. Rivers were swollen and treacherous to cross, while lush wet paths made covering his tracks almost impossible. Yet, his heart surged, and his mind wheeled in blissful contentment as he climbed, scrambled, and slid up and down one ravine after another.

Approaching cautiously, Tavin could see that the partially burned-out cabin had been improved. Images of Mary's smiling face and Wolfe's beard, bristling like a porcupine, flooded his memories. He paused, leaning on his musket, sadly imagining the tragic events that had taken place just months earlier. Wolfe and Mary murdered by Leeds. Momentarily gazing over at two graves on the hillside, he shook off the sorrow, giving a quick signal yap and called out, '*Heyŏnŏhsoödahdŏh*'

Asch stepped from behind a tree, his white teeth gleaming with a huge smile, "*Once again you are as subtle as a charging bear. I heard you coming for miles.*"

Tavin laughed, "*Everything I have learned, you have taught me. Maybe I need a new teacher.*"

They greeted each other with a warm embrace. "*Brother, it is good to see you,*" said Asch. "*And you,*" Tavin replied as they approached the cabin.

"*What news do you bring us?*"

Just then Tavin noticed Liza standing in the doorway, with her arms folded, smiling. "*Liza! I bring news of Agnes. She extends her heartfelt love.*"

"*You found Agnes?*" questioned Liza, her face radiating joy, as she reached out to give him a hug.

"*Well, actually, she found me. It's a long story.*"

"Please come inside. Sit by the fire. We have repaired much of the damage within."

Stepping inside, the glow of a warm fire blazed in the hearth. Tavin knelt and rubbed his hands over the hot flames. *"You have resurrected this place in such a short amount of time."* He smiled at the small bouquet of wildflowers arranged in a pewter mug in the center of the scorched table.

"Please tell me of Agnes," pursued Liza, anxiously.

Once Tavin concluded with the details of his trip to Reading, including the bounty on his head, Liza cried out, *"This is all my fault!"*

"Nothing has happened that God has not ordained, and He will work it out for His glory. Through it, Agnes informed me that she is no longer betrothed. She is free. I was able to tell her the things that I have long held to myself. We have an understanding. A spoken love for each other."

"Finally!" huffed Asch.

Liza laughed, *"The Lord is so good!"*

Liza then continued, *"I will go back, alone. I will clear your name and tell the truth of that night and then you and Agnes will begin your lives together."* She glanced at Asch who sat stalwart, his grey eyes clouded dark with disapproval. Tavin picked up his mug, pushed the bench back and stood from the table.

"I had no doubt that you would persist in returning. Agnes and I discussed this and have agreed. I will take you back. Asch will remain here," asserted Tavin.

"No!" yelled Asch, jumping to his feet.

Tavin continued, *"Hear me out. If God wills, I'll be arrested and not shot on sight. Mr. Hoch, the man who attacked Liza is not only prominent and influential, as we first suspected, but apparently, he is also acutely protective of his good standing in the community. He will very likely brand me a liar and defame Liza's reputation, rather than admit his own sin. Though Hoch's lies are a certainty, the truth must be heard. We stand as vessels of God's mercy, and we will pray that He rights these wrongs."*

Liza interrupted, *"I am sorry that you have been involved in my troubles. Take me within a day's walk, and I will travel the rest of the way alone. This is too dangerous, and it is my problem, not yours. I will clear your name, but I must go alone to ensure that you are no longer implicated."*

"Liza, I admire your selflessness, but no. The matter will be settled, and I will be there. We'll leave in a week."

Asch vehemently shook his head, "I won't sit by and watch you both take this risk. I am leaving with you," reaching for Liza's hand.

"Asch, Mr. Hoch will pitch irrational hatred on your head because of your blood. Your presence will insight rage and blind people's eyes to the truth, complicating the situation. It will be better that you are not with us or the whole matter will likely be twisted to fall wrongly on you," responded Tavin with firmness.

"Stubbornness holds you, like a mule refusing to budge. I have seen it before and always your God steps in and delivers the day." Asch responded to Tavin, enfolding Liza in his arms, he continued, "But this time you risk more than your own life."

"May God grant us His mercy," said Tavin, as he tossed a log into the hearth and silently watched as the flames grew higher.

★ ★ ★ ★ ★

Agnes knocked boldly on the door. A house-servant, young and thin as a rail, answered, wiping her hands on her linen apron. "May I help you?" she asked.

"Yes. If you please, I am here to see Mr. Hoch. Would he be available?"

"Mr. Hoch has gone out for the day."

"May I inquire as to his whereabouts?"

The girl shuffled her feet, unsure whether to answer the question, her eyes darting nervously.

"Please," Agnes added, "I simply wish to trouble him briefly over a matter of concern to both of us."

Glancing toward the parlor behind her, the girl whispered, "He'd be at the Red Owl this time of day. He be all but a slave to rum, but don't tell him I said so."

"Thank you. You have been a great help and your secret is safe with me," Agnes smiled broadly, reaching out and patting the girl's clinched hands.

Foolishly determined, Agnes began walking. The Red Owl was situated several miles outside of town and Agnes felt nervous as the sun bent closer to the horizon. It was further than she had expected and upon hearing a wagon coming up from behind she prayed that it be a kindly sort. A friendly *"Hello!"* and Agnes's prayer was answered. The elderly farmer with a slumped back, and dirty clothes called out again, *"Ride?"* The afternoon air had been crisp and with the coming of dusk, a chill came on the wind. She pulled a light shawl loosely over her shoulders, her brown hair catching hints of amber, as the rays of the setting sun cast long shadows across the road. *"Yes. Thank you, sir."*

The farmer was a mild-mannered man, whose idea of conversation was an amazing usage of single words conveying his thoughts, questions and even opinions. She was grateful for his peaceful way, but especially thankful for the ride. Her feet were sore, and she was tired. Reaching the door of the tavern just as the perfect orange sphere dropped behind a stand of birch trees, she turned and thanked the farmer, who nodded and offered, *"Farwell"*. Pushing the door open, her eyes adjusted to the dark, smoky room. Curious eyes gawked.

Clearing her throat, she stepped toward the bar and smiled anxiously at the plump matron, who stood wiping a glass clean with a cotton towel. The room smelled of liquor and tobacco. *"Excuse me, but I am looking to speak with a man who frequents your establishment. His name is Mr. Hoch."*

Raising one eyebrow above her wire spectacles, which Agnes found intriguing in and of itself, the woman set the glass down and scurried to the end of the bar where Agnes stood. In a quiet voice she warned, *"Mr. Hoch has been drinking a fair amount this day. I think you should refrain from engaging him in any sort of conversation. What is your business?"*

Agnes quickly realized who the woman was. *"Mrs. Demerest, I ordinarily would not presume upon you, nor would I divulge personal affairs with a stranger, but my business with Mr. Hoch indeed concerns you and your husband, as I am here to discuss the indentured girl, Liza Schell."*

Mrs. Demerest tipped her head in interest. *"Well, aren't you the curious one. Let's hear what you have to say, but my caution remains. Mr. Hoch is unpredictable and ornery when he's drinking."* Peering through her squinting, small eyes and scanning the room she finally called, *"Mr. Demerest!"* and waved the thread-like man over.

Having hurried over at his wife's summons, Mr. Demerest stood close to Agnes. A little too close and Agnes took a step back. Mrs.

Demerest eyed him irritably and said, *"This young lady wishes to discuss Miss Liza with us and with Mr. Hoch."*

"Is Liza found? That poor girl. First carried off by Indians and then kidnapped by a crazed, wild man," Mr. Demerest anxiously spewed.

Agnes lifted her head confidently, *"There is much to talk about. Could you please point out Mr. Hoch?"*

"He is sitting over there, in the middle of a card game."

"Could you please ask him to join us?"

"I will but he's not apt to leave a game."

"Inform him that I know the truth about Liza. That should entice him enough."

Stepping over to the table, Mr. Demerest bent down and whispered in Mr. Hoch's ear. *"What?! What are you babbling about old man?"* Pointing to Agnes, he took a nervous step back, as Mr. Hoch peered around him to look at Agnes. Agnes waved. Sliding his chair noisily back from the table, *"What is this about?"* scoffed Hoch to no one.

Agnes quickly moved to an empty table in the corner. Sitting with her back to the wall, she folded her hands and rested them lightly on the table's surface. Mrs. Demerest called for a tavern girl to take her place behind the bar and Mr. Demerest scurried to sit across from Agnes. Mr. Hoch ambled over, the buttons on his vest puckering over his belly, with a glass of red wine in one hand and a smoldering pipe in the other. *"Please, sit,"* said Agnes.

"I don't know who you are young lady, or how you think you know me, but I can assure that you have nothing to say that is of any interest to me," said Hoch, taking a noisy sip from his glass, and wiping his sand-colored mustache with the back of his fleshy hand. He continued to stand.

Mrs. Demerest squeezed onto a chair next to Agnes, eager to hear what this was all about. *"I do hope that you are not wasting our time with some nonsense."*

"I came here in good faith to right a wrong, if that is possible," Agnes said, staring boldly up into Mr. Hoch's suspicious eyes. She continued, *"I am Agnes Bowen. Liza Schell is a friend of mine. We were captives together at the Indian village of Chinklacamoose, liberated through the efforts of the man you described as 'a crazed, wild man'."* Looking at Mr. Demerest, she continued. *"My father was Mathias Bowen, a well-respected man of industry, turned farmer, who lost his life along with my mother and brother last October.*

Mr. Hoch," Agnes directed her words at him, *"I believe that you will recall my brother, Thomas. He incurred a sizable gambling debt, which my father settled with you."*

Hoch pulled a chair out and sat down in disgust. *"I remember your brother, Thomas. He was a fool and bad at cards. But, your father, indeed, resolved the issue of payment. I do not understand what any of this has to do with me anymore. The problem was decided in an amiable and fair manner. Your father was a man of integrity."*

Turning to both Mr. and Mrs. Demerest, as if to dismiss Hoch, she replied, *"I do not reference the gambling debt to debate or justify my brother's actions, but only to confirm, as Mr. Hoch has validated that my name comes with credibility. I am my father's daughter. I only begin there, because what I tell you will contradict what Mr. Hoch has claimed and I need you to believe me."*

"Go on dear, tell us what you came here to say," Mrs. Demerest anxiously crooned, leaning forward eagerly.

"This is absurd. This girl can know nothing!" Mr. Hoch exclaimed with dramatic waves of his hands. Redirecting his remarks to Agnes he continued, *"But please, go on, let us hear your imaginative tale,"* wiping sweat from his forehead with an embroidered hanky, pushing his grey wig off center on his greasy head.

"Mr. Hoch attacked Liza the night she disappeared. Mrs. Demerest, if you recall, Tavin Shire, the man who is accused of attacking Mr. Hoch, and kidnapping Liza Schell, arrived here asking for Liza. You sent him to the barn where Liza was milking the cow. Unbeknown to Tavin, Mr. Hoch had previously entered the barn and began forcing himself on Liza. Tavin's friend, an honorable Seneca warrior, by the name of Asch Wolfe, saw what was happening. Asch entered the barn and fought with Mr. Hoch. Mr. Hoch pulled a gun and was about to shoot Asch when Liza struck him over the head with the blunt end of the hatchet that Asch had dropped. Liza then ran with Tavin and Asch. Willingly. She was not kidnapped."

"Preposterous! An inventive story to be sure!" yelled Hoch.

"Young lady, if this is true, why did Liza run? She could have told her story and continued to work here. There is much work to be done." Mr. Demerest espoused.

Mrs. Demerest firmly scolded her husband, as he sank sullenly down in his chair. *"Is that all you can think of right now? Work? That sweet girl was attacked, and you are worried that she could have remained here to fulfill her obligation!"*

Agnes continued, *"She could have remained, but who would have believed her word against the word of a wealthy, prominent man like Mr. Hoch?"*

"Indeed, the girl is a liar. My reputation far exceeds any claim that this servant girl may lay at my feet." Hoch boasted.

"What is the true purpose of your coming here? Liza is gone," interjected Mrs. Demerest.

Turning her head, to address the plump, red-faced matron, Agnes firmly stated, *"I want Mr. Hoch to drop the charges against Tavin Shire. Renege the bounty on his head and I will retain the truth of the circumstances concerning that night. I will share it with no one. If he refuses, I will shout it from the rooftops, proclaim it wherever I go and declare it to anyone who will listen, 'Mr. Hoch attacked a young innocent girl in his drunkenness and sin!'. My own reputation as well as the status of my father will carry credibility. Gossip and scuttlebutt will abound over Mr. Hoch's character, and if he recovers from it, I will see to it that Liza presses for legal action concerning attempted rape and murder. This whole thing can be dragged out or it can go away. It can hunt him down for years or quietly be put to rest."*

"You cannot threaten me!" shouted Hoch.

"Threat or option, however you choose to see it. Think about it. I can arrive at your home tomorrow for your answer. Perhaps I will have the pleasure of meeting your wife at that time," Agnes replied with a gleam in her eye.

His face reddened in anger and through gritted teeth, Hoch muttered with a hiss, *"Do not come to my home. I shall give my answer now. This is fabrication of the highest degree, but I will not see my good name, or my family suffer hearsay chatter or unproven accusations. The wild man who attacked me can go free. I will rescind the charges and renege the bounty, just to be rid of you."* Pushing his chair violently back from the table he stormed out the door, leaving his card game unfinished.

"And what of Liza?" Mr. Demerest hesitantly asked Agnes, glancing timidly at his wife for approval.

"Liza wishes to return here. She is determined to honor the Lord by fulfilling her obligation of two more years. As you know, her life has been a series of unfortunate and painful events. Yet by God's grace, she has found love. I have been told that the man I mentioned aforehand, Asch Wolfe, has made clear his

respectful intentions to make her his wife. He will wait for her." Agnes took a deep breath and continued, *"That being said, the Lord has prompted me to become her proxy and thus, purchase her freedom. She is unaware of my intentions. But with your permission I humbly ask that I be allowed to fulfill her requirement for these two remaining years."*

"When can you begin?" Mr. Demerest quickly responded.

Mrs. Demerest reached over and pinched his scrawny arm. *"Hush!"*

CHAPTER

28

Full of sincere advice and reluctant good wishes, Mr. Gehman loaded Agnes' bags onto the bed of the carriage. *"My dear girl, I can't help but believe that this choice is not in your best interest."*

Agnes smiled up at him as she stooped down to hug Liddy, three-years-old, and the youngest Gehman daughter. Giving her an extra hard squeeze Agnes whispered in the child's ear. *"Always give the Lord His praise, little one, no matter what comes."*

"I will, Miss Agnes," Liddy replied with tears welling up in her innocent eyes.

Rising and brushing her skirts smooth, Agnes picked up the heavy satchel next to her and walked toward the cart, her back ramrod straight, feeling blessed and surprisingly serene. *"Mr. Gehman, I believe that you are correct. This choice is not in my best interest, but it is in the best interest of my friend and this I must do. God will see to my future. I thank you for your kindness toward me. May God bless you and your children as you embark on your approaching marriage."*

The ride to the Red Owl was slow and bumpy. Agnes felt sickeningly faint as the afternoon sun beat down in unrelenting brightness framed in a cloudless sky. The driver was a chatty man in his fifties whose continuous conversation, fixed on the atrocities sweeping the frontier, did not amend the waves of nausea welling up inside of her. His lively descriptions of the tortuous, maimed, and ruined lives only further agitated her already tenuous stomach and she clutched her belly tighter with every bounce of the cart.

She thought back to the tranquil wagon ride she had enjoyed with the elderly farmer two weeks earlier. She missed his gift of modest conversation. This current driver thought it his duty to fill every silent moment with rattling nonsense and brutal stories. A profound relief swept over her whole body as the Red Owl came into view.

Stepping through the door, the rusty hinges squeaked. Mrs. Demerest was the first to spot Agnes. *"Miss Bowen! You are here!"* she hollered, with surprise in her voice. *"Goodness knows we need the help!"* Mr. Demerest snorted in recognition and quickly moved toward Agnes to help her with her bags, as his feisty wife frantically, impatiently had motioned for him to do so.

"My apologies for the delay. I had planned to arrive last week, but circumstances prevented my departure until this day. My former employer required more time to secure a new governess. I only hope that I may now be of good service to you. I will lean greatly on your expertise as my experience in this work is very limited," said Agnes.

Mrs. Demerest preened with pride, *"I will teach you everything I know my dear girl and we will make extra certain that our patrons maintain decorum and dignity with proper behavior. Liza was a precious girl, and it burdens my heart that she was abused in such a deplorable way. We should not have the same fate in your case."*

Mr. Demerest escorted Agnes upstairs to a sparse room in the back corner. A patchwork quilt lay neatly across a small cot. A washstand stood on one wall with a ceramic pitcher and basin. Centered on a small side table adjacent the cot, a single, tapered candle had burned down to the pewter holder, leaving thick layers of creamy melted wax drippings. A Bible sat next to it. Agnes couldn't take her eyes off it.

"That was Liza's. I don't know if she knew how to read, but she was mighty grateful when Reverend Riegel gave it to her," offered Mr. Demerest.

"Reverend Riegel?"

"Yes. He's new to these parts, but what with a shortage of ministers, we are happy to have him, although he does hold to some unique and controversial beliefs. He spent time with the savages. Interesting man. German Reformed."

"And these other items also belong to Liza?" asked Agnes, noting a tattered woolen cloak and a knitted shawl hanging next to a white linen apron on a hook near the door. *"She certainly did not have much did she?"* A sadness could be heard in Agnes's voice as she choked down a silent sob and glanced around the cramped room.

"Nope. She was indentured for a reason. Didn't have anything."

"Thank you, Mr. Demerest. I will be down shortly to begin work. My prayer is that I am not a disappointment. Liza was so very special, and I could never hope to match her capable ways and joyful spirit, but I will work hard."

Mr. Demerest muttered something and walked out the door shaking his head.

Tucking loose strands of hair up inside her mop cap, Agnes pulled the apron hung from the hook. Tying it around her waist, she took a deep breath. The stairs were narrow and steep to the tavern below, and as she descended into her new world, she silently prayed, *"Father God, I pray you give me strength to fulfill this privilege for the sake of Liza."*

The atmosphere was cheerful. As far as Agnes could tell, most of the men seemed honest, bold and hearty, filled with jokes and laughter. She could imagine her brother Thomas here, joining in the merriment. She felt no threat or reason for caution. These were good men. Family men. Hard working. Patriotic men from all walks of life. A group of Provincial officers sat off in a far corner, hunched tightly together, conversing over some seemingly important matter, without the frivolity that the rest of the room exhibited, yet they too appeared civil and polite. Agnes felt encouraged.

"Ready so soon my dear? I am pleased to see that. There are rooms upstairs requiring attention. Bed pans to empty and wash basins to fill. Tomorrow, I will show you where the wash tubs are located, and you can begin laundry duty. Follow me," Mrs. Demerest called out with a lilt in her shrill voice and a bounce in her bulky step.

★ ★ ★ ★ ★

The old chestnut tree was wet and mossy. Tavin leaned against the soggy bark and scanned the valley roads below for signs of patrolling watchmen. They had earlier avoided detection by a party of rambunctious volunteers, diligently scouring the countryside for merciless raiders. The sun was now high, displaying the glittering droplets of the mornings rain across the forest floor. A warm breeze came in from the south. *"The inn is there,"* Tavin pointed, *"at the east end of the valley below."* Turning to Liza who leaned against the opposite side of the tree to catch her breath, he smiled and added, *"We'll stop here and travel the main road at dusk, we should make it just before the sun sets in full."*

"Thank you! I need the rest! These days have been strenuous." she exclaimed and laughed.

Tavin had set a brutal pace and she'd struggled to keep up, yet never complaining. It was important they travel quickly. The sooner they reached the Red Owl the better, while caution was required, especially at this point in the journey. The bounty on Tavin's head was an enticement for anyone, and now, the watchmen forming a make-shift defensive perimeter along the arc of valleys and mountain ridges made matters all the more threatening.

Liza was optimistic, as was her nature. *"God will see to our safe arrival. And then I will explain what happened. Surely my words will be weighed with the utmost attention and truth will prevail."*

"We strive for the best end, and by the best means available to us, yet the scales may be tipped against truth in favor of lies," mumbled Tavin.

Liza smiled up at him, and quoting in German she recited, *"Trust in the Lord with all thine heart; and lean not on thine own understanding. In all thy ways acknowledge Him and He will direct thy paths."* Adding, *"The God of Heaven will not turn from us. Alles ist gut."*

"All is well", Tavin mused. *"My mother used that phrase often. It irritated me at the time. Her faith was paramount, and everything came back to trusting God. I was bitter and angry. I couldn't see life the way she did. When she was murdered, a burning fury exploded inside my heart, and I could see no use for God. What use was it to pray or to seek Him?"*

He paused, shifting his musket behind his back. His blue eyes glowing, triumphant, he sat down and thoughtfully continued, *"I see His hand everywhere now, just the way mother did. Sometimes there is only the hard way, and I am tempted to howl, 'Woe is me!' and then the cries of a crucified Christ bring me to my knees in humbleness before the throne of the Father. The demands for redemption and justice are satisfied in Christ and any suffering I endure cannot compare to His."*

With the darkening blue of the sky, they ventured on toward the Red Owl. Mud puddles lounged periodically across the path reflecting the golden rays of the setting sun. Billowing clouds grabbed the light in displays of deep yellows, lavenders and pinks. Leaping gingerly over each colorful puddle, Liza felt like a child again. Tavin nonchalantly commented as they continued to move along the well-traveled path, *"You can walk around those you know."*

"One cannot forget to enjoy the simple pleasures of life!" she laughed.

Picking up their pace as they approached the Schuylkill Valley, Liza thoughtfully asked, *"Do you think that Asch will be alright? I mean, he is so concerned for you, and for me."*

"Do I think Asch will be fine? Yes. Do I think he's sitting back over those mountains calmly waiting to see what happens? No. I believe he has tracked us all along. He's not too far behind. But he'll remain up in the hills, hidden."

"What? He's following us?"

"Absolutely."

"How do you know this?"

"Because that's what I'd do."

The Red Owl was now in front of them. They had encountered no trouble along the journey and Tavin breathed a sigh of relief and a prayer of thanks. He pushed the heavy door open. The rusty hinges squeaked, and he stepped inside; Liza was close behind. Adjusting his eyes to the dark room, he recognized the stout woman behind the bar. Motioning Liza forward, they passed several tables of interested men who eyed Liza, ignoring Tavin. Liza, oblivious, smiled broadly and greeted Mrs. Demerest, who seemed delighted and perplexed at the same time. *"Liza!"* she squealed.

Liza eagerly began, *"Good evening Mrs. Demerest. Deepest apologies for my sudden and unexpected departure, but once I explain the true circumstances, I believe that your kind and considerate nature will comprehend the distress and danger of my situation. But I assure you, I am here now to satisfy the contract."*

"Oh my!" cried Mrs. Demerest, adding, *"Miss Agnes told me that you would return. I just didn't believe it."*

"Agnes? Agnes was here?"

"She lives here. She works here. She's upstairs as we speak cleaning rooms for new patrons arriving by coach tonight."

Rubbing her head, her glossy green eyes strained for understanding, Liza questioned, *"You must forgive me, but I am speaking of Agnes Bowen. There must be some confusion."*

"Yes. Yes, Agnes Rose Bowen. She arrived here a week or so ago. If I had even a little of the gumption that girl has, I wouldn't be working in this tavern. She came in here, challenging Mr. Hoch to his face. He backed down too, as quick as a wink. That's what told me she was telling the truth about you being attacked and that this young man, she nodded toward Tavin, *"was innocent all along."*

"Liza! Tavin!" came a loud cry from the top of the stairs.

Leaping down the steps, Agnes crossed the room, her skirts and apron waving wildly as she ran, throwing herself into Tavin's embrace, while at the same time stretching an arm to hug Liza's neck. *"I've been so anxious for you. You are both free! The truth was told and charges against Tavin are dropped. I have so much to tell you both."* her words seemed to tumble over each other in a chaos of energy.

Laughing, Tavin enfolded her tightly, *"You have liberated all decorum, Agnes Bowen,"* he whispered in her ear, noticing the blurry-eyed judgment of several nearby patrons.

Releasing her grip on him, she glanced around the murky room. *"It matters not. My joy cannot be contained."*

Tears flowed down Liza's flushed cheeks. *"It is so good to see you, Agnes. But what are you doing here?"*

Mrs. Demerest boldly interrupted, *"She serves as your proxy. I tried to talk her out of it, but she is a stubborn girl, insisting that she fill your position. She has indentured herself to service here for the duration of your contract."*

"No. I cannot allow you to do that Agnes. This is my responsibility."

"And now, it has fallen to me," Agnes firmly stated. *"My life has been one of ease and privilege in comparison to the tragedies and hardships you have endured. This is not to say that I have not agonized through grief and loss. I have. My parents and brother were murdered. I was carried off to suffer as a slave in an Indian village, just as you."* Agnes took both of Liza's hands in

hers, and added, *"Yet the Lord has taught me so much through my anguish. He showed me what a silly, selfish girl I was, with my head so easily turned by the prospects of wealth and status. Through you, Asch and Tavin, God showed me what it means to truly follow Him. Jesus gave his life to pay my debt and now please allow me to pay this debt for you. I honor Him in doing so. Please do not take this from me."*

Stunned, Liza had no words. Tavin interrupted the silence, *"Mrs. Demerest, may I beseech you to allow Agnes a few hours of personal time. There is much needed sorting."*

"Of course. Her upstairs chores are almost complete. She may take some time before the coach arrives this evening."

Stepping back outside, Tavin breathed in the brisk evening air. Gloomy, wet clouds spit rain and the wind caught Agnes's apron, whipping it up over her head. Laughing, she pulled it down, while her mop cap loosened and spun up into the air. Tavin ran to catch it as it merrily tumbled across the road. *"Let it go!"* called Agnes. *"I've never liked a cap."*

Liza pointed toward the barn, *"We can find shelter to talk there."*

The barn immediately imposed images of that dark night so many weeks before. Quickly pushing the memories from her mind, Liza asked, *"Agnes, could you please explain the considerations that have brought you to this place?"*

As Agnes explained, Tavin's jaw tightened. He was released from the assault accusations leveled at him by an evil and manipulative man, Mr. Hoch. He no longer had to hide from a bounty. And yet now this man, Hoch, was free to live his life with no further accountability. There was no justice. Agnes had cut a deal removing the legal charges against Tavin, while allowing Mr. Hoch full liberty. *"God will see to justice,"* was Agnes's calm reply, reading Tavin's thoughts. A recollection momentarily flashed across Tavin's mind as those very words had come from his own mouth convincing Asch to trust God before seeking revenge on Leeds.

Liza excused herself, *"You two need to talk now. I will wait with Mrs. Demerset. I am certain that she is eager to hear of my circumstance."*

Mr. Hoch was not the only issue that caused Tavin's anger to swell. Agnes had bound herself to servitude. Just when the pieces of his life seemed to fall into place, there was another hill to climb, another obstacle to overcome. The Demerests could grant permission for Agnes to marry, if they saw fit, but what kind of life was that?

As Agnes had predicted, Tavin had truly become a man of the wild. Living peacefully as a farmer in the valley was no option. Farming was no longer an ambition. His mind spun in loops with conflicting thoughts and feelings. Truthfully, he had no idea who he was anymore. All he knew was that Asch and Liza could now be together, while he and Agnes would be forced to wait two years. Tavin had dreamed of marriage and a home with Agnes. Now she was describing a call from God. A call that did not include him.

"This is not acceptable!" he angrily spouted.

"Tavin, I understand your frustration. None of this is a matter of fairness or justice. My love for you remains, but this is honoring God and placing someone else above my own wants and desires. I can do no less. I do this for Liza and for Asch. Their future will be fraught with more challenges than we will ever know. The time they have together will be hard, but at least they will have a chance to create a life in this moment…right now…for whatever time God allows. I have spoken with Reverend Andreas Riegel…."

Tavin perked up from his slumped posture, *"Wait! What name did you say?"*

"Reverend Riegel. He is new to the area, having lived with the Seneca, at Shamokin Village, before returning to the Tulpehocken Valley and now here…."

"Yes. I know the name," Tavin interrupted, reflecting on his conversation with Drake after Job was killed along the riverbank. *"It was Riegel who first shared the gospel message with Do:hsetweh, dubbing him 'Job', due to the tragedies of his life. I would very much like to meet him."*

"God's hand is always working!" Agnes beamed. *"Reverend Riegel has agreed to perform a marriage, having great empathy for Indian people, despising the prejudice and hatred coming from so many of the German, Dutch and English. When I explained the circumstances, he was most sympathetic. Since neither Liza or Asch have family to grant the customary approval and since Liza is no longer indentured, he has consented to marry them with the authority of a license."*

"You have been busy since I left you two weeks ago," said Tavin, shaking his head.

Walking with Tavin, hand in hand back to the tavern, the conflict concerning her indentured position rested between them for later discussion. Agnes sat down at a table in the corner with Liza, explaining the details and circumstances of the past weeks in animated enthusiasm. Tavin watched and wondered at the change in Agnes. No longer timid to stand on her own beliefs, nor held down by social dictates, she seemed freer and more alive than Tavin had ever seen her. With her feet planted on the solid ground of faith, her joy could not be contained. He couldn't help but smile to himself.

"The Lord has been so good!" Agnes all but yelled.

"What do I do now?" asked Liza, feeling overwhelmed with the flood of information.

"Well, for the moment, I will verify whether Mrs. Demerest has a spare room. If not, I can fix up a pallet on the floor of my room and you can sleep in your old bed tonight."

"I would argue but I am truly exhausted, and I can see that you are now no one to disagree with!" laughed Liza.

Tavin stood next to Agnes with his hand resting on her shoulder, *"I will go back up the mountain. I have no doubt that I can find Asch up there."*

Just then the stagecoach from Easton pulled to a stop in front of the Red Owl Inn.

CHAPTER

29

Heavy snorts steamed from the nostrils of horses; glistening sweat dripped from their noses. Jumping down from his seat, the driver loudly announced, *"Red Owl Ordinary here! Your rooms should be ready. Enjoy your stay."* Tavin paid no attention to the commotion in the darkness of the evening.

"You have only just arrived. Can't you wait until morning to go?" pleaded Agnes.

"Better to find Asch sooner than later. Who knows what kind of trouble he'll find without me," laughed Tavin. Gathering up his pack and bow as he slung his musket across his back, he reached out and wrapped his arm confidently around Agnes's waist, pulling her tight. *"You are an amazing woman. You will be my wife, whether now or two years from now."*

Agnes gave a coy smile, *"I was hoping you'd come to that decision."* Her hands cupped his face and she pulled him down closer. *"I know that you are still angry, and I am sorry. Truly, I am."* He kissed her firmly and bolted across the shadowy yard, leaping over a fence to cross a muddy field. Agnes watched until she could see the shadow of him no more, her heart overflowing with a love she thought she'd never have. Liza stood next to her. *"Your sacrifice for my sake is too much."*

Smiling Agnes quoted, *"walk in love, as Christ also hath loved us, and hath given Himself for us an offering and a sacrifice to God for a sweet-smelling savor.' Walking in love as Christ walked in love. This is my sacrifice, which is also my joy."*

Liza hooked her arm through Agnes's, *"You make it hard to disagree."*

"Yes. Yes, I do," laughed Agnes. *"I'd better get busy. Mrs. Demerest will want my help in the kitchen."*

"If it is alright with you, may I presume upon your kind offer and rest on the cot in your room?"

"Sleep there tonight. I will comfortably make do with a pallet on the floor."

The following morning Agnes rose before dawn, as was her custom. Spending time in prayer, a candle sputtered and flickered on the table, where she sat in the corner of the tavern. Once finished, feeling refreshed and alive, she tucked her hair inside the new mop cap Mrs. Demerest had provided, and mumbled to herself, *"Of all the things about this whole situation, this unavailing cap vexes me the most,"* and then giggled to herself.

Stepping outside Mrs. Demerest was busy stirring a large cauldron of porridge over an open fire with a slender teenage girl assisting. *"This will be ready soon. Agnes, bring some bowls and scoop up servings for our guests. Hot water for tea is in the kettle. Hurry."* Mrs. Demerest was always a little scattered and frantic with overnight guests. *"Yes ma'am."*

Several men had already gathered around tables waiting for food. *"It won't be long. Breakfast will be here shortly,"* Agnes assured, as she steeped tea leaves in the boiling water for several minutes, before pouring cups of the dark brew into pewter mugs. A pleasant looking man in his forties, politely replied with his thanks while the others seemed to ignore her altogether, as she served them.

"Mr. Leeds, what is it you say that you do again?" came a question from the other side of the room. A mug slipped from Agnes's hand. It dropped to the floor, spilling hot tea around her feet. Eyes turned to her. She smiled nervously, *"Not to worry gentleman. Clumsy on my part."*

Pouring a fresh cup, she ambled to the table where the man, Leeds, sat. *"Would you care for more tea, sir?"* she asked while eyeing the man carefully. *"Yes. Set it down."* Agnes noticed a deep scar stretching across his forehead and his thick brown bristly beard. A black tri-cornered hat sat on the table. But what struck her most were his eyes. Rigid, close and narrow.

Having never seen him, Agnes knew who Leeds was. Tavin had told her enough. Her heart began to pound with anxious worry. *"If Tavin and Asch see him, there will be violence. They will never let Leeds go, not again."* Her mind swirled with what to do. Finally, she prayed that Tavin and Asch would not return to the Red Owl until Leeds was gone. Reaching in to remove dirty plates and mugs, she overheard him say that he was going to scout for a Provincial advance to reinforce the newly constructed Fort Swatara.

As she listened it became clear that Leeds was a trusted companion. *"I am here to help guide our troops to defeat those French scoundrels! We shall soon take Fort Duquesne!"* he boasted and pounded his fist on the table. His zeal and charisma were convincing, although Agnes knew his true intentions. He was spying for the French.

She purposely cleaned a nearby table where Leeds sat crowing of his exploits and condemning French occupation. Laughter and robust slaps on the back encouraged his deception. Slowly replacing candle stubs with new tapers, her ears strained to catch every word. A Provincial officer stepped over and joined in the conversation, notably offering his admiration, as Leeds continued in his verbose tales. Agnes listened to catch the officers name, hoping to speak with him later, but it never came. *"If I could only have the chance, maybe Leeds could be arrested as a spy before Tavin and Asch realize that he is here,"* she silently thought, while just as quickly realizing that she had no proof, only second-hand knowledge. No one would take her word.

★   ★   ★   ★   ★

Suppressing a smile, Tavin knelt on the creek bed. *"Can a man not even get a drink without you sneaking up behind him?"* turning to see Asch casually leaning on his musket. The misty fog of morning molded eerily at his feet, rising in soft ghostly wisps over his body, and swirling up toward the illuminating sky.

"It is good to see you, my brother," offered Asch.

"You as well. It is no surprise that you followed. I expected to find you skulking around up here, close by."

"You travelled alone with the woman who is to be my wife. I was not going to just let you leave with her. Figured she'd need more protection than you," said Asch, squatting down next to Tavin to scoop water into his mouth. Tavin chuckled.

"I have news. Seems that you may be a husband sooner than you thought. Liza is free. Agnes has taken the indenture and arrangements have been made for your marriage. She is indeed a formidable force, as stubborn as a dog with a bone!" Both admiration and irritation could be heard in Tavin's voice.

"Maybe she learned from watching you," said Asch, with a slight smile. *"But what arrangements do you speak of?"*

"Reverend Riegel, the same man who lived at Shamokin, Agnes has spoken with him, and he is sympathetic to your plight. Liza waits with Agnes at the Red Owl for her groom to arrive. I am amazed at how God wraps our lives to His will and demonstrates His sovereignty through the circumstances we find ourselves in."

Asch thoughtfully nodded, *"God twists things in strange ways."*

"He does!" exclaimed Tavin. *"I do not understand so much. I see His hand at work, and I am angry. How can I be happy with Agnes's decision? She has sacrificed her future. She has ignored my feelings and moved ahead without considering me at all. Please do not misunderstand, I am happy that you and Liza will be together, but it comes with loss. I will lose two years waiting for Agnes."*

"This is hard. It seems God continues to go against you, and Agnes follows."

Tavin stood and reflected for a moment. Finally, he spoke, seemingly to himself as much as Asch, *"I know that God is not against me, and I respect Agnes and her faith in God's leading. My faith is feeble, and I am ashamed to say that I doubted Agnes and God."* He picked up his pack, grabbed his musket and slung it over his head, firmly stating, *"Agnes has acted in selfless sacrifice and God has proven Himself over and over. How can I be bitter? Your words have helped me. Although I cannot say that I have resolved my feelings to a permanent measure. It will take time."*

Asch stood and shook his head in bewilderment, *"As always, you are a confusing man. What now?"*

"Now, we go! You are getting married!"

★   ★   ★   ★   ★

Birds chirped merrily relishing the morning sun after a heavy rain the night before. Reverend Riegel remained true to his word in performing a Christian ceremony for Liza and Asch. Tavin marveled as they solemnly pledged their loyalty and love to each other. There had been no traditional courting, there was no financial future, no dowry, and no expectations that they would meet any social norms at all. None of that mattered. The only thing that appeared to be important was their deep devotion to God and to one another. They were indeed free, just as Asch had predicted.

Agnes stood behind Liza wearing a light blue linen dress, with a square neckline, lined in delicate lace. She held the bouquet of white and yellow spring flowers she had picked alongside the Red Owl. Delicate curls framed her pretty face, and tears rolled down her flushed cheeks as she caught Tavin's stare. Sun streamed in through a small window, outlining her body and Tavin thought she looked like an angel, just as she had so many months before in Bethlehem as she sat on the seat of that borrowed buggy.

He gave a knowing smile and redirected his attention to the words of Reverend Riegel. *"Please recite this pledge; I take you as my spouse and promise to you my faithfulness in all ways. I will keep you in sickness and in health and in whatever condition it will please the Lord to place you, and that I shall not exchange you for better or for worse until the end."*

"Amen. You are now husband and wife." Riegel coughed as he pronounced the final words, jolting Tavin back to attention, his mind having wandered once again. Agnes squealed with joy as Asch kissed his new wife, looking every bit the regal Iroquois warrior that he was.

Liza's face beamed with happiness as she adjusted the ivory embroidered wrap around her neck, a gift from Agnes. Agnes's mind floated back to the day she and her mother had packed to escape the raids. She had folded that elegant wrap, her grandmother's, and carefully stored it in the trunk. As warriors pilfered through the belongings, they thoughtlessly discarded it as worthless. It meant nothing to them, yet Agnes saw it as a thread of promise, of life.

It was the same ivory shawl that Tavin had wrapped around the Grover's infant girl as he discovered her on that bloodied path. Agnes was amazed and stirred with gratitude when Tavin returned it to her. Mrs. Grover had surmised that it might mean something special to Agnes. She was correct and now Agnes had given the most meaningful thing she owned to Liza as a wedding gift. *"You are a beautiful bride! May God bless you and Asch with His love and mercy! I shall miss you so very much!"*

Mrs. Demerest filled the doorway with her bulk, waving frantically. Liza twisted around, almost losing her balance on the plodding horse, and waved back. Her wide eyes as green as the budding spring leaves, matching the deep green of her fitted wedding gown, a gift from Mrs. Demerest. Liza was humbled at the generosity.

Asch tightened his grip on the reins of the old broken-down horse, and continued walking. Uncomfortable in the open space of the well-travelled road, he was eager to get higher into the lush mountains. Asch firmly led the aging mare, an endowment from Mr. Demerest, who had planned to put her down that week. She resisted the quick pace, pulling back and throwing her head, while Asch's eyes continually darted back and forth, alert for trouble. White vigilantes or painted Lenape raiders all offered a threat. Survival had always dictated his life and he was especially aware on this trip with his radiant wife.

Agnes peered through the upstairs window. She'd said her good-byes earlier and couldn't bear to watch as Asch and Liza rode away, although now she found herself pressed up against the cloudy glass with tears flowing freely. The wedding ceremony had brought no fanfare, and no one in attendance except for Tavin, Mrs. Demerest and herself. It was a marriage made between two of the most unlikely, and wonderful people Agnes had ever known and now she watched as they disappeared over the first rise of the road. Her mind went back to Adoniram Leeds, and she thanked the Lord that no one, except for her, knew that he was now in Reading.

Smoothing her skirts, she reached for her apron hanging on the hook. The bright room felt dingy and cold. Wiping her eyes, she donned her mop cap and frowned to herself. Downstairs Mrs. Demerest sat alone at a table, crying into her white hanky. Looking up as Agnes slumped down the steps, her naturally ruddy cheeks flushed to bright red, she sniffed and murmured, *"My dear girl, should we all be blessed with such a love as I have witnessed this day between those two precious youngsters."*

"Indeed, my heart soars with joy for them as well. I only pray that they see long years together. They come from two different worlds. The road will not be

easy, but their love holds them tightly and their faith sustains their future, no matter how difficult."

"I have never had a love like that. Mr. Demerest is a fine enough man, but love was never a consideration at our marriage."

Agnes was quiet, not knowing how to respond. Finally, she simply said, *"Life is often fraught with regret and doubt. Trusting in God is our only solace."* And at that, she went to work scrubbing the tables.

★ ★ ★ ★ ★

Stepping into the makeshift building masquerading as a church, Tavin called out, *"Is anyone here!?"* There was only silence and dusty sunshine streaming in through a small window on the side wall. Walking toward the front, he observed the crude pulpit and wondered at the simplicity, having paid it no mind a week earlier. He returned now to have a conversation with Reverend Riegel. He had questions. Lots of questions.

A voice suddenly called from outside. Tavin stepped out and found Reverend Andreas Riegel sitting awkwardly atop a slouched-backed mare. *"Mr. Shire, what can I do for you?"*

Tavin smiled and scratched his head, *"Well, first I want to bring my gratitude for performing an unconventional marriage. Controversial, I'm sure. And then, I wonder if you recall a man, an Indian, by the name of Do:hsetweh?"*

Riegel's eyes lit up, *"Yes! Job! I lived at Shamokin. While there I met Job. He had toiled under great cruelties and God worked a miracle in his dejected and desolate heart. I am curious, how do you come to know him?"*

"It is a long story, but Job saved my life, as well as the lives of others, while sacrificing his own. When I heard that you had known him, I wanted to understand what had happened at Shamokin."

"It is God who effects change in a heart. I am only a vessel, a servant, placed in this world to do all the good I possibly can." Riegel paused for a moment and thoughtfully continued, adjusting himself in the saddle. *"Job's life had been pressed almost to death, first naturally, by smallpox and then by his own hand. God's mercy guided him from a lonely desert to the springs of life. The sacrifice of Jesus Christ covered the depravity that dwelt inside of Job, as it dwells in us all. Job became a true believer. Make no mistake, he remained a fierce Iroquois, while at the same time he sought to live for God's glory, not*

his own. He didn't do it perfectly, of course, none of us do. I am sorry to hear of Job's death. But I have confidence that he arrived gloriously in the Father's house." Reverend Riegel took a deep breath, pulling a handkerchief from his pocket he coughed violently into it. Perspiration glistened on his forehead.

Tavin smiled, *"You have confirmed what I had come to believe about Job."*

"And what of you, Mr. Shire? I sense a great unsettledness in you." Riegel coughed hard once more and uttered, *"Pardon me."*

Tavin noted how thin Riegel was. His rumpled clothes hung on his gaunt frame and his skin appeared sallow. Dark circles ringed his eyes. He was obviously suffering an illness and was not offering any complaint or explanation. Tavin could respect that. He answered Riegel's question, impressed with the man's keen perception. *"It's true. My faith falters. Yet just when it seems I am on the brink of giving up, He washes over me with His goodness. Agnes, whom you know, is to be my wife. I am trying to come to terms with the fact that I must wait two years for her. Choosing to trust God is difficult, even after He has shown me His faithfulness over and over."*

"You have time. Don't waste it. God has a purpose," said Riegel.

"I plan to approach the command in Reading. I will offer to gather intelligence of the enemy's strength and movements, while obtaining greater knowledge of where and how captives are held. Scouting. I have been back and forth over the mountains many times and know the land."

"I have no doubt that your experience will come as great aide. Sadly, vast numbers have lost their lives or been carried off. British forces have been bolstering up in support of Provincial militia and are currently building guardhouses along the ridge of the Blue Mountain. I have heard rumors of plans for an insurgence north. Perhaps you can join them. Several Indian scouts as well as an experienced English tracker are ready to guide them through."

"Thank you. God willing, I can be of assistance. As you said, I shouldn't waste the time when there is so much suffering."

Riegel coughed again, *"If it will help, I can speak with Captain Smith in Reading. He may have some influence in seeing to the number of scouts that Mr. Leeds recruits."*

"Leeds? Did you say Leeds?"

"Yes, he arrived two weeks or more back from Easton. An interesting and engaging man, whom I would not want to cross!"

Tavin shuffled his feet, looking at the ground, gathering his racing thoughts. *"Again, I thank you. You have been a great help. And may God bless you in your work here,"* he calmly said, taking the reins of the fidgety horse, borrowed from Mr. Demerest. The horse snorted and threw her head as he swung into the saddle and rode directly for Reading.

CHAPTER

30

June 1756

The town was bustling. Warmer temperatures brought people out from inside their houses, and they filled the streets. Children played games of hide-and-seek, leapfrog, and tag. Ladies sauntered about together in casual dresses wearing hoods, mop-caps or high brimmed straw hats with colorful ribbons to protect their fair skin from the sun. Militiamen stood on corners eyeing women and making quiet comments to each other. Winter had been bleak with terrible news of massacres and kidnappings. Now, the new life of spring brought with it new hope. As Tavin looked around he knew it to be a misguided expectation.

Finding command headquarters, Tavin boldly approached, his resolve driving his confidence. *"I need to speak with Colonel Weiser immediately."*

A stalwart guard asked, *"And who might you be?"*

"My name is Tavin Shire. I recently returned from a scouting expedition for Lt. Colonel Clapham with the Third Battalion Pennsylvania Provincial Regiment, at Fort Augusta along the Susquehanna. I have valuable information." Tavin weighed his words carefully to give the best impression, standing straight and tall.

"I doubt that he will see you, but you can wait here." The private scurried inside the unimpressive limestone building and returned in quick order. *"The colonel will see you."*

Lt. Colonel Weiser sat comfortably behind a small desk, with papers and maps scattered across it. He stood when Tavin entered and extended his hand. *"Clapham informed me of your reconnaissance at Fort Duquesne. Your report was passed on to me. Was there something more to add?"* Weiser was a direct, no-nonsense man. Sitting back in his chair as Tavin began, he folded his hands across his belly and listened with consideration.

"A Lenape raiding party attacked my family near the Swatara, last November. My mother was killed, my sisters taken and my brother severely injured. With the help of three Iroquois friends, I was able to retrieve my sisters. While returning them back across the Blue Mountain, to Bethlehem, I was befriended by a man named Adoniram Leeds. Leeds portrayed himself as a patriot and loyal to the crown but was discovered to be a spy for the French. He is instrumental in the murder of innocent people. He has inspired Lenape and Huron raiding parties and is now here, in Reading, preparing to scout for the regiment. His allegiance stands with the French, and he should be detained. He is a spy." Tavin spoke in nervous, quick sentences, aware that he sounded unstable at best, a madman more likely.

"Thank you, Mr. Shire. I shall take this to my commanders and investigate your claims."

"I beg your pardon sir, but I must tell you. Leeds is crafty and convincing. If it comes to my word against his, I fear that I will be dismissed."

"Do you have any other witnesses to Mr. Leeds' loyalties?"

Tavin thought for a moment, hesitant to bring up Asch, then replied, *"I do. A friend. He was there. He saw what Leeds did and knows who Leeds is. My friend's mother and father lived near the Mahantango. Leeds murdered them."*

"Well enough. Bring him in and we shall dispose of this matter quickly."

Tavin pressed further, *"I will need time. My friend is over the mountain with his wife. There is another thing. His mother was Seneca and his father white. Will his word be honored?"*

Weiser did not hesitate to answer, *"It will."*

"And will Leeds be detained until we return?" Tavin pushed again.

Weiser adjusted his grey powdered wig with both hands and stood, impressed with the persistence of this rough-hewn young man. *"Other than Captain Smith, whom I shall confer, we will keep this between the two of us and we will see that Mr. Leeds is not dispatched until your return. But I must tell you, an expedition to retake Fort Duquesne is intended once additional support arrives. Upon this consideration, I cannot impede this singular objective. If you have not returned to that point, Leeds will go with the advance."*

"I understand. Thank you, sir," said Tavin as he turned to walk out.

"Mr. Shire," Weiser called after him. *"Your services may be valuable in the future, as they were for Clapham at Fort Augusta. When you return, I'd like to discuss some possibilities."*

"Yes sir. Once this is resolved, I'd be pleased to speak with you further."

Weiser nodded and promptly turned his attention to the maps on his desk.

Stepping out into the warm sunshine felt somewhat calming to Tavin's pounding heart. He stood, turning his face upward, allowing the warmth to wash over him, as he whispered, *"Lord, help me to do your will. Walking away while Leeds is so near goes against every fiber of my being. I could find him and inflict my own justice. This is my temptation, to spare Asch from further danger."* Images shifted between Leeds standing over Job's lifeless body and killing Asch's family. He took the dirty beaded pouch that Leeds had left next to Wolfe's body and turned it in his hands. Asch had given it to Tavin, to remember why they searched for Leeds. Shaking off the troubling thoughts, Tavin walked briskly toward the horse that Mr. Demerest had named Gris. Taking the chestnut's bridle, he rubbed her neck before mounting into the worn saddle. *"Gris, we have a trip to make."* Kicking her sides, he rode northwest for Asch, without further reflection or preparation.

★ ★ ★ ★ ★

Liza chopped frantically at stubborn clumps of dirt, her white apron swinging with each determined motion. She had tucked her dark skirt up into her waistband, exposing beaded moccasins rising almost to her knees. A straw hat sat precariously on her head, tied with a pink ribbon under her chin. Tavin called out from the hillside, *"Liza!"* Straightening her back, she recognized him immediately and began

221

waving enthusiastically. *"Tavin! It is good to see you, although it has been but ten days!"* she laughed, her wide eyes sparkling. *"I did not expect to see you so soon. Is all well? Agnes?"* Her voice was hopeful, while guarded.

"Alle sist gut. Agnes remains under the watchful care of Mrs. Demerest. After your experience, I'm surprised she lets Agnes out of her sight. As protective as a mother hen." Tavin dismounted and asked, *"Is Asch here?"*

"He left early this morning to hunt. I expect him back soon. Please come inside, you look spent. Have you come with no supplies?"

"I'm afraid I left in a hurry without giving much regard."

"Well, you are here safely now. I have tea brewing and a stew in the cauldron, although there is very little meat in it. My hope is that Asch brings home a deer or elk."

Tavin stepped inside the cabin. The table, still scorched from fire, and the long benches pushed neatly under it, brought back memories of Berta and Katherine sitting mesmerized by Mary. Tavin walked to the stone fireplace and turned to look toward the door, imagining Leeds gun jamming and Wolfe getting off a shot. Looking down at the floor, dark brown stain droplets remained where Leeds had been hit in the leg. So much had happened in only a few short months."

"Are you ok?" asked Liza.

"Yes. Just remembering."

"Asch will often drift off in the same way, deep in thought," said Liza as she reached out to hug Tavin.

Just then Asch walked in. *"If you are trying to steal my woman, you'll have to fight me,"* he laughed.

"I would never dare fight you. You are too weak. You could get hurt," Tavin jabbed back.

The two friends laughed together in natural and familiar understanding. *"You have restored this cabin in a good way,"* said Tavin, accepting the mug of hot tea that Liza handed to him.

"Wiyóaje'," Asch replied. *"It's improving,"* he translated, looking at Liza.

Liza smiled and nodded her head. *"Asch is helping me with his language. It is very complicated!"*

"And Liza is teaching me of God from the book."

"*I pray that God gives you many years together and many children!*" Tavin exclaimed, toasting into the air with his mug. Liza blushed and Asch beamed.

The sun set and the night gave way to cooler temperatures. Liza stoked the fire and the three sat at the table sharing news and anecdotes. Fresh wildflowers cascaded over the edges of an old pewter cup on the center of the table; a taper candle burned low next to it. The brightness of the hearth danced shadows on the walls in seeming merriment, until Tavin came to the point of his visit. "*I come here for more than camaraderie.*"

"*You have news. Unpleasant news,*" suspected Asch.

"*That depends on how you look at it. I have found Leeds.*"

The muscles in Asch's jaw tightened. His grey eyes narrowed and through gritted teeth, he asked, "*Where?*"

Tavin carefully explained what he had learned and the conclusion of his conversation with Weiser. Liza reached out and took Asch's hand, sliding closer to him on the bench, her eyes soft. "*I knew this day would come. I prayed it would not be so soon.*"

"*We can leave in the morning,*" Asch abruptly replied, gazing with hatred at the door as if an unseen enemy stood ready for retribution.

That night, Liza curled close to her husband and whispered, "*Vengeance is bitter medicine, Asch. I would ask you not to go, but I know you must.*"

Asch sat up and wrapped his strong arms around her, pulling her tightly against him. "*I want to do what is right. Leeds killed my parents in this cabin. Justice must come.*"

A long silence followed and finally Liza pleaded, "*I beg only three things of you. Do not murder Leeds. Trust God. And don't die.*"

Asch smiled in the darkness. Sensing Liza's face turned up toward him, he leaned down and kissed her. "*You would have me release Leeds from facing a reckoning. He deserves to die at my hand.*"

"*God calls you to seek justice, but not vengeance. It says in the Bible, "O man, what is good; and what doth the Lord require of thee, but to do justly, and to love mercy, and to walk humbly with thy God."*"

Asch tensed, "*There will be no mercy for Leeds.*"

"*All I am saying is that God is the ultimate judge, and He will exact His reprisal to those who deserve it. It is not yours. Eternity will right the wrongs of time here on earth."* Liza tightened her arms around him, *"No matter what happens, you have my love, forever."*

He quietly replied, whispering, *"I will consider your words."* The silence lingered and they fell asleep embraced in each other's arms.

CHAPTER

31

A rooster crowed. Agnes stretched and yawned before swinging her feet onto the cold wood floor. The sun had yet to peek over the horizon, while illuminating the eastern sky with subtle hints of gold. The floor creaked as she walked to the water basin and splashed her face. Smoothing the wrinkles of her cotton nightdress, she quickly pulled on a petticoat and tied a pocket around her waist. Reaching for her white apron, she suddenly remembered that she had washed it the day before and it hung on the line outside.

Breathing in the cool morning air, Agnes strolled barefoot toward the clotheslines, hoping that the dew hadn't been too heavy the night before. As she reached for the apron, a familiar voice called her name, *"Agnes!"* Spinning around, she covered her eyes against the brightness of the rising sun to see Tavin jump the fence and cross the road. Running toward her, the fringe on his buckskins waving as wild as his hair, Agnes caught her breath. *"Tavin!"* she called out.

Tavin scooped her up into his arms. She laughed, *"Where have you been? I have been so worried!"* Asch came around through the gate of the fence, leading Gris and the old nag that the Demerest's had gifted, and called a greeting, his white teeth shining with his smile.

"It's a long story." Tavin answered. *"Asch and I are headed for Conrad Weiser, but I wanted you to hear what was happening first. Besides, I missed you."* Agnes threw her arms around his neck.

As Tavin explained the circumstances of how he had discovered Leeds, Agnes listened attentively, silently debating whether she should admit to seeing Leeds when he had first arrived. She had withheld that information from Tavin for fear that violence would result. She did not regret it, yet she felt guilty.

Her prayer now was that the Provincial militia would exact the rule of law, arresting Leeds as a spy, sparing Tavin and Asch the revenge that drove them as sure as a hawk searching its prey. *"Come inside. A hot breakfast will do you well,"* she quickly insisted.

Agnes heaped large portions of cornmeal porridge into bowls, topping it with maple syrup that was reserved for special guests. Pouring hot tea into mugs, she peppered the two hungry men with questions. *"How is Liza? Is she happy? Is the garden planted? Will Colonel Weiser honor his word? Will he believe Asch? Will they seize Leeds?"* Tavin gave Asch a quick smile and patiently answered her flurry.

Mr. Demerest entered the room with a scowl on his sunken face. *"Are these paying customers?"* he questioned. *"You may add another day to my indenture if that will satisfy the bill,"* Agnes responded without hesitation and giggled. No one could throw cold water on her warm heart. Seeing Tavin brought calm to her worried mind, and she silently praised God for His goodness.

An hour later, she said goodbye again, and watched as they rode on down the road, their horses plodding indifferently. *"Father God, hold them in your loving care,"* she prayed, silently nervous that the eager volunteers combing the countryside might mistake Asch and Tavin for hostiles.

★　★　★　★　★

"Your words are compelling," said Weiser. Tavin and Asch sat expectantly, waiting for Colonel Weiser's final decision. *"I have spoken with Mr. Leeds, not disclosing your accusations and only gathered from him his dedication as a patriot, loyal to the crown, which of course is contrary to what you have testified here."* Weiser sat behind his desk and shifted in his chair,

pushing some papers aside. *"That being said, I believe that he is, as you have stated,"* Weiser nodded toward Tavin, *"as crafty as a fox."* Tavin let out his breath, unaware that he had been holding it.

"I have been in communication with British command and the consensus is to allow Mr. Leeds to remain in his position, providing him false information to relay back to the French. The line of forts intended for the ridge along the Blue Mountain are essential for the protection of the population. Any disruption or delay would be detrimental to this objective. In addition, an expedition to retake Fort Duquesne is well into the planning stages."

Asch stood, leaning over Weiser's desk in anger. *"You are letting him go?!"*

Weiser lifted his hand in a gesture allowing calm, *"In a sense. Yes. I understand your frustration, but if we can deceive the French with false intelligence, it will give us an advantage. Once circumstances change and we surmise that Leeds is no longer of use, he will be arrested for espionage and dealt with appropriately."*

Asch straightened, the veins in his neck pulsing and his fists clenched. *"Leeds is a killer. He murdered my parents. He cannot be allowed to escape,"* he yelled.

"I assure you. My officers will see that he is watched carefully," pledged Weiser. Shifting papers around on his desk, Weiser continued, *"Now, there is another matter. Two days past, Fort Granville was descended upon, seized, and destroyed. Led by Francois Coulon de Villiers with over fifty French regulars and Indian allies, they took approximately thirty prisoners, including women and children. The garrison commander, brother to Lieutenant Colonel John Armstrong, was killed. Armstrong is currently readying an expedition of three hundred Pennsylvania Provincial troops to go against the Lenape village of Kittanning, a staging point for attacks across the frontier. Your knowledge of that part of the country would be valuable to this effort."* Glancing back and forth between Tavin and Asch, Weiser waited for a response.

Asch replied first, *"I will not aide a military excursion against a village where women and children will be harmed or killed."*

Weiser responded, *"My sentiments are in accordance with yours."* He paused and lit a pipe. *"Armstrong is going whether we like it or not and my hope is that Kittanning will be destroyed but with caution and restraint given to women and children. Once they realize that we can reach so deeply into their* territory, they will concede to British authority. And as far as the white captives," Weiser looked at Tavin, "I know of your concerns for their recovery. This is an opportunity."

Tavin glanced knowingly at Asch and thought for only a moment, "I will serve as a guide for the expedition, if it means bringing back those who have been taken, but I will not murder innocent people in an unsuspecting village."

"I assure you, I would not want that. If anything, I would hope that you could bring a voice of constraint and objectivity. And as far as Leeds, he will be given false intelligence to pass along. I assure you my officers will see that he is watched carefully," vowed Weiser.

Tavin and Asch left Weiser's office feeling angry and apprehensive in this plan, as well as cheated. Walking back toward where Gris stood wide-eyed, harnessed to a hitching post, and Asch's old mare hung her head in exhaustion, they discussed the turn of events. "I was prepared to challenge Leeds with the truth of who he is and see him put in shackles," Tavin thoughtfully commented.

"I have dreamed of the day that I can avenge my parents." Asch paused, reaching up to swat pesky flies off the ears of his sorry horse, and continued, "But a voice will not leave me, whether it is you, Liza or God, I cannot say for sure. It repeats, 'vengeance is mine'. Maybe this is God's way. It is hard. I want to see Leeds under my hand."

"Your anger is righteous. Evil has shown its wicked face and your rage is justifiable. I feel it too. But where we take that blameless rage is what matters to God. He waits for us to give it to Him. We are slowly learning to listen to His voice. That is a good thing." Tavin paused as if realizing something for the first time, "I am ashamed to admit, my anger toward Agnes's decision to indenture herself is based on selfish motives, not a righteous cause. My pride is offended. She didn't consider me. Walking humbly is my curse. I stumble with it." Tavin reached for the reins and untangled them from the post. Gris snorted and pulled back, happy to be free.

"What will you do now?" asked Asch.

"I will return this borrowed horse," said Tavin as he swung himself into the saddle. "I have pushed the limit of Mr. Demerest's patience. Then I will figure out how I can explain my plans to Agnes. She will not be happy, but I believe God has set this before me. I'll join the advance with Armstrong and continue to wait for plenty of 'opportunity'," joked Tavin.

Asch smiled, rolled his eyes, and eagerly exclaimed, "I return to my wife. And I may just leave this horse alongside the road somewhere. I can move faster without her dragging pace."

"Be well my brother and, God willing, I will see you soon. Take my regards to Liza."

CHAPTER

32

March 1757

Thinning clouds cast an eerie halo across the face of the moon. Winter snow clung against the north side of hills glowing like a white blanket framed by the stark blackness of the forest. Wolves mournfully howled in the distance. The wind sighed its cold breath.

Tavin's mind drifted to Agnes, as it so often did when surrounded by unrelenting silence. Rubbing his hands vigorously over the hot coals of his concealed fire, his stiff fingers tingled and gradually regained feeling. Pulling his cloak tightly around his shoulders he shivered and whispered, *"Agnes. How I miss you."* An owl hooted. Tavin looked up and saw nothing but the twinkling of a million stars through barren branches.

The past months embraced a blur of memories. Tavin had never dreamed that scouting for the Provincial Militia and His Majesty's army would take him so deep into the Ohio Country for so long. Kittanning continued to haunt his dreams as he trekked across the wilds of an unsettled land. September 8, 1756, seared into his mind and resounded in his nightmares. Screams and panic, explosions, and fire. The entire village engulfed in flames.

Some called it a massacre, while most heralded Captain Armstrong and his force as heroes, bringing the Lenape to their knees and killing a prominent war chief, Tewea, known as Captain Jacobs. Tavin saw it as something in between. While there were atrocities committed that could not be washed away, or denied, the surprise attack also yielded the recovery of eleven gaunt men, women, and children. All in varying degrees of physical anguish. Yet most of the white captives were not so fortunate. Ferried north across the Allegheny and then on foot deeper into the Ohio Country, they were beyond reach. While military action could defeat an enemy, it was not the finest tool in recovering prisoners.

Armstrong thanked Tavin for his contribution in guiding them secretly to Kittanning. Tavin nodded politely, feeling a twinge of regret. *"My prayer is that this will be the only incursion necessary to detour the marauders. Both Indian and white alike suffer too much,"* said Tavin. Armstrong made no response but turned to bark orders for his men to withdraw. There was concern that another war party could descend, he wanted to reassemble and move quickly.

Choosing to separate from Armstrong and his large column of men and go his own way, Tavin breathed a deep sigh. It felt like freedom. His recourse was clear: continue to gain intelligence concerning French and Indian movement, strength of force and surmise the locations and number of captives being held. While frustration and conflicting ideals remained, he saw no alternatives. Solutions were short to come by. Nothing more could be done to help those poor souls seized in violent raids, held so far out of reach to the northwest and into New France. Tavin prayed a treaty might be struck and soon.

He had lost track of how long he had actually been gone, but with spring approaching he figured that it was seven, maybe eight months. Truth was, his future felt mired within the circumstances of time and tragedy. Images of emaciated, withered and beaten men, women and children seared into his mind. He had crisscrossed from the French Fort Machault to Fort Le Boeuf with its eight six-pound cannon in each bastion, to Fort Presque overlooking Presque Bay on Lake Eerie. From Indian villages at Kittanning to Logstown, Saucunk to Muskingum. His only communication with other human beings belonged to random couriers, young, scared and most often fresh off the boat from England, Ireland, or Scotland.

He missed Asch's companionship and the months away from Agnes brought a loneliness to his current existence that weighed him down as nothing ever had before. He was eager to return to her. He was anxious to hear news. Jakob, Henryk and Berta pressed upon his thoughts, and he longed to see them again. The exhilaration of narrow escapes, daring feats and treacherous exploits waned after weeks of solitude holding him within an unforgiving, monotonous wilderness. He was ready to go back. Back to civilization. Back to the people he loved. Back to Agnes.

There was one more stop before riding on toward the Schuylkill Valley. Fort Northkill.

★ ★ ★ ★ ★

Agnes woke with a start. Listening. There it was again. What was that noise? She sat up in bed and listened quietly. A hard pack of snow hit her window and she jumped with a start. Swinging her legs over the edge of the bed, she padded across the room, her bare feet on the cold floor. Wiping frost from the glass with the sleeve of her nightgown, she cleared enough to peer through. Asch stood below. He motioned for her.

Pulling on her robe, she scurried softly down the steep stairs, avoiding the spots that squeaked. Lifting the latch, she opened the door. Covered in freshly fallen snow, Asch held a worn woolen blanket, a bundle, safeguarded tightly in his arms. He pushed past her to enter, his eyes as a madman.

"What has happened?" Agnes loudly whispered, fearful to wake the Demerests who slept in the back. Asch did not answer, but gently laid the bundle down on a nearby table and rushed to stoke the embers of the fading fire. Rattled and scared, Agnes began to carefully untangle the tightly bound blankets, while Asch focused on bringing the flames in the hearth back to life.

Gently unwrapping the rough woolen blanket, a newborn squirmed inside of a soft mink pelt, eyes closed. Pulling the pelt open, the ivory embroidered scarf, dirty and soiled, swaddled the child. *"Liza?! Is Liza safe? What has happened?!"* Agnes all but screamed.

"*Liza has gone to God. She is gone,*" Asch replied, his words almost indiscernible.

Tears flowed down Agnes's cheeks as she rewrapped the infant, a boy. She picked him up and tenderly carried him to the warmth of the blaze. "*Asch, please tell me.*"

"*Childbirth. She died in my arms, holding our son. My heart is darkened with a sadness as deep as the grave that now holds my beloved Liza.*" Ashes' voice was weak. He tucked his hands inside his heavy matchcoat to hide the shaking and stared at the wooden planks of the floor.

Agnes slowly and methodically responded as one in shock. "*My heart is broken for you and your child. I loved her so much. I once asked her how she could be so joyful when her life had been wrought with such trouble. She smiled and told me that under the shadow of God's wings she could sing for joy. That is where her help and comfort came. Now she rests in His presence, still singing.*" Her rote words spoke a hard truth and did little to ease the grief. Great shudders racked her body, as she clutched the newborn, Liza's baby. She felt sick to her stomach and weak in the knees.

The baby squawked, jolting Agnes. "*Asch, what do we do now?*" she sobbed.

"*I have no means to care for an infant. I leave him here, with you. You will be his mother. He has no other. You are the only chance he will survive,*" said Asch his voice cracking.

"*But you are his father. He needs you!*"

"*He needs a mother. Liza wanted me to bring him here. You were as a sister. She trusts you with our son. I trust you. He is yours. I will be going.*"

"*But where will you go? What will you do?*" Agnes asked, bouncing the infant in her arms like she had done it all her life, her dark eyes darting from Asch to the restless baby.

"*Where I go does not matter. I do what I must do,*" he said.

"*Asch, no. Please. It does matter! If you go after Leeds or Mr. Hoch, you put yourself in danger. Let it go. You have a son to consider. God will see to justice. Liza would want you to live your life free from the burden of seeking retribution. Please stay!*" Agnes pleaded.

Asch stood silent for a moment. Gold flecks from the blazing fire in the hearth now glinted in his moist grey eyes. He finally spoke, "*I will honor your arrangement with Mr. Hoch. His attack on Liza deserves punishment, yet I will let him be. God can deal with him. But Leeds. There is a greater evil found in him. Revenge may be a portion of my motive, nevertheless, he continues to plot violence. War is war."*

Agnes stumbled over her words. *"Fighting evil is a dangerous business. It is not only your life that is put in great peril but you risk descending from righteous duty to become entangled within the snares of evil itself. I fear that you may stretch the boundaries of God's laws even to the point of crossing them."*

Asch smiled a knowing smile. *"I understand your fears. They are the same as Liza's. I believe that God would have me find Leeds and stop him. I can do nothing less."* Reaching out he stroked the top of his infant son's head and quietly recited, *"May mercy, peace and love be multiplied to you."* Turning abruptly, he bolted out the door.

"Wait, Asch!" screamed Agnes, but to no avail. He was gone.

Weeks past and the infant boy thrived under the care Agnes and Mrs. Demerest provided. All the while Agnes prayed that Tavin would return. There was no sign of Asch and Agnes feared the worst for both. After so many long months, she'd heard little word from Tavin. Only once in November. Weiser had provided a letter, stating that Tavin was safe and hoped to return soon. April approached and there was still no news. Spring teased and snow fell again, covering the hills after hoodwinked daffodils and tulips poked themselves up from the ground.

Nerves were on edge with reports of war swirling. Indian and French attacks increased. Yet it seemed a world away inside the Red Owl. Mrs. Demerest placed a wooden rocker in Agnes's room, saying, *"No need to fret over your work, dear. The little one needs your attention. Let Mr. Demerest fume all he wants. God would have us do everything we can to help."* Agnes was grateful. Hour after hour she sat humming a tuneless melody, staring lovingly down at the beautiful smooth face. Soft black hair covered his perfectly round head and long lashes waved when he blinked his eyes. Agnes was sure that they were green, like his mothers.

★　★　★　★　★

The wheeze of handsaws hummed like buzzing bees in the distance. Tavin noted the darkening sky as snow began to spit. Kicking the sides of his grey mare slightly, she began a rhythmic trot. He was grateful for the horse on these last few legs of his journey. She made travel more comfortable, and the deeper more treacherous rivers were behind him. Only mountain ridges and the lower lands lay ahead. He often mused on how he came to own such a fine mount. A month earlier a crusty French trapper spotted Tavin. Obscenities carried on the wind as the terrified trapper fled in apparent fear for his life, coming quickly to his demise by charging headlong into a low hanging tree branch. The horse kept going as her master lay deceased. *"More spit than wit,"* Tavin had thought to himself. Tracking the horse, she was now his. That was the way of it. The frontier offered no promises, no forgiveness, no place for the weak willed or dim witted.

As Tavin approached the small clearing, a detachment of men could be seen hard at work felling pines. A buckboard wagon sat nearby, ready to be loaded and transported back to the fort for firewood. The men did not notice Tavin as he passed.

Fort Northkill, at the base of the Blue Mountain, situated equally between Fort Henry to the west and Fort Lebanon to the east, was a necessary, and unpleasant assignment. Berks County, heavily populated, demanded this stockade be built. Set between the two more substantial forts, which were effectively twenty-two miles apart, it offered a more adequate sense of protection, if only a sense. Tavin smiled cynically and thought, *"The utmost vigilance of these three garrisons will do little to deter a merciless enemy although it appears that even vigilance seems to be lacking at Fort Northkill."*

"Take it easy girl, we don't want some over-eager recruit taking shots at us," he said, pulling the reins back and leaning forward to whisper close into the skittish horse's ear. The garrison came into view as the snow came down harder. Standing on a small rising ground, a half mile from Northkill Creek, Fort Northkill was not much of a fort at all. The stockades were ill-fitted in the ground and open in many places. Roughly thirty feet square it offered extremely crowded conditions for the twenty men, give or take, who served there, along with refugees seeking protection. An inadequate, poorly constructed log house, with no chimney, offered little shelter in bad weather. Standing close to very thick woods, as near as forty yards, Tavin thought to himself, *"Fort Northkill is playing high stakes with a losing hand!"*

Approaching the garrison, Tavin understood his appearance from a distance could easily be mistaken for an enemy. His caution was well founded, as a shiny Brown Bess musket was indeed posed and ready. A young sentry, not much older than Tavin, appeared red-faced and jittery before hiding himself behind the post gate. Tavin called out, *"I bring intelligence from Fort Lebanon."* Waving a greeting, the sentry stepped out, smiled and with a thick Scottish accent replied, *"You had me nervous there for a minute mister. Thought for sure that you were one of those bloodthirsty savages."* Tavin cringed. The use of the word *"savages"* never settled well with him. Ignoring the comment, he bluntly asked, *"Where can I find your commander?"*

"Tha'd be Sergeant Swadling. He's not here. Off on patrol."

Making a blunt observation, Tavin commented, *"Your bastions appear unstable. You are dispatched from Fort Lebanon to secure this place as a refuge are you not?"*

"We are. First Battalion of the Pennsylvania Regiment, commanded by Colonel Conrad Weiser, detached from Captain Morgan's company," he proudly stated, and added, *"The ground is solid as rock. Too hard to dig new posts."*

Tavin nodded absentmindedly. *"I saw three men cutting about a half mile back. Where is everyone else?"*

"Most everyone is gone. Five are on leave, three are at Reading, two went off to their own homes and the rest are off with Sergeant Swadling. There's only eight of us here, with the duty sergeant," the young sentinel replied, brushing snow from his sparse red beard, and adjusting his tricorn black hat.

Tavin felt as surly as the gray clouds above. His icy blue eyes flashed in annoyance as snow gathered on his lashes. *"I'll need shelter and a dry place for my horse to stable and feed. Been on that rock-strewn road from Fort Lebanon for eleven miles or more. I could use rest and some food."* Dark circles ringed Tavin's eyes. His posture sagged from exhaustion, while his expression held a hardness that made the sentry uneasy.

Stammering, unsure of how to respond to Tavin's rigid, cheerless demeanor he finally pointed to the log house and a small, covered stable next to it. *"I should check with my sergeant first sir. But since he's not here...., wait, you can't just ride in!"* the sentry hollered as Tavin was already halfway to the makeshift stable and rough-hewn cabin. A hot fire burned outside with an iron kettle sitting on a makeshift grate. Steam rolled from the kettle's spout. The steady snow silently built with intensity. The fire sputtered and smoked.

Quickly stabling the horse, he wiped her down, tossing some loose hay at her feet. Stepping inside the cabin, the room smelled of perspiration and musty damp clothes. A haggard looking woman sat in one corner holding an infant, quietly singing a lullaby, while another stood at a long table pounding out bread dough. Three children played a game with glass marbles at her feet. No one looked up when Tavin entered. Four militiamen sat at a corner table playing cards. Candles burned randomly across the dark and gloomy room.

Without taking his eyes off his cards, a heavy-set middle-aged man flatly commented, *"We are low on provisions. Waiting for supplies from Reading to get here."*

Tavin dropped his musket and pack on the floor and sat down heavily in a nearby chair. He pulled his powder horn and checked its dryness, *"I'm tired, cold and wet. Need to sleep for a while. Later I will require food,"* he stated.

"Take that cot over there," the man pointed to the back corner. *"Haggerty won't be back for a long time. Taking some leave."*

"When your commanding officer returns, wake me," stated Tavin.

The man absentmindedly nodded and threw down a card. *"Pay up!"* he laughed. His three companions moaned and tossed coin on the table.

Sleep came as a sweet relief, an escape from the solitary life Tavin had embarked on and was now done with. He'd seen too much, gone too far and now all he wanted was to be home, wherever that was… it didn't matter, as long as Agnes was there. Impatience stalked him, like a fox hunting a mouse. He felt an urgency that he could not shake. It would fall upon him when he least expected it. This was one of those times. Feeling ill-tempered, sleep provided a welcome respite. His dreams brought him comfort and in an odd way, companionship. Visions of better days and the ones he loved surrounded him in the floating surreal pleasures of his sedated state.

A hand shook him roughly. *"Sergeant Swadling is here, mister. You've slept through the night and half the day,"* the young sentry said.

Tavin sat up. A rough woolen blanket lay across his shoulders. He glanced around the room. A woman, with a child sitting on her lap, smiled slightly, her lost eyes, blank and expressionless as she nodded. The kindness struck Tavin, lifting his downtrodden spirits. He stood, picked up the blanket and walked over to where she sat. *"Thank you for the cover. Your consideration is greatly noted."* Handing the blanket to her, she reached up to take it and quietly replied, *"You were shivering and calling out names. I thought the blanket might bring you comfort."*

Tavin smiled genuinely, the first he had in a very long while. Turning to the young sentry who was now sitting at the table stuffing his ruddy face with fresh bread, he said, *"Looks like they brought you in out of the snow finally,"* and slapped him on the back in friendliness. The young man responded with surprise in his Scottish accent, *"Yes sir."*

"Now if you would be so kind, show me to your Sergeant Swadling."

The sergeant sat outside slumped in a chair near the firepit with something steaming from a mug in one hand and a smoldering pipe in the other. His clothes were rumpled and dirty, his hat sat crooked on his head and his mustache totally covered his lips so that Tavin could barely see his mouth. It was hard to say how old he was, but Tavin thought maybe in his fifties. *"What news do you bring from Fort Lebanon? We get regular reports from there and I don't see any reason you should be sauntering in here with anything new to say. I don't know you and you don't look like Provincial Militia in the least,"* Swadling sourly stated.

"I'm not with the militia. I scout on my own terms. I have been in direct communication with Captain Morgan, at Fort Lebanon. He has concerns about the competence of command at this fort. I can see why, yet I am not here to discuss your capabilities or lack of it. I am on my way back to the Schuylkill Valley. Captain Morgan asked that I stop here with orders for you to increase your patrol." Tavin handed Sergeant Swadling a sealed envelope, adding, *"The dismal state of the people, afflicted with sickness, want and fear are crying out for greater vigilance. They cannot protect themselves as houses and barns are burned, cattle destroyed, and they are carried off or killed,"* Tavin firmly quantified.

Silence hung in the cold air for several moments. Finally, the sergeant slowly stood, his eyes ablaze. *"You need not lecture me as to the state of the frontier. I have witnessed atrocities that haunt my dreams!"*

Ignoring the Sergeant's defensive response, Tavin was already at the entrance of the shoddy stable, ready to saddle his horse, eager to leave.

The weather had cleared sometime in the night. The early morning sun sparkled like diamonds on fresh white snow. A deep sense of relief came over Tavin, as he guided the plodding mare along the rough road from Fort Northkill. He was going home. Not to a building or even a town. He was going to Agnes. She was home. He didn't know how long he would stay; it didn't matter. She was the place of comfort and peace. He needed her and something deep within told him that she needed him.

CHAPTER

33

It had been a restless, interrupted night. The rocking chair squeaked an easy rhythmic cadence, until Agnes's head dropped in slumber while the baby slept in her arms. Fretful dreams came as they so often did, waking her in a cold sweat, compelling her to plead in prayer, *"Father God, I beg your aid."* But this time, she didn't wake from the disturbing scene. The vivid nightmare played itself out in images of raw terror. Forest prowlers crept toward the baby with blurred, menacing painted faces, ripping him from her arms. She screamed, *"Tavin! Help!"*, as she swirled in jolting, helpless circles on a barren hillside, stumbling and clawing in desperation. Tavin was nowhere and the baby was gone. *"No! No!"* A hand reached for her shoulder, and she jerked with a start.

Shaking the clouds from her mind, she clutched the baby, who had awakened with her cries. He whimpered. She lifted him to her shoulder, rocking again and patting his back, *"There, there. All is well. Alles ist gut."* From the corner of her eye, she caught the shadow of a figure, perfectly still. The man stepped into view. He stood gazing down at her and the baby boy, his eyes lined with softness, his lips holding a subtle, sad smile. *"Tavin,"* she whispered, unsure whether he was real or simply an extension of her frantic nightmare.

Tavin's voice cracked, *"Mrs. Demerest was downstairs. She told me. He's beautiful, but even more so in your arms."* Once again, as it had happened twice before, she looked as an angel. Morning beams streamed from the window, a dusty halo framing her sunlit face.

"Tavin!" she gasped. Bewilderment, joy, anger, and sadness flooded her heart and mind, drowning her in a torrent of emotion. She held the baby tightly against her chest, dropped her head into his soft neck, with uncontrolled weeping. Tavin dropped to one knee and wrapped them both in his strong arms. *"I'm here. It's going to be alright. I'm here."*

He waited, saying nothing more, until Agnes regained her poise. Tears washed her cheeks, as she lifted her head. *"Where have you been?! I needed you. Asch needed you. Liza is dead!"* her soft words, filled with weary despair.

As the morning sun followed its path across the blue sky into late afternoon, they finished saying the painful things that needed to be said. Sharing sorrow and grief, it seemed the world had gone mad. Finally resting in each other's presence, love tugged at their hearts and eased their minds. Tavin held the baby boy tenderly and marveled at his tiny hands and perfectly shaped head. *"What is his name?"*

"He doesn't have a name. Asch said nothing about a name, and I haven't felt it was my place."

"Agnes, you are his mother now. Asch trusted you with his son's life. It's right that you should name him."

Her throat closed with emotion. *"How can I? He is Liza's. Asch is his father."*

Tavin took her hand, and gently uttered, *"Liza is gone. Asch is lost in his heartache. This child is yours. Name him."*

Agnes straightened her slumped posture, *"I will think and pray on it."*

Tavin did not hesitate, *"Yes. In the meantime, call him Wolfe."*

"That's not a name for a baby." She suppressed a laugh.

"It's his father's and his grand-fathers name. For now, it'll be fine."

The Demerests welcomed Tavin's arrival, especially Mr. Demerest who was pleased when Tavin negotiated a trade: physical labor for room and board. Agnes found herself watching Tavin as he worked, repairing broken fence posts, fixing the broken barn door and chopping boatloads of wood. The muscles in his arms flexing with each stroke of the axe and swing of the hammer.

She had to watch. She had to memorize him, searing his frame into her mind before she let him go. She knew he waited for her to say it. He was patient, although she saw the edginess and anxious worry in him. Their eyes would lock, and unspoken knowledge would pass between them. They both knew the truth. It had to be done. Tavin had to go.

A week passed when she finally braved the words that she had resisted, *"You must find Asch."* She didn't look up as she sat staring into the dancing orange flames of the fire, the baby snuggled against her. Strands of her dark hair hung down across her face and she pushed them back before adjusting the cotton blanket around the tiny legs and feet of Asch's child. Of Liza's child. Of her child. Tavin's heart felt as if it would burst. His love for her overwhelming.

"Yes, I will go. Asch needs my help. Marry me."

"What?" Agnes responded, wrenching her head around to face him, unsure of what she had heard.

"Marry me. Marry me now. God has given us this time. It may not be perfect, but it's ours. We need take it and not wait another year."

"You are not thinking clearly. You can't live here, and I can't leave, not until my indenture is complete. The Demerests have been kind in allowing me to keep the baby even though it limits my expected duties, but I doubt they will allow me to marry. They don't even fully trust you," Agnes explained, knowing that she was right.

"None of that concerns me. I want to be with you, in whatever way the Lord has for us. I have seen too much suffering. Too much lost. Marry me."

Pausing a moment, she replied, smiling, *"I will."*

★ ★ ★ ★ ★

Securing the license from the county clerk was easy with the written consent of the Demerests, who resisted and took some serious convincing, refusing to agree until Tavin agreed that he would not take Agnes and the baby away. Several months remained of the indenture. Mr. Demerest was a stickler for Agnes to continue her work, while Mrs. Demerest only cared that Agnes and the baby remain for her love of them both. Once Tavin promised, they readily signed.

Tavin then went to see Reverend Riegel. Knocking several times, a weak voice eventually called for him to enter. The small house was sparse of furniture. A lone chair was pushed up against a wobbly looking table on one side of the room, wax erupting down the sides of a burnt down candle flowed over the sides of the pewter holder and over the table's edge. Riegel laid on a narrow bed in the corner, looking sweaty and pale. He smiled weakly, recognizing Tavin.

"My apologies, Mr. Shire. You haven't found me at my best," said Riegel, lifting himself to a half sitting position.

"I had become aware that you were suffering an illness last year at the marriage of my friends. My prayer had been that you would regain your health," Tavin woefully commented.

"Yes, my physical condition deteriorates yet the Lord gives me strength to endure to the end. I will see His face soon. But enough about me, how is it with you?"

Tavin proceeded to explain all that had occurred. Reverend Riegel empathized, hanging on every word as Tavin spoke, weakly interjecting genuine comments of comfort and encouragement. Finally, Tavin pointedly asked, *"We would never want to impose, but there is no one whom we would wish to perform our marriage ceremony but you. Are you well enough?"*

"Indeed. It would be my honor. Is tomorrow too soon?" he coughed.

"Tomorrow is perfect. To save you effort, we will arrive here, if that is suitable to you. We can bring a witness. Mrs. Demerest will be happy to serve."

"Yes. And perhaps Mrs. Demerest could bring along some venison stew. I've heard that she is a fine cook."

"I am certain that she would be very pleased to do that." Tavin smiled and made a mental note.

★   ★   ★   ★   ★

Riding through the streets of Reading with a confidence that he had not possessed a year earlier, Tavin easily ignored the stares and whispers his appearance incurred. Aware that he looked more like a primitive trapper than a civilized gentleman; it mattered not. The refined and sophisticated people of the town were content with the social structure they had created for themselves, and he was just as comfortable with his own. God had led him to a place where his confidence was not his, it was the Lord's. He walked with assurance. He suspected that Asch would first seek information concerning Leeds from Colonel Weiser. It was a logical place to begin his search for Asch.

Conrad Weiser stood when Tavin walked in. *"Mr. Shire, your timing is perfect. I have just returned from my homestead this very day. I am happy to see you. The reports I have received speak well to your abilities. Your reconnaissance has allowed several successful ventures. We only pray that this war will soon end."*

"Yes sir. That is my prayer as well."

Weiser sat down. *"Please sit. I assume that there is more that you wish to discuss."*

"I will get to the point. Has Leeds yet been arrested for espionage? Is he detained into custody?"

Weiser cleared his throat, *"I am sorry to inform you, through a series of unfortunate events, Leeds has escaped. A year ago, April, before he came to Reading, he had joined the Lenape leader Shingas in a raid against Fort McCord and the Cumberland Valley. While the raiders traveled their prisoners toward Kittanning, a young man from a family named Knox, managed to break free. He then joined the militia and was here in Reading when Leeds arrived, posing as a patriot. Two days after I informed you that we would watch Leeds and use him to relay false intelligence to the French, Knox recognized him on the street. Before we could stop him, he betrayed Leeds identity and Leeds escaped. The young man almost saved you the trouble and killed the scoundrel. Fired a musket ball at his head and missed."*

"Leeds is out there somewhere, free as a flying bird. Totally at liberty," Tavin stated bluntly, his eyes narrowing in anger.

"That is so. I assumed that your friend told you. He was here several weeks back, and I explained it to him."

Tavin responded, *"My friend is in a bad way. If I find Leeds, I'll find my friend, my brother. Have you had any reports as to Leeds whereabouts?"*

"No news. Finding him will be a difficult and dangerous task. How will you go about it?" Weiser asked, genuinely curious and concerned for this young man whom he had come to respect so highly.

"I will confer with my wife and decide. I only know that I cannot sit back and do nothing."

"May God go with you."

"Always," stated Tavin.

Stepping out from Weiser's dry hot office into the cool air, Tavin caught his breath. Leeds had escaped, again, and Asch was hunting him down. Of that, Tavin was certain. He had prayed that it would be over. He had begged God to exact justice on the murderer Leeds, so that he and Asch could be free of him.

Slipping his foot into the stirrup, Tavin swung his leg over and kicked the gray mare's sides, recalling the conversation with Weiser over in his mind. Suddenly he smiled. He had uttered the words, *"my wife"*. It had come so naturally. So easily. It felt good.

The marriage ceremony itself had been a simple, almost comical, even if pathetic event, and yet for Agnes and Tavin, the most perfect day. Reverend Riegel, confined to his bed, his face sallow, his words weak, spoke of God's love and pronounced the two united, one flesh. Mrs. Demerest dabbed her eyes while holding the baby boy, whom no one could really bring themselves to call *"Wolfe."*

"Thank you again Mrs. Demerest for the venison stew. Your reputation precedes you," Reverend Riegel commented with a grimace as he shifted his emaciated body.

Mrs. Demerest grinned and held her head high at the compliment. Tavin took Agnes's hand and they all stepped out just as a warm afternoon sun untangled from looming clouds. *"I can take care of this little bundle tonight, Agnes. I'm sure that you and this young man would like some privacy,"* Mrs. Demerest said with a wink.

Agnes blushed and answered, *"I am very grateful."*

★ ★ ★ ★ ★

The room was dark, except for a flickering candle on the nightstand. Quiet breathing came from the cradle next to the bed, interrupted with occasional sucking noises. A cool breeze drifted in through the open window fluttering the thin curtains. Crisp air brought relief to Tavin from the stuffiness of the room. *"Are you sure it's not too cold for the baby?"* he whispered in Agnes's ear.

"He's bundled tightly, perfectly comfortable."

"You are a good mother to him."

"I worry about his future. I worry about his father. I want Asch found, but how will you find him? Where will you look? You'll risk your life to search over

the mountains, while the possibility of finding him is so remote. I love Asch and I want him safe, but I believe it's useless effort. You have pushed yourself for the sake of others to a point where I fear you won't come back this time," whispered Agnes. Tavin pulled her closer, hearing the tremor in her voice.

Silence stood between them as they laid together listening to the soft inhale and exhale of the innocent baby boy sleeping, peacefully unaware of the heartache surrounding him. Finally, Tavin answered, *"You are my wife and my love for you begs me to remain here. But Asch is my brother. He is lost in his grief and drowning in his anger. He is chasing Leeds, who is most likely deep within the Ohio Territory, possibly even as far as the great lakes. I cannot abandon Asch. God would have me go. Do you understand?"*

"I understand. I understand it all. I'm just tired. Tired of this war. Tired of waiting for you to return. Tired of not knowing."

"I won't leave you for long. If I haven't found him in two months, I will come back. Mid-May. By then, you will be close to finishing the indenture with the Demerests. By God's grace, we will begin our lives anew."

"Two months. You promise. Just two months."

"I promise."

CHAPTER

34

April 1757

God's presence moved as the wind in the trees. Tavin heard His voice, *"Don't give up."* The rain had stopped, and sunbeams streamed through the forest canopy offering blinding hues of greens and yellows. Looking up, Tavin prayed, *"Lord, I hear you. I need your guidance."* The wind again rustled through the treetops, casting a shower of water off the wet leaves. Tavin wiped his face. *"Alright Lord. I will trust you and keep moving."*

When Tavin left Agnes and the baby, he had instinctively travelled west. The French remained in control of Fort Duquesne, and it made sense that if Asch were hunting Leeds, he would head in that direction. That was over a month ago and Tavin had seen nothing of Leeds or Asch. Feeling like he was chasing his tail, frustration grew to the point of despair. It was only God's voice that morning that had rejuvenated his spirit.

There had been an attack by the French on Fort William Henry in March, destroying many buildings and watercraft, yet the British colors held. Much of the war had settled into the northeast. Tavin contemplated. Leeds may very well have escaped in that direction to avoid arrest in Pennsylvania. Asch would have thought of this, and he had relatives in New York, near Lake Ontario. *"Lord, it's hundreds of miles over dangerous territory and mountainous terrain. Would you have me travel that far?"* he asked and waited.

Tavin had made a promise to Agnes. Two months. Time was against him. *"Don't give up."* The words rang across his spirit again. Wrestling with the dilemma, Tavin took a deep breath, adjusted the pack on his back and started north for the Seneca village of Kanandarque. *"Please forgive me Agnes,"* Tavin mumbled to himself as he clamored up a steep knoll.

★   ★   ★   ★   ★

Coming upon a shallow outlet to a large lake, Tavin stepped across a crude bridge formed with poles and sticks. He dropped to one knee on the marshy ground and scooped water into his mouth, before proceeding up an embankment. Grey smoke rose above the trees a mile or so to the north. Proceeding with caution, Tavin advanced closer. Twenty to thirty dwellings ornately decorated in red symbols of deer, bear, turkey and wolf sat beautifully situated on top of a hill. And he could see several log houses with chimneys. *"There are whites living there,"* he thought.

Building his courage, he decided to reveal himself and prayed he would be accepted. Chatter and agitation exploded in a flurry of chaos once Tavin was spotted on the edge of the town. The rush was violent as he was tackled and kicked. Shouts and accusations teemed while a horde of people swarmed over him. Covering his head with his arms, Tavin yelled, *"Ögwádéó'shö' ! Ögwádéó'shö' ! We are friends!"*

Suddenly a strong arm pulled him to his feet. *"Sea'he't!"* a firm voice bellowed. Men stood back in respect, women solemnly walked away, and children reluctantly ran back to their childish games. Tavin brushed himself off. Rubbing his sore ribs he stammered, *"Kaendae, it seems that you are always pulling me up from one catastrophe or another."* Kaendae gazed at Tavin, confused and curious, a leather strap around his neck held the familiar beaded pouch at his hip. Tavin had almost forgotten the power that Kaendae's presence held.

After communicating with the limited amount of the Seneca language he had gained from Asch, Tavin was able to piece together the first scraps of helpful information he had come across in almost two months. After the village at Kittanning had been attacked and destroyed by Armstrong, Kaendae had parted ways with the French, Lenape and Shawnee and returned to his Seneca family. Tavin was relearning that loyalty proved very fluid, depending on which side could offer the most. Kaendae had satisfied his vengeance on the British for Drakes death. Now, it seemed the French were losing ground in the war, especially after their defeat at Fort William Henry. Better to go with the British.

A Moravian missionary stepped forward smiling. *"Welcome sir,"* he exclaimed, his arms flung wide in greeting, his fleshy cheeks clean shaven, revealed pock marks and scars. Tavin flinched. Feeling unsure as to why this man felt he had the right to offer a welcome in this Seneca village, while at the same time grateful for someone who could possibly translate, Tavin curtly responded, *"Thank you. Have you lived here long?"*

"Two years, give or take," said the toothy man, still smiling.

"Could you please render my words so that Kaendae will understand?"

"You know Kaendae?"

"Yes. We are friends."

"That is very interesting. I have found he is very troublesome. He has not welcomed me here and has discouraged others from hearing the good news of the gospel."

Kaendae stood straight and tall, scowling. Tavin responded, *"Kaendae has seen tragedy, and known sorrow. It hardens a man."*

"Yes. Yes, indeed. Well, if he is amiable to it, I will be happy to translate for you. My name is Herrmann."

Tavin and Kaendae entered Herrmann's cabin and sat down on benches near the fire. Recalling the events of the past year, Tavin quickly explained the circumstances that brought him to this village. Kaendae listened intently, never looking at the missionary, but rather, studying Tavin. His eyes narrowed. The bitterness in his voice was palpable, *"Leeds is a vile man. As cunning as a fox and venomous as a snake. Leeds killed Do:hsetweh. He has caused much suffering. He deserves to die."*

"I agree. Leeds practices evil, but God exacts justice. I do not seek Asch to help him kill Leeds. I am his friend, his brother. I came here to bring him back to his son. To bring him back to his senses and a place of peace once again."

"Asch will not have peace until Leeds is dead."

"I know this is hard to understand. I don't even understand it fully myself. All I know is that God is above all. His word is final. Trusting Him is all I can do. Seeking Him and His ways, His justice, His goodness, and His love will be the only way that true peace comes. All rectitude belongs to Him. Asch believes that too, but his grief has overpowered him. I want to find him before he destroys his life."

"He was here."

"What?!" yelled Tavin.

"Two days past. You are correct. Heyonosodahdoh is seeking Leeds and has gone to Kanadesaga, where rumors say that Leeds scouts with the British army. They help to fortify the village there against French invaders. Leeds is cunning and fools many." Kaendae waited with irritation as Hermann translated and then added. *"Heyonosodahdoh is a strong warrior."*

"This is true. He is brave and determined. But I cannot abandon him. How far is this village, Kanadesaga?"

"Maybe twenty miles east."

"Thank you. I will go now."

"Leeds is slippery. I will join you in finding him. Do:hsetweh and my aunt cry from the grave for retribution. I failed them. When Drake died, my heart was heavy, and I stopped searching to return to my people. Heyonosodahdoh begged me to remain back to allow him time to discover Leeds alone. I honored his wish, but no more. I go with you. We will find Leeds. This will end."

Tavin thought to correct Kaendae. He was looking to stop Heyonosodahdoh (Asch), not exact justice on Leeds, but chose to be silent. He had perplexed Kaendae enough already with his verbose explanation of God's sovereignty. Better to be quiet. The missionary, Herrmann, offered a prayer before Tavin left. Kaendae stood respectfully silent.

Tavin and Kaendae walked a half mile along the edge of the lake, lined with trees adorned with lush wild grapevines, loaded with countless clusters of ripening grapes. Coming to a large field of cleared and cultivated land, Tavin marveled at the abundance of corn, squash and beans sprouting from the earth. The air felt fresh and Tavin's hopes soared. Maybe he would find Asch at Kanadesaga.

The next morning brought menacing clouds threatening a storm. The wind picked up and by noon a driving rain pelted them, slowing their progress along the worn and muddy Seneca trail. Tavin was happy to have Kaendae as his guide. This was a foreign land, unfamiliar territory with uncertain allegiances.

Stopping to drink from a fresh flowing spring, Kaendae indicated that the village was near. Once they reached the crest of a nearby mound, a large lake appeared, grey and dismal in the heavy rain. Kaendae pointed to the north. There, the village sat along a shallow flowing creek. Tavin's heart pounded with apprehension.

Tavin and Kaendae ambled through the village with little attention given excepting for a dog who feigned attack and sprinted away with his tail between his legs at the wave of a hand. A small battalion of soggy British soldiers wandered about in a seemingly unconcerned manner, while others scurried around performing their muddy tasks, dodging the rain as best they could. Tavin's cold-blue eyes darted cautiously around. Looking for any sign of Asch or Leeds, he pushed his dripping straw-colored hair off his face with the back of his wrist and followed Kaendae. A timeworn chief stepped from the long house and gave a greeting. Lively, friendly words were exchanged, and they were invited inside.

The dwelling was cramped, humid, and musty. A fire burned under a hole above their heads. Smoke curled toward it like a snake until the wind refused to accept it, forcing it back down and filling the room with its choking greyness. Tavin's eyes stung. He rubbed them and blinked, adjusting to the smoky dim light. They sat down on the grass matted floor. A pipe was passed, and no one spoke until it was finished.

The chief was Guy-yah-gwah-doh and he was a powerful Sachem among the Seneca. Tavin could only snatch bits and pieces of the conversation that ensued, but from it he gathered that Asch had arrived the day before. Kaendae concluded the discourse with polite gestures of respect and stood to exit. *"Leeds is here with the British regiment."*

Tavin filled his lungs with the fresh, damp air as they passed back through the village. The rain had stopped, leaving mud everywhere, but none of it mattered. He had the first real news. *"If Leeds is still here, where has Asch gone?"* Tavin asked out loud, more to himself than to Kaendae.

Walking past the dingy white military tents, Tavin stopped a disheveled soldier, questioning him, *"Do you know the scout Leeds?"*

"I have no personal acquaintance, but I know who the man is."

"Do you know where he'd be right now?"

"I saw him head into the forest earlier. Looked like he was going to hunt. That way," the soldier offered in his thick British diction and pointed toward a worn path.

Tavin considered whether to inform the commander of Leeds identity, a spy for the French. But Kaendae kept walking without giving any notice of the British presence in the village, a grimace on his tense face.

Once well outside the village, Kaendae stooped down to study the ground. Tavin recalled Kaendae's extraordinary skills when it came to tracking. Kaendae motioned forward and Tavin continued to follow. Unsure of how Kaendae was differentiating tracks, as there seemed to be so many, yet he did not question, trusting his friend's abilities.

Suddenly a musket blast rang out. It wasn't far. An overriding terror gripped Tavin as he and Kaendae leaped across a sodden fallen pine, sprinting through mushy undergrowth and over tangled vines. Adrenaline pulsed through Tavin's body, his lungs burning with dread. Praying as he ran.

Through the dense hardwoods ahead Tavin could see Leeds. He stood calmly priming the hot barrel of his flintlock, when he spotted the two men rushing toward him. He quickly dropped to his knee and hurriedly rammed the paper wad into the barrel. Without slowing down, Kaendae pulled an arrow from the quiver on his back, loaded his bow let the shot fly. It soared over Leeds head and embedded into the trunk of a tree behind him.

Leeds quickly stood, took aim, and pulled the trigger, sinking the ball deeply into Tavin's thigh. Tavin tumbled and rolled across the mossy ground, a boulder stopping his momentum. Excruciating pain throbbed through his leg as his head spun in dizziness.

Kaendae released another arrow, striking Leeds. Leeds eyes bulged in disbelief. He sank back down to his knees, his hands grasping the shaft protruding from his chest. Collapsing forward in death Leeds made no sound.

Using the rock to prop himself up, Tavin tore a strip from his shirt and quickly wrapped it around the open wound, grimacing in agony.

Lifting himself up, he limped toward Kaendae. Leeds lay motionless, his face buried in the leaf covered ground, while Kaendae knelt over a body a few yards away. Tavin's heart began to pound in dread. *"No! No! No! No, God please!"* he pleaded. Forgetting his own pain, he ran and fell to his knees next to Asch. Leeds aim had been true.

Laying on his back, Asch smiled weakly up at Tavin. His grey eyes watery, and bright. *"Why am I not surprised that you are here?"* he softly gurgled.

"Don't talk. We'll get you help. There is a doctor in the village with the British. He can fix you." The words rushed from Tavin's mouth in panic and grief.

Asch lifted his hand and put it on Tavin's arm, *"Your God is my God. I go to Him now. I go to Liza. Mercy, peace and love be multiplied in you. Raise my boy in goodness,"* he whispered, letting out his last breath.

Tavin shouted in agony *"God! Why?! You told me to not give up looking for him only to watch him die?!"* Falling onto his back, next to Asch, his hands over his face, he wept. Kaendae stood soberly nearby, waiting, watching. Tavin shuddered, finally wiping wet tears from his swilled cheeks, he stared unmoving at the sky above. Dark clouds swirled in ominous power above the treetops, writhing and reaching, as if being commanded. He never knew if it was real, or if his grief-stricken mind invented it, but the tumult parted, a brilliant bolt of sunlight shot through the dismal gloom and a clear voice declared, *"Awíyo'hé'öh"* A moment later the slit of blue sky disappeared, and darkness sealed the heavens again.

★ ★ ★ ★ ★

Agnes loaded the last bits of her meager belongings. She couldn't help but feel the weight of her life closing in. So much had happened, so much was lost. The baby happily squealed in the basket sitting on the ground next to her feet, reminding her that she couldn't give in to weakness. She had purpose and a blessed responsibility. *"It's just the two of us now,"* she gently said, bending down to tuck the blanket around his active legs.

Mrs. Demerest emerged across the threshold of the tavern's doorway carrying a pail packed with boiled goat's milk, bread, and cheese. *"For *the trip,"* she managed to voice, lifting her wire rimmed glasses, and wiping her tearful eyes with her familiar worn hanky. *"It seems all I do is cry these days,"* she admitted.

"Your tears have been a comfort to me. 'Weep with those who weep' the Bible tells us. I thank you, Mrs. Demerest. Thank you for everything. Your kindness and generosity have far exceeded my ability to repay you."

Mrs. Demerest's words cracked with emotion, *"Oh my dear. You forget that you have selflessly worked for Liza's sake, first taking her indenture, and now raising her child. God has used you to show me what it truly means to live a life of sacrifice and love. You have repaid more than enough."* Mr. Demerest came around the corner of the inn, in his usual jittery manner, as if he had somewhere important to be but forgot where. *"God's still working on HIM though,"* whispered Mrs. Demerest as she laughed, breaking the somber moment.

Agnes turned to Mr. Demerest who continued to appear distracted and sour, exclaiming, *"Mr. Demerest, releasing me from the final months of my obligation is a fine and honorable act."* Mr. Demerest mumbled something about his wife making decisions without him and how no one listened to him as he walked away. Agnes gave Mrs. Demerest a concerned look.

"Gloom is his constant companion. He'll be fine," assured Mrs. Demerest.

Agnes gingerly lifted her skirts so as not to catch the hem on the step and climbed onto the seat next to the driver. The muslin canopy fastened with strings on the sides of the two-wheeled cart reminded Agnes of a sunbonnet. She was happy for the shade. Mrs. Demerest removed the baby from the basket and hugging him one last time, handed the boy to Agnes. *"May God be with you my poor girl."*

"And you as well, Mrs. Demerest."

The bearded, middle-aged driver snapped the reins and the horse started with a jerk. Travelling the fifty miles would be a strenuous journey on the bumpy, muddy road for two days. The driver, a local farmer with only a few baskets filled with butter, eggs, and vegetables to sell at market in Philadelphia, accepted payment of a shilling to transport Agnes with her baby to Germantown. It was all that Agnes had and a risky venture, but one she knew she had to make. She would find Tavin's family.

CHAPTER

35

July 1757

Infection spread across Tavin's thigh. Vicious tentacles clawing and climbing. Laying on a cot inside the dirty, yellowed British canvas tent, he was unaware of days passing or people coming and going. Fever ravaged his body. A musket ball had lodged in his thigh. It was deep and Tavin had lost a lot of blood. The young surgeon, by the name of John Morgan accompanying the British battalion at Kanadesaga had done everything he could think to do. Now, there was nothing else, but to wait. Amputation would certainly see him die.

In a surprising gesture, Guy-yah–gwah–doh approached Morgan. His English broken, but understandable, he offered a pouch filled with a mixture of blueish clay and various herbs. Morgan accepted the poultice with hesitation and thanked the Sachem for his thoughtfulness. Setting the poultice aside, he gave it no true consideration.

Tavin continued to decline. Disorientation and hallucinations came with a raging fever. Kaendae had left him in the care of the British surgeon two weeks earlier. With rudimentary provisions and inadequate medicines, Morgan removed the slug. Recuperation went well until the vicious infection began to spread its poisonous tentacles. Morgan liked

Tavin. He was impressed with the young man's stalwart countenance, resolute faith, and evident knowledge of frontier life. Spending many hours in conversation, Morgan recognized that Tavin held an intuitive knowledge of and a unique position among the Seneca, which explained why a powerful Sachem like Guy-yah-gwah-doh would go to such effort for a dying white man.

Frustrated with his own failure in healing the festering, toxic wound, Morgan glanced over at the leather medicine pouch, still sitting untouched on the table next to Tavin's cot. He grumbled to himself, scratching his black bearded cheek, *"There is nothing to lose,"* and picked it up. Applying the poultice liberally across the infected area, Morgan rewrapped the thigh and prayed, as Tavin fell deeper into delirium.

The next day saw no improvement. Tavin's fever spiked, and he lay sweating and thrashing on the narrow cot. Morgan reapplied and prayed again. On the third day, the fever broke. On the fifth day, the infection was all but erased. Tavin sat up, hungry and thirsty. *"I think I need a bath, he joked."* Morgan laughed, *"Indeed you do."*

The thought of cold, clear lake water washing over his body energized his weakened state as he weakly made his way to the water's edge. Stripping off his clothes, he stepped in. Catching his breath against the chill, he dove headfirst, feeling alive and free. Scrubbing his body with sand, he washed away the stains, dirt and sweat. Doing the same with his clothes, he spread them out on a large boulder to dry in the warm afternoon sun. Soaking in the heat and peace of the day, his mind wandered to Asch.

"Don't give up," he was sure God had said. Tavin thought that message had meant one thing. God meant it as another. Mulling it over, Tavin suddenly saw the gift and understood the word he had heard from the heavens. "Awíyo'hé'öh" He was there when Asch died. It was good. He'd heard Asch's last words. A gift of good-bye. A gift to Asch; he didn't die alone. *"We will meet again. In God's heaven, we will meet again."* Tavin stretched his sore muscles and soaked in the sun's warmth, feeling at peace for the first time in as long as he could remember.

With his leg sufficiently healed and his strength regained, Tavin limped around the village looking for Kaendae to no avail. He was gone. The wildness that possessed Kaendae had taken him again and he had joined his fellow Seneca in support of Fort William Henry. As he packed to leave the village and head south, Morgan gave him some advice. *"Continue to keep an eye on the leg."* He paused and added, *"No strenuous exertion."* Tavin laughed and responded, *"I am going back over rugged mountainous terrain. I think strenuous exertion cannot be avoided."*

★   ★   ★   ★   ★

Travelling the rough, mountainous miles on foot with a wounded thigh took longer than Tavin wanted. The late July sun beat down on him as he finally reached the Schuylkill Valley, tired, sore, hungry, but mostly relieved and thankful. Approaching the Red Owl Inn, his emotions caught up with him. The events of his life bubbled up and pressed against his wounded yet rejoicing heart. He quickened his limping pace in the sweltering air.

Mr. Demerest spotted him coming down the dusty road. Squinting to get a clearer image, he finally recognized the tattered hobbling man. *"Saints be praised. It's the ghost of Tavin Shire!"* he shouted.

Tavin gave a quick wave, wiped the sweat from his forehead with his sleeve and as he got closer watched as Mr. Demerest disappeared around to the back of the inn. Soon Mrs. Demerest came rushing out from seemingly nowhere, hollering, *"Oh dear! Oh dear! Oh my! You are alive! We were all certain that you had met your demise. Agnes is gone!"*

"What do you mean 'gone'? Where is she?" demanded Tavin, confused and worried.

"Gone to Germantown. She is released from her final months of indenture. She took the baby and went to find your family. Word came of your grandmother's sudden death and Agnes felt it her duty to see to your brother and sister there. She believed that you had met some terrible fate. I told her she should wait, that maybe you were just late, but she insisted that if you weren't back in two months, you weren't coming back. Said you'd promised."

"Yes. That was a promise I had no right to make. It is God who wills and directs, not me. I'll be on my way. Thank you."

"Please, it's late in the day and by the looks of it you've had a rough go. Let's get you cleaned up, some food in you and a good night's sleep. Agnes's room is still empty. I haven't had the heart to hire her replacement yet. You can head out in the morning."

As much as Tavin wanted to continue to Germantown, he knew that Mrs. Demerest was correct. It would do him well to pause, eat and rest. A candle stub burned in the center of the table as Tavin scooped up the last bits of gravy with rye bread. Sitting in the corner, it quickly dawned on him that returning to the statutes and norms of white society was going to take significant adjustment. He watched and listened as hearty men gathered, eating, drinking, playing cards and sharing boisterous stories. He didn't feel a part of it and wondered if he could ever fit again.

A maid filled a large basin with heated water and carried it to the room where Tavin readily washed the dirt and grime from his body with lye soap. Mrs. Demerest had laid out a white shirt, tan britches, stockings, and a pair of Mr. Demerest's old leather shoes. Tavin dressed and stretched out on the small cot that had been Agnes's for almost two years, his feet hanging over the end. Their wedding night came to mind, and he smiled into the darkness of the room. It was a last glorious thought before sleep overtook him.

Morning came with a rooster crow. The smell of bread baking filled the air and Tavin's stomach grumbled. Splashing his face with water, he limped down the steps. Mrs. Demerest waved her arm and pointed to the same table in the corner. A young servant girl, with a shy smile and missing teeth, served him bread, butter and cheese.

"*I know you are in a hurry, but a few more minutes to eat properly won't hurt,*" Mrs. Demerest called out from the other side of the room.

"*I can't pay you.*"

"*Not to worry. It is an honor to help.*"

"*It seems that I am forever in your debt.*" he laughed.

"*No debt. Solvency is gained through sweeter ways than the Kings currency. God has taught me more through knowing Liza, you and Agnes than I could have ever gained on my own. That is payment enough.*"

★ ★ ★ ★ ★

The oxen strained under the heavy load as they snorted and finally came to rest in the center of the market square. With agility and blithe the driver jumped down and hollered over to Tavin, who had leaped off the other side of the cart, which was loaded with flax to sell, *"Been nice having the company. Good luck to you!"*

Tavin thanked him and brushed dust from his breeches. The ride had been slow and filled with the constant chatter from the verbose and overly opinionated driver, but it was better than walking. Tavin missed the grey mare. Selling her had been a financial decision he had made before crossing over the mountains to find Asch, so many months earlier. He had given most of the profit to Agnes. The small amount he kept for himself allowed for the purchase of supplies and gave him some leverage on his journey, but leverage that didn't last long and now he regretted the sale.

Pulling his pack from the back of the cart, Tavin began walking toward his grandmother Shire's home. Linen sellers and weavers called out to him as he passed by, hawking their wares. He wished that he had enough coin or some commodity for trade to buy something for Agnes. A gift seemed appropriate after the pain and worry he had caused her.

Germantown was as impressive as Tavin remembered it being when he had delivered Henryk and Berta into the loving arms of family, in what felt an eternity ago. He marveled as he walked by two-and three-story brick mansions residing grandly along cobblestone streets. The Immaculate landscaping and pristine front entrance columns, with large chimneys flanking the ends of each house, felt like a fairytale realm compared to the rustic wilderness empire.

The sun, golden as a summer harvest, dropped close to the horizon as Tavin turned onto a rough narrow street. This neighborhood was simpler. No mansions. Only comfortable two-story row houses. His heart pounded. His breathing quickened. Children played games in front of brick structures, spilling onto the dirt street with sticks and balls. Their laughter bright and contagious, reminding Tavin of the children at Kanadesaga.

A swirling mass of energetic progenies, circled, spun, jumped, and squealed. He scanned the blond heads for Berta or Henryk. *"Do I see a phantom before me or has my brother Tavin returned?"* a baritone voice came from behind him.

"Henryk! I hardly recognize you." Tavin exclaimed wrapping his arms around the little brother who had grown almost equal in height. *"I*

expected to find you out here playing battledore, tag or leapfrog. It never occurred to me that in two years you would have sprouted like a weed."

"I'm not a child. I'm fourteen."

"Yes, I can see that." Tavin smiled and wrapped his arms around his little brother.

"I thought you dead. It is good to see you. Agnes is inside with Berta and the baby." Henryk pointed to the familiar house that looked so much like every other one nestled tightly between its neighbors.

Tavin took a deep breath. *"It seems that everyone has assumed that I met my end."*

"You're late. You must be dead."

Tavin laughed. Henryk was taller, with a deeper voice, but the same. Few words and his thoughts were clear. As Tavin turned to walk toward the house, Henryk caught his arm. *"Tavin, when you leave again, I will not be left behind. I will go with you."*

"We will be together," Tavin stated with a firm and sure voice.

Memories of his grandparents flooded his mind, as he walked up the three short steps to enter the house. Suddenly struck with an infinite hope he whispered, *"God has been our guide through the generations. He was faithful and He is faithful, now and forever."* Gently opening the door, he stepped inside and quietly closed it behind him. The room throbbed with silence. Gilded rays of the setting sun mingled with smoke escaping from the hearth, casting a melancholy aura. A large cauldron hung over a blazing fire in the center of the room. It was hot and Tavin stood sweating on the threshold listening, hesitant to call out. Finally, voices echoed from outside. Tavin crossed the small room, passing the steep steps leading upstairs, to an open door at the back of the house.

Agnes sat on a low stone wall, a bowl of peas in her lap, her back to him. A white picket fence ran along the back of the house. Berta played with the baby in the grass next to her. Agnes laughed at something Berta said and Tavin stood mesmerized. His voice caught in his throat as he watched the peaceful scene in the dimming light of dusk. It was all so reminiscent, exactly as his delirious dream on the banks of the Allegheny with Asch. Agnes, a white picket fence and children. Berta stood and lifted the baby into the air, high over her head, spinning in happy circles. The baby giggled. *"Careful Berta, Jude is almost as big as you,"* Agnes teased.

"Agnes," called Tavin, quietly. Agnes, startled, jumped off the wall, the bowl of snapped peas spilling across the grass. Loose chickens scurried to the unexpectedly delectable meal.

"Tavin! I knew you weren't dead!" shrieked Berta running to Tavin. He stretched out his arm to hug her, his eyes never leaving Agnes.

Agnes stood motionless next to the stone wall, facing Tavin, her arms wrapped around herself, as if to hold herself together, her dusky eyes held a soft wonder, *"You look so different. Your clothes,"* she murmured, her voice shaking.

"The Demerests insisted that I should have proper attire. I'm not sure this is me anymore. Proper, I mean." Tavin fumbled for words and shifted his weight. *"I promised you two months, Agnes. I have been gone almost four."*

Berta took several steps back, giving Tavin and Agnes space. Wide-eyed and unsure of what would happen, she waited, bouncing the baby on her nine-year old hip.

"I thought you would not break that promise and when you did, I believed that you weren't coming back."

"I know. You have every right to be angry."

"Listen to me Tavin Shire." Agnes dropped her arms and wrung her hands. *"I grieved over you, with the prayer that maybe, just maybe, you were still alive. And maybe you found Asch. Time went on and there was no news. When word came that your grandmother had passed away, I knew that my place was to be with the children, Berta and Henryk. That is why I am here. You didn't return!"* she cried, her words intense and filled with torment.

"I can explain."

Agnes raised her hand for Tavin to stop. Her voice rose, *"Let me finish. The Lord reminded me that you have no master but Him, and no law but His will. The promise you made to me, was not in your control, but God's alone. You are two months late. But this I know, if you could have been here, you would have. You were doing what God called you to do. I cannot argue. I cannot be angry."* her voice softened back to the whisper, as she hugged herself again, *"Are you alone? Asch is not with you?"* she asked. Tavin sadly shook his head.

Agnes dropped her arms and rushed into his strong embrace. Burying her head into his neck, she wept, clinging to him as tightly as she could, never wanting to let go. After several minutes, Berta spoke up, impatient, *"I want a hug too!"* Agnes hesitantly released Tavin and took the baby from Berta's arms, wiping her eyes. Tavin knelt and Berta threw herself at Tavin with a joyful squeal.

Standing, Tavin tousled the baby's black hair with his hand and asked, *"You call him 'Jude'?"*

Agnes nodded, *"Yes. I remembered that one of Liza's favorite verses came from the book of Jude. She used to say, 'mercy unto you and peace and love be multiplied'. I wanted a name that spoke to his mother's faith,"* her dark eyes shining.

Lifting the baby from Agnes's arms he gazed into the small, sweet face. Bright eyes twinkled back. *"Jude is a perfect name. Asch's last words to me came from Liza. He repeated that same verse and added, 'Raise my boy in goodness."* Tavin gave a gentle smile.

Agnes sobbed in weary heartache while Tavin wrapped his arms around her again, with Jude squeezed in between them, wriggling in confusion. Berta threw her arms around them all, confidently declaring, *"We are a family, like it's supposed to be. No more foolishness."*

Tavin laughed, *"No more foolishness, but remember, there is no folly with God. His ways are straight, His promises true. He has been faithful even through the trials we have faced."*

"What will we do now? Where will we go?" asked Agnes, worry crossing her smooth face. *"We do not belong in Germantown. People have been kind, yet there is a void. The frontier has become home, and I believe that it's where Jude will thrive."*

"I want to go home!" Berta piped up.

Henryk stepped into the yard. *"I, as well."*

"We will find our place. Tomorrow, we pick up the pieces of what is left, and we begin our life together," stated Tavin.

"It matters not where, as long as we go as one." There was loving firmness in Agnes's voice.

Jude squirmed and reached for Tavin, his eyes green as his mothers, his hair as black as his father's. Taking the baby in his arms, Tavin smiled down, *"I am your father now, but I will never let you forget where you came from. You will be a fierce warrior, a strong hunter, a devoted friend, and a good man. You will carry unwavering faith, that holds you tightly through every test. In this you will honor the love and sacrifice of those who came before you."*

A wind rustled through the trees overhead, bending them in swaying rhythm. Long shadows danced across the ground and Tavin felt the pull, the pull to go back. A wildness had settled too deeply inside. And yet this time, he knew, he wouldn't go alone.

ACKNOWLEDGMENT

There are approximately 30-70 fluent speakers of the Seneca language in America. Fortunately, there are significant ongoing efforts toward revitalization through structured teaching, as well as the production of audio and textual documentation of this rare and vanishing Native American language. For this writing I have taken the liberty of using the *"English-Seneca Dictionary"*, compiled by Wallace Chafe, with the collaboration of many others listed in the online dictionary, and ONONDOWA'GA:' *GAWE:NO'*, New Reference Edition, by Phyllis E. Wms. Bardeau, from the Seneca Nation Education Department Cattaraugus Territory.

With great respect, I have endeavored to use the language dictionaries as accurately as my limited abilities have allowed. On a few occasions the capability to produce the exact punctuations was beyond my reach. If I have misrepresented or misused any words or phrases, it was not intentional, and my apologies go out to the Seneca community.

Printed in the United States
by Baker & Taylor Publisher Services